Nightmare in Time

Erik Bergson

* * *

Published by BBJF Publishing
www.bbjfpublishing.com

First published in paperback in 2022

A catalogue record for this book is available from the British Library.

ISBN: 978-1-7396628-0-6

Chapter 1

Littlehampton 20 August 2005

Jamie inhaled the warm summer air, the salt pricking at his senses. As his hand rested on the edge of the car's boot lid, the sun's early morning rays sparked the ever-growing rust to a crimson flame. He creaked the lid down, but it didn't click shut. It never did now. He lifted the boot again and slammed it shut. The car was only meant to tide them over after his redundancy, but four years later it was still with them.

'I still like the colour,' his wife said. Julia always knew his thoughts, her patient smile reassuring.

The green was now hidden under a permanent layer

of dirt and rust. 'Yeah, you're right, it's a good colour.'

Jamie looped the fishing rod case onto his shoulder and picked up the large tackle box. 'Ready to catch some big fish?' he asked his son.

William nodded, took hold of his hand, and led the way through the car park. Julia and their daughter, Holly, followed at their own pace. Tufts of people had already settled on the beach, with their multi-coloured windbreakers adding spots of colour out towards the sea. Jamie tasted the salty air as they walked along the promenade, listening to William's excited chatter of catching a huge fish. The shops at the end of the promenade were already busy. Their displays of vibrant coloured toys — spades, buckets, and glittering beach windmills spinning in the gentle breeze — caught William's attention as they headed towards the harbour.

The morning was hot and humid. William stood on the harbour pier jigging his fishing line. Holly stood next to Jamie as he shared a cold orange with her, the citrus aroma reminding him of fishing with his father when he was about William's age.

Julia sat on a bench behind them. 'Bored yet?' Jamie said, turning round. She smiled and nodded. 'The radio said there'll be a thunderstorm this afternoon,' he added.

'Here's hoping it comes sooner,' she laughed.

'You love it really.'

She pulled a face.

They fished into the afternoon with the humid air slowly giving way to a freshening westerly breeze, making things cooler. The dark clouds, when they came, rolled in fast.

'I'm glad to say that's a lot of rain heading our way, and we need to go,' Julia said as she walked up behind them.

Jamie looked out at the ominous clouds. 'I know, but such a glorious morning. Come on you lot, time to pack up, and quickly by the looks of it.'

Holly nodded, but William protested, insisting he liked the rain.

'Come on, Buster.' Julia said and took William's hand.

As Jamie picked up William's line and began winding it in, a small jerk drew the line tight.

'William, you've got one!' Jamie felt a sudden rush of excitement.

William raced over. 'I got one!'

Jamie handed the rod to William.

'Quick, grab the net!' Jamie said to Holly, who dug through the bag and pulled the net out. They seldom unpacked it.

The heavens opened, large raindrops splashing on his face. The sky had become much darker, on the brink of merging with the sea. Holly shoved the net towards his hand, but she dropped it before he could take hold of it. Julia stood under a large golfing umbrella, and Holly sprinted over next to her. William gripped the fishing rod with Jamie close. The fish struggled as it came to the surface.

'That's it, William. Bring it in slowly, not too fast.' Jamie bent down to pick up the net. 'I've got the net ready, so pull him in gently.' He extended the net fully.

It wasn't a big fish, but William worked with intent concentration, pulling the fish closer.

The sky suddenly illuminated with stark, veined lightning accompanied by a terrific boom of thunder. It made everyone jump. William dropped his rod, but Jamie grabbed hold of it.

'Don't let go, William! We're nearly there.' Jamie leant over the edge of the pier at a full stretch. 'Bit more.' William's excitement touched him. He scooped the fish into the net and whisked it onto the pier.

William let go of the rod. 'I've caught a fish. I've caught a fish, Mum. Did you see?' He ran over to Julia, pointing to the fish in the net.

Jamie reached in and pulled the flapping fish out. 'William, over here, it's your fish.'

William rushed back to Jamie. Jamie extracted the hook and placed the fish into William's outstretched hands. He giggled as he held the wriggling fish.

'Look, Mum, I caught a huge fish.' William's smile was wide. The rain had soaked them both.

'We need a picture before we put him back in,' Jamie said.

'But it's pouring,' Julia replied, standing next to Holly under the umbrella.

'Come on, one quick picture.' Jamie threw the net over his shoulder and leant against the pier railing. William stood in front of him, grappling with the fish. 'Hold on to the fish and make sure we can see it when Mum takes the picture.' He turned to Julia, 'Hurry up, it's wet out here!'

As Julia pulled the camera out of her handbag,

another sharp crack of lightning lit the sky. Jamie didn't react as an intense heat and brightness engulfed his body. The brightness lasted an instant, but the heat remained.

His legs gave way, and he collapsed on the pier. The dark clouds above poured down unceasing water. The wetness consumed him, was drowning him. Breathing became difficult. Julia, having dropped the camera and bag, appeared above him, her face contorted and though her mouth moved, there was no sound. Something was wrong. The deluge continued. He saw the fish flapping on the pier and, for a moment, wondered if it was trying to swim away. Julia grabbed hold of his shirt and pulled him up, but though he wanted to stay, the water was pulling him away. Her face blended into the dark clouds above.

Chapter 2

A green bottle held him. A bottle with thick glass walls and a violent, disturbed liquid raging against them. Time was irrelevant in this dream. The liquid heaved him against the walls, a constant turbulent tide, receding only briefly into the depths of the middle. There were no coherent thoughts or peace, only an endless mixture of crashing emotions. A dream without control, taking him on an unwilling journey.

Then, without warning, a crimson light flooded the area as the bottle melted away. A field appeared and someone was there with him, close by and with a strong purpose. But the crimson field flickered into a harsher light.

A moment of sharp lucidity brought him to the surface of reality, and as the mental fog dissipated, a growing consciousness swept over him. His eyes opened a crack, but the sharpness of the light forced them closed again. The light hurt less each time he opened them and as his focus improved, strips of light in the ceiling became clear. In his peripheral vision, he caught a rush of movement.

A smell became clear, only a hint at first, growing gradually stronger. Quiet murmurs of noise and feeling filtered through his senses. Crisp sheets under his head led to a tingling through his body as the stiff fabric became more apparent. Time became irrelevant. All these senses flowed over him – all calm now, unlike the green bottle.

Then the smell connected – a hospital. He was in a hospital. A door opened and a myriad of thoughts and images ran through his mind. One image stood out. A connection – a key. The rust. His rust. On his car, an ever-spreading seam on the boot. The rust took him back to the car park in Littlehampton. His mind struggled to connect the events which had put him in hospital.

A face appeared above him. A stranger, wearing an old-fashioned nurse's cap.

'Can you hear me?'

He nodded but didn't speak.

She smiled. 'Welcome back, dear. You rest, I'll get the doctor.'

A few minutes later, another stranger appeared in a white coat with a stethoscope around his neck and wearing oversized glasses. Old-fashioned, out of place.

'James, can you hear me?'

Again, Jamie nodded.

'You've been asleep for a while.'

'Julia,' Jamie said, his voice frail.

'Don't speak, just rest for now.'

'Julia, fishing, where's she?' The words were mumbled and confused.

The doctor put his hand on Jamie's shoulder. 'Rest, I'll be back.' He nodded to the nurse and left.

'Julia...' Jamie tried again.

'Is that Julia you're saying?'

Jamie nodded.

'You're asking for your family?'

Jamie nodded several times.

'Leave it with me. You just rest for now,' the nurse told him.

Her hairstyle bothered him as she walked away. It looked so out of place. So many fragments of information, but none of them connecting into a coherent thought.

The ward looked odd – the uniforms, the hairstyles, the equipment. A dark and unsettled awareness continued to grow. The surrounding air seemed strange and different. The images of Littlehampton flitted through his mind, piecing together his last memory.

'Can you hear me, dear?' A gentle nudge on his shoulder interrupted his thoughts. The nurse repeated it.

He nodded, his mind tired and still confused.

'Your family is here.'

A movement caught his eye as his parents walked up next to his bed.

'James,' his mother said, 'we've been so worried.'

This dream was so real. They were younger than the

last time he saw them – before their accident. And they were alive. It looked and sounded like his mother, and his father was standing behind her with a gentle smile.

'Mum!' he said, his voice low and frail.

'We've been so worried. You really scared us. You've been asleep for so long.' Her voice was clipped, nervous.

'Mum?' What he saw made no sense. A disconnect from reality. 'Mum, it's you!'

She nodded and smiled.

'Can't be.'

She reached out, and for an instant he experienced a strange disjointed connection as she touched his arm. He pulled his arm away in reaction to the sudden coldness.

'Oh James, we've been so worried. We nearly lost you.' She reached out again towards his arm. 'I'm just glad Billy was there to save you.'

'Billy's dead. Can't be.'

'Sorry, love, couldn't quite hear you.'

'Billy's dead.'

'What? Billy's dead?' His mother paused. 'Billy's fine. The doctor said you'd be confused. It'll all come back to you; it'll be alright.'

For a moment Jamie smelt oranges, his father's smile bringing back memories of the fishing trips from his childhood, which gave him a little sanity to hold on to.

'Julia?' Jamie said.

'Julia? Who's Julia?' his mother said.

A coldness crept around his thoughts.

'My wife.' Jamie raised his voice despite the hoarseness.

His mother didn't reply for a moment. 'You're confused. I don't know who you mean.' She paused again, her eyes sad, worried. 'You're not married, James. You're just confused. It's the terrible accident.'

'No, no, no!' It hurt when he raised his voice, but the walls of his sanity began to crumble. 'Julia, my wife. No, no, what year? What year is this?'

'Oh my goodness, Malcolm, get the doctor! It's 1985, James, October 1985.'

'No! Can't be.' The information made no sense. The gap between what he knew and what he was experiencing now widened. 'It can't be 1985.'

'It is, my love. You've just started your final year.' She touched his arm again, but this time there was warmth. A nurse came over with his father.

'A dream, must be a dream,' Jamie said, trying to get some grasp on reality. 'Got to get back to Julia, wrong place, got to get back.'

'Relax, my dear, the doctor's coming,' the nurse said.

An inner strength, or panic, took over. Jamie screamed, but it was more of a howl. He grabbed the IV tubes and ripped them out of his arm. The panic drove him on, his head spinning as he sat up. This was a dream, so it didn't matter. 'I can't be here. Wrong place, wrong time, have to get back!'

He tried to get off the bed, but his strength failed him. The nurse put her hands on his shoulders. Flecks of blood appeared on her uniform and the sheets from the ripped out IV tubes.

'Sorry.' Jamie lay back, his voice now hushed.

'That's alright, dear,' the nurse said. 'Let's get you settled.'

His head pounded and spun until he knew no more.

Confused thoughts skated around his mind as he prized his eyes open. Wild dreams invaded his thoughts. The obscure green bottle and then the dream of his mum and dad, which had seemed real but couldn't have been.

A man appeared wearing a rumpled white coat, open to reveal a bright wide tie, something Jamie hadn't seen in a long time. Despite his unkempt hair and the large round glasses perched on his nose, he looked serious, but his smile was friendly and reassuring.

'James?' he said in a gentle voice.

Jamie nodded.

'I'm Dr Johnson. I'm a psychiatrist. Nothing to worry about. I'm here to help you. OK?'

Again Jamie nodded.

The doctor pulled a chair around and sat down.

'Where is Julia?' Jamie said, his voice clearer, but still hoarse. 'Please, where is Julia?'

Dr Johnson paused. 'OK, let's start at the beginning. Do you remember what happened before you woke up in the hospital?'

'Yes.' It still hurt when he talked, but he spoke in clipped sentences about fishing in Littlehampton, his kids, the thunderstorm, the fish on the pier, and waking up in hospital.

'Who's William?'

'My son.'

'And you were in Littlehampton?'

Jamie nodded.

'How long have you been married?'

'A long time.'

'How long? Can you remember?'

'About fifteen years.'

'Right.' Dr Johnson nodded while he scribbled in his notebook. 'Describe Julia, your wife.'

'This is wrong. Where is she?'

'Do you know what she looks like?'

'Yes! Why so many questions?'

'Bear with me. Describe her, please.'

A desperate tiredness crept over Jamie as he said, 'Brown hair, brown eyes, a contagious smile. Where is she?'

Dr Johnson sat still, silent, and looked at Jamie, studying him.

'When did your accident happen? The date, do you remember?'

'It was a Saturday in August, the 20th, I think.'

'What year?'

'2005.'

'Right.' He paused for a while. 'I need you to rest for now. I'll be back shortly.'

'What about Julia? Find Julia, please.'

'I'll see what I can do.'

He smiled, stood up, glided the chair sideways and left Jamie to his thoughts. It was all wrong. He just didn't know how it was wrong. No one knew who Julia was. His mother said it was 1985, and his sanity was rolling towards the edge of madness.

Dr Johnson appeared again with a nurse who attached a syringe to his cannula.

'James,' Dr Johnson said, 'you've had an accident which has caused you to experience a vivid dream.'

'The green bottle?' Jamie couldn't remember if he had mentioned the green bottle.

'What green bottle?'

'My dream.'

'Yes, your dream. When I asked what year you had your accident, you said 2005. Do you still think it's 2005?'

Jamie nodded.

'Well, it's October 1985. You're in your final year at university. You're not married.'

'Sorry?' What the doctor said didn't register.

'We're in 1985, not 2005.'

'There's a mistake. Either you're all crazy or I am.' A twinge shot down his back as the nurse and doctor stared at him. No, he was the crazy one. 'No, no, it's 2005. It's summer 2005, that's the last memory I have. Of Julia, my wife.'

'You don't have a wife. I'm sorry, but you don't.'

'I do!' What the doctor said made little sense. A dark undercurrent touched the edges of his sanity.

'James, I need you to do something for me.'

Jamie nodded as Dr Johnson picked up a mirror and handed it to him. 'Here, have a look in the mirror.'

Jamie stared into the mirror. An icy terror ran through his body as he saw himself, but twenty years younger.

'What's going on? This can't be!' Jamie's voice was loud, driven by anger and a deep fear. The wrong face stared back from the mirror. 'This is a dream. It's a dream, isn't it?'

'No, this is not a dream.'

'This has to be a dream!' His voice became louder and more desperate. 'I'm twenty years too young. I need to get out of here. I need to find Julia and my kids.'

As he tried to pull himself out of bed, he saw the nurse depress the plunger of the syringe. The raw panic subsided, and he couldn't help but submit to the calmness and relax into a deep sleep.

He awoke to find his mother next to him, smiling.

'Can you hear me, James?'

He nodded.

'Good. You're sleepy, I know, they've sedated you. They said you got so angry again about some kind of dream you're having. The doctor says you think you have a wife and children, and you had your accident in 2005. I don't know what to think.'

Jamie nodded as his mother chatted on, but he wasn't listening, his mind in turmoil. Was this dream real? Or were the past twenty years of his life the dream? Every time he became agitated, they would sedate him. He needed to stay calm and take control...

When he woke, the ward was quiet and dark. As he tried to lift himself off the bed, his entire world spun. He called out in a quiet, feeble voice and waited without hope.

'How are you feeling?' a nurse said as she appeared out of the gloom.

'Rough.'

'Alright, my dear. I'll page the doctor and we'll make you a little more comfortable.'

'Thanks.' Jamie became tearful.

'Come on now, you'll be fine. I'll be back in a minute.'

'What's the date?'

'The date?'

'Please.'

'It's the 29th October.'

'No, what year?'

'1985.'

'Thank you.' Jamie felt desperately lonely.

The nurse reached over and placed her hand on his forearm. 'Come on, dear. It's always hardest at night. I'll get something to help you sleep. You'll feel better in the morning.'

She returned with a small pill container a while later.

'No, don't put me to sleep again,' Jamie pleaded.

'It's a little medicine to help you sleep, and you'll wake up refreshed in the morning.'

'But I won't,' he said to himself.

The ward was busy when he woke, with bright light flooding in from the windows, lifting the earlier darkness. It helped lift his mood and made him feel a little stronger.

Breakfast was unappetising, accompanied by a few sips of water. The headache had gone, his mind was clearer, and the spinning had stopped. The ward was different. Definitely not 2005, but it no longer felt like a dream. Dr Johnson came again mid-morning.

'How are you this morning?' Dr Johnson said.

'Better than yesterday.'

A nurse walked up to the bed with a tray holding a syringe.

'James, when we talked yesterday, I had to sedate you for your own good. You became so agitated. I need you to remain calm so we can figure this out.'

Jamie nodded. 'OK.'

'Yesterday you thought it was 2005. Yes?'

'I had my accident in Littlehampton, August 2005.'

'Alright. When I showed you the mirror yesterday, what did you see?'

'Myself, but so much younger. It makes little sense.'

Dr Johnson smiled and relaxed back in the chair. 'Let's go back to basics. You say your accident happened in 2005, which would mean you were in your forties. Do you agree?'

'Yes.'

'But when you looked in the mirror, you are clearly not in your forties. You are a young man in your early twenties. So you see the misalignment. On the one hand, you have a proven fact you didn't have your accident in 2005. But you think you had an accident in the future. Do you agree?'

Jamie nodded again. It somewhat made sense, but he didn't believe it was right.

'So the problem we have is one of fact versus the mind. I think when you had your accident, something happened with your mind to give you this vision, this vivid dream of something not real.'

'But it is real, it's not just vivid, I have lived every day through to 2005. All the emotions and living over the last twenty years must be more than just a dream.' The agitation returned, but Dr Johnson's logic restrained him.

'You think it is real. The mind is a hugely powerful instrument, and it can play a lot of tricks on you. Don't concentrate on what you think. Concentrate on logic and the facts. You're in your early twenties, you have started your final year at university. These are facts we know. We have physical proof of these facts. Do you agree?'

Jamie nodded.

Dr Johnson paused for a while. 'Who is Prime Minister in 2005?'

'Tony Blair.'

Dr Johnson paused; his face showed no reaction to Jamie's answer.

'What about America and the Soviet Union? Is the Cold War still in place?'

'The Soviet Union breaks up in 1991. There are other wars now.'

'How old are your children?'

'Holly is eleven and William is seven.'

'What does Holly look like? Describe her.'

'She has brown hair, her mother's brown eyes and the same beautiful smile.'

'What's 2005 like? Have we got colonies on the moon?'

Jamie hesitated, not sure how to answer. 'No colonies

in space,' he said eventually. 'The internet was invented instead. Mobile phones, digital everything, cheap holidays, cheap money.' He felt exhausted and confused. He couldn't understand or even believe the conversation he was having.

'Interesting. Do you still think it's 2005?'

'I had my accident in Littlehampton, August 2005. I can't explain why I'm here or why it's 1985 or why I seem to be twenty years younger. I see what you're saying, but it's still 2005.'

Jamie felt relieved when he was left alone. The entire conversation had disturbed him. He wasn't mad or crazy, just in the wrong time. Remain calm, Julia would be along once he woke from this nightmare.

Lunch was no more appetising than breakfast. Afterwards, he struggled out of bed and staggered around the ward on weak legs. Dr Johnson came round later, and they talked again – all the same questions and Jamie tired of them. They didn't help.

In the late afternoon, his parents visited again. It wasn't real, none of it was. After their accident he had grieved for them, but now, after ten years, they sat in front of him – he wanted to believe, but couldn't.

'I'm so worried about you. The doctors keep talking about your dream. James, how are you feeling? I'm really worried.' His mother paused.

'Mum, I'm fine, but tired. I'll be alright.'

'I'm glad you're feeling better. I was saying to your father, we don't know what you've been through this week.'

His father pulled out a couple of oranges and placed them on the table next to Jamie's bed and smiled. Jamie returned the smile and the tiny connection relaxed him.

'You and those bloody oranges. It won't help him with these dreams. Honestly, Malcolm.' She turned back to Jamie. 'Ignore him. The doctors will make you better.'

Jamie drifted off into his thoughts as he struggled to accept his parents were with him again. His mother's chatter faded into the background as she talked about the neighbours, what was on TV and what the papers were saying. In the end, he closed his eyes. On opening them, he realised he was alone once more.

Suddenly, Billy appeared – another shock which rattled his sanity.

'Billy! It's you!' A rush of emotions caught Jamie's breath.

'You're one lucky sod. Thought we'd lost you.'

Billy dragged a chair over to Jamie's bed, pulled open the bedside drawer and darted a look left and right. 'Thought you could use some proper medicine,' he said as he placed a small brandy bottle and cigarette packet in the drawer.

'Christ, it's good to see you! Take my hand.' Jamie reached out.

So many years since he had last seen Billy, Jamie had forgotten how big he was. This was how he remembered him best. Scruffy, long unruly hair, unshaven and smiling. Happy and easy going. Not how he remembered him the last time he saw him.

Billy looked confused and uncertain as he looked at

Jamie's outstretched hand.

'Come on, I'm going nuts in here. I just need to check something. I'll explain later.'

Billy hesitated.

'Come on, give me your hand.'

'OK, OK.' Billy took hold of Jamie's hand.

Jamie squeezed his rough hand. He felt a coldness at first, but a warmth spread through it as he let go.

'Thanks, mate. Right, I need you to help me. I need out of this hospital. What I'm about to tell you is going to sound weird. Really weird, but I need you to listen and then help me. OK?'

'Yeah, sure. Whatever you need, even if holding your hand helps.'

'Right, we're in 1985,' Jamie said, and Billy nodded. 'Well, I had my accident in 2005.'

Billy stared at him for a moment. 'You've been through a lot, mate. You almost died. You've got a lot to get to grips with.'

'I know it sounds unbelievable, but it's not just the last memory I have of Littlehampton, it's the next twenty years I remember clearly.'

'You're just confused, not surprising.' Billy paused. 'So if you remember the next twenty years, what happens?'

'OK, here goes. You know Julia Parker?'

Billy shook his head. 'Not really, but I know who you mean.'

'Well, you haven't met her yet, neither had I, but we get married and have two kids.'

'You're right, this is unbelievable.'

'Look, Billy, I need to get out of here. They think I'm nuts and keep jabbing me with drugs. I need to pretend I'm fine, otherwise they will never let me leave.'

Billy nodded.

'What happened? How did I get here?'

'You don't remember anything?'

Jamie shook his head. His last memory was of Littlehampton.

'I was convinced you were dead. No, I knew you were dead when I pulled you out of the water.' Billy paused before continuing, 'I don't know how you came back.'

'What water? How?'

'It was last Friday. We were in town. You'd had too much to drink and wandered off. I thought I'd find you passed out on the way back. But, for whatever reason, you ended up in the river. The police were there with torches. They'd received reports of a person falling in.' Billy paused.

'The person – it was me?'

'I sort of knew it was you when they told me. I sobered up real quick. I ran down the path, downstream by instinct. It was dark, but then one of the torches just caught something as it swept over the river. Your shoe maybe, but it was enough, and I dived in. When I pulled you out, there was no pulse. I know I was probably still drunk; it was dark, and all shit was happening, but I was convinced you were dead. I pumped your chest; water came out your mouth, but there was no heartbeat. I can't remember how long I was there, maybe half an hour, but when the ambulance arrived, they couldn't find a pulse either. Then there was a heartbeat. It was as if your heart stopped for half an hour and then started again. Scared the shit out of me.'

'Not as much as you're scaring me now.'

'What do you mean?'

'The last thing I remember was fishing in Littlehampton with Julia and the kids, getting struck by lightning and waking up here twenty years in the past. I have no recollection of what you just told me.'

'Maybe you died for a moment and your mind got fried, made up some other life, like a really screwed up dream. It's blocked out what happened.'

'That sounds a bit like bullshit.'

Billy laughed. 'Unlike the bullshit you're telling me.'

Jamie smiled. 'You're right, I'm not in a good place. I've got to get out of here. I need to pretend I'm fine, otherwise they'll keep me in a straitjacket forever. Or better still, I'll wake up.'

'What?'

'Never mind. I need you to tell me the latest from Uni, who everybody is.'

'What do you mean?'

'It's been twenty years; I can't remember everything or everyone clearly. I need to get my mind straight.'

Billy spent the next half an hour relaying all the gossip from the first few weeks of term. Jamie remembered people long forgotten, but some he couldn't recall at all. He struggled to accept everything Billy told him. It seemed so real, but the next twenty years seemed just as real. Then his thoughts went back to Julia, and he interrupted Billy.

'Billy, have you seen Julia recently?'

'I don't really know her. I might have seen her in the Union bar.'

'What does she look like?'

'This is definitely weird. You know what she looks like.'

'I do when she's forty. I can remember when we first went out, but it's a long time ago.'

'So when do you two get together?'

'The Christmas Disco.'

'Well, she's probably as lovely as ever. Let's get you out of here and you can see for yourself. You need a few pints down the King's Head to sort you out.'

'You're right. That's what I need. Got to get out of this place first.'

Jamie smiled, but a few pints wouldn't dispel his crazy thoughts. Billy left him exhausted and confused, his mind bubbling with turmoil as he looked for perspective in this crazy world. They sedated him again that evening.

The following morning, Jamie woke refreshed and stronger with a clear head. Breakfast was more appetising, and later Dr Johnson came to see him.

'How are you this morning, James?' he asked, pulling up a chair.

'I feel much better and my head is clearer, but I can't remember much of the last few days.'

'Do you remember the accident on the pier?'

Jamie tried to look confused. 'What pier? I'm talking

about taking a dip in the river.'

'Oh, you thought you were in 2005 when you woke up.'

'Did I? I can't remember.'

'What year is it?'

'1985.' Jamie saw a hint of disappointment on the doctor's face.

Dr Johnson asked him questions about the accident and his dream. Jamie feigned no knowledge of Dr Johnson's questions about his life in 2005. In the end, Dr Johnson concluded Jamie must have had a delirious dream induced by his medication. Jamie agreed with whatever he said.

The doctor discharged him later that afternoon. His parents came to pick him up. His mother gave him a stern look as she packed the bottle of brandy along with the rest of his things. Jamie dressed slowly, still unsteady.

'Mum, if you drop me off at Uni, I'll be fine,' Jamie said as they made their way out of the ward.

'I won't hear of it. You'll spend a few days at home where I can make sure you're well enough to go back to university.' She gripped his arm to emphasise her point.

However, as he walked out into the fresh air, a deep tiredness came over him. 'You're right, I need to go home for a few days,' he said as they reached the car.

'Of course you do. You sit in the front, it's more comfortable.'

'I'll be alright in the back.'

'Nonsense.' She opened the door and guided him into the seat. He flopped in and felt drained, both physically and emotionally.

The old world flashed past him as his father drove back home. All the cars were old, but looked new. There were no modern cars. It felt so wrong. His mother was how he remembered her, as was his father, but he felt an odd detachment. He had already grieved for them; they were already gone. The world looked old, empty fields stood where roads and houses would be built. He was too tired to become distressed and needed to go home and sleep. Tomorrow this dream would be over, and he held on to that thought as they made their way home.

Chapter 3

Jamie didn't wake from his dream. The nightmare was now his reality. Back at Uni, his old room looked familiar but different somehow. At home, fitful sleep interspersed with dreams from his real life had been a struggle. Awake and he was in the nightmare of this other world.

His desk was littered with paper, books and music cassettes. He picked up a cassette and placed it into the music player, pressed play, and heard the cogs turn. Tinny music blared out of the tiny speakers. The music was new, different, or maybe he had just forgotten it. He hit the stop button.

A pad of paper on the desk had notes scrawled across the page, nearly illegible. Books lay strewn across one side of the desk and scattered on the bookshelves.

As he turned away from the desk, the large mirror on the wall reflected a youthful face. At home, he had stared into many mirrors, trying to find something old within. But only a youthful face stared back at him.

The door flew open.

'You're back!' Billy said, almost ploughing into Jamie. 'You alright now?' Billy swerved around Jamie and crashed down on the comfy chair by the end of the bed.

'No, I'm not alright. I'm forty and the last thing I remember is fishing in 2005. When I woke up a few days ago, I'm in 1985. So I'm about as far from alright as can be.'

'You're really not making any sense. I thought they'd drugged you in hospital and you were just hallucinating. You don't still believe that crap you're saying, surely?'

'I don't know what to believe. I've already lived for the next twenty years.' Jamie paused. 'That sounds crazy, doesn't it?'

Billy lifted his eyebrows. 'Yup, sounds a little touched saying shit like that.'

'None of this is rational. It's not a dream; I remember every moment.'

'Must've been some powerful drugs they gave you if you can still remember it all.'

'There were no drugs, Billy. I'm married to Julia. We have two kids.'

'Don't you think that's a little unhinged, as you haven't met her yet? If you said you wanted to marry her, that'd be OK.'

'No, no. I am married to her.'

'You see, that's just crazy shit you're saying.'

'I know it is, but it's true.'

'You sure you're not high on something? You can tell me, I wouldn't mind trying some myself.'

'No, no, no. None of this can be true.' Jamie buried his head in his hands. Billy stood up and grabbed Jamie by the shoulder.

'This is real, Jamie.' Billy shook him. 'This is real. You need to get a grip. I'll see you in the Union bar in half an hour. We need a few drinks and we need to talk.'

The door shut and Jamie looked into the mirror again. A rush of goose bumps ran along his arms as he sat down on the bed. Confused thoughts consumed him once again.

The door flew open and Billy burst in. 'Come on, mate! I've been waiting for you.' Billy pulled Jamie off the bed.

'Has it been half an hour?' Jamie felt a little disorientated.

'More like an hour. Let's go!' Billy pushed him out the door.

They walked over to the Union. Each step seemed intimately familiar. There was no clear memory of the walk to the Union, but as he walked with Billy leading the way, it all seemed like a step into a familiar dream.

'Two pints of bitter, Alan,' Billy said, catching the eye of the barman.

'Make mine a lager,' Jamie said.

'Lager?!' Billy turned to Jamie. 'Since when do you drink lager?'

'I got a taste for it about ten years ago.'

Billy stared at Jamie for a moment in disbelief. 'Make it one bitter and one lager,' he said to Alan, then to Jamie, 'you are really screwed up. I mean, really screwed up!' Billy shook his head.

'We change as we get older.' Jamie shrugged his shoulders.

Billy paid for the drinks and they sat at a table. Billy pulled out a packet of cigarettes and took out two, giving one to Jamie.

'I've given up.'

'No, no, you're just winding me up now. Not funny.' Billy looked worried. 'You don't just give up; you can't give up.'

'They're bad, Billy. I gave up about ten years ago.'

'You hadn't even started smoking then. You are in some crazy shit place.' Billy continued to stare at Jamie. 'You really don't want a fag?'

'Nope.' Jamie shook his head.

'Shit, something bad has happened to you. You drink lager now and have given up smoking. This is seriously screwed up.' His face was serious as he drained half a pint straight down, putting the glass back on the table.

Jamie drank some of his lager while Billy lit his cigarette and blew the smoke out to the side. Jamie had no desire for one.

'So, you hungry for a burger?' Billy said after a while, 'or have you gone veggie?'

Jamie smiled, remembering their staple diet. A greasy hamburger with greasy chips. 'Come on, I'm starving.'

As they headed towards the stairs, he almost walked

into Julia.

'Julia!' He stopped in front of her. She halted, and he had to take a step back.

A desire to put his arms around her grew in intensity, but she was different – so young. All he could do was stare.

'I'm Jamie,' he said after a few moments.

'You had that accident a couple of weeks ago?' She stepped back a little more.

Jamie nodded.

'Are you OK now?'

Jamie said nothing, as he wasn't OK, far from it.

Billy's large hand landed on his shoulder and pulled him away.

'He's not all OK yet, bang on the head,' Billy said, dragging Jamie away.

Jamie felt detached from the unfolding events, diving into emotional failure. Billy pushed him up the stairs towards the food bar.

'Come on Jamie. You don't know her yet, and you were way too close. I thought you were going to put your arms around her. "I'm Jamie,"' Billy mocked. 'You come out with lines like that and she'll never go out with you. Let's eat.'

Billy kept hold of Jamie and pulled him into the recess of the food counter. They grabbed a burger on a yellowed tray.

'So you believe you were married to Julia?' Billy said as they sat down.

'Yeah, we were, but we don't get together for another

few months, at the Christmas Disco. You're right, she doesn't know me yet. It's the strangest feeling, seeing someone you have spent twenty years with, and then meeting them with everything erased. The next twenty years are so clear. It's not a dream, but this doesn't seem like a dream either. I suppose one must be.'

'I don't know, mate, but as far as I know, this is real.' Billy leant forward and pinched Jamie hard on the arm.

'Shit! What're you doing?!' Jamie said, snatching his arm away.

'This isn't a dream, so your other life must be one,' Billy paused, 'or you've entered some multi-dimensional world, and you've slipped back in time.'

'You're taking the mickey now!'

'No, I'm not. But what you're saying doesn't make any sense.' Billy paused and considered. 'Who knows though, you might be the sane one and we are all crazy. Maybe the world we know isn't what it seems and, if we knew more, what's happening to you would make sense. I'm starting to sound like you.'

'So you don't think I'm crazy?'

'I'm open to all ideas, always have been.'

'So you're a bit crazy as well?'

'Suppose so.' Billy smiled and took an enormous bite of his burger, tomato sauce oozing out the side of the bun.

Jamie picked up his burger and bit into it, the taste better than he remembered. They didn't talk for the few minutes they ate. As soon as they finished, Billy stood up, stuck a cigarette in his mouth, and lit it with an enormous lighter.

'Let's get going. Don't want to hang around here if we've got serious things to discuss,' Billy said, blowing out a lungful of smoke.

The brisk walk to the King's Head at the top of the town refreshed Jamie. They settled down at a table in the corner with their drinks.

'So what's happening?' Billy said, lighting the first of his many cigarettes for the evening. 'Say, I believe you're from the future. Tell me what happens in the next twenty years. What happens to me?'

'Do you really want to know?'

'Yeah, why, is it bad?'

'Sometimes it's best not to know what the future holds.'

'It's bad.' Billy leant forward. 'You can tell me; I want to know.'

Jamie paused. 'You start work in London, and you do really well.' Jamie paused again, picked up his drink and took a swig. He didn't say anymore.

'And?' Billy asked.

'You do well, really well.'

'Don't bullshit me, Jamie. I know you too well.'

'OK, you...' Jamie paused again, 'you develop a bit of a drug habit.'

'A bit of a drug habit. How big is my bit of a habit?'

'Quite big, really.'

'And do I recover from this habit?'

Jamie drank from his pint with no answer.

'What happens?' Billy broke the silence. 'Oh, shit! When you have your accident in 2005, am I still in your world?'

Jamie didn't respond, apart from a slight shake of his head.

'When? When do I leave?'

'I can't tell you, I just can't.'

'That's one big load of crap to land on somebody.'

Billy stubbed his cigarette out and drank the rest of his pint in one, slamming the finished pint down on the table.

'Shit, need more drinks,' he said and pushed his glass towards Jamie's half-finished pint.

Jamie finished his drink and went to the bar. Billy had another cigarette in his hand when he returned.

'You making this up?' Billy said as Jamie sat down.

'No. But if it's a dream, there's nothing to worry about.'

'I know, and it doesn't make any sense apart from being a dream. But I'm a little spooked. I might start believing what you're saying.'

'It's probably the drink.'

'No, I've only had a few pints, it's not that,' Billy said. 'Tell me about your life over the next twenty years and what happens in the future. I want to know, this is weird.'

'I suppose my life really started at the Christmas Disco. I met Julia.' Jamie paused. 'Nothing was the same after that. We were actually in here for a few drinks before going to the Disco. Julia turned up with her friends. There was an altercation at the bar, and we got involved. I ended up talking to her, and we never stopped talking for the rest of the evening.'

'But you've already met her, so how's that work?'

'Yeah, that's a bit difficult. I had seen her before, but not to talk to. When I met her that evening, we connected. You know what I mean.'

Billy laughed and winked.

'No, not like that. She was...' Jamie paused, 'like no one I'd ever met before.'

'And she felt the same?'

'Yeah. We got married and had two kids.'

'So what did you do when you left here?'

'I started as a temp in the back office of Grant Shievers, in the City. They took me on full time. I ended up on the dealing floor and earned good money.'

'So you did well?'

'I did until the dot-com bubble burst.'

'The what bubble? What are you talking about?'

'The Internet start-ups. I'll come to them later. There was a huge stock market crash. In the aftermath, a lot of people lost their jobs, including me.' Jamie turned his glass around in his hands. 'I felt a huge sense of failure which never left me. A lot of bastards on the floor managed to hang on. That grated on me.'

'You sound genuinely bitter, mate.'

'I was, about losing my career, the lack of money, and failure. It affected us all.'

Billy said nothing and drank the last of his bitter.

'What I've left out is the important stuff, like all the emotions which come with twenty years of living. I'm not the same person,' Jamie said.

Billy stared at Jamie for a few moments. 'I need to get some more drinks,' he said. 'You need to finish your pint.' Billy stood up and headed to the bar.

As Jamie drank, his mind tried to make sense of what was happening. This felt real, but wrong at the same time.

Billy returned with two pints and some crisps. 'You not finished your drink yet? Come on, mate. You can't have changed that much.'

Jamie gulped down the last of his pint and took a sip from the new drink straight away. No, he had changed.

'So what's this Internet thing then?' Billy settled back on his chair and lit another cigarette.

'It's difficult to know where to start. The Internet becomes big, really big. There have been huge changes. Technology has advanced so much you wouldn't recognise the world I left. How about this? You know the Walkman you use now?' Billy nodded. 'Well, now we have a small device, smaller than your fag packet, where you load music digitally. You can load more music than you can ever listen to, thousands of songs.

'Digital cameras. You can take thousands of pictures and store them on a card a fraction the size of a credit card. Everyone has a mobile phone. They now have a digital camera. You can phone and send texts, even take a picture and send it to other mobiles. It's amazing.' Jamie drank his beer. Billy stared at him with an amused expression.

Jamie continued, 'And then there is the Internet. This revolutionises the world we live in. Imagine millions of computers all around the world, all connected. It changes everything. You have a browser on your computer, and you can use a search engine to type in any question, or anything you are looking for, and you'll get the answer instantly. Imagine all the libraries in the world in one place and whatever information you want, you could access it instantly. You can shop online and message people anywhere in the world.

'Satellite TV becomes huge, with sports, films, music and everything in between. Hundreds of channels. DVD replaces videos. And video games – you would love them! TV devices and handheld ones, with more games than you would ever be physically able to play.

'Satnavs are great as well. It's a small box for your car which tells you where you are, and you tell it where you want to go, and it gives you directions as you drive to get you there.

'People go mad with credit. The world becomes risk free, or so they say. It's a different world to the one now.' Jamie took a long drink of his pint. Billy stared wide eyed, genuinely astounded.

'Well,' Jamie continued, 'there were huge political events like the fall of the Berlin Wall, the breakup of the Soviet Union, Princess Diana, nine-eleven—'

Billy put his hand up. 'Whoa! What are you on about? That sounds just nuts, wacky stuff for a sci-fi novel. You think this actually happened to you?'

'It has happened to me, and to you. I know it sounds crazy, but in twenty years' time, in this very pub, it will sound perfectly normal. Nobody would bat an eyelid; everybody would know what I was talking about.'

'Either you had one mother of a dream and you should switch courses to a science fiction one, or you are from another world. I don't know which.' Billy stubbed out his cigarette and drank from his pint. 'This is heavy stuff, mate. Come on, drink up. It's your round.' He smiled.

Jamie braced himself and downed the rest of his pint. When he came back with the refills, Billy had finished his bag of crisps.

'Cheers,' Billy said. He wiped his hands on his jeans and drank a good portion of his pint before he lit another cigarette. 'I've been thinking, if this is real, like you're from the future and we know what's going to happen, then we could become rich. What about sporting events? Do you remember who won the big competitions? Horse racing? We could bet our way to riches.'

'Do you believe me?'

'No, but if we could make some money, then I could be swayed.'

'I hadn't thought of anything like that.'

'I'm just bringing in the possibility of different ideas which may explain what happened to you. So let's go along with the get rich scheme.'

Jamie considered the glib way Billy approached his unbelievable situation. Billy didn't believe him, and he himself didn't know what to believe, but he considered Billy's point.

'For it to work, we need to assume the future is predetermined and everything will happen in exactly the same way,' Jamie said.

'Yeah.'

'I can remember a lot of the football finals and some of the other big sporting events. So if they all turn out the same, then we could bet in confidence and get rich.'

'Ace plan, mate.'

'Or the future could be random,' Jamie continued. 'This new future is totally different and betting on sporting events will be the same as betting on events which have not happened yet. So the future I know differs from the future which lies before me. I've already met Julia, months before I should. Does that make any sense?'

'Yeah, looks to me like we've got a situation we can only win with. If the future is the same and you know what's going to happen, then we can become rich, really rich. Or, if this future is going to be different, random, then you've got twenty years of experience to use against graduates like me.' He paused.

'You said you screwed up your career and never made it big,' Billy continued. 'Well, now you get another crack at it, but you know what to do this time. Maybe I could come along for the ride.' He stood up. 'I'll get some more drinks while you ponder that thought.'

Jamie found Billy's simple acceptance of something as outlandish as time travel a little disconcerting. The dream of the next twenty years wasn't fading, even with the effects of the drink. He remained in his forties and he lived in a dream now. But neither were dreams, they were both real.

Billy interrupted his thoughts as he placed the drinks on the table. Jamie picked up his glass and drank, stood up and nodded towards the toilet. When he returned, Billy was smoking another cigarette.

'Interesting thought, isn't it?' Billy said. 'This could all be a massive dream? You just don't know. One thing to bear in mind though, if you remember the next twenty years clearly and worked in finance, you can use your experience to get a first in your degree. You're barely scraping a pass at the moment, so if you do get a first, you'll know it wasn't a dream. Do you follow what I'm saying?'

'I think I do.'

'Yeah, look at it as if you've got another shot at life. This time, don't make the mistakes you made last time.'

'What about Julia?'

'You know Julia better than she does. It shouldn't take you too long to persuade her to go out with you.'

Billy made some sense in this weird situation. Or maybe he had drunk too much.

'So let's work on the first assumption we can become rich. Who wins the football league this season, for example?' Billy leant forward.

Jamie started racking his brain. He needed Google, but that was a long way off.

They talked on about future sports events, with Jamie trying to remember who and what had won different types of events.

'I need to see Julia,' Jamie said, as they eventually staggered back onto the campus. Billy stopped.

'It's almost midnight and you're drunk. What are you going to say to her? Hi, I'm your husband from the future.' Billy looked at Jamie, who shrugged his shoulders. 'Well?'

'No, it doesn't sound good, does it?'

'You think! She'd think you were a right nutter, and she'd never go out with you.'

'But I feel like a nutter, so what difference does it make?'

'You can't go and see her. Come on, I'll get you back to your room. You need some sleep.'

Jamie sat on his bed when Billy left his room. The drink had helped, but his crazy thoughts rushed back as the alcohol wore off. He didn't feel tired; he was too restless. He felt a sudden need to get away from the constraining walls, and a few seconds later the coldness of the night surrounded him. Few people were about as he walked across the campus. The late-night coffee shop was closing and when he stopped, he stood outside Julia's Halls. Yellow curtains defined her room, with a pale light illuminating from within. The instinct to go up was strong, but to say what? He couldn't go and see her so, instead, ambled back to his room with his anxiety rising as the frosty night continued to drain the alcohol from his head. It would be another long night.

Jamie stood amongst the gathering crowd. A cold night, as Bonfire Night should be, and dark, but the streetlights at the edges of the field, combined with all the sparklers people held, cast a moving light amid the shadows.

Yesterday, he went to his first lecture for twenty years. Most of the people he recognised, but not all. Maybe he had forgotten, but they seemed so different, like there was no link to his previous life. The lecture seemed more interesting this time round. Some ideas were a little outdated, but it took his mind off all the craziness. Then more lectures today and he even started to write an essay.

A group of them had come to the bonfire, friends he had long ago lost touch with. Although the numbers in the crowd grew, Jamie felt alone. They were faceless people in the dark, people you see in your dreams. With his eyes closed, he wished for his life back.

Through all the noise of the crowd, he heard her voice. A distressed voice, he recognised the nervous edge to it. He opened his eyes, looked left and took several steps forwards. He saw Julia and a few of her friends.

Big Pete, the captain of the rugby team, stood next to Julia with his usual gang of followers. They were drunk. Julia was trying to pull away from Pete, who had his arm around her, but she was having little success.

'Julia,' Jamie said, striding over. 'Everything alright?'

'Jamie!' Her voice sounded surprised, but he noticed relief in her tone as well.

'Big Pete bothering you?'

She said nothing, but a small nod of her head was all the answer he needed.

'Fun's over, Pete,' he said. 'Leave them alone.'

'What's it got to do with you?' Pete puffed himself out and stepped towards Jamie.

'They're not enjoying it, so it's got everything to do with me,' Jamie said.

'Bit of bother, Jamie?' Billy said as he came over.

'Pete and his boys were bothering these girls, but he's about to leave now.'

Pete looked up at Billy. 'I'm bored now. Come on lads,' Pete said, and walked away with his boys in tow.

'Shame,' Billy said. 'You guys OK?'

'Yeah, fine,' Jamie said and laughed. Then turning to Julia, 'OK?'

'I am now. Just couldn't get rid of them.'

'They're gone now, but maybe best if you stay with us for a while.'

'If you don't mind.'

'Come on, the fireworks are about to start,' Billy said.

The first fireworks burst skywards; their fiery bloom illuminated the darkness with an ephemeral light shining brightly, but quickly faded back to the darkness. Then the sky exploded again, and then again.

For the next fifteen minutes, the fireworks held everyone's attention. And when the last few fireworks were sent skywards, the bonfire crackled into life.

As the heat of the fire spread, so the crowd moved back. Julia nudged Jamie's arm and pointed to the fire, and they moved closer. The warmth of the fire was fierce compared with the cold of the night. Hot flames licked their way around the wood. The fire crackled and hissed out its heat. As he stood next to Julia, the warmth and contentment of being close to her proved reassuring. The wife he once had, in some other place or time, was the same as the woman next to him, but also wasn't. Not yet.

Eventually, as the flames died, so the crowds diminished. The cold hit them as they walked away.

'Thanks for earlier, you know,' Julia said.

'That's alright, Pete's just a bully. Unfortunately, a big bully.'

'I'm glad you stepped in.'

'So am I.'

They all walked back together. Jamie talked with her, making her laugh, which was easy, as he knew her so well.

They fell behind from the main group, and as they crossed the railway bridge to the campus, he noticed Pete and the boys by the entrance.

'It's him,' Julia said and grabbed Jamie's arm. 'Should we turn around?'

'No, we'll be fine. He's just a bully. I'm not walking away from him. Come on.'

'Well, look who it is,' Pete said as he stepped forward, blocking the path. 'Not got your big mate with you this time.'

'You're drunk, Pete, just leave it,' Jamie said with a steady voice.

'I might not want to leave it. No Billy this time.' He was slurring and as he turned to his boys, his big bulk swayed.

Jamie stepped back as Pete turned. Pete stumbled forward and, as he did, Jamie grabbed Julia's hand and slipped past him. They were through the gate before Pete knew where they had gone.

'That was easy,' Julia said as they hurried towards the Union.

'He's just a drunk idiot,' Jamie said with a grin.

She laughed. 'Isn't he going to come after us?'

'No, he probably won't remember anything, anyway. Forget him, let's get a drink. I could use one.'

'Same here.'

* * *

On Friday, returning from his last lecture of the week, Jamie finally saw Julia walking alone towards him. The few times he had seen her since Bonfire Night, she had been with her friends and it would have been awkward to speak more intimately.

'Finished for the week?' he said, as they stopped on the path leading from the lecture theatres.

'Yes, still struggling to get back into the routine of lectures and essays.' She smiled.

The sun was low in the sky. An icy edge signalled the closeness of winter.

'Yeah, I know, I'm struggling as well.' He paused. 'I know we've only just met, but do you fancy going out for a drink over the weekend?'

For a moment she paused, then took a tiny step back and looked down. 'I've got a boyfriend and I'm seeing him this weekend. Sorry.'

The impact took a full second to hit, like an express train at full speed, and though he tried to recover, he couldn't. His breath shortened.

'I enjoy being with you and talking with you.' She paused for a moment. 'I suppose I wanted you to know, well, just so you know.'

His legs gave way as he sat down on the path. Both an emotional and physical response to what she had said left him unable to control his reaction. Her books fell onto the path as she immediately knelt down.

'Oh God, are you OK?' Her arm supported him around his back. 'Are you alright?'

He tried to get his voice back, tried to regain some

function, but struggled for breath with a pounding head.

'Are you alright, Jamie?' Her voice became more urgent.

'Yes,' he finally said with a voice so hoarse he hardly recognised it. 'Yes, I'm OK. It's what you said. It means everything is different.' She didn't understand the significance of this, but for him, a huge realisation dawned. The past was different. In his first life, she had already spilt up with her boyfriend in the summer.

Julia held tighter. 'Relax, deep breaths.'

The deep breaths helped. He regained some composure, but the emptiness remained.

'I'm alright,' he said, pulling himself into a crouching position. He stood up but still felt lightheaded, with unsteady legs. She held on to him.

'Let's get you back to your room. I'll help,' she said, picking up her books.

'No, I'm alright, I'm fine now.'

'Well, I'll make sure you get back to your room.'

'No, honestly, I'm fine. I don't know what happened.'

She squeezed the material on his sleeve so hard it tightened around his forearm.

'Honestly, Julia, I'm fine now. It was just you said you had...'

'A boyfriend?'

'Yes.'

They stood there for a moment longer. Julia held the sleeve of his coat and Jamie stood sheepishly in front of her.

'Do you need help back to your room?' she whispered.

'No, I'm fine.' Physically, he had recovered, but his mind started to disintegrate as he smiled weakly. 'I'll see you next week, and I promise not to fall down again.'

She returned his smile. 'I'll see you.'

A wide chasm opened up as she moved away.

The next thing he knew, a hand landed on his back, snapping him out of his isolation.

'Alright, Jamie,' Billy said, 'you OK, standing here on your own like a statue?'

The sun was setting; it was dusk.

'How long have I been here?'

'Dunno, but Roger said he spoke to you about ten minutes ago and you were like in a trance.'

'It's all different. This world is all wrong.'

'What are you talking about?'

'I asked Julia out, but she's got a boyfriend.'

'So?'

'She didn't have a boyfriend when I met her.'

'You said you don't meet her until Christmas, so she might be single by then.'

'No! She broke up with her boyfriend in the summer. I don't know what all this means. The past is different, and the future is already changing.'

'You're sounding weird again. The future can't be different. It's not happened yet.'

'It can be if it has already happened.'

'OK, we both need to get a drink. You need some perspective. Come on.'

'Yeah, you're right. Just need some perspective.' Jamie turned to follow Billy, but his legs still felt weak.

Jamie sank into despair as the weekend progressed. Billy took him out drinking, but it made little difference. He buried himself in his coursework, the only thing which diverted his mind from all the crazy thoughts tearing him apart. The essays were easy this time, and he wrote one after the other.

Sunday afternoon he spent walking. The town was quiet, with few people about. As dusk drew in, he walked around the campus, eventually sitting down outside the main lecture theatre. People walked past, some of whom he recognised. Thoughts of Julia and her boyfriend tore at him. Then someone sat next to him.

'You seem miles away,' Julia said.

'More like a lifetime away,' he replied wryly.

'That is a long time.' She laughed, then paused and put her hand on his arm. 'Are you alright, after Friday? I thought about it a lot over the weekend, as I couldn't understand your reaction. It did leave an impression, I must admit.'

'I'm sorry. I didn't mean to embarrass you.'

'You didn't. I was worried. I don't know why you got so upset when I mentioned I had a boyfriend.'

'It's not so much your boyfriend, more that things have changed.'

'I still don't understand.' Julia said.

'I like your company; I enjoy being with you. I don't want to lose that.'

'I still want to see you, you're so easy to talk to.'

'Maybe we could just hang out as friends?' Jamie said.

'I'd like that.'

'Drink? You can tell me about your weekend, preferably the bits without your boyfriend.'

'His name is John.'

'OK then, without John.' He smiled.

'Come on then,' she said and stood up.

She placed her arm through his as they walked to the Union. 'I don't want you falling down on me.'

'I'll try not to fall for you.' They both laughed.

Friends would have to do. For now.

As the weeks rolled on, autumn turned to winter and the days became colder and darker. Jamie remained in turmoil and every time he saw Julia, his heart would lift and sink at the same time. They would chat outside lecture halls, grab a coffee, or have a drink in the Union when they saw each other.

His course provided his only escape. He wrote at least one essay a night and rather than picking one essay from several choices, he did all of them. A renewed interest in his lectures rekindled his desire to learn more.

Towards the end of term, he received a note to see his tutor. Paul Hitching had arranged an appointment and as Jamie entered his office, he saw the head of department, Professor Fox, was there as well.

'Come in and sit down, James,' Paul said, gesturing towards an empty chair.

Jamie sat down, aware the mood was serious.

'Right, James, we have a little problem which we are concerned about.' His tutor accompanied his statement with a dry cough before continuing. 'This essay, handed in a couple of weeks ago.' Jamie recognised it as one of the first essays he'd written since the accident.

Paul carried on, 'Well, this is an A+. It's an excellent essay. Which is good, but looking back at your previous coursework you've never had an essay above a B-. In fact, most of them have been just about passable. So going from average to a work of excellence is perplexing. I have to ask if this is your own work, because we don't think it is. Think carefully before you answer.' He placed the offending essay on the desk.

Jamie thought for a moment about what Paul had said. He had a point, but they wouldn't believe anything he had to say.

'It's my work. After my accident, everything became clear and I write these essays without thinking too much about it.' He saw they didn't believe him; the arched eyebrows gave it away. 'I can't explain. The knowledge is just there, crystal clear.'

'It's not much of an explanation. This is a serious issue and if we don't believe you, we can exclude you from this course. Do you want to try again?'

'It is my work, and it's the best explanation I can give. Give me another essay title and I'll write it here and now if that's the only way I can prove it's my work. You choose a title, and I'll have a go right now.'

Professor Fox looked over at Paul and nodded. 'Seems fair to me. I'll pick the title.' He paused and thought for a moment. 'Write me an essay on the impact of Technology on the Economy in the next decade, say three thousand words.' He had always been a bastard, Jamie thought, but they had laid the gauntlet with a gift of a title.

'OK, if I can have access to the word processing room, I'll get cracking right away.'

Professor Fox half smiled, 'Good luck and let's hope it's as good as this essay, otherwise we will have to continue this conversation afterwards.' He nodded as he stood up and strode out of the office.

'Shit, what are you up to, Jamie? It's a shitty title for three thousand words with no prep.' Paul said.

'It'll be alright.'

'OK, good luck. I'll check the word processing room.'

Five minutes later, Jamie sat in front of an old word processing green screen. The technology was antiquated. He typed the title on the flickering screen. Paul Hitching sat in the corner marking papers.

Jamie spent a few minutes planning and then started typing. Three hours later, he hit the print key and went over to the huge dot matrix printer, slowly feeding the perforated pages into the machine.

'How many words?' Paul asked as he walked over to Jamie.

'About three thousand. If it's too much, you'll have to throw away half of it,' Jamie said with a slight smile. The printer kicked into life and they watched page after page fold out of the machine. When it had finished printing, Jamie tore off the perforated side of the feeder strip and tore the pages apart one by one. He handed the finished essay to Paul.

'You certainly know how to handle a word processor, and physically producing this many words is impressive.

But the proof of the pudding, as they say, will be in the content. Both the professor and I need to read this. I hope it's good, Jamie.'

'Well, if it's not, then I might as well do something else,' Jamie said, a little overconfident maybe, but he didn't care anymore.

The following day, he had a note from Paul to see him urgently. Jamie popped into the department and, within a minute, was sitting in the same office as the day before. Moments later, Professor Fox walked in and sat down, throwing his essay onto the desk. 'This is extraordinary,' he said. 'I had to give it A+ and more. Your ideas were well thought out, painting a new economic order. Fascinating. Three thousand high-quality words in three hours. I'm impressed. I don't know what happened when you had your accident, but your mind has certainly opened. Keep up the excellent work.' He stood up and walked out of the office without another word.

'Bloody good essay,' Paul agreed. 'I don't know how you did it, but keep up the good work.'

Jamie met Billy later in the Union for a burger. They had intended to go into town for the night but, after a few pints, decided to stay put.

'So what's all this about Professor Fox and Hitch?' Billy asked, lighting a cigarette. 'Everyone is talking about it. Carol spilled the beans, caused quite a stir in the department. I hear you wrote an essay that impressed even Foxy. What did you write?'

'It was easy. I've already lived through the new

technology advances, so it was simply a running commentary on the next ten years.'

'So what happened, exactly?'

Jamie told him.

'Shit!' Billy said as he pulled out another cigarette. 'So they thought you'd been cheating? And Foxy gave you an A+, must be a first!'

'I'll let you read it if you want.'

'I'm not that interested,' he said with a laugh. 'So what's up? You still on about your time travelling life?'

'Yes, I still have my life twenty years from now, a wife and kids. The craziness has worn off a little, but I'm still crazy. Going to lectures and writing essays takes my mind off it.'

He sighed, took a long drink from his pint and finished it, picked up Billy's empty glass and headed towards the bar. As he crossed the floor, a group of people entered.

'Hi, Julia,' his voice lifted as he stopped next to her, 'I haven't seen you all week. How about a drink tomorrow night?'

'Hi, Jamie,' she said, looking a little distracted, 'this is my boyfriend, John.' A large, dark-haired man stepped next to Julia, staring at Jamie with narrow eyes containing no hint of friendliness.

'Alright, mate,' Jamie said, trying to keep his tone light-hearted.

'I'm not your mate!' John glared at Jamie, menace in his voice.

'Clearly not!'

'Who is this arsehole, Julia?' John asked.

Julia looked embarrassed. Jamie smiled, not wanting to cause a scene, and moved to leave.

'What are you smiling at?' John said as Jamie moved past him.

'Not you, mate,' Jamie answered without thinking. A hand grabbed his shirt and pulled him round.

'I'm not your mate!' John repeated.

Jamie saw a fist approach his face faster than he could move away from it. The full impact hit his cheek, and then he took another blow to the other side of his face. He stumbled away from John, his head spinning, and he put his arms out to stop his fall onto the ground. Part of him wanted to get up and beat John, take out all his frustrations. But not wanting to embarass Julia he stayed where he was. There was an eruption of shouting; Billy was trying to pull him up.

'You alright?' Jamie heard Billy ask. 'You alright?' he repeated, when Jamie didn't answer.

'Yes, I'm OK.' Jamie grabbed Billy's arm. 'Don't hit him, promise.'

'Oh, I'll just give him a slap.'

'No, leave it. Promise.'

'OK, but can I at least give him some verbal?'

'Yeah, just don't hit him.'

'OK. Can you stand?'

'Yeah, I'll be alright.'

Jamie watched as Billy went over and pushed his way between John and Julia, gesticulating wildly.

The crowd grew, as did the noise level. Billy was right

up next to John, but the rest of the people were just blurs. Jamie felt out of control, the pain in his face of no consequence. The melee was getting louder, and he needed to get away from all this madness. Pulling himself up off the floor, he stood still for a moment and let his senses return. He skirted around the large crowd in the middle of the Union and slowly made his way outside into the night.

He needed some solitude and headed up to the top of the campus. A row of benches looked out over the town. It was quiet as he sat down, a contrast to the Union. With heavy breaths, he tried to let his mind empty itself. The pain became more obvious as his breathing slowed. This never-ending dream was out of control, the events of the last few weeks rolling around his mind.

Footsteps approached, and he knew it was Julia before he opened his eyes.

'Jamie! I've been looking all over for you. Quite a few people have. Are you OK?'

'I'm fine. How did you find me?'

'Just luck, really. I saw someone sitting up here.' She sat down next to him. 'It all got out of hand. I don't know what got into John. I've never seen him like that.'

'Fairly short tempered.'

'No, I've never seen that before. He shouldn't have hit you. Billy was furious. He told me you'd asked him not to hit John. Why was that?'

'I wanted to protect Billy from getting into trouble again.'

'I don't think that was the reason...'

Jamie shook his head but said nothing else.

'It's freezing out here. Aren't you cold?'

'Not really had time to think about it, but now you mention it, yeah it is freezing.'

'Come on, let's get back to the Union. John has gone back to my room. I don't think he'll venture back there. I'll deal with him later. You need a drink.' She stood up. 'Come on, I'm frozen.'

'Come on, Jamie,' Billy said as he pulled Jamie off the chair and out the door of the King's Head. 'She's not coming, we need to get to the disco.'

Jamie resigned himself to not meeting Julia in the King's Head and followed Billy outside. Things were unsettlingly different. The last few weeks of term had gone by in a haze of essays interspersed with moments of sanity spent with Julia.

The Union was heaving, with the Christmas Disco drawing in the whole campus. The heat flushed his face as he pushed his way in. Jamie searched the mass of faces, looking for only one as he made his way deeper into the throng of people. The loud music and all the shouting made his head buzz.

Billy pulled his arm and pointed towards the bar. 'Drink?' he mimed.

Jamie nodded and, as Billy headed into the melee around the bar, he pushed deeper into the mass of people. As he moved away from the bar, the crowds eased and in the hazy light he spotted Julia. But Pete was there as well, harassing her again.

Pete was next to her with his arm around her shoulder. She moved away from him, but he followed. Jamie forced his way through the last knot of people and caught Julia's eye, seeing a flash of relief on her face.

'You OK?' Jamie said, his voice raised as he reached Julia.

'I am now.'

'Oh, look here, mister big man,' Pete said with a drunken swagger.

Pete moved closer to Jamie, pushed him hard, and assaulted him with an incoherent string of abuse. He then turned round and garbled something to his friends.

'Let's get out of here. He looks really pissed!' Jamie said, realising Pete was distracted.

'I'm right behind you.' Julia said.

He grabbed her hand, and they forced their way through the crowds towards the exit. As they approached the doors, the warmth of her hand and the rushing cold exhilarated him.

He dashed into the shadows opposite the entrance, slipping around the corner so he could see if Pete was following them. Julia pressed up next to him, her hand still gripped in his.

His breathing was hard, and he felt the pulse of his heart beating as they stood still. Eventually, Pete burst out of the doors and ran forward before stopping, his boys right behind him.

'Where are you?' His voice was loud and slurred. 'I'm gonna find you...' He continued to curse.

'He's pissed,' Jamie said as he leant close to her ear.

'We need to go somewhere quiet and let him calm down,' he whispered.

'Where to?'

'Come on, my room. I don't think he knows where it is.'

She nodded, and he led her away from Pete, keeping to the shadows. A few minutes later, he locked his door. Julia put her hand on his as he went to turn on the light.

'Better to keep the light out,' she said, her voice quiet and close to his ear. 'No one will know we're in here.'

Chapter 4

Jamie walked back from his first lecture of the new term. Christmas had been a struggle at home and he needed to be back at university, a little closer to Julia. Over the last few days, he had already written up most of the course work for the term. How he used to struggle with those essays the first time, but they seemed so easy now. Snow was imminent and the cold bit into him. As he walked across the campus, he saw Julia with some of her friends.

'Julia, wait up,' he said, quickening his pace.

'I'll catch you later,' she said to her friends, who waved and carried on.

'It's good to see you,' Jamie said as he stopped next to her. 'How was Christmas?'

'It was great,' she said. 'And you?'

'Yeah, it was OK, thanks.'

They were both silent for a few moments, enduring an awkwardness between them. She looked down at the ground and he wanted to say something about their night together.

'Let's walk,' she said, to break the tension. 'I think we should walk.'

Flecks of snow swirled around them as they walked down past the lecture halls and out of the campus. The hollow cold reflected his torment.

'I like you, Jamie, but that night shouldn't have happened. I don't know what I was thinking. I'm sorry, it was wrong.'

'It didn't feel wrong to me.'

'Jamie, it was,' she said with a raised voice. 'I've got a boyfriend. In fact, I have a fiancée. We got engaged on Christmas Eve.'

'No, you can't be engaged. It's not how it's supposed to be.' He looked over to her, but she was looking down at the ground.

'I want us to be friends, not lovers,' she said.

He sat down on a railing and she stopped next to him. For a brief moment, his head was in free fall. It was all wrong. But she hadn't married John yet; he still had time to win her round.

'Are you alright?' she asked.

'Yes, I'm OK.' He stood up and smiled. 'I want us to stay friends. Just friends, if that's what you want. I don't want one night to change that.'

'Good, I want that as well.'

'No dark rooms for us then, and it'll be fine.'

She smiled. 'Come on, we're nearly in town. Let's get a hot drink to warm us up.'

'Sounds good to me.' The snow was heavier as they headed into town, the cold reflecting his dark mood.

Billy returned to university the following weekend and on the Sunday night they went into town for a few drinks.

'I've been thinking about all this time travel stuff. You still believe you travelled from a life in the future?' he said.

'Every second of every day.'

'Well, I think we need to get serious about testing it. Were you into horse racing?'

'No, not really. Only the big races.'

'What, like the Grand National, the Derby?'

'Yeah, but I can't remember who won what and when.'

'Doesn't matter. I've been reading about the subconscious mind. I reckon if I read out the names and riders, somehow your mind will make a connection with the winner. Somewhere in the back of your mind, you'll have stored it all and, with the right coaxing, we can unlock those secrets.'

'I'm up for it, but I'm not sure it'll work.'

'Look, we'll start easy, pick the big events to bet on, but maybe we could practise on other smaller events. See if my theory works.'

'Sounds a bit crazy.'

Billy raised his eyebrows and smiled.

'OK, not as crazy as me. Drink?' Jamie said.

Over the next week, Billy bought the Racing Post

every day and read out all the riders and other big sporting events to Jamie. At the end of each race Billy read out, Jamie would say, 'nothing there,' to humour him.

Early on a Friday afternoon, when Jamie and Julia were in the cafeteria, Billy charged in, Racing Post under his arm.

'There you are,' he said. 'I've been looking all over for you.'

'I've been in lectures.'

'Hi, Julia.' Billy squeezed in next to Jamie and unfolded his paper. 'Missed some races today, but still a few to go.'

'Sorry about this,' Jamie said to Julia.

She smiled, 'It's alright.'

'Here we are. You two carry on talking. I'll whisper the riders into your ear.' Billy leant close to Jamie's ear and read out the runners.

'Right, where were we before the mad one turned up?' Jamie said.

'What about Billy talking to you?'

'Oh, it's OK, he's got some theory about the subconscious mind or something. I'm not listening to him, anyway.'

She laughed, and they carried on as Billy read out horse names in a monotonous voice beside them. At the end of each race, Billy would pause and Jamie would turn to him and say, 'nothing there, mate.' Unperturbed, Billy would start the next race in the same voice.

When he finished all the races, he stopped and flicked through the paper to read out the football matches for the weekend. Jamie and Julia carried on talking, but when

Billy read out Manchester United and Ipswich Town, some pathway into Jamie's brain suddenly opened and, before he could even think, he said, 'Ipswich win.'

'What!' Billy popped his head out in front of Jamie. 'You sure?'

'Don't know how I know, but Ipswich win.'

'They've got no hope. It's eight to one,' Billy insisted.

'Well, you've been reading all these names to me for the last week and this is the first one which has triggered a reaction, a tingle.'

'OK,' Billy said, his voice excited, 'time to put this into action. Ipswich Town it is. Let's get down the bookie and get some money on.' Billy folded his paper and stood up. 'Come on then, let's go, people.' Jamie looked over at Julia.

'OK, let's get going,' she agreed with a smile and stood up. Jamie was a little surprised, but quickly followed behind as they headed into town.

'Come on, you'll be alright,' Jamie said as he sensed Julia's reluctance to enter the betting shop. Billy went in without hesitation. She nodded and followed Billy inside. A few old men sat in the small room with heads bent over their newspapers. A stale odorous air greeted them, with the four drab walls lined with newspapers. Billy walked over to the wall where a big whiteboard had prices scribbled all over it and stopped by a little shelf which held the betting slips and short stubby pens.

'OK, Jamie, you're sure about this feeling?'

'I suppose so. I haven't done this before, but I'm as sure as I can be.' Jamie didn't feel sure at all. 'So how much money are you putting on?'

'Me? Come on, it's all of us. We were all together when you got your premonition, so we have to see it through, together. It's eight to one, so if we say four pounds each, we're near a hundred.'

'OK, if we're all in this, let's make it a fiver. What's left over after the hundred is a meal and drink.' Jamie turned to Julia, conscious she might feel uncomfortable, but she had already pulled her purse out.

'I'm in for a fiver,' she said. Billy smiled.

'One for all and all for one,' he said as he bent over the betting slip and scribbled across it.

Billy led the way across to the counter.

'We need to pay the tax up front, a quid fifty,' he said.

Billy gave the betting slip with the fifteen pounds to the girl behind the counter and gathered the money for the tax from the other two. A large man came over to the girl and looked at the betting slip. He nodded and huffed.

'They've got no chance,' he said to Billy, not unfriendly but not smiling.

'I know, but I feel confident.'

'We'll see,' said the man, who moved away into the back of the office. Billy paid the tax and received his receipt for the bet.

'We're all totally mad,' Julia said as they walked back to Uni.

'No, he's the one who's totally mad. I'm just trying to profit from his craziness,' Billy said, pointing to Jamie. Julia laughed. There was a renewed step in their walk, all of them somehow linked.

* * *

The next day, they met in the Union for lunch and a few drinks. Billy was excited and anxious. 'Too much of a long shot,' he kept muttering. They went back to Julia's room to watch the results on TV. Billy had a small radio he had tried to tune in for some news of the results, but in the end, he gave up and resigned himself to wait for the results on the TV. Billy remained focused on the TV while Jamie and Julia sat behind him, chatting.

'Ssshhh!' Billy hissed, 'Listen.'

Jamie caught the reporter announce the shock of the afternoon: Ipswich was one goal up with a quarter of an hour to play.

'Holy crap!' Billy said, and jumped up and down. 'Holy crap,' he kept repeating as he turned around to Jamie and Julia. 'Did you hear that?'

Jamie didn't know what to believe. 'There's still fifteen minutes of play Billy, game's not over yet.'

'Oh, shit, shit,' he said and sat back in front of the TV again.

The next twenty minutes ticked by with Billy now silent in front of the TV. The reporter came back on. Big upset of the day, Ipswich had won by one goal to nil. Billy sat there for a moment, then exploded into a series of jumps and screams.

'You're a crazy mother, but a gold-plated genius,' he said as he calmed down. He grabbed Jamie and kissed him on the forehead, then turned to Julia and did the same. Jamie turned to Julia, who beamed.

'We won!' she said, ever so quietly, and leant over to kiss Jamie on the cheek.

'Let's get down the town; we've got some money to collect,' Billy stated when he calmed down enough to speak coherently. They walked into the town and dodged through the throng of Saturday shoppers. Billy went into the betting shop and came out a few minutes later, his smile broad.

'Right, your fivers back and then forty quid each,' he said as he counted out the money. 'I think my theory is going to work.'

'Beginner's luck,' Jamie said, and Julia nodded.

'We'll see. Let's chip in a tenner for a nice meal and drinks.'

'Sounds good to me.'

'Same here.'

After an excellent meal with plenty of drinks in the pub, they arrived back at Uni. Jamie and Billy walked Julia to her room, but they didn't stay.

'Right mate, I'll see you tomorrow. We're going to be rich,' Billy said as he slapped Jamie on the back and stumbled off to his room.

Jamie walked back to his room, drunk but satisfied. The first good day in a long time.

The weeks rolled past with Jamie, Billy and Julia spending more time together. The days mostly consisted of Billy reading endless runners and teams from the Racing Post. Normally, Billy whispered in Jamie's ear in the cafeteria. Billy said they needed to keep the same routine, despite Jamie saying it didn't matter. The next three bets were winners. Each time Billy read out a specific name, Jamie felt a tingling sensation. A connection in an indescribable way which he couldn't understand. They built a pot of money, which Billy reverently told them to keep as a betting pot to use when the right one came along.

Jamie went to lectures and wrote essays, the only activity which kept his mind off his first life. As time went by, he thought the memories would fade and he would gain some understanding. But they didn't – they didn't lessen. The weeks fell through February and into March with the first signs of spring. Every bet was a winner. Billy used all the bookies in town and also caught a train to other towns to put bets on there.

March brought the Cheltenham festival, and Billy couldn't contain his excitement for this big horse racing event. He said they had to go to Cheltenham to get the feel for the horses. Billy had no doubt in his conviction of this being the big one, and he told them continually. Jamie's indifference changed when Julia became equally excited. Billy proved his conviction right when Jamie had a premonition about one horse which came in at twelve to one, followed by the last race at ten to one. They left jubilant with their winnings, but for Jamie, being close to Julia was what was important. The one thing Jamie had not won yet was Julia, but he was convinced it would come.

It had gone ten o'clock before they arrived back. Julia invited them to her room for a coffee – a final celebration. Billy declined with a slight nod to Jamie when they parted. She made Jamie a coffee, and they settled into her room talking about the day and the excitement of winning. Julia turned around as a loud knock rocked the door. She stepped over and as she turned the handle, the door flew open. John charged in.

'What's he doing in your room?' he said, loud and aggressive.

'Well?' John said after a moment of silence. 'Is this one of your cosy nights in with *him?*' He asked contemptuously.

'John,' Julia said quietly.

'Need to get your excuses sorted out, don't you?' John focused on Jamie, who hadn't moved since John burst into the room.

'Look, John, we were just having a coffee toge—' she began.

'Shut up!' John cut her off.

'John,' Jamie said eventually with a clear voice, 'why don't you piss right off!'

'What?!'

'You deaf as well as stupid? I said, why don't you piss off? Right off!' Jamie said.

'You little shit!' John launched himself forward.

'Stop!' Julia shouted, her arms extended out to each of them. 'Stop this nonsense. I'm getting annoyed with both of you, but particularly you, John. What do you think you're doing?' She stared at John. 'Jamie, can you please leave? I need to talk with John, and I'll see you tomorrow.'

'You sure, Julia?' Jamie said, not wanting to leave.

'Yes, please. Now!' Her voice was angry and insistent. Jamie glared at John, his anger simmering.

'Alright, I'll see you tomorrow,' Jamie said as he turned and walked out. Dark thoughts followed him back to his room, and with the many times he walked back to Julia's halls, those thoughts grew heavier. Only when her light was out did he find some peace in sleep.

He didn't see Julia the next day; he couldn't find her anywhere. When he told Billy what had happened, Billy's only suggestion was as they had money now, they could deal properly with John. Jamie didn't think it was a serious suggestion, but with Billy he wasn't entirely certain.

'Julia!' Jamie said when he finally caught sight of her the following Monday. He ran to catch her up.

'Hello, Jamie,' she said, as he came alongside her.

'Where have you been? I've been worried about you.'

'No need to worry about me. I'm fine.' She had a sharp edge to her voice as she continued on her way.

'Julia, stop, please. Talk to me.'

She stopped and turned to face him. Her eyes were sad and stern.

'Look Jamie, I'm going out with John. We're going to be married, and I'm spending my time getting involved with you and your crazy friend, Billy. It can't happen. I don't think we can be just friends, but I'm willing to try. We can grab a coffee in the Union and if we bump into each other, we can stop and talk. But that's it, OK?'

Jamie didn't believe a word of it. 'This is all John's doing, isn't it? His jealousy is driving a wedge between us. He's the one with the problem, not us.'

'Jamie, please.'

'But it's true. He's no good for you.'

'How do you know what's good for me? I can make up

my own mind.' Her voice became even sharper.

'I'm sorry,' Jamie said. 'I thought we were getting on so well. I enjoy your company and I don't want to lose you.' There was a slight waver in her stance but then a renewed stiffness in her posture.

'I think for the next few weeks, I need you to keep your distance so I can sort myself out. OK?' Jamie didn't answer. 'OK?' she insisted, a little softer this time.

'Yes, I suppose so,' he said and left abruptly. He couldn't bear the situation. He walked back to his room and started another essay. He had to get his mind off Julia.

The last few weeks of term were slow and painful for Jamie. Only on a few occasions did he see Julia, but they never went for a drink and only spoke briefly. She remained cool towards him and Billy. When he talked to Billy about it, Billy ignored what he said and continued to read the runners out of the Racing Post, looking for the signal of a winner. A week before the end of term, Billy rushed into Jamie's room and urged him to come with him.

'What is it?' Jamie said.

'Come on, you'll see. Quickly!' Jamie grabbed his coat and walked across the campus with Billy towards the car park.

'Well, what do you think? She's all mine.' Billy said, pointing towards a battered-looking red car.

'Bloody hell, Billy, she's a wreck.'

'A wreck?' Billy looked at Jamie. 'She's just experienced.'

'OK mate, let's see what she's got.'

Billy grinned, reached into his pocket, pulled the key out, and went around to the driver's door. 'Hop in, mate, and get ready for the drive of your life.' He ducked into the car and popped the lock on the passenger's door. Billy started the engine and drove out of the car park, the car screaming under his heavy foot. Although it looked a wreck, it drove well, Jamie thought as Billy threw the car around town and along country lanes.

The Easter Disco, as always, was on the last Thursday of term. With a few drinks inside him, Jamie went looking for Julia, feeling the need to tell her how he felt. As usual, the place was packed, and he shoved his way through the crowds, becoming more desperate in his search. In the end, he found one of Julia's friends and had to shout above the music.

'Where's Julia?' he repeated several times.

'She's gone home,' her friend told him. 'She's gone back to John.' Then she leant closer to Jamie. 'You're not in his league. He's rich. You're wasting your time with Julia.' She shrugged and walked away into the crowd.

He felt let down, annoyed and hurt that she hadn't said goodbye. Billy listened to Jamie's woes, but his only solution was to buy him more drinks. None of it helped to blot out the miserable world Jamie had ended up in.

The week before Easter, the campus quietened with only some of the final year students remaining. Jamie stayed as he struggled and felt uncomfortable at home. Billy also stayed on site and they would meet up in the evening for a drink, with Billy continuing to read from the Racing Post.

Nothing seemed to work for Jamie as hollowness stalked him. Julia always loomed large in his mind.

Early Easter Saturday morning, Jamie headed off to the newsagent for a paper. The freshness of spring all around him contrasted with his grim mood. As he passed the residents' reception, he saw Ron the caretaker sorting through the day's post.

'Alright Ron,' Jamie said as he entered reception.

'Alright, Jamie. You still here?'

'Going home today.'

'I have a letter for you somewhere, not much post today. Hang on a sec,' he shuffled through some envelopes, 'here it is.'

'Cheers mate, have a good Easter.' Jamie took the letter and recognised Julia's handwriting.

'Same to you, Jamie. I'll see you next week,' Ron said, and turned back to his post.

Jamie didn't hear him. He walked out with his heart racing, tore the letter open, and pulled a cream page out of the envelope.

Dear Jamie,

I'm so sorry for the way I've been the last few weeks. There has been so much to deal with. I've had to avoid you so I could think clearly. When you read this, I will be married. John has organised an Easter wedding on Saturday. It's been a whirlwind, but he says it's time to move on with our lives. My time at university is nearly over and I'm starting my next life. It's the right thing to do, and though I shall miss our chats and adventures, it's time I moved on.

I hope we can still be friends, but obviously things will be different. Hopefully we can talk when I get back and I'm sorry for how this has turned out.

Julia,

P.S. I think you're crazy, but I like that.

A heavy weight exploded across Jamie's mind. He read the letter again and looked at the postmark: Thursday. She must have thought, with the Easter holidays, there would be no post on Saturday and it wouldn't arrive until after Easter. Then the penny dropped. The wedding was today.

'Oh shit!' he said out loud. He sprinted for Billy's room, charged up the stairs, and banged on the door. He turned the handle and pushed against a locked door.

'Billy! Wake up.' He banged on the door again and continued to shout.

After a while, he heard some movement from the other side and the door opened.

'What's so important this time of the morning?' Billy peered out at Jamie. Jamie barged through the door and only stopped when he saw Lisa from the language course in Billy's bed, who pulled the sheets up to cover herself.

'Why don't you come in, mate?' Billy said sarcastically as he wrapped a small towel around his waist.

Jamie felt bad for bursting in on Billy, but pushed the feeling aside. 'I'm sorry, Billy, but this is an emergency. Julia's getting married later today. I need your help. We've got to get to Southampton. Like right now.'

Billy stared at him, confused.

'I'm sorry,' Jamie said as he waved towards Lisa in the bed, 'but this is an emergency. My whole life is on the line here. We've got to get moving, Billy. I'll fill you in later. Get dressed.'

Billy continued to stare.

'Look, I'll put it another way. If you don't get dressed right now and drive me to Southampton, there'll be no more racing tips. Now move!'

'OK. Reading you loud and clear. Give me a few minutes to get dressed,' Billy said, eventually snapping out of his confusion.

Jamie waited for Billy outside in the spring air. He paced back and forth, then walked round in a big circle as he tried to think where she would get married. Would it be in the same church they got married? It must be, he told himself. But they couldn't get their first choice, a pretty church somewhere in Hampshire which Julia was desperate for. He couldn't think of its name or where in Hampshire. They went there once, fifteen years ago – a long time ago. It must have been ten minutes or more before Billy appeared.

'See you later,' Billy said to Lisa as he kissed her.

'Right mate,' Billy said as he turned his attention to Jamie. 'What's the emergency?'

'I got this letter from Julia this morning, but I think I should have received it on Tuesday. She says she's getting married today. I need to stop her.'

'OK, I'm with you. So where do we have to go?' Billy

pulled out his cherished car key.

'Don't know. Somewhere in Hampshire, probably not too far from Southampton.'

'Right, I'll drive straight there,' Billy said. 'Would be helpful if you could be a little more specific.'

'I know where we got married, so we'll try there first, but it wasn't Julia's first choice. We couldn't book it when we got married, but maybe they have this time. I've got a vague idea where it is. I'll work it out as we go.'

'OK, let's get going. Lisa was a little pissed when you burst in.'

'This is an emergency, life-changing stuff we're involved with here. You can see Lisa when we get back.'

'Cheers, mate,' Billy said and laughed.

'Come on, let's just get going.'

Jamie hurried him towards the car park. They stopped for petrol after about half an hour and also bought a map, which Jamie looked through when they were on the road again. He found the route to the church where they were married. They drove in silence, Jamie preoccupied with finding Julia and trying to remember the location of the other church. He jabbed at the rattling map on his knees and read out the names of villages. But there was no recognition of the names he read out. For the next hour, Billy drove and Jamie gave directions to the church where he married Julia fifteen years ago. They stopped outside the church at midday.

'I'll see if I can find the vicar,' Jamie said as he climbed out of the car. 'You stay here.' Jamie walked up to the church, tried the handle, and pushed through the doors.

'Hello, anybody here?' he called out as he walked further into the church. There was some movement by the altar as he walked along the main aisle. Memories flooded back from fifteen years ago, combined with a sudden pang of fear. Julia should be next to him, not John.

'Hello, excuse me.'

The vicar at the front of the church turned.

'I'm sorry to interrupt, but it's an emergency.'

'Right, I see,' the vicar said. 'What exactly is the emergency?'

'Is there a wedding here today?' Jamie said, emotions straining his voice.

'No, there's no wedding here today. What is it?'

'It's my wife, no, I mean my girlfriend. Well, she's not even my girlfriend yet. She's getting married today and I've got to stop her.'

'Why?'

'Because she's my wife.' The vicar looked at him, puzzled. 'It's a long story. I need to find her before it's too late.' Jamie paused. He didn't have time to hang around. 'I'm sorry, thanks for your time, but I've got to get going.' Jamie turned and ran out of the church.

'No wedding here today,' Jamie said as he pulled out the map.

'Where to?'

'I don't know.'

'What about if I read the villages out to you, like we do with the horses, and you listen and see if anything comes to you?'

Jamie nodded and passed the map to Billy.

‘Right, let’s start in the top right-hand corner. I’ll work my way down and across and read out whatever village I see. This is the right page?’ Billy asked as he settled the map in front of him.

‘I think it’s somewhere in this area.’

Billy read out the names of villages, landmarks, basically anything which had a name to it. For the next five minutes, Jamie listened and let the names wash over him. Then a tingling sensation shot up his arm and he jolted upright in the seat.

‘The last name. What was it again?’ Jamie said.

Billy read it out again.

‘That’s it.’ Jamie looked over, and Billy pointed at the map. ‘How far are we from there?’ Billy ran his hand down to where they were.

‘Must be a good half an hour, maybe a little more. You sure? We’ve only got time for one shot?’

‘Yeah, we’ve got to go with it, haven’t got time to read through all the names. No, I’m sure, let’s get going.’

‘I wish we could get a bet on this one,’ Billy said as he pulled out onto the road and drove hard out of the village.

Jamie concentrated on the map and gave garbled directions to Billy, becoming more agitated as they drove. He became louder as the traffic slowed them down.

‘Come on, Billy, pull out!’ Jamie said as they waited at a junction.

‘Look, calm down,’ Billy turned to him. ‘I’m going as fast as I can. If I pull out without waiting, some bloody eighteen-wheeler is going to squash us and we will go to the church, but not for a wedding. OK?’

'Right, what's the plan?' Billy said as they pulled into a lay-by outside the village some sixty minutes later.

'I don't know, just get to the church.'

'No, mate. If any of this is going to work, we have to have a plan. She's getting married. You can't go in there as she stands at the altar and say, "Oh, Julia, before you say I do, why don't you leave John and spend the rest of your life with me?" And she'll say, "Of course, Jamie, how silly of me." It's not going to happen. We need a plan because you've only got one chance at this. And John isn't going to stand there and say, "Fair enough Julia, you run along". Also, John isn't going to be on his lonesome, is he? He's got mates, quite a few I should imagine. So you see, Jamie, we may have to be a little cunning and have a plan.'

'OK, we need a plan,' Jamie eventually admitted. 'But I can't think of one.'

'Right, let's assess the situation. Julia may be getting married at the church down the road. We have to assume if she is, then it'll be in the next few hours. We need to drive into the village and park the car somewhere near the church. I'll scout the church and see what I can find out. I'll find out as much as I can and when I get back, we can decide on a plan of action. Sound good?'

'Yeah. Let's go.'

Billy pulled back onto the road, and they drove into the village. They passed the church with people outside dressed for a wedding. 'Looks like something's going on.' Billy pulled around the corner and parked in a road nearby.

'You stay here,' Billy said. 'I'll check out what's

happening in the village, and who's actually getting married. We need to keep an eye out for John. We don't want him recognising us.'

Jamie nodded as Billy got out and walked back to the church.

'You're bang on,' Billy said as he climbed back into the car five minutes later. 'She's getting married here at two o'clock.'

'Which only gives us twenty minutes,' Jamie said as he looked at his watch. 'Shit!' He could lose his wife.

'Right, we need to come up with a plan real quick. What exactly do you want to do?'

'Stop her getting married.'

'OK, I know, but how are we going to achieve it?'

'I can't think of a plan now. I need to talk to her and tell her about us, how I feel, how she felt the first time.'

'You're sounding a little scary there, and she might think the same. Are you sure this is what you want to do?'

'Absolutely,' Jamie said, a tingling sensation running up his arm. He felt a renewed energy. 'I think we need to get over there and when the opportunity is right, just go for it.'

'Just go for it?'

'Yeah, I've not come all this way just to drive home. I have to do this.' Jamie jerked open the door and stepped out of the car. They walked back towards the church. As they approached, Jamie saw a half-hidden bus shelter in amongst overgrown shrubs.

'Perfect,' Jamie said as he stopped by the shelter. 'We'll wait here for a while. We can see the church and we'll know when Julia arrives. Maybe I can catch her and talk to her.'

Billy nodded and squeezed next to Jamie. More and more people arrived and milled about in front of the church. Several men in top hat and tails came out and guided the guests into the church. Then Jamie saw John, in his tails, come out of the church. As the guests arrived, he shook their hands and waved them inside. At about five minutes to two, only the ushers stood outside the church.

'Looks like we're waiting for Julia now,' Jamie said as he looked along the road in both directions.

'Any ideas?'

'I can only rely on my instincts; I can't think straight at the moment.'

'OK, I'll be behind you, whatever you decide.'

Jamie nodded and kept his eyes focused on the road. At ten past two, Jamie noticed a white limousine turn the corner to the right of them and proceed down the road towards the church. Jamie ducked into the shelter and watched as the car pulled past them. Julia sat in the back. His heart leapt – she looked as beautiful as on their wedding day.

'Are we going?' Billy whispered as Jamie stood frozen.

'No.'

'Time's ticking, we need to do something soon!'

'I know.' He tried to find his way back from the sight of Julia preparing to marry someone else. Julia walked up the path and into the church, her white dress flowing behind her. Jamie continued to stare as she disappeared into the church. The spell broke, and he jolted awake.

‘Shit,’ he said, the tingling sensation back in his arm. He rushed out of the shelter towards the church, a new urgency moving him up the path to the doors as he heard the bridal music.

‘Shit, shit, shit,’ Jamie said.

‘You can say that again.’

‘The plan is to wait for the music to stop, and then go,’ Jamie whispered.

‘And go?’

The music stopped. ‘Yeah, go,’ Jamie said and pulled on the door. The heavy door glided open, and he stepped into the darkened porch, then through to the main aisle where he stopped. Julia stood next to John with people on either side of them. But he focused only on Julia. No one had noticed him. For the next moment he stood still, a thousand emotions stabbing at him.

‘Julia,’ Jamie called in a loud voice.

‘Julia, you can’t get married,’ Jamie continued, his voice loud and steady despite the mayhem inside.

‘Jamie?’ Julia said through the silence. Her voice sounded surprised, awkward.

‘Julia, you can’t get married now. He’s not the right one.’

‘What do you mean? Why are you here?’ Julia’s voice became stronger.

‘I mean, you don’t want to get married. It’s not right yet, and John’s not the right person,’ Jamie said.

John snapped out of his shock. ‘Stuart, Adam, get him out of here!’

Two of the ushers came at Jamie, grabbed hold of

him, and lifted him off the floor. As he struggled against them, they slowly pushed him towards the door.

'Julia, I love you with all my heart. Like no other,' he screamed. More hands landed on him, dragging him backwards. 'I love you!' he roared again, but this time from the depths of his heart.

As Jamie fought against the hands which grabbed at him, his attention shifted from Julia to the surrounding melee. Billy was further towards the door. As a hand came around his neck, a rush of emotion gave him new strength. Pushing sideways to regain some foothold, he launched himself forward into the knot of bodies around Billy and rolled clear. Billy was a few feet away, one usher still holding on to him.

'Great plan!' Billy said. 'Why don't we get the hell out of here?' Billy shook the usher off as Jamie scrabbled up and broke free of the hands grabbing at him. Jamie ran for the door, but a body smashed into his back, knocking his feet from under him. The granite floor knocked the breath out of him and as he struggled, the person behind held him fast. Billy's foot flew into the body of the usher who held him. The grip slackened and Jamie pushed with all his strength to break free. Billy grabbed his arm and pulled him up. They burst out of the door and stumbled down the steps to the church path. Jamie glanced around and saw several men behind them.

'Not a great plan, mate!' Jamie said to Billy as they ran through the gate of the church.

'I wouldn't go quite so far as calling it an actual plan.'

They ran down the road alongside the church and when they looked round, the group of men had stopped by the church gate, their job done. The big usher stepped onto the path, shouting at them.

'Now what?' Billy asked as they watched the men return to the church.

'I've said my piece. I can't drag her out.'

The adrenaline rush had lifted him out of his emotional stupor. His thoughts were clearer, but he had no idea what else he could do. They could do no more, and he had only ever assumed Julia would want to be with him. The thought hadn't occurred to him she would want anything else.

A tingle raced through his arm. Movement caught the corner of his eye and from the back of the church, Julia came sprinting towards them. He pulled Billy round.

'What?' Billy said as he saw Julia.

'Quick! Get the car!'

'I'll be waiting,' Billy said, racing down the road.

The mass of material from Julia's white dress billowed behind her as she ran. She pulled off her veil and threw it away. Jamie vaulted over the wall and ran towards her.

'I'm yours, Jamie!'

Julia leapt into his arms. He held her close for a moment, then grabbed her hand and pulled her towards the wall. People were pouring out of the church and running down the path in pursuit. His hand clasped hers as they scrambled over the wall and ran across the road.

'We need to get away from here!' Jamie said as they reached the pavement on the other side.

'You lead and I'll follow,' she said, her voice like his – breathless, excited.

They ran down the road. Jamie looked back at the posse of people running towards them.

'Hurry!' he said as they reached the turning, 'down here!' As they sprinted down the road, Billy drove into a road on the left.

'He's leaving us!' Julia shouted.

'No, he's waiting round the next corner so they won't see what car we've got. He's smart, our Billy.' They covered the last twenty metres and turned the corner where Billy waited with the rear door open.

'Lift?' Billy said and smiled as they threw themselves onto the back seats.

Jamie reached over and grabbed the door, pulled all the material from Julia's bridal dress into the car and managed to shut it as Billy screamed away. The car shot down the narrow road and they hurtled round the next corner. Jamie pulled himself straight as Julia fought against the folds of excess material.

'Bloody hell!' Billy said from the front. 'Now that's a plan, mate!'

Jamie helped gather some of the material aside so Julia could sit more comfortably. She smiled.

'I've got a thousand questions,' she said with a laugh. 'The first of which is, why?'

'Easy answer. I love you. Why did you change your mind in the church?'

'That night of the Christmas Disco, I wasn't drunk. I remember every moment and though I denied it, I couldn't shake the feelings I had for you. When you screamed you loved me, I understood my true feelings. I love you, not John. My heart got my legs going and the rest sort of followed.'

'Do you want to go back? You've got to want this.'

'I'm yours, Jamie. This morning on my wedding day I was excited, but my heart has never beat so fast as when you screamed you loved me.'

She put her hand behind his neck and they kissed, her warm hand trembling on his neck. 'And I wouldn't want to miss Billy's driving. He's going to kill us, isn't he?' She laughed as they sat back.

'Probably.'

Billy glanced round, smiling. 'I'm not even going fast yet.' He swerved around to the left and headed out of the village. 'Maybe we should find a bookie. Jamie's hot today,' Billy laughed as he put his foot down.

After half a mile, he turned off the main road onto a smaller road.

'Where are we going?' Jamie asked.

'They'll probably come looking for us, and the cars parked around the church will easily catch my baby, so if we stay on the main road, it won't be long before they're behind us. I don't know where this goes. It's random, but it's the best chance we've got of getting away without any further company.'

'You done this sort of thing before?' Jamie asked.

'What, stealing the bride away from the altar?' Billy said and laughed.

'Running away from people?'

'No, it's instinctive I suppose.'

'So where do we go now?' Jamie said.

'It's Easter and I'm going home. Nobody knows where I live. Spend the night there and I'll drive you back to wherever you want tomorrow. If you two are OK with that?'

'Sounds fine by me, as long as I'm with Julia.'

'Same here for me, obviously with Jamie, not me...' she giggled.

Jamie put his arm around her. And in the confines of the small rattling car, a little of the crazy pain he'd felt for the last six months eased.

Chapter 5

Jamie awoke early with Julia asleep next to him. The window was open, as it had been a warm night. He slipped out of bed and pulled the curtain back. The sun was already up, warming the cool early morning air of summer. Easter seemed a long time ago – the wedding, his first night with Julia... again. The complicated and uncomfortable weeks which followed had been rough on Julia, but she didn't regret it for a moment.

The final results were being pinned up later that morning. Julia had organised a picnic for the afternoon with some of her friends and insisted he and Billy come along, although he knew her friends weren't keen on them.

He would leave university soon and start the next stage of his life once again. William and Holly crept around the fringes of his thoughts. Over the last few months, he had pushed them into the outer recesses of his mind. The thought they were not yet born, or what happened to them, was something he couldn't resolve within himself.

Julia slept peacefully, and it comforted him. His relationship with her differed from the first time. The conversations they had were different from the ones he had with his Julia twenty years in the future. But she was his Julia.

He closed the curtain, went back to bed, and put his arms around her. Feeling her warmth as she stirred, the disturbed thoughts slipped away.

Jamie sat in the shade of a huge old oak tree on the edge of campus as Billy read out the names of the horses for tomorrow's races. It was late afternoon, and the mood was jubilant. He had passed with first class honours. Julia did better than last time, as did Billy. If his first life was a dream, or in some way real, this life was different. Julia talked animatedly with her friends further away. It had been a good day. Billy had paused and looked at him, waiting for a response.

'Billy, stop reading out the names. We need to talk about the next stage of our lives.'

'Right here,' Billy said, pointing at the paper. 'I thought we were already on the next stage.'

'It's not racing. We need to move on.' Jamie shook his head.

'We're making money and if we can ramp it up, we'll

earn good money.'

'How much are we going to make betting on horses? Couple of thousand, tens of thousands, or until no bookie will touch us and we're scratching around putting on ten, twenty-pound bets?'

'Sounds good. Tens of thousands will do nicely.' Billy looked bewildered.

'No, Billy, I want to make tens of millions or even hundreds of millions.'

Billy stared at Jamie. 'You're not serious, are you?'

'Yes, very serious. We can bet on the horses for a bit of fun, but I want serious money. And we're not going to get rich punting a few horses.'

'How?' Billy shook his head. 'How can we do that?'

'We need to join the biggest bookie in the world.'

Billy's eyes lit up at the mention of a bookie.

'I mean the financial markets: stocks, bonds, and currencies,' Jamie said. 'There, we can place eye-watering bets and make real money. But we have to join the market first.'

'How?'

'We work there. Start off as juniors in the back office and work our way onto the trading floor. If my money-making tingle is as good trading as it is with horses, we should have our own hedge fund in five to ten years.'

Billy looked disappointed. 'What do you mean by a hedge fund?' he asked.

'If you had fifty million pounds in your bank account in ten years, would you feel it was worth it, or would you prefer to mess about making a few thousand on the horses?'

Billy thought for a few moments. 'OK, it's the first one, but do you think it's possible? I know we can win money on the horses. I don't know what you mean by a hedge fund or how we could make that much money. So what's your plan?'

'We need to start in the dealing room, ideally at different banks. We can run the same positions and start building a reputation. Once we've got a track record, we can ask for money from investors and we invest that money. We get a slice of the profits and a management fee every year. Might not sound a lot, but if we can get, say, a billion dollars to invest and we take a two per cent management fee, that's twenty million. With a twenty per cent performance fee over some benchmark, there could be another twenty or thirty or more million. Not bad for a year's work. Once we've done that, the next year we'll have five billion to invest and so on. I know these numbers work, Billy, it's what happens in the early nineties. We've got time to get the experience – and importantly contacts – to make this happen. But we need to concentrate on making it happen. Drinking and reading the Racing Post won't get us there.'

'OK, I see what you're saying. It's just I naturally thought we would be betting on horses and sporting events.'

'We can on the weekends as a bit of fun, but if we want to make real money, we need to be more focused. What do you think?'

'I'm with you. If that's your hunch, I'm right behind you.'

‘Well, let’s enjoy the last few weeks of Uni.’

‘OK, but tell me if anything tingles when I read out the five-thirty Kempton runners.’ Billy picked up his paper.

Jamie sat in the office at the recruitment agency, filling in the form exactly as he had done twenty years previously. He had moved into a flat with Julia three weeks ago, after leaving university. Julia was already working, a different role this time. It unsettled him a little, and he wondered if his old job would come up by the end of the week.

After he completed his application form, he handed it in at the reception desk. The girl behind the desk said they would be in touch.

‘Any chance of seeing one of the consultants? I’m desperate to work at Grant Shievers, in the back office,’ Jamie said with a smile, trying to appeal to her.

The girl shook her head, telling him they were all busy.

‘Who’s desperate to work at Grant Shievers?’ a woman asked as she walked past the reception desk. Jamie recognised her as the lady who found him his job last time. ‘Let’s have a look at your CV.’ The receptionist handed over the paperwork. ‘Come on, let’s find an interview room.’

Jamie sat down opposite the lady.

‘Bit of a coincidence, I just came off the phone from Grant Shievers, and they’re looking for a back-office clerk.’ She paused as she looked through his CV. ‘Excellent degree. Why didn’t you go through the graduate entrance route?’

'It would take too long. I want to work in the back office, learn from the inside as it were.'

'Interesting. They are desperate for someone by Monday and since you're desperate, well, maybe fate has decided. I've a good feeling about you. You ready to start Monday?'

'Absolutely.'

'Excellent. Strange how things work out.' She smiled.

'Yes, certainly strange.'

'You wait here and I'll get the paperwork sorted out.'

Jamie smiled to himself, looking forward to going back to his old job. He was determined things would be different this time.

On Monday morning, Jamie sat in Grant Shievers' reception. After a fifteen minute wait, a young woman came out of the lifts. The receptionist pointed over at Jamie.

'James Harding?' the young woman said as she approached. Jamie rose to shake her hand. 'I'm Louise. Come on and I'll take you up to the madhouse.'

'It's not that bad, is it?' he said to make conversation, although he remembered the nickname of the department the moment she said it.

'It has its moments,' she commented with a smile as they walked over to the lifts.

When he walked into the department, all the memories of working there years ago flooded back. He recognised faces, not necessarily names, and the whole place felt familiar. People looked up as he walked through. The first time it had intimidated him, but this time he felt confident – he knew these people and knew he had the edge.

Louise took him into the deeper reaches of the department to the corner office. Edward Harris sat behind his desk talking on the phone. They stopped outside the office for a moment, but he waved them in.

'This is James Harding,' Louise said, as he came off the phone. He stood up and shook hands with Jamie.

'Pleased to meet you, James.'

'Good to meet you, Mr Harris. Please call me Jamie,' Jamie said, hoping this time he wouldn't insist on the more formal version of his name.

Edward looked at him for a moment. 'Call me Edward. We're not formal around here. Do you have any experience with FX back-office operations, in particular confirmations?'

'No, not really.'

'Straight out of uni?'

'Yes.'

'What did you study?'

'Economics.'

'Well, at least it's sort of vaguely related. You're probably the best the agency has. Louise will show you what to do.' He turned to Louise. 'Sorry, it's your turn with the new one.' She shrugged her shoulders. 'Go with Louise, and she'll get you started. Good luck.'

Louise showed Jamie to his desk. It was a different desk to where he had sat the first time. A little unsettling, but he was back in his old department. Louise spent the next hour explaining his job. Jamie listened with a keen ear, everything flooding back.

He was a little rusty at first, but by the middle of the week he could undertake most of his duties without thinking. On Friday morning, he saw Louise in Edward's office before she came over.

'You've certainly picked this up easily. The only thing I'm left with is the dealer queries. I've spoken to Edward. He's happy for me to take you onto the dealing floor and once you can sort the queries on your own, you'll have the whole role to yourself. You're doing well.' She smiled. 'Once you've got the queries together, I'll take you onto the floor.'

A rush of emotion hit him as he walked onto the dealing floor. It seemed such a long time ago. The main dealing desk ran down the middle of the room and several desks ran off the main spine. The dealers were so young, but he recognised most of them. He noticed his old boss, a young graduate on the end of the forwards desk. Louise turned and came back to him, and only then did he realise he had stopped.

'Are you alright?' she asked, her voice only just discernible over the noise circulating around the room.

The environment took him by surprise despite spending so many years in this room. The fabric of the room wrapped around him. It was familiar, but also new in a way. Again, he felt a stab of pain from the future, his body frozen as his mind tried to find a resolution to his crazy thoughts. Most of the time, he kept busy and enjoyed his new life. But at times like these, he began to lose control just when he needed to hold it together.

'Jamie?' Louise repeated, a little louder.

Through the noise, he heard Louise calling his name.

'Jamie?'

'I'm sorry,' he said, pulling away from his consuming thoughts. 'The size of the room and the noise surprised me. Was I gone long?'

'No, no, you just stopped and looked. It's OK, come on.'

They walked over to the middle of the forwards desk. Jamie recognised the desk head – a man who had always hated him.

'This is Geoff Stiles, chief dealer on the forwards desk. This is Jamie, he'll be taking over the confirmation queries from next week.' Geoff looked up at Jamie and turned back to the screens.

'Anything for me?' he said in his booming voice as his eyes remained on the screens.

'No, a few for Tom, Grant and Steve,' Louise said as she looked down at the print off.

'It's always Tom. He's bloody useless.' Geoff turned to his left and shouted over to Tom, 'Do your job!'

This reminded Jamie of how much Geoff hated Tom as well. Louise moved down the desk and nodded for Jamie to follow. Geoff had always been a bastard.

'Jamie, this is Steve,' Louise said.

Steve nodded to Jamie and turned to Louise. 'Alright, darling, what you got for me today?' He pushed back from the desk. 'Don't tell me you're not coming round to see me every day.'

'Afraid so. Jamie will take over on Monday.'

'Shit, no offence, Jamie, but you just don't look the same.'

'None taken,' Jamie said, smiling awkwardly.

They went through the queries and moved on to Grant, a morose and sullen individual. He didn't acknowledge Jamie in the slightest, and after a difficult five minutes with him, they sorted out the one query against his dealing ticket.

'He's always painful,' Louise said as she leant close to Jamie's ear. He nodded as they walked towards the end of the desk and Tom, his future boss.

'Right, this is Tom, the youngest dealer on the desk and the nicest to deal with.' She leant forward to Tom and whispered the last part of the comment. Tom grinned, stood up, and shook Jamie's hand.

'Hi, I'm Jamie.' Tom's fresh and young eyes were not the hardened ones he would see in fifteen years' time.

'Good to meet you. What have I screwed up this time?' Tom said with genuine good humour.

'Well, as always, there's about seven or eight queries we need to sort out.' Louise replied.

She placed the printout on Tom's desk, and they worked through the deal tickets. Jamie stood behind Louise and looked on, but his mind was elsewhere, his eyes wandering around the dealing room.

It was chaos as people stood up and shouted, picking up the phones and continuing to shout. He had forgotten the noise level from the early days of his career. In twenty years' time, it would all be different. The hairs on his neck lifted as the buzz of the old dealing room drove into him again. Some of the old faces sat at their desks looking, of course, so much younger. It seemed strange that he knew what happened to their careers and their lives. But not all of them. A lot of youthful faces seemed unfamiliar as he scanned round the room.

But maybe it would be different this time. The dealing room felt familiar, but just a little different. He couldn't put his finger on it. Maybe the air smelt different, maybe the carpet a little thicker.

'Jamie!'

'Sorry, just taking in the noise and buzz of the dealing room.' Louise's voice dragged him back from his momentary trance.

'Don't blame you,' Tom said as he stood up. 'Where were you working before?'

'Just graduated.'

'First job then?'

'Yes.'

'Come on, Jamie, haven't got time to chat,' Louise said with a smile.

'Right, I'll see you Monday, Tom,' Jamie said.

'You probably will.' He smiled and sat down to his screens again.

'What did you think?' Louise said, as they came off the floor.

'Impressive.'

'It is, just takes a little while to get used to it. Will you be alright on Monday handling the queries?'

'I think I will.'

'You can always ask Tom. He'll help you. He's nice.' Louise said. Jamie smiled.

Jamie had his break in early February 1987. He had built his contacts on the forwards desk and even Geoff Stiles talked to him. Jamie had come onto the floor with the dealing queries on the Tuesday morning.

'What's going on?' Jamie asked as Tom put the phone down.

'It's just me and Geoff today,' Tom said, pointing at his flashing dealer board.

Jamie sat down at the desk next to him and grabbed a line. As he answered, he recognised the voice from Anglo.

'Simon,' Jamie said, 'it's Jamie, we're short on cover today. What can I do for you?'

Jamie waited a few moments with no response.

'I want dollar/mark points from Feb 25 to Mar 18 in twenty,' Simon boomed through the earpiece.

'Just getting the points,' Jamie said and clicked the phone to mute. He grabbed a large desk calculator and looked up the market prices on the screens in front of him, tapping out the numbers on the calculator as fast as he could. This wasn't the first time he had done this since his other life. Practise over the months made this feel natural now. The numbers came to him, and he checked back to the screen.

'What are you doing?!' Geoff said as he stood and clicked his phone off.

'Your dealer boards are going mad. I can get quotes out. I can do this. Don't worry, I won't screw it up.'

Geoff and Tom stared at him.

Jamie didn't wait for an answer and clicked the phone on.

'Twenty eight / eighteen,' Jamie said into the mouthpiece.

'Is that the best you can do?' Simon's voice boomed down the phone line. 'You're way off the market.'

Jamie heard anger in the voice coming over the line. If he didn't know Simon, he would have crapped himself.

'Look, mate, it's bang on the market. Quote changes in the next five seconds.' Jamie saw Tom's jaw fall open.

'Alright, you little shit, yours in twenty,' Simon said. 'Your name again?'

'Jamie.'

'You're alright, speak soon.' The phone went dead.

'What did he say?' Geoff asked.

'I'm alright and mine in twenty at twenty-eight.'

'Shit,' Geoff said and looked down at the screens. 'Shit.'

'Phone lines are flashing. Am I on board or what?' Jamie said.

'Go!' Geoff said, sat down and grabbed a flashing line.

Tom hit a line, and Jamie hit the Taylor's line. Probably Johno and he looked forward to taking a few points off him. The strange tingling sensation was building inside him, maybe the buzz of dealing again, or maybe it was his betting mojo.

'Jamie here, we're short on the desk and I'm covering. What can I do for you?' he said as the sharp tones from Johno bit down the phone line.

Jamie spent the rest of the morning on the desk with

the three of them on the phones. Jamie wrote out the deal tickets as quickly as he could. It felt like coming home again. As New York came online and took some of the calls, the pressure eased by two o'clock. The dealer board had stopped flashing, and the three of them stared at their screens.

'Where did you learn to deal?' Tom asked.

'Sort of picked it up the last few months watching you guys,' Jamie said.

'Shit!' Geoff stood up on the other side of the desk. 'Did you make any money?'

'Yeah, I did.' Jamie added up the deal tickets he had scribbled down on a notebook he had grabbed. His old way of tracking his profit and loss was so ingrained he hadn't thought about it when he picked up the phone earlier. 'About eighty thousand.'

'Shit!' Geoff sat down.

Tom came over to Jamie and looked through his deal book. 'Let's check these tickets to make sure we're all up to date. Any queries on these deals and you'll have to sort them out,' Tom said and laughed.

'Shit, I've still got the queries from yesterday. I'll get bollocked being away for so long.'

Geoff stood up. 'I'll have a word with Edward later. You did good.'

'Best get these queries sorted out,' Tom added with a smile.

The next morning, Edward called Jamie into his office and told him Geoff Stiles wanted to see him. As Jamie went to leave, Edward stepped forward and shook his hand. 'Good luck. You've certainly made an impression.' Jamie walked down to the dealing room and over to Geoff.

'You want to be a dealer?' Geoff said in his gruff, straightforward way.

'Too right I do,' Jamie said, as he saw the hint of a smile on Geoff's face.

'Good, you start right now. That's your desk, and they've set up your dealing code. I've spoken to Edward. He's on board with your transfer. We'll sort out the employment details later on. Janice from Personnel will be down later with all the paperwork. Right now, I need your arse at your desk making money.' Geoff turned back to his screens. Jamie stood still, a little stunned, but he saw the empty desk next to Tom's.

'Welcome on board, mate,' Tom said, smiling as Jamie sat down. It was a genuine smile Jamie knew Tom would lose over the years. It felt strange to be next to him, but he enjoyed his early company. Tom showed him his log-in and a brief introduction to the dealing system. It came back quickly. The phone board flashed.

'Come on, new boy,' Geoff said as Jamie picked up his phone straight away.

'Jamie here.'

The next few months, Jamie worked hard. He already knew most of the clients, and it was like coming home. He made money every single day, never experiencing a daily loss. His intuition always led him in the right direction. In July, with the release of the US trade figures, came his second big break. He felt the downside in the US Dollar/Deutsche Mark currency all morning and had built a short position to trade out after the figures. Geoff had looked through the positions on the desk.

'Jamie, you've got a limit short position on the dollar/mark.'

Jamie stood up and nodded.

'That a good idea with the trade figures ten minutes away?'

'It is if they are bad numbers,' Jamie answered.

'And what makes you think they are bad numbers?' Ross Wilson, head of the proprietary trading desk in London, sauntered up to the desk. He was the second most senior person in the dealing room. His voice was loud, and the room sensed a junior dealer about to be picked on, the noise level decreasing a few notches.

'It's a tingling feeling I have,' Jamie said before he had time to formulate a more appropriate response.

'A tingling feeling, eh?'

Jamie nodded.

'So how much would you bet on a lower dollar/mark?'

'My whole limit, as I have already.'

'OK, let's test the strength of your tingling feeling. You can have my whole limit, one hundred million dollars, to sell dollar/mark. But if I lose money, then you may well be looking for a new job.'

The room neared silence.

'OK, it's still sell dollar/mark before the number,' Jamie said, trusting his instincts.

'Sell one hundred million dollar/mark!' Ross said to

the spot desk, who jumped on to the phones. Ross turned back to Jamie. 'Let's see how your tingling feeling works.'

Jamie recognised the slight smile on Ross's face, a sort of enjoyment when a bet was more than a bet. He nodded as Ross walked back to his desk.

'Shit, Jamie, what are you doing?!' Tom said.

'I hope to hell you're right,' Geoff said as he stood up. 'I don't want to lose you.'

The room silenced a few seconds before the data release.

'It's way below consensus, shit. Sell dollar!' the dollar/mark trader shouted. For a heartbeat, the whole dealing room had at least one eye on Jamie. The room exploded into activity. Jamie sat down and grabbed a line from a board suddenly full of flashing lines. The dollar/mark plunged.

A few minutes later, Ross came over to Jamie. 'What's your tingle factor?'

Jamie checked the dollar/mark rate on his screen, down two big figures, a million dollars up. 'You got a dollar; I'd take it now!'

'Buy my dollars back!' Ross said to the spot desk as he ran over there.

Later in the afternoon, as the room calmed, Ross came over. 'Great call, Jamie. I don't know if it was just luck or not, but you took the gamble. I want conviction in traders.'

'You're not having him.' Geoff stood up, tension in his voice.

'Not yet, anyway. I'll be keeping my eye on you. You

impressed me, doesn't happen often.' Ross nodded to Geoff and walked back to the prop desk.

'Don't listen to him, he's just a reckless risk taker,' Geoff said to Jamie and sat down. Jamie thought he might be a risk taker, but he's one rich risk taker.

The months fell through the summer. Jamie enjoyed work, and he enjoyed his time with Julia. He kept in close contact with Billy, who still worked in the back office.

Jamie toned down his dealing. Every important economic number they would ask him what his tingle factor was. Most of the time, he said he didn't have a view. It wasn't his money they were gambling, which meant he didn't get any of the reward. This time round, he was smarter. There was always a tingle, and every now and again he would let on just to keep them interested. He did well on the desk. He made money.

As summer became autumn, they rolled towards Christmas. Jamie worked hard; his energy totally focused on his job. He made money, and he made contacts. He went out most nights during the week, meeting people from his bank but also, more importantly, people from other banks. Billy moved into the front office as a junior spot trader. The weekends Jamie always spent with Julia. He felt guilty for being out so much, but she accepted it. The extra money he brought in was a tangible result of his obsession with work.

In the second week of January 1988, Jamie sat down with Geoff for his first review.

'You made a fantastic start last year. We're all pleased.

You're a natural and as you get more experience, you will become a more integral part of the dealing team at Grant Shievers.'

Jamie sat and listened while he bullshitted away. He wanted to interrupt him and ask him for the numbers. They were the only important part to him.

'Right, let's get to the numbers. Your salary will increase by five thousand to forty-five thousand pounds. In terms of the bonus, because you've been at the bank for less than two years, bank policy is you're not entitled to one. So I'm afraid it'll have to be next year.' Geoff had lost a little of his confidence.

Jamie looked at him, his eyes fixed, and held the silence of the room for a few moments.

'Are you taking the piss, Geoff?' Jamie said through his anger.

Geoff looked at him, a little shocked.

'I've made more money than you and the rest of the team put together. I might be a junior dealer, but don't you dare treat me like a mug! Did you think I would be happy with this review? You bullshit me about how good I am and give me zero compensation. All the money I made goes against you as head of desk, so they base your compensation on my money-making ability. And you expect me to be happy with this?'

Geoff continued to stare at Jamie, speechless.

'Look Geoff, this is how it's going to be played out. You will go back to Personnel and Andrew, tell them to double my basic and give me a bonus with at least six figures in it. If they say no, I walk. With my contacts, I'll have a new dealing job by the end of the week. This is not negotiable. I will sit at my desk and await their answer.' Jamie stood up and walked out.

Jamie sat at his desk, seething, but not surprised. He knew he had the upper hand. Geoff had expected Jamie to be quiet and bow to his bullshit. Telling him how next year he would reap his rewards. But Geoff would reap Jamie's reward this year. Two hours later, he received a call for a meeting on the seventh floor. As he entered the plush meeting room, Geoff, Ross, Andrew Gold, the head of the dealing room, and Janice from Personnel, sat behind a large conference table. The faces were grave, angry, Jamie thought, as he sat down opposite them.

'So what's this bullshit you've been giving Geoff?' Andrew said, his voice angry. Jamie remembered how terrified he had been of this man for the first few years he had known him.

'No bullshit, Andrew. I just want fair compensation for my work.' Jamie's anger drove his confidence as he stared straight at Andrew.

'You've just started! Been doing the job for less than a year, and you sit opposite me telling me you want more. You cocky little...' Andrew stopped short as he looked over at Janice. Jamie knew he always shouted. He was nothing special on Andrew's anger scale.

'Exactly! I've only been doing the job for ten months, and I've made more money than the whole of Geoff's desk made in twelve months. So, in effect, Geoff is getting his bonus based on my dealing ability, and I get nothing. Zilch! It's nothing personal, but I want just rewards for my efforts. I've made real money despite being just a junior dealer and I deserve reward for that.'

Jamie waited for Andrew to come back. He didn't, instead turning to Geoff.

'Is this true about the money?'

'Well, sort of.' Geoff became flummoxed. 'As a junior dealer, he is supervised by me and the team, so we consider his profits the teams' until he's more experienced.' Geoff pulled himself together.

'Tell you what, Andrew, you can easily check my deal calls and deal tickets. I'm no junior dealer.'

'You are a junior dealer,' Andrew said. 'Janice, explain the policy to him.' He pointed at Jamie.

'You are a junior dealer grade, and there is a no bonus policy for the first two years.'

They were not going to move on the compensation. This was his second chance. He took a deep breath – all or nothing.

'OK, here's what I'm going to do. I'm walking out of this bank now. You have until noon tomorrow to phone me at home and offer me a sensible review. Otherwise I will not come back.'

Andrew gave a snort of shock, while Ross was almost smiling. Jamie didn't bother to look at Geoff. 'You want to know why I'm such a cocky little shit? Ross, dollar/mark will be two big figures higher by close of New York. Buy it now, sell at the New York close and go short to pick up at least one big figure by nine o'clock London. Do it, it's this tingle I get. I'll be by my phone until twelve o'clock tomorrow. Then I'll be at lunch.'

'This isn't how things are done. We have procedures,'

Janice said.

'No offence, Janice, but I couldn't give a shit about procedures. I make money, that's why you will call me.'

He stood up and left the room in silence, walked over to the lift and out through reception to the pub. It was time for a stiff drink.

He mentioned nothing to Julia. There was no point in both of them worrying. She didn't question him in the morning when he told her he would go in later. The morning was unsettled for him. Reading the papers was pointless, as he couldn't to take his mind off work. The things he said yesterday had burnt bridges unless they came round to his terms. They were bound by all their policies, so he wasn't so sure they would. But he wanted to move forward and couldn't afford to wait another year while Geoff and everyone else took advantage.

He would make a few phone calls in the afternoon and felt confident he would get another job. Eleven o'clock came and went, and his anxiety rose in proportion with the passage of time. Eleven thirty and the phone rang.

'Jamie Harding,' he said as he picked up the receiver.

'Jamie, it's Ross.'

He hadn't expected to hear Ross at the other end of the line. 'Morning, Ross.'

'Quite a show you put on yesterday. Geoff's pissed off; it warms my heart to see him in such a stew. Look, I'll come straight to the point. Geoff doesn't know shit from gold. Your little bet worked as you said it would. I made about half a million on it, and your past calls have been scarily accurate. I like your style. You're one of only a few dealers who have left Andrew speechless. Come work for me on the prop desk. It's where you belong. I'll double your salary and chuck you a hundred grand bonus.'

'Whoa, yes!' Jamie said before he could contain himself.

'I take it that's a yes?'

'What about Andrew and Geoff?'

'Andrew's on board. I think Geoff hadn't given him the full details of how much money you had made. Don't worry about Geoff.'

'When do you want me to start?'

'Get your arse in here now.' The phone went dead.

An hour later, Jamie sat at his new desk. Geoff was brooding at his desk, and Jamie decided to go and clear the air.

'You cocky little shit! You screwed me!' Geoff said, anger in his eyes.

'You screwed yourself,' Jamie replied, all the resentment for Geoff from his first life rushing up to the surface. 'I was a temp in the back office a year and a half ago. Now I've got my own limit on the prop desk after demanding a decent pay rise and a bonus that you tried to screw me out of. So you, my friend, better watch out because who knows where I'll be in another few years.'

He paused, a little uncertainty in Geoff's eyes suddenly. 'Who knows? I might be your boss. Think about it,' Jamie added.

He noticed the unnatural silence in the room. All eyes were on them. Geoff was in a tough position, and Jamie felt a little sorry for him. He thought of Geoff's wife, Mary, who had to put up with him, and loved him for her own reasons. Geoff was a bastard and a sly one, but Jamie had boxed him in. Did he want to go for the kill and humiliate him completely? He saw the anger leave Geoff's eyes, replaced by a hint of desperation.

'It's up to you, Geoff. I only want to make money. I don't want a war.' Jamie stepped back and held out his hand.

Geoff hesitated. Jamie knew this wasn't the end of it. A few moments later, Geoff put his hand into Jamie's and they shook. Neither said anything. The end of the first battle between them. But Jamie had put down his marker, not only with Geoff, but with the whole dealing room. He turned and walked back to his desk.

In early spring 1988, Julia and Jamie stood in the kitchen of the show flat.

'Can we afford it?' she asked. 'I love it.' The flats were brand new and Jamie had already decided. In his first life, he could never have imagined buying a flat like this so soon.

'Yes, we can afford it. In a couple of years, this place will be worth about thirty per cent more. I'll get a few more bonuses in and we'll sell up and buy a bigger place, maybe move out of London.'

'I love this place,' Julia said again.

'Right, if you're on board, we'll sign the papers.' She nodded. Six weeks later, they moved in.

Two weeks after they moved in, they were in the

BMW showroom. Jamie signed the final document and took delivery of his brand-new, dark green car. The newness of the car and the smell of the leather were intoxicating. It felt good, success felt good. He looked over to Julia as she nudged about in her seat.

His thoughts opened the door to his first life. Spring 1988, they were still renting. He still worked in the back office and his salary was a fraction of his current earnings. They would buy their first car at the end of the year – an eight-year-old Ford which never started on cold mornings.

A quiet roar ripped through the bonnet as he started the engine. Julia smiled and looked happy as he looked over at her. But then he remembered when they picked up their old Ford she had looked just as happy – maybe she was happier now, though. The thought stayed with him for a few moments.

'Alright?' he asked.

'Absolutely!' she said.

He smiled and put the car into gear. They pulled out of the garage and he felt pure joy as they accelerated down the road. The shiny bonnet reached out in front of him. The paint work gleamed, no rust on this car. Suddenly, the car park in Littlehampton flashed across his mind – the last morning of his first life. The rust on his old car. It had a strange pull he hadn't felt for a long time. He had to stop at the side of the road.

'Are you alright?' Julia leant over and placed her hand on his forearm.

'Yeah, yeah, I'm fine.' However, Jamie felt unease run through his body.

'Maybe you're coming down with a cold,' she said, rubbing his arm.

'It's probably the excitement of the new car.'

She smiled, put her arm around his neck, and drew him in for a kiss. The crazy thoughts slipped back into the depths of his mind. Don't think about it, he told himself. The nightmares were still alive, but he needed to forget about them. He indicated and pulled out, pushed the accelerator firmly, and enjoyed the instant motion from the car.

Jamie sat alone in their flat on a grey February evening in 1991. Thick dull clouds smothered the land, and a biting icy wind swirled around the naked trees. Julia was out. He had just received his bonus, so he should have been euphoric. But he wasn't. An unsettled feeling sat with him, a dark foreboding.

After his annual review, he had taken Julia out for an expensive meal. His bonus was one million, his salary had increased to a quarter of a million, and he had been promoted to the youngest Vice President in the bank. But Julia wasn't happy. When he pressed her, she was evasive, but it came down to them spending so little time together. Work consumed him. He was out every night, and she never saw him. A despondency hung over him. He worked hard so they would never have to drive around in an old rust bucket in twenty years' time and scratch around for money.

It had been a bad day right from the start. His instincts hadn't been right in the morning. All his trading positions felt wrong. He closed all except one, which he decided to roll forward before going home to get his head straight. Geoff shouted out the quote for his position roll.

Jamie looked at the screen and for a moment, he thought he had heard wrong.

'Can I have the quote again?' he said.

The same quote as before came back.

'Have I got a different market from you guys? It's way off the market.' Jamie walked over to the forward desk.

'That's the quote you get from this desk,' Geoff said. 'You tosspot!'

'What's your problem today?' Jamie said, sensing another argument.

'You strut around the room like you're somebody. They made you a VP and you're barely out your nappies. It's not right, that's my problem.'

'Whether or not I'm in my nappies, I still want a quote in the market, not some piss-take number.'

'The quote stays. Take it or leave it.'

Jamie wasn't in the mood for Geoff's crap today.

'Just because you're shit at making money,' Jamie said, his voice loud and accompanied by a drop in the room's noise level. 'Do you know what your problem is? Deep down, apart from being a moron, you tried to screw me out of my bonus the first year, but I wouldn't let you. I screwed you instead. That's your problem. But it's your problem, not mine.'

'You little trough feeder, you're only twelve and walk round here like you own it. Don't shout at me you jumped up little shit.' Geoff stood up next to Jamie, a few inches taller. Jamie saw a glint in his eyes, a sinister streak he had never noticed before.

'You've got to get over it, Geoff. I earn more money and am senior to you because I'm a better trader. Deal with it.' It was maybe harsh, but after taking crap from Geoff for years, Jamie didn't care anymore. 'You've spent years digging away at me, just because I wouldn't let you walk all over me when I worked for you.'

'Who are you to talk to me like that? I need to teach you some humility, you little shit.' Geoff stepped up to Jamie and pushed him back several paces.

'I don't have to take your crap anymore!' Jamie said, as he regained his composure. 'One of us has to go. We'll let Andrew decide who he wants to keep.' Andrew stood at the door of his office, watching.

'You stay, Jamie. Geoff, in my office now.'

Jamie went back to his desk and watched the animated discussion between Geoff and Andrew. Ten minutes later, he received a phone call from Andrew's secretary.

As he approached the office, he noticed two security guards further down the corridor. Jamie sat down on the chair next to Geoff in Andrew's office.

'You two have real differences you need to resolve. Geoff has calmed down, and I need the two of you to sort out a working relationship.'

Clever, thought Jamie. You don't want to make the decision. Geoff had realised his job was on the line. But Geoff hated him and would screw him at any opportunity. The solution wasn't to shake hands in front of Andrew. Jamie decided to play his hand, realising he had to see this through.

'No, Andrew. He's a spiteful shit who will say whatever he needs to keep his job, and next week he will continue screwing with me. I don't need people like him around me. One of us goes, you choose.' Geoff stared at Jamie with eyes wide open. Jamie saw fear, or pure anger. He couldn't decide which.

A silence followed for the best part of a minute. 'Geoff, I've got to let you go. It's about making money and you're just not in the same league.'

Geoff leapt up, and Jamie felt himself lifted out of his chair. He fell sideways, hit his head on the glass wall and rolled on the ground with Geoff holding him fast, despite his efforts to break free. It took the two large security guards to pull Geoff off him.

'Get him out of the building!' Jamie heard Andrew's booming voice as he sat against the glass wall, a little dazed. Geoff's power had shocked him, and he was glad the security guards had been in the corridor. Ross walked into the office.

'You alright, mate?' Ross asked as he went over to help Jamie up.

'Yeah, I think so.'

'Did you get any better points?'

Though shaken, Jamie couldn't help but laugh.

'You go home, have a couple of days to get sorted. I'll speak to you tomorrow.'

As he poured the last of the bottle of wine, opened earlier in the evening, the morning's events seemed a long time ago. The dark foreboding rushing around his head seemed to grow. Speaking to Julia earlier that afternoon, she was brusque with him and said she was going out in the evening. It wasn't the first time.

As he drank the wine, he hoped it would numb all his crazy emotions. The TV flickered in the corner, but they were only moving images in front of him while his mind fought his demons.

A loud knock at the front door brought him back to the present. He looked at the wall clock as he pulled himself off the sofa – it was nearly nine o'clock. It would be Julia coming back, forgetting her key as she always did.

Opening the front door, for a moment he just stared. It wasn't Julia. A blur approached his face and, before he could move, he felt the full force of Geoff's fist.

He reeled backwards into the hallway and suffered another sharp thud to the head, followed by blows to the body. His mind couldn't keep up with events. Then, just as suddenly, it stopped. His head spun, and he stumbled to the ground. Red spots dripped down over the cream carpet, and he tasted blood in his mouth.

'You little shit, you cost me my job, you jumped up arrogant bastard!' He heard Geoff screaming at him, his words slurred but loud. He turned his head and tried to focus on where the sound came from. Geoff stood beside him and had bent down while he shouted.

'Geoff,' Jamie said, blood spraying onto the carpet. 'Why are you here?'

'Because you need to be taught some humility, and not be such an arrogant bastard. You really are a piece of work. All the rest of us work hard, put the time in and appreciate our rewards as we receive them. But you just waltz in, screw me over without showing any respect, and then continue to shove it in my face day after day, week after week, year after year.'

Jamie tried to piece it together. The pain swam through all his thoughts as he struggled to think coherently.

'Why are you here?' Jamie asked again, 'and who is that?' Jamie looked at a large man next to Geoff.

'You still don't get it, do you, you little shit?' Geoff rained down more blows. 'Don't you understand? You cost me my job! You don't know what you've done – look what you made me do. Just because you had no humility. No fucking humility...'

The other man stepped forward and grabbed Jamie, pulling him off the floor by his shirt. His arm pulled back and Jamie could see his fist approach, the impact throwing him across the hallway and into the lounge, landing on the coffee table. The glass inlay shattered, and he crumpled onto the floor. He put his hands up to his face, but it was numb. His hands shook as he pulled them away. They were covered in blood. A slow nausea crept into his throat.

'Jesus, Mick, you've taken half his head off!' Jamie heard Geoff shout.

'I only hit him once.'

Jamie saw Geoff looking down at him.

'Jesus, Mick,' Geoff said as he leant down and stared at him.

'Help me,' Jamie mumbled, his mouth full of blood.

'We need to get out of here,' Geoff said. 'Mick go, go now!'

Then Jamie was left alone with his pain. He tried to focus his thoughts, but couldn't. The blackness came in spots but slowly blended to crimson. The pain eased, and he felt a familiarity to that colour he had experienced when he travelled back in time. A specific colour he could feel. It grew in intensity and through the calmness of the crimson, he saw shapes begin to grow.

Unfocused images developed around him as a new world unfolded, a world he had never seen before. There was a familiar kinship to it, though. He stood on the edge of a cliff with a castle opposite. An old castle, a ruin. Rolling fields stretched away from the castle; the horizon seemed to run towards an infinite line. A void lay between the castle and where he stood, a chasm of nothingness. As he looked into the darkness, he felt despair, which seemed to want to draw him in. With difficulty, he pulled his eyes away and looked back over the landscape. A crimson colour overlay this entire world. The fields were green but crimson as well, the castle a beige grey colour with a crimson hue. This place gave him a sense of contentment he hadn't felt for a long time. He couldn't move, he didn't need to.

There was someone next to him and, though he stared hard, he struggled to focus.

'James,' the person said as he moved closer and became clearer. A man, tall with blond hair.

'Who are you?' Jamie asked, his voice clear.

'You can call me Gabriel.'

'Where am I?'

'You are between timelines, this is indeterminate time. Time doesn't exist here, and this is how you represent it. A dream world.'

'I don't know what you're saying.'

Gabriel appeared to smile. 'You are an anomaly.'

Jamie stared at the man, who seemed to glimmer. Kindness and a calmness radiated from him.

'You have slipped between timelines and now you are stuck in an ever-increasing time loop.'

'I don't understand.' Jamie felt sure it must be a dream, but it felt real.

'In your first timeline, you died on a fishing trip and when you woke up in hospital, you were back in 1985. Before you woke up in hospital you briefly stopped here, but you didn't become self-aware before you jumped. It will become clearer each time you return. You believed your life was a dream, although you knew it was too real to be one. The world you were in was the same, but also a little different. Yes?'

Jamie nodded.

'You see, the world comprises an infinite number of different timelines. Every decision made is a choice causing two or more outcomes, and ever more decisions compound these. Every decision causes a divergence between the timelines and every world has the results of all those choices, whether intentional or not. Some worlds are similar, whilst others are completely different. The only fixed constant is you all die at the same point, all the

Jamies, in all timelines. This keeps the time continuum in place.'

Jamie listened, but it made no sense.

Gabriel continued, 'In your original timeline you lived past the point you should have died – 25th October 1985. When you had your accident, you didn't actually die. In fact, you lived another twenty years. When an anomaly occurs, like you, an inconsistency develops.'

'How did I live past my time?'

'Well, that's the anomaly. Because all timelines are simultaneous, all events in all timelines occur simultaneously. We don't know exactly how it came about. There is another anomaly from a different timeline, another person like you. There is always a link.'

'I still don't understand any of this. Why don't you ask the other person?' Jamie shook his head.

'I'm not able to. You are the cause, and I can only talk to you at the moment. I haven't time to explain now.'

'Who are you?'

'I'm a guardian. I exist only in this world, and I have to keep the time continuum intact. When an event like this threatens a timeline, I have to put it right.'

'I still don't understand.'

Gabriel began to fade. 'You are about to jump again.' His voice trailed off as he merged into the crimson world.

Then he saw her in front of the castle, on the other side of the void. A woman dressed in crimson. He saw her clearly. Her dark hair framed her warm face. Not only could he see her, but he could feel her. Her calmness, her kindness, flowed across the void. She smiled, her face becoming animated. He sensed a familiarity, although he had never seen her before.

'Hello, my darling Jamie,' she spoke, her voice soft.

'Hello?'

'Don't be afraid, Jamie. Don't be afraid.'

Jamie wanted to ask her questions but didn't feel the need. He let the aura from the woman flow over him.

She reached out her hand across the void. 'Don't be afraid, my darling,' she repeated.

Jamie again felt the words wash over him. 'Who...' he asked.

'You know my name.'

Suddenly, the scene shifted. The woman smiled as he descended into the void. A panic rose through him. She was still there, but further away and above him. He felt an instant loss. He didn't want to leave; he wanted her calmness. The void rushed up around him as he plunged into nothingness. A familiar green liquid wrapped itself around him. But he wasn't afraid.

Chapter 6

25 October 1985

Jamie woke with someone on top of him, hitting him on the chest. An overpowering smell filled his nostrils, an unpleasant, wet, rotten stink.

'What the fuck are you doing?!' Jamie said.

'Sarge, you're back.' The person jumped off and landed next to him. 'We all thought we'd lost you, but I knew you would come back. You wouldn't leave me in this shithole.'

At first glance, he thought the person was a man but, as he focused, he realised the fine features were of a woman, despite her short hair. Before he had time to speak, another person appeared, their face covered with a mask. They gripped his wrist and flashed a bright light in each of his eyes.

'Christ, trooper, looks like you've pulled him back from the dead. He must have been out half an hour, but he's fine now. Get him out of here so we can have the bed.'

'Come on, Sarge, I'll give you a hand.'

She hauled him up into a sitting position, her sinewy strength surprising him. She put her arm under his shoulder and round his back, and pulled him off the bed. At first, his legs felt weak, but her arm gripped him tight. As he recovered his balance, he looked around the large room.

He was in a hospital of some sort, tables lined up in rows with groups of people huddled over them. All the tables had severely injured people on them. And they all wore green uniforms. Army uniforms, not one he recognised. As he looked down, his open tunic was similar, with what looked like blood on the front and other parts torn. The woman who held him wore the same uniform.

'Where are we?' he asked as they hobbled out of the room.

'Sarge?' She looked puzzled. 'We're in the forward field hospital. You nearly took a direct hit. We thought we'd lost you when your heart stopped,' she said, edging towards the door.

The cold began biting into him and as he looked up, he saw the canvas. They were in a big tent. A thousand questions spread through his mind as he tried to comprehend this new situation. Hundreds of unfamiliar smells bombarded his senses and there was a creeping difference to any world he knew.

Fleeting recollections of the crimson world flashed through his thoughts. A man had talked to him, telling him about different worlds. He tried to remember his name but couldn't recall it. Also, he'd felt calm with the woman who told him not to be afraid.

Only what seemed like moments ago, Geoff had attacked him and left him bleeding on the lounge floor. As real as now and just as frightening. His second life had been real, as real as his first. Now he was in yet another world.

'Come on, Sarge, we've got to get out of here. The quicker the better,' the woman said with a determined push towards a doorway.

The smell and air improved once through the door. They had entered a small reception room containing a table with a man sat behind it.

'Sergeant Harding, he's back with us,' the woman said.

'Welcome back, Sergeant,' the orderly behind the desk said. 'We need as many soldiers as we can muster. They're getting closer.'

A loud explosion shook the ground under his feet. To Jamie, it sounded as if the world ended. His ear drums rang. But neither the woman nor the man behind the desk flinched. 'Theirs,' the woman said.

'You're checked out, Sergeant, and good luck. Don't want to see either of you two back here.'

'Me neither,' the woman said, and with a firm hold of Jamie, she strode out through the exit into the cold and dark night. People and vehicles criss-crossed between the large tents which surrounded them. The vehicles looked like old Jeeps. She guided him down the road and stopped when they came to a Jeep parked by the side of the road. Two occupants jumped out.

'You're back, Sarge!' one of occupants said. 'We heard they snagged you.'

'They didn't. He's not left us!' the woman said. 'Let's get back.'

Both men jumped into the front of the Jeep. The engine started as the woman guided Jamie into the back of the open top vehicle. Before he had time to settle into the seat, the Jeep jerked out into the road. Music blared out from the front, a song he thought he recognised. The woman pulled Jamie closer to her and took hold of his hand. The night was cold, but refreshing, away from the smell of death. There were a lot of questions he wanted to ask, but the noise from the Jeep and the music drowned out any such attempt. After five minutes, the Jeep pulled up as they approached scattered lights in amongst the woods. The woman let go of his hand and helped him out of the Jeep.

'Good to have you back, Sarge!' one man shouted as they drove off down the road.

As she led him across a field, some of his strength returned, the fresh air clearing his nostrils and head. Sounds of explosions drifted in from the distance as the long grass brushed against his legs.

'Where are we going?' he asked.

'Back to the front line, Sarge. Back to our unit. Are you alright?'

'Fine, a little stunned, I suppose. How much further?'

'Just a little further. The woods are just over there.'

'I can't remember what happened to me. It's a blank. Can you help me, just between the two of us?'

'Yes, Sarge. You took shrapnel and your heart stopped as they patched you up. The doctor gave up after a few minutes, but I wouldn't let you go. I knew you would come back, and I got you back. I kept beating your chest until it started again.'

'How long was I dead for?'

'I don't know exactly, about twenty minutes, maybe half an hour, I think.'

'Probably why I can't remember much.'

'Oh, I see what you mean.'

As they approached the edge of the woods, he saw movement in amongst the trees. Scattered tents and people were on either side of them as they walked through the camp. The woman stopped outside a tent, pulled back the cover with one hand and held him firm with the other as she guided him into the tent. The tent was small, with a camp bed on one side. He sat down as the woman fiddled with a small object on the other side. The atmosphere was cold and damp, and he shivered as he sat in silence. The sound of a striking match caught his attention as the contraption in front of him let out a puff of heat. She stepped back and sat down.

'Are you warm enough, James?' she said, her voice a whisper. 'Oh God, I thought I had lost you.' She put her arms around him. 'The heater will soon warm us up.'

Her voice was soft and gentle, far more intimate. The heater pushed out a cloud of warmth and gave the tent a faint glow. For the next few minutes, they sat in silence with the woman holding him tight.

He was, or had been, rich with a big bonus and set on a course to become extremely wealthy. Julia was unhappy with their relationship, but he could have fixed that. Then it was all gone, and he was plunged into a crimson world with a man who told him about time. And the mysterious woman who he tried to picture. Don't be afraid. Those words were clear as the crimson world floated around the fringes of his mind. The thoughts gave him goose bumps all over and made him shudder in the woman's arms.

She held him tighter.

The heater warmed the tent, but not enough to stop his shivers. A dampness permeated throughout. He wanted to ask her name. He was sure he knew it, but couldn't recall.

'What time is it?' he asked instead.

'It's just past midnight,' she said as she checked her watch against the faint glow of the heater.

'I'm so tired,' he told her. She stood up, laid him down on the camp bed, and squeezed next to him with her head tight against his neck. There were still so many questions, but he relaxed. The woman from his crimson dream repeated, 'don't be afraid' as he drifted off to sleep.

He woke with a start. A sudden coldness to his left side, with the woman gone. Weak light filtered through the walls of the tent. The heater had gone out, and the dampness remained. The last twelve hours had been insane, unreal, and his mind tried to make sense of it as he lay still on the bed. Probably less than twelve hours, but it felt like a lifetime. The tent poles above him drew his eyes, with the damp canvas pulled tight across them.

A thought snapped back from the crimson world. The man had said he died in October. The thought held clear for a moment, and then the crimson world receded again. Twice now he had lost Julia, and he was now in a totally different world, the air different from anything he had felt before. These thoughts spread wildly around his mind as he tried to find something to hold on to.

The tent flap opened, and the woman came in and sat down on the bed.

'Morning, James,' she said, kissing him on the mouth. Despite the cold, her lips were warm and tender. 'How are you feeling? Quite a night.'

'More than you could ever imagine.'

Despite the short hair and dirt and blood on her face, she had an attractiveness he couldn't quite put his finger on, a certain familiarity.

'God, I thought I'd lost you last night. I nearly fell apart when they brought you back injured. I keep wondering what life would be like if we weren't fighting and dealing with this shit every day.'

'Don't,' he said. He knew how she felt, in a way closer than she could imagine. 'What time is it?'

'It's about seven thirty, clear skies, another beautiful day. A lot of talk out there about how close they are and when they will attack. I don't think we've got enough here to withstand them.'

All he had were questions within this strange world.

'Last night, when my heart stopped, something happened and I need some help. What's the date? I need to get a few reference points.'

'OK, I think it's the 26th October.'

'What year?'

'1985,' she said, with a slight narrowing of her eyes.

'Where are we?'

'We're on the south coast, close to Hastings.'

'Sussex. Who are we fighting?'

'Are you sure you're alright?'

'Well, not really, but I need to know who we're fighting.'

'The Reich Army.'

'The Reich Army?!' As he said it, a part of his brain, or the other Jamie's brain, flooded in a stream of memories. Of course, they had always been fighting.

'Yes, we've fought them for the past forty-five years,' she said.

'Shit!' This different world sunk deep into his consciousness, a strange fear seeping into his being.

'Do I need to take you back to the field hospital? I'm worried again.'

'No, I'm fine. They can't help me. I'll be fine. I'm just a little woolly at the moment.'

'I suppose you nearly died last night, so I'm not surprised you're a little confused. I'm sorry, I'm just worried.'

'What happened yesterday, before I woke up in the field hospital?'

'We were on patrol yesterday afternoon. There were

reports of enemy activity around Westfield and we intercepted them south of there. We exchanged fire, and you took the forward unit to give chase as they retreated. They had a fall-back line which hit you with rocket grenades. I was with the second unit. Harris and Jones took a direct hit, you and Wilson took shrapnel. Roberts and Smith dragged you two out under covering fire.

'By the time I saw you when we rendezvoused with them, you were unconscious, but still with us. We pulled you and Wilson back to the line and took you to the field hospital. They patched you up, and you seemed to get better, but then your heart stopped. They gave up, but I wouldn't let you go. I beat your chest. I wanted you back. And God, when you woke up, I felt like I'd stepped on top of the universe. I've seen so much death I thought I'd hardened to it, but when you nearly died, I felt as if my heart had been ripped out.'

He placed his hand on her arm, and although he knew her name, it flitted just out of reach. The other James loved her, he felt it, but couldn't tell her he had gone. She needed hope in this place. A damp atmosphere enveloped them, dank and desperate. Death stalked all of them. He pulled himself off the bed and stretched his cold muscles, but he felt strong, stronger than ever.

'Are you alright?' she said.

'I feel strong. It's just my head's a bit weak.'

'Well, as long as you're strong in the body, we're OK.' She smiled, her white teeth contrasting the dirt across her face.

'I'm hungry, though.'

'It's on its way, James. I've persuaded Steve to find some eggs and bacon for you. You need a hearty breakfast after yesterday. I need you to get all your strength back. Last night I realised how much I need you, how much I love you. I'm sorry, I shouldn't...' She kissed him on the lips as Steve came in with a covered plate. Pulling off the cloth, the aroma of scrambled eggs and bacon filled Jamie's senses.

'Glad you're back with us, Sarge. This should give you some fighting strength. Rumour is they're coming today.' He handed the plate to Jamie, nodded, and left before Jamie had time to sit back on his bed.

The woman handed him a small knife and fork and he tucked in. It tasted good. He gulped down a couple of mouthfuls, but then stopped. 'I'm sorry – have you eaten? Have some of this.' He pushed the plate towards her.

'No, you need it more than me. I'm fine. I'll get something later.'

He saw her hunger, but with the rich flavours filling his mouth, he took little persuasion to finish. He put the plate down on the floor and stood up.

'I need to get some air, stretch my legs and see whether they still work.'

'Put your coat on, it's cold out there. I fetched it from the hospital this morning. There's some blood on it, but it'll keep you warm.'

She reached over and picked it up from a small chair at the bottom of the bed. A thick coat with worn decorations around the lapels and shoulders, and some faded and ripped braiding on the sleeves. He pulled it on with the woman's help.

He stepped out into a brighter light. Tents and troops filled his vision. Soldiers turned to look. 'I'll take the plate back and see what there is to eat. I'll come and find you.' She smiled and turned to go. He stepped forward, but she stopped him with a hand on his arm. 'Have you got your pistol?' she said.

'I don't know.'

'You must have lost it yesterday. Don't move.'

She ducked back into the tent and came out with a pistol in one hand and a rifle in the other. She pulled his coat back, holstered the gun and handed him the rifle, which he took naturally. He was about to say he had never held a rifle before, but as his fingers wrapped themselves around the stock, it felt natural, like he had held it all his life.

'Perfect. It'll be good for the troops. You are invincible and fighting fit.' With a sharp turn, she strode off amongst the tents.

The camp was in a wooded area, not exactly a forest, with tents slotted in amongst the trees. The cold had a rawness to it and the damp canvas added to the desolate feel. The air tasted different as he breathed it in. The woman disappeared into a tent without sides, steam and smoke billowing out.

As he hurried through the camp, people acknowledged him. He nodded in response and carried on. Within a hundred yards, he reached the edge of the camp, which led on to some fifty yards of open ground. A deep trench dissected the ground on roughly an east to west line. Eight-foot-wide and five or six deep, he reckoned as he walked up to the edge of the trench. The weeds suggested it had been dug a long time ago. Across the other side, another fifty yards of open space led into a similar thinly wooded area. Two soldiers huddled in the trench, but they were asleep. The strange atmosphere continued to permeate his senses.

Yesterday, he sat in a luxurious flat, drinking a fine wine, waiting for his wife. Now, less than twenty-four hours later, he stood in a Sussex field in the middle of a war, some six years earlier. The bleak landscape did little to comfort him, and as he surveyed the woods opposite, he noticed movement deeper into the woods.

As he watched, there was further movement, then he saw a figure at the edge of the woods. The hairs on his arms tingled, and a slight foreboding flitted across his mind. Several more figures appeared in amongst the trees and one raised his arms. A puff of smoke from the figure coincided with a searing sensation in his shoulder. A streak of red appeared as he looked down. Another puff of smoke and he heard a whizz past his head.

An instinct from somewhere deep inside jolted him out of his stupor and he threw himself into the trench. The depth of the trench winded him, and as he looked at his shoulder, the red had spread. Another body crashed into the trench, landing next to him. The woman, with all the kit she had brought scattered on the floor.

'They're attacking. Just got the alarm from the forward scouts. Oh no! Oh no, you're hit!'

'Yes,' he said, but he felt no pain. A sense of the unreal swam through his mind.

She grabbed hold of his coat and pulled it back, revealing his shoulder. The pain kicked in as she felt around the wound. 'The bullet is out. Skimmed your shoulder, you're lucky, but you're scaring the shit out of me. Troops are on the way,' she said as she pulled his coat back over his shoulder. 'Have to deal with that later.'

She handed him a combat belt with ammunition, and he instinctively slung it round his waist and clipped it on. For some reason, it felt natural, even though he had never touched a combat belt. An instinct at the forefront of his mind came from somewhere, maybe the other James. A head full of anticipation of what was to come next.

Suddenly, his mind opened, a thousand thoughts running simultaneously along the neural pathways. One by one he processed them, each little random snippet given careful consideration: his children, his weddings, the fishing trip, the dream in the green bottle, time travel, his first big bonus, being rich, being poor, fighting for Julia, losing Julia, shot in the shoulder. But they all, equally quickly as they burst into his mind, converged into the dream last night. And the woman he saw. She told him not to be afraid, and she became his only thought.

Then a strange rush of energy burst through his body, unlike anything he had ever felt. Explosive energy. Before he had any conscious thought, he stood up against the edge of the trench, his rifle naturally in his hands, and opened fire. He fired at the movement in the woods until the bullets ran out. As he ducked back down in the trench, he reloaded his rifle from his combat belt in one smooth motion. There was no conscious thought of how. More soldiers crashed into the trench. Without hesitation, he stood back up and opened fire. Once the rifle emptied, he looked over the open ground towards the trees, but there was no movement. Three dozen soldiers knelt with him in the trench. All eyes were on him.

The woman leant forward and whispered in his ear, 'You're in charge. Lieutenant Reece died last month, and you've been in charge since then. You've always been in charge.' She stepped back and joined the others.

They waited for orders. He stood up and leant over the top of the trench, searching for some sanity. The woman stepped up, grabbed his shoulder, and pulled him back into the trench seconds before an explosion behind them. An intense sound wave blew across the trench, adding to his confusion. Another explosion, this time in front of the trench.

'Shit!' The woman broke the silence.

The woman from the crimson castle flooded back into his mind. Don't be afraid – he understood he had to go forward.

'Don't be afraid!' he said as he pulled himself over the top of the trench and charged across the open ground. The ground was rough, but his legs pounded the dry earth as he felt an emotional release. Halfway across, he opened fire with the woman right next to him, her rifle in action. Close beside her, the rest of his platoon. As he approached the tree line, he heard more explosions behind him.

They reached the woods and he dived for cover, again naturally reloading his rifle. There was movement deeper in the woods, and he led the platoon forward. At first cautiously, all his senses heightened, but gradually his pace increased. As they reached the edge of the woods, a dozen enemy soldiers were clearing the next field and heading towards the next wooded area.

The rest of the platoon fell in behind him. Adrenaline still pumped through his legs and he charged across the field, closely followed by his soldiers. The enemy stayed ahead of them as they crossed several more fields.

At an elevated position on the edge of one field, he could see the enemy continuing to retreat. The woman handed him a pair of small binoculars.

After surveying the retreating enemy, he passed the binoculars back to her. 'What do you think?'

'Probably a decoy unit. Didn't think we would charge straight at them. Must have shit themselves,' she laughed. But it was a sad and tired laugh. 'Don't know if they'll be back.' She scanned the landscape in front of them in a slow side-to-side sweep.

'You know you saved us all with that wild charge out of the trench. If we had stayed a few more seconds, those mortars would have taken us all out. We all know.' She touched his hand.

'Are you alright?' Jamie asked.

For a moment, she was silent. 'You are all I have in this shithole we call our home. The last twenty-four hours have made me realise how quickly I can lose everything.'

He felt an instant sadness for her and for everyone around him. A soldier came next to him with two faded stripes on his sleeve.

'Sarge?' he said.

'Perkins.' Suddenly, he knew the corporal's name.

'Send a couple of scouts after them, say half a mile, to make sure they continue to retreat with no more enemy troops out there. Send the rest back to the front line and pick up the mortars and rounds they left.' The order came from the new Jamie.

'Yes, Sarge,' he said and disappeared a moment later.

'We'll stay a little longer to watch the scouts go out,' he said to the woman.

Two soldiers circled out into the field. They headed out towards the next wooded area, and he watched them disappear into the woods.

'There is something I need to tell you. Please listen carefully. It will sound completely crazy, but I need to tell you. I'm not exactly sure why.'

As he was about to ask her name, it came to him out of nowhere: Judy.

'Judy, I don't quite know where to start. Your James, the one you love deeply, died last night. His heart stopped, and he died.'

'But—'

'Please, listen, let me finish. I'm part of James's soul, in a way. I jump through different time dimensions. I can't explain further; I just don't know. Yesterday I was in 1991, wealthy and living in a luxury flat in London. But I was attacked and died.' The man from the crimson world flitted through his mind. 'I'm an anomaly, a time anomaly,' he said as he made the connection. The man was just out of reach.

'When your James died, I jumped into his body. It sounds strange and unbelievable, but it's the truth. How long had James's heart stopped? Think about how long.'

'About half an hour,' she said after a moment.

'That's a long time.' He paused to let it sink in. 'I can feel your James inside me. I've never handled a gun or rifle and certainly never fired one, but I can now with no idea of what I'm doing. I can't explain why or how this happens, but you have to take my word for it. I feel sad for your loss of James in a place like this. I can feel his love for you, from your James, and I feel anguish he has gone. If I hadn't jumped into James, he would have died last night and most of the platoon would have been killed this morning. It must have happened for a reason.'

'I don't know what to believe. You're not my James?'

'No.'

Her hand gripped his, all her strength channelled into a desperate grip. 'You can't leave me; my James is in there somewhere. I know he is.'

'Yes, he is, but you need to be strong enough when I'm not here.'

'No, you can't leave. You are my James. I don't know what to believe, but I need to hold on to you.'

He didn't say anymore, each alone with their thoughts. The two scouts came back through the woods.

'Sarge, not many, and they're all heading south. Can't see any new troop movements.'

Again Jamie knew what order to give, the other James somewhere inside him. 'Retreat to our line. I'll follow behind.'

'Yes, Sarge, will do,' one scout said, and they disappeared through the woods.

'Your wound needs dressing. I'll do it now,' Judy said.

'OK, but have we got any food in all this gear?'

'We've got some oat cakes.' She opened her backpack and pulled out a packet. The cakes were dry, but he devoured them, his hunger back again. She passed him a water bottle, and he drank. The water was warm, but it helped with the dry cakes. An eerie silence spun around them as they ate. The troops had fallen back, just him and Judy.

'James, what you told me earlier, is it true?'

'In a way, I suppose it is, but I'm struggling to know what the truth is anymore.'

'All I know is I need you more than I could ever say. You're scaring the hell out of me.' She reached over and touched his cheek; her skin was rough, but he felt a gentleness.

'Take your coat off. Let's have a look at today's wound.'

Ten minutes later, he had his coat back on with his wound dressed. The pain throbbed through his shoulder.

'How bad is the pain?'

'It's OK,' he said and lay back on the grass, the clear blue sky above.

'You ready to get back?'

'Let's stay a little, the pain is easing lying here.'

She slipped down next to him on the flattened grass. The long grass swayed around them, forming a small room with only the sky above. She held his hand as they shared the quiet intimacy.

The minutes ticked by. The silence flowed over them

and time seemed to spill away with no trail left behind. Then a tiny disturbance, so small, a gentle puff of air on a still day.

'Shit, we've got a lot of company coming our way,' he said, sitting up and peering over the long grass.

'Shit, shit,' she said, so close to his ear he felt the warmth of her breath.

A dozen enemy soldiers at the far end of the field, some three hundred yards away, walked steadily towards them. Behind them was a large swathe of soldiers.

'There must be several battalions coming up from the coast. The rumours of new troops landing must have been true,' she said.

'We need to get out of here now!'

They grabbed their combat gear, crawled back to the tree line, and then withdrew deeper into the woods.

When they returned, the whole front line was a mass of activity. Reinforcements were arriving. An officer walked along the trench line shouting orders. Jamie and Judy had joined the rest of the platoon in the trench when the officer stopped in front of him.

'Where have you been, Sergeant?' The young, fresh face annoyed him instantly.

'We went for a picnic in the woods,' Jamie said, adding 'sir,' a moment later.

The officer stared at Jamie, wanting to say something to assert his authority. 'Sergeant, you will position your platoon in this trench and hold it at all costs. It is imperative you hold. Understood?'

'Yes, sir!' Jamie said.

The officer turned and marched off along the trench.

'Hope they shoot him first. We've got a chance then,' Judy said. She touched his shoulder. 'I need to have a look. It's bleeding quite badly again.'

'It'll last a little longer.'

'No, it needs dressing now. Come on, Sergeant, now!'

'Perkins,' he said to the corporal who was next to him, 'get all the platoon commanders over here once that ponce has gone. We need a proper plan.' Perkins nodded and headed off along the trench.

Judy led him back towards their tent. Once inside, she pulled his coat off.

'Sit down on the bed. We need to be quick.'

The pain increased as she peeled back the bandage and, though he couldn't help wincing, she ignored his discomfort. As she lay a small medical kit out on the bed, he looked at his shoulder. The fleshy part of the wound bled. She poured a liquid along the wound and for a moment he felt nothing, then a fierce fire ignited his shoulder.

'Shit!' he said. 'What are you doing?!'

'Shh, it's supposed to hurt. I don't want you dying on me because of some infection. Just sit still.' She dressed the wound. 'It's messy, but it'll do until I have more time.'

The pain remained intense as she helped put his coat on.

'How's that?'

'Painful, but otherwise good.'

'Now, will you stop getting injured! You're scaring the

shit out of me. I don't know what to believe about who you are. You're different in a way from my James, but I love you. You're all I have, so don't you dare leave. OK?'

Her hand squeezed his, her grip strong, and she kissed him.

'Come on, my James, there's another battle waiting for us.'

When they returned to the trench, there were several soldiers standing around. Jamie recognised them as other platoon commanders. All different ranks, but he knew he was in charge.

'We've just seen what we're up against out towards the south when we chased that recon unit this morning. There's no way we will hold them back. HQ up the road is packing up and retreating. They want us to hold the line until they're safely away. Which is fair enough, but no point in everyone dying in this trench today.'

The group in front of him nodded. 'What's the plan then, Sarge?' one soldier asked.

'Split your platoon into thirds, one in the trench, booby trap your camps, second group behind the camp with mortars and the third group up on the ridge over there.' The ground sloped up from behind the camp to a ridge some two to three hundred yards higher.

'The trench line holds with the mortars slowing the advance. When the time comes, shouldn't take too long, all fall back to the ridge. Run like the wind, and with the booby traps in the camp slowing Fritz down, hopefully most should make the ridge. Put the Gatlings up there on the ridge, and that is the real defence line. If that breaks, which it might, then fall back as best we can.'

There was general agreement and after a few questions followed by strategic co-ordination, they set the plan.

The trenches were silent. Everyone crouched down on the ground. The last twenty-four hours had been intense, emotional, confusing, helpless, powerful. And then there was Judy. The other James loved her – he didn't know her. The dislocation within him was unsettling.

The mortar line behind them began the onslaught of shells into the woods. Jamie felt himself tense. He was a coiled spring, his heart pounded, his grip on his rifle so hard it hurt. Judy leant close to him and whispered, 'stay with me.'

The mortar shells fell on the enemy as they approached through the woods. Everyone focused on the look-out scout. The minutes ticked by and then the signal came from the look-out. The trench moved as one, every second soldier up against the parapet, rifles aimed across the open ground. In front of them, the field was full of enemy troops.

A roar of gunfire erupted from the trench, and the return fire sliced through the surrounding air. A soldier to his left flew backwards and as Jamie glanced round, he saw a bullet wound in his left eye. The enemy fell on the open ground, but there seemed an endless stream of soldiers coming through the woods to replace them.

The mortars fired continuously into the woods. Jamie rolled away from the parapet as his rifle emptied, and the second wave of soldiers resumed the onslaught. Reloading was automatic, his breath hard. The young soldier lay next to him, one bullet having ended his war. A disturbing thought struck him. If the other James had died last night, would the soldier have been somewhere different and maybe been alive now? The crimson breeze brushed against him. The man said our time is fixed across all dimensions.

'Sarge!' Judy shouted to get his attention, slipping down next to him.

'It's not going to hold,' he said, 'too many.'

As he looked along the trench, numerous soldiers were on the ground. So many. They both stood up and fired again until their rifles emptied, then crouched back down into the trench, reloading in an instant.

'We can't hold them!' he said. 'We have to go!'

She nodded furiously.

Most of his soldiers were down in the trench and looking at him. They knew as well.

'Retreat!' he said a couple of times.

He reacted mechanically, grabbed Judy by the shoulder and they ran half crouched across the trench. The rest of the unit was right behind them as they scrambled over the top of the trench. Fifty yards of open ground under heavy fire. They sprinted towards the tree line. He turned around and opened fire as he ran backwards, aiming at the advancing enemy.

He lost his footing and as he tried to regain his balance, he tripped and landed hard on his back. As he struggled up, Judy grabbed him and pulled him towards the cover of the trees. The rest of the soldiers crashed into the tree line, turning and firing at the approaching enemy who were crossing their trenches now.

'We can't stay here – move!' Jamie shouted above the noise of the gunfire. 'Up to the ridge, now! We'll cover!' He reloaded, Judy next to him, and they opened fire, giving the soldiers some time.

The soldiers moved with speed and caution back through their camp. The mortars fell but were slowing.

'Come on, James!' Judy said as she moved away from the tree line. 'Now!'

As he stood up and turned, he stumbled and fell to his knees. She was next to him and grabbed him under the arm, pulling him away from the tree line.

'Come on, James!' she said, dragging him through the tents, choosing the pathways carefully. 'Are you hit?'

'I think so.'

She stopped and stared at his front. 'Oh shit!' she said. 'Can you still run? We have to get back to the ridge.'

'I can.' There was no pain, just a detached dizziness.

'Come, quickly.'

Once they cleared the edge of the camp, the ridge was about a hundred yards in front of them. The field was full as the soldiers ran for cover, everyone's intention to reach the safety of the defence line. Multiple explosions in the camp were slowing the enemy. Exhausted, Judy pulled Jamie through a gap in the defence line.

'Come on, James, we need to look at your wound. Over there by the trees. Can you make it?'

He stumbled along the field towards the trees as his

breathing became more laboured.

'Come on, we're nearly there.'

'No, I need to rest,' he said as they reached the edge of the woods, his legs giving way under him.

The light was fading fast. Judy was next to him, desperate to stop the blood loss.

'Try to hold still. This isn't as bad as it looks.'

A cold pain crept into his body, a sinister cold.

'There's not much I can do apart from trying to stop the bleeding. I need to get you back to the field hospital.'

'There is no field hospital. They've gone.'

'Yes, there will be, there has to be.' Her hands pressed the bandages down on his wound.

Terrific gunfire emanated from the second line, and he struggled to keep track of how long he had been there. The rest of his soldiers were spread out in the field in front of them, or at least what was left of them.

'Judy, I need you to listen.' She stopped pressing the bandages on his stomach and looked at him. 'There's no field hospital to take me to. You need to retreat further back and try to regroup with whatever units you can.'

'Shut up,' she said. 'I'm not leaving you, so just shut up.'

'There's not much time.'

She applied more bandages, then pulled his shirt and coat back over him. The pain stopped him rolling over onto his stomach and he ended up half on his side with his head stretched towards the second line.

'How's that?' she asked, her face close to his.

'It hurts, but I'm OK.'

Gunfire and mortar explosions erupted further away, but he couldn't tell if the line was holding. They would know soon enough.

'You're going to die, aren't you!' It wasn't a question, and she said it with sad resignation.

'Yes, I'm bleeding out and there's no field hospital to take me to. You know it. I know it. Please promise me you will retreat with the rest of the unit; this is a crap place to be. I can fire off a few magazines if they break through.'

She moved closer to him. 'I will stay to the end; nothing matters beyond us.' She raised her head up towards the field. 'Anyone want to make a retreat? Free choice.'

There was only silence.

'What about you, Perkins?' she said.

'I'm tired of running. This is as good a place to die as any. Not much left of our unit. We're together now and we stay together until the end.' His voice was rough, but loud and clear. Several other voices came back with similar replies.

Jamie struggled to understand the logic. 'But I'm dying. If they break through, you will all certainly die as well, but if you leave now, you will live to fight another day.' Jamie paused and waited for a response. There was none. 'OK, take me with you. Get Perkins or someone to carry me while we all retreat.'

'No, you're too hurt. We're all tired of running. You are different from my James,' she said, frowning, her voice quieter. 'We would never think like that. There is only us, our unit, nothing beyond us matters. If they come, I will die next to you.' Her gaze was fixed, determined, and he felt uplifted in a strange and inspired way.

'I'm sorry.'

'I know you're in pain, and though it's all sort of strange, you are still mine, aren't you?' Her facial features had changed in a moment from fierce determination to an altogether more vulnerable expression, or maybe a terrified one. He wanted to save her, but his pain only increased.

'Yes,' he said, his breath shortening, 'deep down inside I am still yours.' The pain increased again, his breathing became shallow, and he struggled for breath. 'Hold me.'

She put her arms around him and pulled herself closer. As the green liquid rushed over him, he heard her last cry.

He fell. The green diffused towards red. Crimson. Another world unfolded and he was back on the edge of the cliff with the castle in front of him. The fields stretched out from the castle into the infinite horizon. He felt the same calmness he had last time.

Then Gabriel was next to him.

'James.' His voice was soft, but clear.

'What's happening?'

'You died again, and you are back to my world, in-between time dimensions.'

'It still doesn't make any sense. This is just a dream, but I live in different worlds. What is real anymore?'

'It's all real, James. It's just you can't comprehend it.' Gabriel paused. 'You are an anomaly. There are an infinite number of timelines, and every soul has a time when they die. Throughout all the time dimensions. It is a constant. But something happened in your original timeline. You survived past your time and it has left you in a time loop. As you die in one timeline, you jump back to the same point as another of your souls die in their timeline. You can't die, you leave one world and jump into another James who has just died. You need to stop this anomaly. It's critical you do.'

'Why can't you stop it?'

'I can't control the actions of souls in each time dimension. Only you can control your actions. You need to undo the event which caused this.'

'What event?'

'I don't know. Only you will know. You need to undo it.'

'This makes no sense. Who is the woman I saw by the castle last time?'

'She is the other anomaly. When you jump, you both come to this indeterminate time. You will meet her in one of the time dimensions you jump into. In some way, the two of you are linked, the cause of the anomaly, but we don't know exactly how it happened. You need to undo it.'

Gabriel's voice became quieter and, as it did, he drifted away from Jamie, then disappeared.

Jamie turned back to the castle opposite him and the fields radiated out from there. There was no sense of time as he waited for the other woman. The fields drew his attention hypnotically across them. As he turned back to the castle, she stood there. She wore the same clothes and looked the same as the last time he saw her. She smiled;

her face lit up.

'Hello, my darling, Jamie,' she said, her voice quiet but clear.

'Who are you? What's going on?' Two of many questions he wanted answers to.

'There's no time, Jamie, no time. We will meet soon. Don't be afraid. I am with you.' Her smile comforted him, all the questions and torment tearing him apart abated. He didn't want to leave this world.

'What's your name?'

'You know my name. It's Amelia. We've only got a few moments more. I'll explain everything when we meet.'

'When?'

'Soon, Jamie...' her voice trailed off.

The void was below and ready for him.

'I don't want to go,' he said, the calmness replaced by the panic which had become all too familiar. Her arms stretched out towards him and as he tried to reach for her, the nothingness of the void enveloped him. The familiar green liquid engulfed him. Thoughts of Amelia and the calmness she gave him swam with him, but faded as he looked for his resolution.

Chapter 7

25th October 1985

The eternity of green liquid which held Jamie turned darker. The temperature dropped, and he stopped swimming against its growing force. Black, icy cold, angry and aggressive. The endlessness of the green bottle gone. There was no sense of his new environment as he tried to move his arms and tried to breathe. He needed to breathe, but there was no air. The liquid battered him, and despite his flailing arms and legs, he was helpless against this unknown force.

A renewed peacefulness crept into his body. The intense cold and the mysterious power of the liquid diminished. As the cold became less intense, a gentleness took the edge off the turmoil all around him. The angry liquid became soothing.

Then he hit something. The liquid lifted him; he spun round and round and then slid along a soft surface as the liquid ran off. For a moment, he felt salty air around him. But a barrier lay between the air he could smell and his ability to breathe. More liquid crashed over him and pushed him further along the ground. As the liquid receded on each wave, he focused up into the dark sky. The stars became brighter. He still couldn’t breathe, but a calmness crept through him, which didn't require any breath. Then the stars began to dim, to swirl, and his world changed again. The cool depth of the green bottle rolled back into his mind as the specks of light diminished. The void opened again, a slip down. Crimson.

Then he was back, coughing, and his first sensation was an intake of wet air. He coughed harder; the water leaving his lungs with air replacing it. More coughing, harder and more intense. With each cough, he felt more in control of his breathing. The green bottle was gone and the waves lapped around him, the salty taste strong in his mouth. As he became more aware, he felt someone next to him. Someone hitting him hard on his back.

‘James, I thought I had lost you.’ He heard her voice, shaky but definitely Judy's voice. He had only just left her. ‘Why did you jump James, why?!’ Sensation returned as her hand beat his back.

‘I'm—’ another cough interrupted before he said, ‘I'm OK.’

Then she was next to him and he recognised her features, even in the shadowy light from the shore.

‘You are alive! You are alive! James, I thought you

were gone.' Tight arms clenched him.

'I'm cold.' The cold was more evident as he breathed more easily.

'Of course. Can you get up?'

'I'll try.' With considerable effort and her help, he pushed off the ground and steadied himself against her. He felt weak, but her arm held him as they walked back up the beach.

'We need to get you to the physicians,' she said, her voice pitched and nervous.

'No, I'll be fine, just help me home. I'll be fine.' The cold bit into him and he shivered.

'I think we should let the physician have a look at you.'

'No, please help me home. I need to get warm and I'll be fine.' The cold was his priority. He needed warmth, and the rest would follow. 'Please help me back.'

'Of course, but I am worried about what happened to you.'

'We'll talk when I'm warmer.'

A more determined arm pulled him closer, and she led him towards the lights.

He sat close to a roaring fire, stripped naked under the two blankets wrapped around him. A large cup of a tealike drink, accompanied by a fiery alcoholic drink akin to whiskey, had helped the inner cold. The fire was hot against his face, but his body still shivered. Judy scuttled about, making him drinks, tending the fire and constantly asking if he was alright. A long silence followed as she sat on a chair next to him. The only sound was from the crackling fire.

Eventually Judy spoke. 'What happened, James? I was terrified you were gone. Finding you was little short of a miracle.' Her voice was soft and steady now.

'What's the date?'

'Sorry?'

'I know this is odd, but I need to know the date, please.'

'It is the 25th of October.'

'What's the year?'

She paused. 'It is 1985.'

'It's always the same,' he said out loud.

Gabriel swept through his mind. He saw the crimson castle and the woman. He couldn't remember her name, but he was sure he knew it. Gabriel had told him about a jump, always at the same time, but he couldn't quite remember what he had said.

'What is the same?'

'It's a long story. You wouldn't believe any of it, anyway.' He smiled and saw the confusion on her face. 'Can you tell me what happened? Please.'

'Well, you seemed quite drawn when you left the public house. You seemed so down and I followed you. It is not the first time you have wandered off feeling down. I am glad I did follow. You headed straight over to the pier, and I had to run to catch you up. But I could not catch you. As I reached the end of the pier, you went over the side. I screamed at you, but it was too late. Never have I been so scared in my life. I ran to the side, but I could see nothing, just the sea a long way down. The pier was empty. I did not know what to do, so I ran back off the pier and down to the beach. I went to the left, then I turned and ran back the other way.

'It was fortunate I did, as I nearly fell over you. You lay on the beach. You were still, and I thought you were dead. I rolled you over on your side. I did not know what to do apart from hit you on your back. It seemed to take forever before you coughed, and then you kept on coughing. I was meant to find you.'

She paused as tears ran down her cheeks. 'What happened, James?'

For a while, he let the warmth from the fire occupy his thoughts. The difference from when he saw her last, to him only a matter of minutes, was stark. Long hair flowed down past her shoulders, a little rounder and not the same sinewy body as the last world.

He always came back to the same date when the other Jamies died and he took over from them. The world he woke to became more different each time and, as he looked around, he felt deeply unsettled. The air he breathed tasted different, and the smells unsettled him. Like a new country, but more than he had ever felt when he travelled in his real life. The thought of Julia was suddenly strong within him, and he struggled to put all the things happening to him into some sort of order.

He couldn't tell Judy the truth, she wouldn't believe him. Even he struggled to believe what was happening to him.

'I'm struggling to know what happened myself. I have a huge blank in my mind, where I am, where I work or anything about my life. I can remember bits. I know you're my friend.' He watched her reaction as she smiled; her eyes softened. 'My life is a blank at the minute. Maybe you can help.'

'Of course, you nearly drowned. I do not know how you survived for so long in the water. It is probably temporary; we should have gone to the physicians.'

'No, no, I'll be fine. Where do I work?'

The concern grew across her features. 'You cannot remember where you work?'

'It's a total blank. I don't even know where I live, which town, or who the Prime Minister is?'

'Well, you live here in Chester-by-Sea, capital of West Downshire.'

'Chester-by-Sea? West Downshire?'

'You do not remember, do you?'

'No, it's all new to me. Who's the Prime Minister?'

'I do not know what you mean?'

'Well, who runs the country?'

She looked puzzled by his question. 'It is King Henry the Fourteenth. He has been on the throne now for nearly fifteen years. The Duke of West Downshire is Lord Selsey.'

Every answer unsettled him more. 'Is it 1985?'

'Yes, it is.'

'Are you sure it's not 1885?'

'Are you mocking me, James?'

'No, no, I'm not. It's just what you are telling me. Who's in the government? Who runs the country?'

'I have told you already.'

'I'm sorry, I can't remember.' This new world was

different, but just as weird as the last one.

'Where do I work?'

'I am quite concerned about you.'

'No, I'll be fine. It'll come back to me. I just need a little help.'

'We both work at the King's Tax Office here in Chester-by-Sea. It is not far away. You are, like me, a junior tax clerk. You must remember.'

'Not at the moment, I can't.'

'I live a few streets away and we have worked there for the last four years. We were at school together, and the King's Selection put us in the Tax Office.'

The cold was easing. Although he had stopped shivering, he pulled the blankets tighter around himself.

'Do we have a radio or television?'

'What are you talking about?'

'Computers?'

'James, what are you talking about? You must have banged your head on the rocks when the sea washed you ashore. You say words I do not understand.'

'What about electricity?' The room had several lit candles mounted on the wall, but there were no light fittings anywhere in the dimly lit room.

'Only the noble officials have electricity. We do not have any.'

Nothing surprised him anymore. 'What actually do we do at the Tax Office?'

She gave him a long look before she answered. 'You are a junior compiler; you are excellent at adding up the certificates, and I am a junior scribe. Do you not remember?' Her voice became edgier. 'If you cannot remember how to do your work, they will end your commission.'

'Losing my commission is bad?'

'Yes, you will not be allowed to work there.'

'Oh.'

'Do you not understand the scale of the problem? You will lose your living quarters and you will be out begging on the street. You will! Master Lock will not hesitate.'

'Who's Master Lock?'

'Oh my Henry, I am now worried.'

'Why are you so worried?'

'Well, we have to be back at work tomorrow and if you cannot remember how to do your work, Master Lock will end your commission.'

'And that's bad?'

'Yes, James, it is bad. Go and get dressed in the warm clothes I have laid out on your bed. You go now. I will scribe out some sample certificates and you can practise adding them up. Quickly.'

As he stood up, he had a proper look round the room where he lived. The only light came from the fire and the candles. A large wooden table stood behind them with several large candles on it, which Judy had just lit. The ceiling was empty of any electric bulbs or fittings. To his left, a door led him into the bedroom.

The bed was on the other side of the room and a large candle on the bedside table lit the room. Clothes were laid out on the bed. He closed the thick door and dropped his blankets to the floor. The clothes were difficult to put on, as his skin was still cold and clammy. They were uncomfortable, the rough material scratching his back. The surrounding smells were so unfamiliar, and as he breathed, he felt ever further out on the edges of insanity. He ran his hand over his hair. It was long and tied back in a ponytail.

Judy sat at the large wooden table when he came out of the bedroom. Sheafs of paper were scattered on the table and she was busy writing on them. The warmth of the fire drew him closer.

'James, I have scribed several certificates with figures. You do know what you have to do with them?'

'I need to add them up?' he said as he sat down next to her.

'Yes, you sort them into date order and you write down the figures in your day ledger. This sheaf is your day ledger. It has four columns, one for the date, one for the certificate reference number, one for the figure, and finally one for the running total. You scribe the first two certificates and add each one to the other as you scribe them.'

He reached over for the day ledger, and as he picked up the pen, which was like an old-fashioned quill, he knew what he had to do. The quill felt natural in his hand, as had the rifle in the last world. As he worked through the papers Judy had prepared, it became easy and natural.

'Yes, you are absolutely fine. You see, it has come back to you.' There was relief in her voice. 'I think you will be fine tomorrow.'

'Do you mind if I sit by the fire?'

'Of course, James. I will get you another hot drink.'

He sat down by the fire and welcomed the warmth. Jumbled thoughts ran through his mind, and he tried to let go as he watched the flames lick and leap up in front of him.

She brought him another steaming hot cup of the sweet tea drink. The taste wasn't unpleasant, but more than anything, it warmed him. She sat next to him and sipped her drink.

'It has been quite a night,' she said.

'Yes, I don't know what to say. It's all a blur of events. What time do we start work tomorrow?'

'We have to be there at nine o'clock.'

'What time is it now?'

'It is well past midnight. I should have left a few hours ago. I hope the patrols do not pick me up.'

'Stay with me,' he said, partly out of guilt and partly because he needed someone with him. He felt increasingly unsettled.

She didn't answer.

'Come on, I'm tired.'

'What do you mean?' she said.

'From what I can see, there's one bedroom. There's nowhere for you to sleep in here, or the kitchen. We'll share the bed; it's plenty big enough. Don't worry, we'll just sleep. OK?'

She stared at him. This new world was weighing heavily on him. The fire had warmed him, but he needed to sleep. He smiled, walked into the bedroom, and stripped off his trousers and jumper. The sheets were cool. He missed the glow of the fire, but he felt utterly drained. After a few moments, he heard footsteps in the room and she stopped next to the bed. Without a word, she removed her outer garments.

'Come on, Judy, we both need to sleep. Thank you for saving me.'

She smiled, blew out the candle and climbed into the bed next to him.

'Why do you call me Judy?' Her voice was quiet.

'What do you mean?'

'My name is Judith. I am worried about what happened to you, and the way you speak is different. You may need to be careful; you know how Master Lock is difficult.'

'I'm sorry, it's been an eventful evening.'

'It has been an eventful evening, James. I hope some sleep will help you remember. I can still see that dark ocean taking you.'

'Sleep now,' he said as he let go of all the thoughts swirling around his mind. Sleep took him quickly.

When he woke, Judith sat next to him on the bed, dressed. She stroked his face.

'You need to wake up, James. We need to leave soon. It has already gone eight o'clock.'

Her face lit up, a smile he hadn't seen before. Different from the last world. She kissed him on the forehead and left the bedroom.

Jamie climbed out of bed and saw his clothes laid out on the other side of the bed. They were still uncomfortable. He pulled the curtain back and peered out into the street, giving him yet another shock. The street teemed with a mixture of horse-drawn carriages and large, clumsy cars. Pavements were filled with people rushing along, and the buildings were a mixture of old wooden houses nestled between sturdier brick-built dwellings. The scene shocked him. He was lost in a strange world.

It took some effort to pull away from the scene outside the window. The large fireplace was cold as he walked back into the main room, which had a musty, burnt smell hanging in the air. Judith came out of the kitchen with a plate in each hand and placed them on the table next to two cups of tea. Each plate had several slices of thick cut bread and a sizeable chunk of cheese. They sat down and ate breakfast in silence.

'It is time we left. I will leave first. You follow on in a few minutes.'

'But I don't know where work is.'

'You cannot remember?'

'No, still struggling.'

'We cannot leave together. You will have to remember.'

'Do I go left or right when I leave?'

'Left to the next road and then right.'

'Thanks, I'll probably know once I get going.' He felt sure the other James would lead him in the right direction.

'I will wait for you at the market, by the clock tower, and we can walk into work together. And remember your satchel.'

She smiled, stood up and fetched the satchel and his inks and placed them on the table. Before picking up the plates, she pulled his long hair tight and tied it back. Then she was out through the kitchen and he heard the door close.

He instinctively picked up a small wooden quill case and placed the inks into it, along with the selection of quills already packed. The case fitted neatly into the satchel. There was a small mirror on the far side of the room, and he couldn't help but look into it. An unshaven face stared back at him, his long hair tied back. It was unsettling to see himself so different. The new James hovered at the back of his mind. As he relaxed, he let him take over, picking up his satchel and coat. Once outside and on the road, the new James led the way.

Judith stood by the clock tower as he came into the square. Market stalls and people filled the area.

'Good morning, Master James,' she said in a formal voice.

'Good morning, Mistress Judith,' he said, not sure where his words came from.

'Will you accompany me to work?' she said, again formally.

Jamie realised the formal behaviour, why Judith couldn't go home late, and why she had to meet him here accidentally.

'I would be pleased to.'

They strolled across the busy square filled with a multitude of people. Despite all mixing together, it was clear there was a strong social order in how people dressed.

'So Master James, how are you today?'

'Not bad, thank you for asking. Interesting night. And how are you this morning?'

'Very well, thank you. I too had an interesting evening.' A smile crossed her face.

As they left the square into a side street, it became busier and they had to squeeze together a little. The whole situation was difficult to comprehend. A world where it felt as if he had travelled back a long way in time. The air he breathed was all wrong. He couldn't put his finger on it, but it was deeply unsettling. As they walked through to the end of the street, it opened into another larger square. A large building stood opposite them on the other side. A stone building, three floors in height, with 'King's Tax Office' inscribed on a marble plinth above the entrance. It felt familiar as they approached it.

The entrance was large, with military guards lining the walls. Their uniforms were formal, and they were armed with swords and rifles. Several formally dressed men stood by a reception desk, with a small door behind them. Jamie followed as Judith headed over to the door. The men acknowledged them by name as they passed through into a small corridor, which led to a set of stairs at the far end.

The stairs led up to another large reception area. Again, guards lined the back wall. Several large prints hung on the wall straight in front of them. The largest, a portrait of the King, lavishly painted with a gold lettered nameplate – His Royal Highness King Henry XIV. The next smaller portrait read 'Duke of West Downshire, Lord Selsey', carved on an oak plaque. It depicted a large, fat man who looked decidedly less regal than the King. The final picture, a small sketch, had a simple lettered wooden plaque, 'Master Lock – King's Tax Inspector, West Downshire'.

He followed her through another set of doors and into the main office – a huge open plan room with a dozen large wooden desks arranged in two rows. Large windows covered two sides.

As Judith turned towards the desks on her left, she nodded discretely to the right. He moved over to the desks on the right and, as he approached, he knew his desk was the third one down. People he passed greeted him and from somewhere inside, he knew who they were, or at least their name.

Two people were already at his desk and he knew them, Master Gordon and Master Philip. They were about his age, and he knew they were his friends.

He pulled out his quill case and placed the pots of inks on the table in front of him.

'What happened to you last night, Master James? You left halfway through the seventh round and you never came back.'

'I'm fine, Master Philip. Thank you for asking. I needed the air, and I walked home instead of coming back. I felt a little drawn.'

'I should think you did, Master James,' Philip said and chuckled quietly. 'You lack practice, or maybe someone took your attention away from finishing the round.'

'Yes, maybe, Master Philip.'

Jamie looked up at the large clock on the front wall.

The hands showed five to nine. The office filled up fast, with an increased level of noise as people settled into their desks and talked. Jamie talked to his friends as he looked over to the other side of the room. Judith sat a little further back from the main doors at the front. She hinted at a smile, but not enough for anyone else to notice.

At nine o'clock, a door opened to the right of the main entrance and in walked Master Lock. Jamie recognised him from the picture. The room became silent as Master Lock walked with deliberate care to the centre of the room. The guards from the reception locked the main doors.

'Good morning,' Master Lock said in a loud and clear voice. 'We have received the East Selsey tax certificates for September, late as usual, but we need to process them by the end of the day. No time to lose, runners please.'

Several doors on the other side of the room opened and runners came out with large boxes. Jamie waited for the boxes to be delivered to the desks on his side of the office. When their box arrived, Jamie had to sign for the sealed box, then both Philip and Gordon countersigned. Gordon cut the seal open and pulled the lid off. Philip reached in and pulled out the contents.

The bundles of paper were tax certificates. He knew the moment he saw them. The several large leather pouches, with a large seal impressed into the leather, held the money. Jamie knew what had to be done. Philip would sort the certificates and Gordon would count the money. He would reconcile the two on his sheet of paper, which he reached for as both Philip and Gordon sat next to him and carried on with their tasks. Jamie picked up his quill, reached for his inks, and drew out four columns.

The room remained busy throughout the morning, and Jamie never had a moment to look over at Judith. Runners rushed between the tables with the boxes. By the end of the morning, Jamie understood every box they reconciled was double-checked by another team of three people on the row of desks where he sat.

The new James was there, somewhere inside, like a subconscious part of him. When he needed to do something, he knew what to do, what to say. By lunchtime, he was starving. The runners cleared all the boxes and at one o'clock, the last box disappeared into the side rooms with the doors closing. Master Lock strode to the front of the office.

'There is much to be done before tonight. You will eat lunch at your desk, the doors will be opened and you may use the restrooms.' He turned and nodded to a guard by the door.

Moments later, the main doors opened and small groups were escorted out to the toilets through the reception area. A group of people handed out small parcels accompanied by a glass of what looked like a beer or cider. Everyone ate quickly, and Jamie realised they would be back at work shortly. By half past one, the remains of the food and drink were collected. Master Lock stepped out to the front of the office with the main doors closed again.

'There is much to do. Runners, please.'

On cue, the side doors opened, and the runners came out with their sealed boxes. It was comical, Jamie thought, but as the first box arrived at their desk, he reached for a sheet of paper and drew up the columns.

The afternoon passed as the morning. Runners rushed in amongst the desks and added to the noisy atmosphere. Every time he needed to add up, he always knew the answer, accompanied by a small rush of pleasure.

Late in the afternoon, he heard a bang on the main door, not loud, but enough to detect above the noise of the room. Jamie looked at the clock. It was five past six. The momentum of the room slowed and, as the noise level dropped, Master Lock hastened towards the door.

A deafening explosion broke the silence as the main doors disintegrated. The shock and heat of the blast blistered across Jamie's face as the force threw him onto the floor. For a moment, a strange stillness engulfed the room.

He lay on the floor, his ears aching. The James from the previous timeline flooded through him, his senses keener, and a moment later he was up. Smoke and debris filled the room. He looked over to where Judith had sat. Thick smoke obscured his vision and as he stared into the smoke, his mind tried to catch up with the events of the last couple of seconds.

Several people suddenly appeared through the main door with flashes of gunfire. Jamie rushed towards them. Through the smoke, he saw a person approach and raise his rifle. Jamie hit him with the full force of his body and they crashed to the floor. Jamie ripped the rifle out of his hands and hit him with the butt. Dropping the rifle, his focus shifted to Judith.

More gunfire erupted from the reception area. Soldier

Jamie wanted to go towards the gunfire, but the present-day version headed back towards Judith. The smoke cleared as he moved down towards the back of the room, and he saw a mass of bodies scattered on the floor. Master Lock lay in the middle of the aisle, dead. Several people on either side of him had also taken the full blast. Jamie saw Judith further down, gripping a wound in her abdomen, her face bleeding from several deep scratches.

'Judith!' He reached for her and took her in his arms. 'Where are you hurt?' His ears rang and he couldn't hear her, only a muffled noise, like being underwater.

He ripped off his tunic, eased her hands away from her stomach, and pushed it against the wound. In amongst the pandemonium, all he could do was gather her up in his arms, and although he wanted to talk to her, he could only hold her tight as she slipped away.

A soldier touched his shoulder and pointed towards the main entrance. Jamie shook his head, and the soldier moved on. The big clock showed it was quarter past six. Jamie held her close and, as he held her, he thought back to yesterday when she had held him whilst he was dying on the battlefield. No! It would have been today in the evening when he jumped. The thought struck him – she didn't survive in the previous timeline. The enemy must have broken through, and she didn't leave him. She probably died at the same time as she had in this timeline, which meant it was fixed, as his time was when he jumped into another world. The Jamie he jumped into had died, always at the same time. Judy died at the same time; it was fixed in different timelines. Gabriel flashed through his mind. Gabriel had already told him, in the crimson world.

Six Months Later

Jamie put his inks away, half a day complete, and he looked forward to his brief lunch. As he stood up, he looked over at Judith's seat. An unconscious act now. The darkness cloaked him, along with all the other heavy thoughts he couldn't shake.

Spring approached summer and the days slowly warmed. It was six months since Judith had died, the aftermath of the attack efficient and cold. Master Lock had died with six of the tax staff. They had sent Jamie home and told him to wait for a message when to return. Less than a week and the Tax Office functioned as normal, all the damage repaired and a new Master at the head. The picture in reception changed, with no further sign of the previous week's attack. No one spoke of the event, and he never knew where Judith was buried. The whole attack was wiped from all records, a cold efficiency which seemed to be the way in this world.

Since then, at least one attack a month breached the Tax Office, although not on the same scale as the first. However, it was only a matter of time before they breached the doors again. He worked, as there was little else to do. Travelling out of the district was impossible, as only the noble class were free to travel. The likelihood of obtaining a permit for someone like him was nil. Julia was always forefront in his mind and he wanted to go to Southampton (now called South Windsor) to look for her. But he had no idea if she was there. No directory enquires; no internet to search. The dawning realisation was that he would remain here for the rest of his life. Everyone he worked with drank every night. It was the only leisure time activity and positively encouraged.

He was part of the educated working class, who maintained the King's taxes and ensured the noble class remained in charge. The uneducated working class farmed and also served the noble class. And the classless, they were the illegals, the rebels. They refuted the King and all the ruling nobles, attacking the King's Tax Office, which Jamie now understood symbolised the King's power. They lived outside the districts, in the countryside, in towns where the King's rule was less secure. Uncoordinated and more motivated by the wish to survive day to day rather than start a revolution.

Jamie kept a low profile. Over the months, his obsession to see Julia had grown. He couldn't go to South Windsor so thought seriously about becoming classless, an outlaw, a rebel. But that was no guarantee he would find her. Even if he found her, he couldn’t have any real relationship with her, as he would be classless. But his life now wasn’t a great deal better. There was a darkness ever present, deep inside him. The latest James, it must have been what drove him to jump into the sea. Those dark thoughts lingered at the edges of his mind and he began to understand hopelessness.

One evening in late May, as he left the Tax Office, a small crowd had gathered outside in the square. The civilians wore fine clothes, and the soldiers were from outside the district. As he stepped out into the square, he saw her.

Julia. Her hair was long and the sumptuous dress she wore made her look different, but it was unmistakably Julia. She wore the dress of a noble and she looked beautiful. Crossing the square towards her, his heartbeat increased. Several ladies-in-waiting accompanied her.

For the briefest moment, he felt a strange stillness. The world in front of him paused for a split second, taking a chilly breath. Then an explosion ripped apart the stillness. Gunfire and another explosion. Everyone else seemed to move in slow motion as he covered the ground towards Julia. Then the whole world around him sped up. Julia still stood when he reached her, staring at one of her fallen ladies-in-waiting. Jamie seized her and pulled her down to the ground. Wide, confused eyes stared at him.

'Julia!' he said, his voice loud above the gunfire and the screaming. Instinctively, he shielded her from the gunfire, with bullets striking the ground next to them.

'Julia!' he said again, and she continued to stare at him. 'Do you trust me? Trust I will protect you?'

She nodded with a spark of comprehension in her eyes. 'Yes.'

'Come with me!'

The noise of the attack grew. Jamie, the soldier, was taking over. The safest place now was the Tax Office, and they sped towards its entrance. Masters George and Harold were either side of the reception door, rifles already drawn.

'Let me through. She needs protection!' Jamie said.

The main window to his left blew inwards with the full force of an explosion crashing them both to the floor.

Glass shards bounced all around them. Jamie was dazed, but his mind was catching up rapidly as he held firm to Julia.

Dust and smoke swirled in the foyer. Masters George and Harold were both on the ground, dazed. As he looked out towards the entrance, he saw several tax soldiers on the ground. Bullets whizzed to the side of them as the rebels approached.

The only cover was behind the thick oak of the reception desk, and he didn't hesitate to drag Julia over and use it. Master Harold's rifle was on the ground, which Jamie snatched up, pressing it tight against his shoulder as he leant out across the desk. Several rebels entered the foyer, and he didn't hesitate. They returned fire, but were too young and inexperienced. His rifle ended their rebellion. He maintained his position and waited for the next wave.

'Are you hurt, Julia?'

'No, I am fine,' she said, her voice shaky.

'Stay down behind the desk and stay close to me.' A hand grabbed his leg as if to confirm she was staying close.

The smoke cleared and the gunfire outside lessened. Several soldiers came through the broken windows wearing the same uniform he had seen earlier.

'I am Captain of the Southway Guard. Stand down!' the first soldier shouted to Jamie.

'I am Master James, a tax scribe. I have the lady safe,' he said, not sure why he included his profession.

The Captain rushed over to Jamie and came around

the desk. 'My Lady, are you hurt?' he said as he knelt next to Julia. 'Where are the Tax Guard?' He looked up towards Jamie.

'No tax receipts today, a limited detail on duty.' Jamie said.

'Simpkins, Walters!' the Captain shouted to two soldiers, who both responded in unison. 'Get behind here now!'

The Captain turned back to Jamie. 'Most of the Southway Guard are with Lord Southway at West Downshire Manor. I have sent a signal to them, but it will be a while before they arrive.'

'This is not a great tactical position.'

'No, not enough guards here and too many rebels out in the square.'

'Through the barracks,' Jamie said, pointing to the back of the foyer. 'I know the way. I use it as a shortcut home. It leads to the back alleys, which I also know well.'

'We need to get out of here,' the Captain said. 'Lady Julia, can you move with us?' He leant down to her.

'Yes, I can, Captain.'

A rebel came through the entrance with his right hand held high. Jamie saw the bomb and fired instantly. His bullet hit the rebel's arm, and the bomb fell to the floor. Jamie shouted to take cover, grabbed the Captain and pulled him down behind the desk as the bomb exploded. The foyer filled with noise and debris.

Jamie shouted to the Captain. 'We need to go now!'

Jamie grasped Julia under her arm and they rushed through the barrack door, the Captain close behind them, followed by the two soldiers and Masters George and Harold. Jamie led the way through several corridors to a sturdy door, where he stopped.

'This leads out into a small courtyard and then a small alley. It can take us anywhere in the city centre. I'll go first and check the situation.'

'No, you stay. We need you to get us to the Selsey Pier on the seafront. The main Southway Guard will come in along the coast road, and we will meet them there,' the Captain said. He turned to the soldier behind him and nodded. The soldier opened the door and slipped out.

'All clear, sir, alleyway is clear,' the soldier said a few seconds later.

'Go!' the Captain commanded.

Jamie took Julia's hand and pulled her out the door, leading the way and moving with a quick pace through the labyrinth of lanes and paths. The few locals scattered as they saw the Southway soldiers.

They ran on for about a quarter of a mile until Jamie stopped as the alleyway opened onto the large promenade down to the seafront. The Captain leant out of the alleyway and looked for signs of the rebels.

'Where to, Captain?' Jamie asked.

He didn't answer as he looked back and forth. Julia held Jamie's hand tightly.

'We need to get on the Selsey Pier. You take Lady Julia to the end. We can cover the entrance from where it narrows. That is the only way on for the rebels if they get here before the main guard.'

'Are you up for a quick sprint to the pier, Lady Julia?'

'Yes, I am, Master James.'

'I will lead,' the Captain said, 'you and Lady Julia follow. When we get onto the pier, I want you to take Lady Julia to the far end and keep her from harm.'

'I will, Captain, with my life.'

'I have no doubt.' He turned to Masters George and Harold. 'You two stay with me,' he pointed to the two soldiers, 'and you two bring up the rear.' They both responded, 'Yes, Captain.'

'Let us go!' The Captain ran out of the alleyway and across the promenade. Jamie followed, pulling Julia close as they ran. As they reached the pier, the Captain shouted for everyone to clear the area.

The Captain stopped. 'Master James, down to the end, find cover and we will hold here.'

Jamie nodded and ran to the end of the pier while Julia gripped his hand. There was a shelter at the end of the pier which looked out to sea and hid them from sight.

'How are you? Are you hurt anywhere?' Jamie said as they sat down on the bench in the shelter.

'No, I think I am unhurt. Shaken though.'

'I'm not surprised after the last few minutes.'

'How do you know me? I feel you know me, more than you should.'

'I'm a traveller through worlds and somehow we are linked through time. I don't understand it all and how it works, but we have been together several lives now.'

She looked at him, slightly breathless, with eyes wide open.

'You obviously don't believe any of it and you think

me completely crazy, out of my mind, which is fair enough. I think I was there in the square to protect you and keep you safe.' He smiled, which broke her gaze, and she smiled back.

'I do not think I have ever quite lived as much as I have the last fifteen minutes. You must have been sent from the Gods to protect me.'

'Not quite the Gods, just some fluke of dimensional time. All the same, I am glad I was there.'

'So am I, sir.'

Jamie looked back down the pier. The Captain stood on the railings and looked towards the promenade.

'Where do you come from again? I am not sure I understand,' Julia said.

Jamie smiled. 'It's a long story and I'm not sure I understand it any better than you. I travel between time dimensions and every world is different, but most of the people are the same, like you. We are connected in some strange way, and as soon as I jumped into this time dimension, I tried to find you. If we had more time, I would tell you it all. But not now.' Julia stared back at him. 'I see I have left you speechless.'

A moment of silence followed. 'Yes, you have, but also curious and a little excited.'

They both looked down at their joined hands, but neither moved. The rebels became less of a concern as Jamie let the calmness of being close to Julia ease his thoughts.

'I should call you Lady Julia, but it's not something I'm used to.'

'I do not mind. You can call me Julia; I like it. Maybe only when we are in private, though.' She smiled and her face glowed.

'I will do, Julia, and please call me Jamie. You always have done.'

'You are strange, Master Jamie, but I like you. You are different and although I think you are a little crazy, I still like you.'

'I am glad to hear it, Julia. I like you too, always have done.'

Jamie stood up, reluctantly released her hand, and walked around the shelter to get a better look down the pier. The Captain still stood on the railing. Jamie scanned the promenade but saw no movement and returned to Julia.

'All quiet on the front. I think we are safe for a while. If we must run again, I'm afraid we will have to swim for it.'

She laughed. 'You are like no one I have ever met. You are so informal, so different.'

Jamie leant back on the bench and settled next to Julia. Neither spoke for the next few minutes as Jamie looked out to sea. The other James must have felt desperate to go over the edge on a cold October night. Part of him understood that this wasn't a world he liked. But he felt some peace next to Julia.

The Captain's voice boomed from down the pier and snapped him back to reality. The Captain signalled him.

'It's the main Southway Guard! Get Lady Julia ready to move. Once we are clear, we will move into the guard and they can take her.'

Jamie nodded and turned to Julia.

'The main Southway Guard is here. We need to be ready to move.'

'I am ready.' She straightened herself and smoothed out her dress.

'Julia, thank you for this moment with you.'

She smiled.

'Lady Julia, are we ready?'

'Yes, we are, Master James.'

Two days later, Jamie received a knock at his door. Since the attack, he had been at home, ready for the call to return to work. He assumed this was the reason for a visitor.

Julia had occupied his mind since he had escorted her to the main guard on the promenade. It became formal, and he said his goodbye with deference. She thanked him for his bravery, but her eyes told him a different story. The small peace he had with her on the pier slipped away as she boarded the coach. She looked back at him a final time before the coach and the whole guard moved off at speed, back in the direction they had come from.

As he opened the door, he expected to see a young messenger from the Tax Office. Instead, several people filled the tiny hallway. The Captain of the Southway Guard stood in front of him.

'Master James, you may remember me,' the Captain said with a smile.

Jamie was a little taken aback. 'Yes, I do, Captain. I'm

a little surprised.'

'May I introduce Lady Julia's husband, Lord Thomas Southway, son of the Duke of West Downshire.'

A tall, well-dressed man stepped forward, in his mid-twenties. Jamie felt instant jealousy, exasperated by his good looks.

'Master James, I cannot thank you enough for your bravery in protecting my wife, Lady Julia.' Lord Southway's voice was polished with both deepness and charm.

'My Lord, I just happened to be there when the attack started and Lady Julia needed help,' Jamie said.

'Not from what I have learnt. The Captain here has informed me of the details of the attack, and other witnesses say you proved bravery beyond a tax clerk. Captain Smith praised your actions highly, and I listen carefully to his voice.'

'Thank you, my Lord.'

'I need people like you. You are smart with numbers and have the bravery and skills of a good soldier. I want you to join my household as a treasurer, with the rank of a sergeant. It is a senior position, and I have authorised it with your Tax Master.' He smiled widely. Jamie felt he should hate him, but found that he couldn't.

'I am honoured at your offer, my Lord, and gratefully accept.' His excited thoughts rushed to Julia.

'Excellent, Master James. My valet will contact you and sort out the arrangements. I look forward to you joining us. Good day, Master James.'

'Thank you, my Lord.'

Lord Southway turned, and Captain Smith gave Jamie a salute. 'Master James, I look forward to you serving in the Southway household,' he said.

'Thank you, Captain Smith. I am honoured.'

When he closed the door, he felt a rush of emotion. He would be near Julia again.

Three months later

The late August sun shone fiercely on Jamie as he walked in the extensive Southway grounds, heading towards the lake and the huge forest which surrounded it. The tall trees provided some respite from the sun. Three months had passed since the attack and though he had seen Julia often in his duties at the House, he never managed to be alone with her. However, knowing she was close provided some small comfort.

He felt hot under his new uniform and longed for a pair of shorts and a T-shirt. The grass looked cool in the shade and he imagined the feel of it on his feet. His rank was a sergeant in the Southway Guard and, combined with his role as a treasurer for the Southway Household, his position had improved considerably. They provided him with a large cottage which came with a housekeeper.

His uniform was a formal affair. Dark blue tunic with a decent amount of gold braid, big brass buttons and the collar high on his neck. A large leather belt held his midriff tight, accompanied by a sword and two large calibre pistols. This was his required uniform at all times. As he was alone, he had removed his cap. The heat was unbearable and no one would know.

With the main household away, he walked out to the lake every afternoon. He stopped under a huge tree, hopeful the shade would cool him a little. The estate was considerable and belonged to just one family.

A movement behind him was enough for him to place his peak cap on and step out onto the main path. In the distance, he saw Julia with two of her ladies-in-waiting. He quickened his pace towards them.

'Lady Julia,' he said formally with a slight bow as he stopped.

'Sergeant James. I am glad I have come across you; my ladies worried about a walk on our own. The weather is too glorious to not walk among the trees. Do you not think, Sergeant James?'

'Indeed, Lady Julia, I walk out to the lake as often as I can. Let me accompany you.'

She smiled and turned to her ladies. 'You can both go back; Sergeant James will accompany me, and I will be perfectly safe. Go and prepare a bath for when I return.'

They both bobbed a curtsey and hurried back down the path.

'What a perfect summer's afternoon, do you not think, Sergeant James? Or may I call you Jamie?' She smiled mischievously.

'It certainly is, Julia.'

'Shall we walk down to the lake?'

'Yes, I would be pleased to accompany you to the lake,' he said in the formal way which everyone used. 'Would you mind if I took my cap off? It's far too hot.'

'No, please do.'

They strolled towards the lake, the path shaded by the large trees.

'It seems a long time since the incident at Chester-by-Sea. I have wanted to speak to you privately ever since you came to work in the household, but you know how difficult it is.'

'Yes, it is difficult, but I am glad we have a little while together now.'

'So am I, Jamie. I feel liberated calling you so informally. It feels quite wrong, but I like it.'

'I've always been called Jamie. In this world, I find it difficult to be formal all the time, like wearing this uniform on a hot summer's day. I would prefer to wear shorts and a T-shirt, and with this soft grass I would go barefoot.'

'What is a T-shirt?' She stopped and looked at him.

'It's like a vest, and you would have writing on the front, something like "Surfer Dude".' He looked at her puzzled expression. 'Never mind.'

'And barefoot, I cannot believe you.'

'Why not?'

He bent down and undid the laces on his boots. Once he had pulled his boots off, he removed his socks, stuffed them into his boots, and tied the laces together.

She smiled. 'I cannot believe what you have done.'

The grass felt cool and soft on his feet. 'You should try it, it feels great. Go on, there's no one around.'

'I could not!'

'Why not? It'll take less than a minute to take off your

shoes. I promise you will enjoy it.'

For a while, she was silent. 'I will try it,' she finally said. 'Can you help with the laces?'

He knelt and undid her laces, eased her boots off and pulled her long socks off. As he stood up, she placed her hand on his arm, and her breath was louder.

'How does it feel?'

'Wonderful, amazingly wonderful.' Her smile was wide, genuine, and contagious. As it always was.

'It is,' he said and pressed his bare feet deep into the thick grass. He picked up both pairs of shoes and his cap. 'Shall we?' he asked as he stepped forward.

'What if there is something in the grass?' she said and hesitated.

'Let's walk and enjoy the summer's afternoon. There may be something in there or there may not. Let's walk.'

Slowly, with one pace after another, they stepped forward. 'I should not enjoy being without boots, but I do. Do you remember, on the pier back at Chester, when I said it was the most exciting fifteen minutes of my life?' He nodded. 'Well, I thought it was the danger, the gunfire and bombs, but I feel the same excitement now. I think it must be you.' After a few more paces she continued, 'I don't know how I can be so candid with you, a stranger.'

'Maybe you feel comfortable with me?'

'Yes, maybe I do. I do like walking barefoot. I am glad Lord Thomas hired you. I praised you highly, as did Captain Smith. The Captain suggested your position and Lord Thomas instantly agreed.'

'I couldn't be more pleased with the position. The

grounds are quite beautiful. I have a comfortable cottage and I can spend an afternoon with you. Go for a walk with you under these magnificent trees, barefoot in the wonderful heat of summer. Now, what could be better?'

'It is perfect.'

They walked and talked freely. As they approached the lake, the path widened out, and the trees gave way to the strong sun. Tall trees and large bushes surrounded the lake through which they pushed to get to the water. The long walk and the heat from the sun became unbearable, and the coolness of the water beckoned him.

He dropped the shoes and his cap, stepped over to the side of the lake, and dipped his toes into the water. The icy cold water made the heat seem worse, and he had a strong urge to dive in.

'The water is cold and refreshing. You should dip your toes in,' Jamie told Julia.

She walked past him, stood by the water's edge, and hesitantly dipped her toes in. As she faced away from him, the urge to dive into the water got the better of him. He quietly unbuckled his belt, undid his tunic and his trousers. As they dropped to the ground, he felt free. He sprinted past her and dived into the lake. The cold water caught his breath, and he cooled down instantly.

'I'm sorry, it was too much of a temptation. It's wonderfully cold in here,' he said as he surfaced.

'You are out of your mind!' she laughed.

'Are you coming in?'

The coldness of the lake was exhilarating as he swam hard to the centre of the lake and then back to the shore.

Pulling himself out of the water, he saw her standing with her dress on the ground.

'You are insane, you have only your undergarment on!' she said.

'At least I kept it on!'

'You are completely insane, but I am hot.'

'Come in.' He dived back in and as he surfaced, she joined him.

'This is freezing!'

'It's beautifully cold,' he agreed. They swam further out into the lake. 'The best part is when we get out, we'll be freezing and the sun will feel wonderfully hot.'

'I think I have reached the freezing part now.'

'Come on, I'll race you ashore.'

They both lay in the sun by the side of the lake, the warmth of the sun now welcome, drying them and their clothes.

'I cannot believe I walked barefoot to the lake, removed my clothes and dived in. What have you done to me? I am shocked at myself.'

'Not too shocked, I hope.'

'No, I am enjoying myself. I feel guilty about it, but it is like the time in Chester-by-Sea – I feel alive and released by you. I met you only an hour ago and already I feel it again. I have never felt this before; all the guilt in the world will not diminish it.' She laughed out loud. 'I have been with you for a few hours at most and I feel frightened.'

Jamie reached out and touched her hand.

'Yes,' she whispered as he held her hand.

His rational thoughts were lost to Julia. Only Julia, as an anchor to his sanity, made any sense. He pulled himself up and kissed her on the mouth.

Two Years Later

Jamie ambled along the path down to the lake, the trees alive with all the colours of autumn. Julia walked next to him. Two years had passed since he and Julia first made love down by the lake. They had been together since then, in secret. He escorted Julia on her many walks, her ladies some distance behind.

Jamie was now a lieutenant in the Southway Guard and Head Treasurer. Attacks were frequent, and he had saved the Duke's life on a journey to London. This earned him an instant promotion, and he now lived in a bigger house with a maid and a cook. The uniform was heavier, but in the colder weather he didn't mind too much.

'I have thought about what you said last time we were together,' Julia said, her voice quiet. 'I understand your intentions are good, but the idea of you leaving me and Southway stabs pain all the way through my heart.'

'Yes, I understand, but we have been lucky these last two years. We were nearly caught in June and it is only a matter of time before we are found out. It will be worse for you. You will lose everything.'

'Nonsense. How can you say such a thing? We both have everything to lose.'

'But I will move on to another timeline, another time dimension. You have a whole life to lead, don't you see? I don't want to leave you, but if I stay, I put you in danger.'

'You gave me life two years ago. I can never go back, for my life is with you, whatever happens. When we are discovered, which in the end we will be, my life will end with yours.'

'But it can't. It's not how it works.'

'What how works? You cannot leave me. I will not live without you, I cannot.'

Jamie felt a little unsettled, guilt nagging him. In the end, he would jump to another timeline. But Julia's life would become unbearable. She would have to renounce him publicly before his execution, then probably stay in the Southway household as a junior maid. One rumour he had heard was of a disgraced lady forced to become a maid to the new wife of her ex-husband. His nagging guilt rested on such an outcome, but though he had tried to convince her of those consequences, she wouldn't be rational.

'We will have to be extremely careful. I feel responsible. I have led you to this point and now we are stuck on a path which will only lead to our destruction. You must at least renounce me at the execution.'

'Of course I will. But we will not get caught. For a long while, at least.'

'I wish I shared your faith. I will not leave, but at least think more carefully about the consequences. Not leaving means I will have to stay at Southway, and as long as I stay here, I will have to see you.'

'And I you. Do not speak of leaving me. We have many unions to enjoy.' They walked in silence for a while. 'What if we run away, leave the country?'

'Every noble in the land will pursue us, the reward on offer will turn every person we meet into an informer. We will always be on the run, and they will catch us. The best and most rational plan is for me to leave Southway and you will be safe.'

'You cannot leave Southway; they will not let you.'

'When I say leave, I mean jump into another time dimension. Leave for good. You will have to get on with your life and have me as a good memory.'

She touched his arm, and they stopped. 'How can you speak such thoughts?'

'We should carry on; your ladies are behind us. We don't want to get caught yet.'

She fixed a sharp stare on him and continued. 'I will not contemplate you leaving Southway. We are together now and together we shall stay.'

Four Years Later

A cool mist lay on the ground and the silence of the dawn waited for the sun. Jamie stood in the field and looked east to the new day as the sun breached the horizon. His hands were bound tight behind his back, the sleeves of his tunic removed as well as all emblems of rank. A large white rectangle had been sewn roughly onto his tunic, covering his heart. They would aim for it.

It was six years since he jumped, and he would soon jump again. They were caught two weeks ago, careless and stupid. All the years together and always careful, but it didn't matter anymore.

Lyddia, one of Lady Julia's ladies-in-waiting, must have seen them. She had probably slept with Sir Edmund Castleton, friend and protector of Lord Southway, and told him. The whole household was away, and Sir Edmund would not have come to the house unless he knew. It was too late now to speculate.

Jamie was charged with treason against the Southway House. The punishment was at the behest of the Southway household, and the Duke was insistent on a firing squad. Julia had to disown him and they would spare her.

The sun crept higher over the horizon and crowds thronged around the field. The firing squad, commanded by the Captain of the Guard, stood in front of the whole Southway household, who faced Jamie. Crowds lined the field on either side, a cross section of West Downshire, witnesses of justice in action if anyone crossed the Southway Household.

As the light increased, he saw more people on either side of him. Many ordered to come out.

The Captain of the Guard walked towards him. It would soon be over. He stopped in front of Jamie.

'James,' he said, his voice low, 'this is an unpleasant business. I am sorry. You did wrong, but no worse than any of the lords do. You are the best soldier I have.'

'Some events in your life you cannot control, Captain Smith. I have no regrets, except for what will happen to Lady Julia. For that, I am truly sorry.'

'Any last requests, James Harding?' he said loudly for

the crowds to hear. 'You may address the Household for your last statement.'

Jamie cleared his throat and said loudly, 'Lady Julia was corrupted by me. I forced myself on her and used my position within the household to satisfy my needs. Any dishonour brought to the Southway Household is purely down to me. Lady Julia should not be allowed to bear any of it. I am ready.'

The Captain leant forward, his voice quiet again. 'Would you like a shot of Garrett?'

'I think I would, thank you.'

Captain Smith stepped closer, pulled out a flask, unscrewed the lid and put it up to Jamie's mouth. He swallowed a large mouthful. The harsh taste burned down his throat.

'Captain Smith, will you make sure they aim well? I know some of them can't shoot for shit.'

He smiled. 'I will make sure.' He leant closer. 'James Harding, you are a man of honour. Godspeed.'

'Thank you, Captain Smith. I am ready for the next world.'

Captain Smith nodded, turned, and marched back to the firing line. Jamie waited in silence. The steady rise of the sun produced a bitterly beautiful morning, and he felt it more keenly as the morning surrounded him. Julia approached from the left in a long dress, the thin material flowing around her as she walked. Two soldiers accompanied her part of the way. Her dress was ripped at the bottom and her hair unkempt, but she looked as beautiful as ever. As she walked towards him, his heart ached. She stopped a few feet in front of him and they both nodded in acknowledgement.

'This man, Master James, Jamie,' she said in a loud voice, 'has not corrupted me.' She paused, smiled and turned towards the Southways. 'From the first moment I met Jamie, I fell in love with him. I loved him more each day I lived, and I will love him until the day I die.'

'Lady Julia, you do not know what you say!'

'Be quiet, my love,' she turned to him, her voice soft. 'Let me speak, it will be fine.' She turned back to the Southways and in a louder voice continued.

'If I have been corrupted, it is the most wonderful corruption. It is a feeling I never knew existed until I met Jamie. He unleashed something so wonderful. If I had a choice to truly love a person for six years and die, or to live in luxury until I am eighty, I would easily choose the love I have for Jamie.'

'Julia, we agreed,' Jamie said.

'Lord Southway, my husband, you are a good man, but I do not love you. Jamie is within me and I will never betray my true feelings.'

Jamie saw a lot of movement from the Southways in front of him. Julia moved over to Jamie. 'I love you; I was never going to betray you. Thank you for letting me live for six years. I can't carry on without you. We go together.'

'No Julia, this isn't how it's supposed to be.'

'Do you love me, Jamie? Quickly, for there is not much time.'

'Julia, if only you knew how much I love you, you are deep inside my soul, no matter what happens.'

She kissed him on the mouth, her body warm against his. 'Thank you, Jamie, I die happy with a world of feeling inside me. Thank you.'

Before Jamie could speak, he heard several gunshots, and he fell backwards with Julia on top of him. Her eyes were wide open. 'Jamie, I'm scared.'

'Don't be. Put your head on my shoulder and think only of the day by the lake, the first day.'

'Yes,' she said as she lay her head down on him. He wanted to hold her, but his hands were tied tight behind him. He pressed his head against hers. A wave of outright panic grew, a loss of all control. Julia couldn't die now; she was supposed to live past 2005. Her body became heavier. His panic grew, and he had to get up. The thoughts lashed him, emotions ripped through his body and he couldn't cope with any of it. He gently pushed Julia off as he struggled to his feet. As he stood up, he gulped in a large lungful of air. A thousand eyes focused on him: the field silent. The three bullet wounds on Julia's back made him feel nauseous as his mind struggled to control his actions. He couldn't let Lady Julia down now. He had to get control.

As his breathing slowed, he stepped forward and looked at the soldiers. The sun was up now, ironically giving light and life to the world. One final glance at Julia and he knew he needed to leave the pain he felt.

'Captain Smith, will you please aim true so I may follow my Lady Julia to the next world.'

Captain Smith grabbed a rifle from a soldier. He took a couple of paces forward, pulled the rifle to his shoulder and aimed. Jamie heard the sound as he felt the impact.

He landed on his back and stared at the blue above him. There was no air as he tried to breathe. He wanted to see Julia, but it went black before he had time to turn his head. The familiar warm liquid engulfed him, the blackness became green and a hopeless eternity swirled around him.

The Crimson Castle slowly materialised as his emotions ebbed away. He stood alone on the edge of the void, the castle opposite.

'James,' Gabriel's voice was quiet but distinct as he appeared.

'What happened? Why did Julia die? It wasn't her time!'

'The only constant is the time all souls die. Her time is in the future. People can die before their time, it causes a small disturbance, a ripple in dimensional time, but when all her souls die, the time continuum comes back into balance. The real problem comes when someone lives past their time. Like you, James. Every timeline you jump into causes an ever-increasing divergence between the various time dimensions. You have to stop it before it's too late.'

'I don't understand. How can I stop it?'

'You are the cause of the anomaly. You will know what to do when the time comes.'

'How do you know that?'

'You have to believe me; have faith you can resolve this.'

'Who is the woman?'

'Amelia, she is part of your anomaly. She is also part

of your resolution.'

'This is all riddles, this is crazy.'

'Have faith, James. It's crazy because you don't understand it or believe it. It's real, but not how you think of real. You are approaching your point of resolution.'

'What do you mean? When?'

'You will know when the time comes. Believe you can make the right decision. Everything depends on you, James.' His voice trailed off as Jamie watched him drift away.

He looked back at the castle and she was standing there.

'My darling,' she said, her voice soft but clear, 'it's been a long time since you saw me. I miss you.'

He felt the warmth of her words and the intimate way she spoke to him. 'I don't understand.'

'I know you don't, but we will meet soon and we will talk. You have to be strong in the next world. It will be a difficult world for you to live in.'

'What do you mean?' He felt instant fear at what she was telling him.

'Don't be afraid,' she said again as her voice faded. 'Jamie, my darling, don't be afraid.'

He looked down as he descended into the void. Amelia slipped away from him and he felt the calmness dissipate as he fell deeper into the blackness.

Chapter 8

25th October 1985

The green liquid swirling around Jamie was different this time. Tiny shocks ran through the liquid, as if surrounded by electricity. The intensity grew over the eternity he struggled within the liquid.

Jamie opened his eyes to another world. Electricity continued to pulse through him, his senses heightened. The air tasted salty, the sea nearby. He lay on a hard surface surrounded by water. Someone was close to him crying, or more like producing a stifled scream, a desperate and macabre wailing. Dim streetlights cast a thin pall of light. The red dream floated close to his senses, but not close enough. Gabriel and Amelia, a memory which should be clear, were just outside his grasp. All this input occurred in a moment, a second maybe, and then he was up. With unsteady legs, he held his balance. The road was empty except for a few cars parked further down. Judy was in the road a few feet away on her knees. Her wailing had ceased, her face frozen, eyes fixed on him. Billy sat on the curb behind Judy, staring.

Jamie took an uneasy step towards Judy and sank to his knees. 'Judy,' he said, his voice a little hoarse. 'Is it you?' It had been many years.

For a few moments, she stared at him, eyes wide open. 'Yes.'

'What happened? I can't remember anything.'

'They electrocuted you,' she said after a pause.

'What do you mean?'

'You died, you were dead! I tried to save you, but you were dead!'

'I'm not dead. I just can't remember what happened.' As he reached over and touched her face, he seemed to snap her out of her frozen stare. 'What happened?'

'The South London Enforcers – there were so many of them, and we weren't prepared. You fought them, but there were too many. They broke protocol and pulled guns. They said they would teach us a lesson, show us what happens when we come up against them.'

'And what happened?'

'They electrocuted you! Poured water over you and put electrodes on your chest. It was horrible – it took forever! I felt so helpless.'

A weakness spread down through his body, his head

dizzy, and he struggled to keep his balance.

She reached over and took hold of his arm. 'Billy! Come quick!' she said.

'I'm fine, a little dizzy, trying to catch up—' A hand landed on his shoulder. 'Billy, it's you! I haven't seen you for so long.' Jamie felt a sudden connection to his previous life, his first life.

'Shit, I don't know what to say! You were dead a few minutes ago.'

'No, I'm fine, I think.' The weakness spread through his body as a mixture of emotions overwhelmed him.

'Billy, we need to get him to the hospital,' Judy said. 'Get the car. Now Billy!'

Jamie lost his strength and crumpled into Judy's arms as she guided him down onto the road.

'Jamie, don't you die on me again, you stay with me! Can you hear me?'

Dizziness surrounded him as he heard her call out, but only blackness followed.

Jamie could smell the hospital before he opened his eyes. It was dark, a dim light over to his left. The tingling electricity from earlier was gone, and his head felt clearer. Judy was asleep in a chair next to his bed, and Billy was asleep at the back of the room.

'Judy.' His voice was hoarse and louder than he intended.

She jolted awake, as did Billy, who jumped out of his chair.

'You're awake!' she said as Billy leapt to the middle of

the room, now with a gun in his hand. 'Billy, it's OK.' He nodded and came closer to the bed.

'How are you?' she said and touched his arm.

'I feel good, feel stronger. I need to get up.'

'No, no. Stay there. It's not a good idea. Wait for the doctor.'

'I need to get up. I'll be alright.'

With a snap of his arm, the bedsheet was off and he threw his legs over the side. The floor felt cool on his feet as he stood up. Strength had returned to his legs, and he took a few steps, but she gripped his arm and guided him back round.

'Back into bed, I don't want you falling over. In you go and wait until the doctor has seen you.'

'I feel good, not like last night,' he insisted.

'To be honest, you look good. I still can't believe you're alive. I thought—no—I knew you were dead, but you stood back up.'

'You're one lucky bastard,' Billy said as he came up to the bed. 'I wish I could have seen their faces when they found out.' The smile on Billy's face was one he remembered well. Another weird connection. 'You alright for a while, Judy? I'll find out what the news is.'

Judy nodded, and Billy slipped out the door.

This was the third time he was with Judy. They always seemed to be close, and he was certain they were again. She would die tomorrow evening. Was he supposed to save her? And if he did, would that make her an anomaly like him?

'So are you alright? These last twelve hours have been

crazy.' She sat down next to the bed and took his hand in hers.

'What happened the last twelve hours? It's all a bit of a blur to me.'

'Well, I suppose it all started yesterday afternoon. We got reports of South London Enforcers in Brighton, down by the harbour, so they sent us out. We drove down to the harbour and along the front, but saw nothing. Later in the evening, there were more reports, again down by the harbour. They had three cars parked in Seaview Place, and we challenged them. At first you fought them, but they breached protocol. We were unarmed, and they drew guns. We were outnumbered.'

Jamie felt an anger start to burn. A violent anger which pumped through his body – a dark energy he had never experienced before.

'They made Billy and me sit on the kerb, and we had to watch as they electrocuted you. It took so long. I thought it would never end. Billy held on to me. I was out of my head with shock, fright, I don't know. They checked you were dead and told us that's what would happen to all of us if we resisted them in the takeover.

'I couldn't believe they had killed you. I went over to you when they left and felt for any life. You had no pulse, dead. I knelt beside you for ten, fifteen minutes, probably more. Then you moved and got up. Scared the shit out of me. I can't believe how lucky I am. I thought I had lost you,' she said, whispering the last sentence.

A silence followed while Jamie tried to understand this world – they were becoming increasingly stranger.

'Have you been here the whole night?' Jamie asked.

'Of course I have.'

'What time is it?'

'It's just gone six in the morning. All hell's breaking loose out there. Rumours of you surviving an electrocution. I've got your guns over there on the chair, under your clothes. Reports are the South Londoners may come back today, come back for you, so we need to watch you. All our enforcers have been mobilised, so don't worry.'

'I'm OK. I need breakfast and I'll be ready to leave.'

'Well, you rest for a while and once Billy comes back, I'll sort out breakfast for you. OK?'

So many thoughts rushed around him as he relaxed. Julia's death yesterday was deeply unsettling. It changed the structure of the timelines. He thought they only applied to him, but he had altered her timeline, shortened it. And Judy would die this evening. Did he have the ability to save her? But then she would become an anomaly like him. These thoughts continued driving through him as he closed his eyes. A moment later, he felt a gentle nudge.

'Jamie, are you awake?'

Judy stood next to him, smiling. 'Are you hungry? It's eight now and Billy's back.'

Jamie pulled himself up in bed. 'I'm starving.' Billy came over and sat down next to Jamie as Judy left.

'I can't believe you stood up after they electrocuted you last night. Neither can anyone else. It's all over the front, and I heard rumours South London is none too pleased. In fact, I reckon they're a bit pissed off. They'll come back, and there may even be a price on your head by now. You did well, mate. Your armaments are under your clothes over there on the chair. It's going to get hot for all of us, especially for you.' Jamie nodded. 'How are you feeling?' Billy continued, his speech remaining excited and fast. 'Do you think you're up to it?'

'I feel good. No headache, but hungry.' It was good to see Billy; it had been a long time.

'More of our enforcers are on their way over here. We need to get you to a safe house for the moment, out of Brighton.'

'I don't think anywhere will be safe at the moment.'

'You're right, of course. It's about time we dealt with the South London. The sector chiefs are coming round to the idea of sector war. We can get stuck in properly – and you're invincible.'

Immortal rather than invincible. The thought struck him hard. It seemed so improbable, but maybe true in a grim sort of way. Billy spoke in short, excited clips about the impending war. Jamie wasn't listening anymore, and his mind wandered away.

Judy came in with a tray of food. The food tasted good, although different in a way he couldn't quite define. For the next hour, Judy and Billy talked about the impending war, mentioning many names, places, and tactics. Jamie half listened. He lay with his own thoughts interspersed with war chatter.

A nurse walked into the room and stopped next to Jamie. He flinched as if he had seen a ghost. Julia smiled.

His memory flashed back to the Southway field yesterday. She had died, so she didn't have to deny her love for him. The whole idea of her dying before her time had never occurred to him, but it had happened. It seemed a world away, and now she stood in front of him again. But he couldn't hear a word she said. She came closer and touched him on the shoulder, which was enough to snap him out of his sudden suspension.

'How are you?' she said.

'I'm fine.'

'I need to check your vitals. Quite a story, from what I hear.'

Judy leant forward to Jamie. 'Look, me and Billy need to get a few things sorted about the safe house and the reinforcements. We'll be back in a bit.'

They left the room as Julia pulled a trolley over to the bed and took hold of his wrist. The warmth of her touch reminded him of all the years at Southway. Part of him wanted to reach out and hold her, but this was a different Julia.

A doctor came in and looked at the chart Julia had filled in. After scanning the chart, he handed it back. 'It all looks fine; I'll be back in a while to discharge him. Get him dressed.' The doctor's manner was gruff.

'He's not had a good day,' Jamie said under his breath as the doctor left the room.

'He must be new. I've not seen him before.' She shrugged her shoulders and placed the chart back on the trolley.

An instant alarm screamed through his body, a long-lost tingle, a survival instinct.

'Can you help me? He's no doctor, he's a South London executioner. I'm their hit and I need to get out the hospital now!' He took hold of her hand. For a moment, she stared at him. 'Please, I need your help.'

'Of course,' she said, a little unsteadily, 'you get dressed and I'll check the corridor.' She walked over to the door and looked out as he ripped off his gown and dressed. As Billy had said, there were two guns under his clothes, which he stuffed into the waistband of his trousers.

'It's clear,' she said as she returned.

His pulse quickened, a dark violence flowing through his consciousness. There was no time for socks and shoes.

'Let's go,' he said and stood up, barefoot, feeling for his guns as he wrapped his coat around him.

With slow and careful steps, they edged out of the room into the empty corridor. Julia proceeded to the right, and he followed close behind. The quickness he experienced earlier was shortening his breath, an almost sinister excitement. As they came to the end of the corridor, Julia slowed and looked round the corner, but pulled back sharply.

'Wait! There's a large group of men down there.'

Jamie slipped past her and peered around the corner. Several men stood further down the corridor, the doctor amongst them, and he immediately knew. The new James knew.

'It's South Londoners,' he said to Julia, his voice low.

'Come this way, quickly,' Julia said.

She moved back the way they came and went past his room into another corridor. At a nurses' station, Julia led him through a door into a storage area.

'Put this gown on,' she said, pulling a parcel off the shelf. Unravelling the parcel revealed a hospital gown, which he pulled over his clothes. She hurried back to the corridor and came back in with a wheelchair.

'I'll push you out the side entrance. Pull the hood up and keep your head down.' Her voice was steady now.

'Thank you.'

She pushed him out into the corridor and turned left, away from the South Londoners. He pulled the hood tight over his head as he scanned for dangers. As they turned the corner, two men stood further along the corridor. They looked up but made no movement and looked away as more people came into the corridor.

Jamie felt his heart quicken again. A violent restlessness grew inside him – this new Jamie was pushing him to take out these two men, and it was difficult to remain in the chair as Julia wheeled past them. Halfway along the corridor, there was a large foyer with double doors leading out to daylight. Without slowing down, she pushed straight through the doors and into the cool morning air. The sun cast long shadows across a small car park, which was full. As they crossed the road, he noticed two cars parked on the pavement. South London cars. He saw the number plate on the first car, and he knew. As they approached, he saw three people in the first car, two in the front and one in the back. An enforcer stood behind the car. The second car contained at least two men, with two more enforcers standing behind. No one paid them any attention as they came level with the front of the first car.

A sudden increase in his pulse quickened his breathing, and he felt an uncontrollable surge in energy, violent energy. All the skills he had learnt and inherited in his past timelines were still with him.

He grabbed a gun in each hand and, before he had time to consider his actions, he stepped out of the wheelchair and fired into the first car. In a couple of seconds, he had shot the front two occupants, the rear one, and the enforcer stood behind the car. Without pausing, he stepped forward and shot the occupants of the second car. Then, with two large paces, he fired at the two enforcers behind the second car. They hadn't drawn their weapons, only belatedly ducked for cover behind the car. But it was too late. Jamie's violent bullets had already found their targets. He was around the back of the second car before the two enforcers had fallen and fired another bullet into the first enforcer as he tried to draw his gun. The second enforcer, with a wound in his shoulder, stared with wild eyes at Jamie. It was Geoff, and for a moment, Jamie froze.

'We killed you yesterday,' Geoff said, his voice low and angry. 'You should be dead.'

Jamie reached down and pulled Geoff's gun out of his holster and without thought or restraint, he pulled the trigger.

'This is for last time.'

For Jamie, he was just a witness to the preceding seconds of violence. The violence flowed through his body, but he felt no remorse, only an unnerved sense of pleasure.

He scanned the surrounding scene. All immediate danger was over. Julia stood upright, frozen. Her hands still gripped the handles of the wheelchair. Jamie stuffed Geoff's gun into his trousers, pulled a gun out of the holster of the man next to Geoff, and strode over to Julia.

'Julia!' he said to get her attention. 'Julia, listen carefully,' he spoke in a quick tone, his pulse racing. 'Get away from here. Go round to the back of the hospital and say nothing about this. Go now!'

'How do you know my name?' she said, letting go of the wheelchair.

'It doesn't matter. Run now! And thank you!' he said.

For a moment, her face was a mass of confusion, but then she hurried through the car park towards the back of the hospital.

Jamie ripped off the medical gown and sprinted towards the side entrance, his instincts guiding him. An image of the two South London men, they passed in the corridor a few minutes ago, flitted across his mind. Opposite the entrance, he knelt beside a parked car. The two men came through the foyer and then the door. With an instant and natural reaction, he fired. The two men fell, and he buzzed with a malevolent rush of pleasure. It was a disturbing sensation. The doctor and the other South London men filled his mind. A small raised wall further down the car park was the cover he needed. He raced over and crouched down against it, the guns heavy in his hands. He tried to slow his breathing and the rush of violence which pumped through his body. Four men come round the corner, the doctor among them.

For a few seconds he waited, breathed deeply, and tasted the bitter sensation rush through his body. Pure violence, nothing fancy, just a level of violence Jamie had never imagined anyone could feel. He leant forward and fired. All four men were down.

Jamie ducked back below the wall. Movement behind him caught his attention, and he spun round with his guns ready. Billy and Judy froze behind him, and Jamie relaxed a fraction.

'Are you hit?' Judy said as she knelt. Billy crouched down by the wall and looked towards the front of the hospital.

'No.' Jamie said.

'What happened?' Judy said.

'I don't know. It was a hit on me in the hospital room, but the nurse got me out. She pushed me out in a wheelchair with a gown and hood on. When we went past the South London cars over there, they didn't see me; they had their guard down. I had a gun in each hand, and I don't know what happened.' He paused and shook his head. 'I was out the chair and before I knew it, I'd fired bullets into all of them, including Geoff.'

'You mean Geoff from last night? Shit!' Judy said.

'You trying to start your own war?' Billy stood up, looking over to the cars. 'You know Geoff is married to Don Michael's daughter. Shit, he's going to be pissed! There are South London bodies all over the car park. We need to get back to base now!'

Judy helped Jamie up as Billy rushed out of the car park, the two of them right behind him.

* * *

Late in the afternoon, Jamie sat in their office. It was a small room with four chairs, a desk in the corner and a large cupboard on the other side, which housed their armaments. It contained several rifles and about a dozen handguns, with several drawers full of ammunition. He was in a big grey square building down by the harbour. Two dozen enforcers were assigned to the base, each unit comprising three enforcers. The corridors bulged with activity, but the office was quiet. The violence he experienced earlier in the morning was concerning, unsettling. A complete loss of control. A perverse, pleasure driven sensation which was shocking.

Julia's execution in the field, twenty-four hours ago in another world, was constantly on his mind. It was a shock; it wasn't her time, and he was responsible. His actions changed timelines. Gabriel's words came back to him. He had lived past his time and now he was, in a way, immortal. The thought jolted him. He jumped from one timeline to another, back in time to take over from another Jamie, who had died at his predetermined time. These thoughts ground into him, isolated his mind, and sent him slowly towards insanity.

Judy came back into the office alone. 'Are you alright?' she asked.

'I'm fine, I think. Where's Billy?'

'He went over to the Port Side base. You know what he's like, has to get in on the latest gossip.' She laughed and sat down on the chair next to him. 'It's been one hell of a twenty-four hours. I can't take it all in. What you did this morning, you were like a one-man army. It's the talk all over the city. You sure got this war started.'

'I don't know what came over me.' He paused for a moment. 'I don't quite feel myself; I felt such a rage when I saw the South London Enforcers.'

'Sounds exactly like you, but your shooting has certainly improved. You were possessed.'

An unease ran through him. The violence in this timeline permeated all his thoughts.

Before he had time to reply to Judy, Billy burst in.

'It's on. War is on. South London has challenged us. William Hudson,' Billy said with real reverence, 'was down at Port Side and told us himself. He mentioned you, Jamie, it's all over the city. The South London hit price for you has just shot up to a hundred grand. Well done, mate. They reckon you'll probably have the highest hit price in the entire southern region.' Billy smiled; his excitement easy to see. Jamie wasn't sure about all he said, but he got the general gist of it.

Billy talked on, his voice quick, and he mentioned names and places which meant little to Jamie. A few minutes later, he left, saying something about needing to see Jack.

'He's excited,' Judy said. 'We need to get out on patrol. Oh, maybe you should stay here. I can team up with Danny's unit.'

'No, I'm fine. We'll go together.' He stood up, walked over to the armaments cupboard and loaded up with weapons and ammunition, accompanied by a violent pleasure at the sight of them.

* * *

The sea air felt cool as they walked along the seafront. It was quiet away from the base. Few people were out on the streets who were not enforcers; the turf war was on its way and everyone knew. The cool, clean air refreshed him as his violence abated. Judy was close beside him, both silent as they walked.

'Let's go down to the end of the pier.' Some resolution drew him and he needed to find it down there.

'You sure? There's no one down there. It'll be dark soon.'

'Come on, let's go down to the end.'

She nodded and as they walked down the pier, he felt suddenly safe, as if he could leave the violent world behind. The cold sea air was thick with salt and it provided some strange comfort. The pier was empty. He felt redness, a strange sensation to feel a colour, but as they walked, it became stronger. Someone else was with him. The dream, the castle... and Gabriel. Yes, Gabriel was somewhere close to him. The red dream was important, but it lacked clarity.

They reached the end of the pier and found a cluster of benches, surrounded by a shelter to give some protection from the elements. Jamie leant over the railings, looked down to the black water as it swayed ominously, then out to sea, the sky darkening and indifferent. Judy stood next to him.

'Are you alright?' she asked. 'You've been so different since last night.'

Jamie turned to her. 'I'm fine, but I am different from last night.'

'What do you mean, different?'

'Let's sit down on the bench over there.'

The bench faced out to sea, and the shelter hid them from the seafront and quelled the westerly wind. If they stayed hidden here past six, Judy would live. The crimson colour circled again, this time stronger.

'What did you mean, you are different?'

Jamie sat next to her for a few minutes, letting his mind settle. 'Something happened last night when I died. You said I had died.'

'Yes, you died. But you didn't, you came back.'

'I had died, for a while at least. It's hard to explain. I suppose it's like being immortal. I died, but I didn't. It's the strangest experience.'

Gabriel prodded his thoughts.

'Are you sure you're alright?'

'Yes, I'm fine.' Thoughts flooded his mind. 'What's the time?' he said with a sudden urgency.

'It's ten to six,' she said, checking her watch. 'What's wrong?'

'Let me ask you a question. If you could, would you want to be immortal?'

'That's a strange question.'

'Please, it's important.' Crimson flooded his thoughts, the colour stronger than before.

'I suppose I would want to be immortal. Why not?' she said after a while.

'Are you sure? Think about it.'

'Yes, you would live forever. That would be amazing.'

'Yes, but suppose every time you die, you wake up in

another world, another timeline. The world you wake up in would be different every time. You would survive, but all the friends you had would be left behind. You would have to make new friends, then when you went to the next world, you would have no friends again. Would you not feel lonely and lost?'

Jamie paused for a moment. 'I suppose you would jump into an infinite number of worlds. There would be no end.'

A hopelessness drew around him as he said this. There would be no end. The bleakness of the sea and darkness of the sky seemed to provide no optimism for his thoughts.

'You would find no peace, would you?' she said, her voice quiet. 'You would never find any peace. I wouldn't want that.'

'No, there is no peace.'

She pressed closer to him. 'You seem different since last night. All I know is I'm glad you're not dead and you're next to me, as you should be.'

Jamie put his arm around her. Thoughts of how to save her raced around his mind, but time was short. 'I'm worried about the coming war. You can feel it on the seafront.'

'I know, but we're together now. I can't think about the future.'

Judy's time tore at his mind, but she was right. There would be no peace, like his nightmare. If he saved Judy in the next few minutes, she would have no peace, either. If he had the choice, would he have preferred to die in 1985, not have lived one full life? A stark question.

He missed his Julia and his kids, but they were gone. And so should he. Instead, he was stuck in this infinite time loop, immortal, and unable to die completely. One timeline to the next, a different world each time. But he also picked up traits from the Jamie he replaced. In this world, he had an unbelievable amount of violence. He could stop the violence, jump into another world. It could be better, or it could be worse. Either way, there would be no peace. And as his mental state continued to fray around the edges, how many timelines before he became completely insane?

Judy would die shortly, and he couldn't shake the thought he could save her.

What would his Julia have done in this situation? Would she have saved him, to become an anomaly and live a nightmare forever? The answer was easy. He couldn't let her become like him; she would need to find her peace now.

As he looked at her, she smiled and he felt a sudden empty sadness for her and, in fact, for everything. He took her hand, surprised by its warmth.

'I think we should get back.' Jamie said.

'Yes, we need to get back.' Judy said as she stood up.

The sea beckoned him again, and he walked over to the railings. The sea stretched out in front of him, its dark waters restless, the stiff wind fresh on his face. There were no answers out in the sea, no sense to all this madness. Judy came next to him; her hand touched his. Again, the warmth of her hand, the warmth of life. So little time left.

Jamie felt doom all around him, intimately aware Judy would die shortly. 'Come on.'

They turned away from the sea and walked back along the pier. Thoughts of the field in Southway flitted across his mind, only yesterday but another lifetime away.

The new Jamie stirred, a brooding aggression. A keener sense of his surroundings developed as a tingle ran along his arms and heightened his expectations of impending events. A few seconds later, two cars sped into view along the seafront. He pushed Judy into a shelter to take cover and reached for his two guns without thinking, one in each hand.

'South Londoners,' he said.

The two cars sped towards them. The first car stopped by the entrance to the pier, while the second stopped further along the road to the right.

'You go down the left side, keep low. I'll go round to the right,' he said, his voice barely a whisper. Extreme violence was already on the rise as his heart rate increased. 'Go,' he said as he hastened down the right of the pier.

Instead of doing as he asked, Judy went with him on the right side of the pier.

'Judy,' he said, louder than intended. Judy stopped.

They stared at each other and, for a moment, he thought the South Londoners hadn't heard them. Then Judy staggered back as the sound of gunfire accompanied her fall, a bullet wound in her chest. An immediate guilt overwhelmed him. The anger and violence flared quickly, and he pounded down the pier.

Two South Londoners stood straight in front of him. He didn't slow. In fact, the violence drove him forward faster, firing both guns. The two South Londoners dropped as he reached the pavement. He fired to his left and hit the next South Londoner, who had started to move. Jamie didn't miss a step and went straight over the top of the car, firing into the fourth and last South Londoner.

He hit the road on the other side, slowed and spun around. Every fibre of his body was alive to every movement around him as he experienced a massive adrenaline rush.

The other South London car was fifty yards down the road. The occupants stood by the car, guns drawn. His legs pumped his body forward, and he fired as he charged straight at the next car. His running coincided with his shooting, his bullets exactly where he wanted them. A mechanical violence. All the South Londoners had fallen by the time he reached the car.

Neutralised.

He sprinted back to the pier. As he approached Judy, his violence drained away rapidly and his movements became laboured, his legs heavy. Judy lay on the pier, her eyes wide open, her hands clutched frantically at her chest. Only a few moments had passed since they shot her, but it seemed longer. He struggled to run and crashed down on the pier as he reached her.

'Judy!' he said.

'Jamie!' her voice was weak, frightened. 'Jamie, am I

going to be alright?'

'Judy, it's your time. There is so much I need to tell you, but there isn't the time or the words to. You will find peace soon; it's how it's meant to be. Do you hear me?' He reached over to take her hand.

'This is how it has to be. It's the only way. I can't explain it. You remember we talked about no peace if you lived forever, now you will have peace. Have good thoughts.

'Good thoughts,' he said again, but he felt a sudden weakness throughout his body. His heart pounded wildly, and he realised he needed more air. There wasn't any, and he fell forward next to Judy.

The sea air rushed through his nostrils, and he was back. He lay next to Judy, but she had found her peace. He stumbled up and grabbed on to the railings for support.

Several people ran towards him. Billy was at the head of the group and, with sudden relief, Jamie sat down on the pier.

'Are you hit?' Billy said as he approached.

Jamie shook his head. 'Judy took the hit. She's gone, she's gone!' he said as he saw two people kneeling beside Judy.

'What the hell happened?' Billy said, catching his breath. 'There are dead South Londoners all over the road down there.'

'They caught us here on the pier. They shot Judy.'

'Who shot them?'

'I did.'

Billy stared at him for a moment and then looked over to Judy.

Jamie looked out of the window onto the seafront. A weariness had crept over him. It was three weeks since Judy's time. The first ten days were frantic. South London Enforcers had come down in huge numbers, but they had held them off. He remembered only a violence filled period. The fighting had calmed over the last week. His aggression had dissipated and now all he felt was a deep tiredness.

They had buried Judy at sea after the first wave of fighting. He and Billy had gone out on the dawn burial boat. It didn't feel right leaving her out at sea, but in the middle of a war it was the best way. He asked the crew to separate Judy's body from the rest. They complied instantly and, from the look in their eyes, he realised his reputation had already spread. A reputation of violence. Once they had discarded the bodies, he asked them to take her further away. Guilt and pain consumed him as she slid into the water.

As he now looked out to the sea which held her, a few people hurried along the quiet seafront. Billy was at the Port Side base gathering the day's news. Jamie watched and waited. An hour passed before Billy emerged from the base and ran along the seafront. A few minutes later, he heard Billy's footsteps on the stairs.

'You're worth another hundred thousand,' Billy said as he came into the deserted room. 'You are worth a fortune. Bets are on how high they'll go.' He paused for a moment. 'You need to watch your back, Jamie. There will be people who will be tempted. I mean people here in Brighton.'

'I know, but I'll be careful.'

'Something else I heard. The nurse who helped you in the hospital. They haven't got her name yet, but they've put a price on her as well. They say she was part of the assassination of Geoff. It's a big price.'

Jamie felt his heart quicken.

'Her name is Julia Parker. I need you to find her first,' he told Billy.

'Is it important in amongst all this?'

'She risked her life for me. I will do anything for her. We need to find her.'

'OK, let me think.' Billy paced the office. 'OK, I know a few nurses at the hospital. I can get down there and see if I can find out where she lives. The price has gone out, so I need to get down there now. I'll find her, Jamie. I'll see you lunchtime. Where?'

Jamie considered it for a moment. 'The Beacon.'

'OK.'

'Thanks Billy. Be careful.'

'You too, mate.'

Jamie stood in silence, alone with his thoughts.

The light had long since faded from the sky as Jamie sat in the car with Billy. Two other enforcers, Joe and Paul, sat in the back. They had been there for the last half hour, watching and waiting outside Julia's apartment building. A few people walked past, but it looked quiet.

'What do you think, Billy?' Jamie said impatiently.

'Don't know, I'm not sure. It looks quiet. Maybe too

quiet.'

'We can't sit here for much longer. Let's get over there,' Jamie said. He felt Billy's uncertainty, but with time short, they needed to get Julia away to a safe location.

'I'm not convinced, but I agree we can't sit here all night. You boys ready in the back.'

'Loaded and ready to go, boss.'

'Let's go,' Jamie said. Gun in hand, he crossed the road. A short path led to the front door and into the large entrance hall. With Billy behind him, Jamie moved towards the stairs and saw a notice pinned to the wall.

Amongst all the other sheets of tatty papers, he noticed this one instantly. It had a crude drawing of the Southway's coat of arms at the top of the paper and read, 'To the Lieutenant of Lady Julia. You will find what you are looking for if you take the last house number from your first life, the House you worked at in your last life and the favourite number of your wife.'

Jamie pointed to the notice. The other two enforcers were in the hallway now and peered out the side windows.

'What does it mean?' Billy said.

'She's at 23 Southway, Flat 9.'

Billy looked at him, confused.

'I haven't time to explain – later.'

'We got company,' Paul said as he stepped back from the window.

'They're upstairs as well. It's a trap!' Jamie felt an uncertain, violent twinge.

He pointed to the fire exit, and they all hurried down

the corridor, Jamie pausing as he took hold of the door handle. There could be someone outside, but he didn't have time to hesitate. He opened the door and stepped out into the quiet night, and they slipped along the back of the building.

'I've got a shortcut,' Billy whispered as he went past Jamie. He led them across to the next building and down the garden to a gate in the corner, which led out onto a small footpath.

'We good?' Jamie asked.

'Yeah, follow me.' Billy led the way down the path.

Jamie pressed himself into the large hedge across the road from 23 Southway. The dim streetlight a little further down provided the half-light to blend into the undergrowth. Billy pressed into the hedge next to him. Joe and Paul were further down the road, crouched behind dustbins.

Jamie stared at the green door across the road. An object leant up against the door – it was a fishing net. For a moment, he felt confused, but it sort of made sense. Someone who knew him had led him here.

'Let's go, Billy,' he whispered as he pushed himself back onto the pavement.

'It could be another trap.'

'No, it's good. I need to get in there.' He turned to Joe and Paul. 'You two keep watch outside.'

Jamie strode across the road to the green door, which opened as he nudged it. He stopped in the entrance hall, Billy behind him. It was empty as he scanned down towards the back of the house. A large clock above the mailboxes showed the time was ten past nine. Jamie climbed the stairs two at a time to the second floor. He approached the door to his left, which displayed a large number nine. He raised his arm to knock, but the door opened before he had chance.

The shock stopped him dead in his tracks. The woman from the crimson castle stood in the doorway of flat nine.

Billy had his gun drawn and pointed at the woman. Jamie put his hand on the muzzle and pushed it towards the ground.

She smiled. Warm and safe. 'My darling, I have been waiting for you for such a long time.'

Jamie didn't know what to say.

'Jamie, what's going on?' Billy asked.

'Hello Amelia,' Jamie said, finally.

'Come.' She stretched her arms towards him. Jamie stepped forward and felt her arms wrap around him, squeezing him as close as she could.

'I have waited over fifty years for you. I couldn't begin to tell you how I feel, touching you, feeling you next to me in body and soul.' Her voice was soft and quiet, but the words travelled with such emotion Jamie couldn't help feeling moved. However, he also sensed a desperation hidden amongst the words.

'What's going on?' Jamie's voice was equally quiet while Amelia held him tight. She didn't answer, only held him tighter, so close he felt her breathing coincide with his.

'Jamie,' Billy said, 'what's happening here?'

'What's happening?' he repeated.

Amelia released Jamie, and he stepped back. 'Come, we need to talk. Come inside.' She lead him through to the kitchen. Julia sat at the table and looked up, confused.

'Julia, are you alright?' Jamie asked.

'I don't know.' She pointed to Amelia. 'She came to my house and told me we had to go before they came for me. She said she was a friend of yours and told me the events of that morning, details only you would know. Before we left, she pinned something on the notice board saying it was the clue for you to find me. She also said you would get here at ten past nine and you did. I don't understand any of it.'

Jamie turned to Amelia. 'How do you know all this? The clues you left, and that I would turn up here at ten past nine?'

'Oh, that's easy, my darling. You told me.'

Jamie pulled out a chair and sat down. 'When?'

'When you meet me in your next timeline. We need to talk. But first we need to get Julia out of Brighton to a safe house and then on to Southampton. Billy, could you escort Julia to the Arundel safe house? You know where it is. Go alone, don't take anyone with you. You need to go now.'

Billy turned to Jamie, who nodded. 'Billy, you need to get Julia away from Brighton, please. She saved my life and now I need you to save her.'

'I will. Are you OK here on your own?'

'Amelia is an old friend. Take Julia and keep her safe.

I'll see you tomorrow back at the Port Side base.'

'Will do, if you're sure everything is OK. This is a little weird.'

'I'll explain it all tomorrow. You probably won't believe any of it, anyway.'

Billy turned to Julia. 'Jamie's right. We need to get you to safety. There's a price on your head, a big price.'

'But I've got nothing with me; Amelia wouldn't let me pack anything.'

'Everything you need will be at the safe house. It'll be fine. I'll wait for you outside in the hallway.' Billy nodded to Jamie as he left. 'See you tomorrow.'

'Julia, thank you, and I'm sorry I involved you. Billy will look after you and get you to Southampton. You'll be safe there.'

She rose from the chair, walked to the kitchen door and stopped by Amelia. 'I feel I should thank you, even though I don't understand what has happened.'

Amelia took hold of her hand. 'I couldn't begin to explain it to you. Accept you will be safe and go with Billy. Try not to think too much about this.' Julia nodded with a scared smile and headed down the hallway.

Amelia walked over to Jamie, took his hand and led him out of the kitchen and into the lounge without a word. A small coffee table held a bottle of whisky and two crystal tumblers. Two large sofas sat at right angles to each other. Amelia led him over to the furthest one and sat him down. Then she went over to the table, opened the new bottle and poured two generous glasses.

'Drink and I'll be back in a minute.' She left the room.

Jamie sat back on the sofa and took a large sip of whisky, swallowing hard and enjoying the harsh taste. He tried to slow his breathing, to calm down and to understand.

Amelia came back into the room a few minutes later and picked up her whisky seamlessly as she sat down next to Jamie, her body close to his.

'I don't know where to start. I've got a million questions,' he began, but she pressed her finger to his lips.

'Relax, my darling. Let's start at the beginning.'

'This is your fifth world.' He nodded. 'It is also my fifth world. You thought you had time travelled back twenty years the first time, but you now know you jump between worlds, different timelines. And the crimson dream, where you meet Gabriel – he speaks to you, tells you about timelines, which you can't quite remember when you jump into the next world. But after each world, it's a little clearer. You have remembered enough to help you work it out.'

'I still don't understand how you know all this. How do you know?'

'You haven't met me yet, but you will in the next timeline. You tell me then.'

'How can that be possible?'

'As you tell me in the next world, all timelines are simultaneous. It happens all at once, but we only experience one world at a time.'

'Gabriel told me about the different timelines.' Jamie reached over for the glass and took another large mouthful.

'You're frightened by the violence which burns inside you. It's like the Jamie you jumped into is trying to take control. You question whether it is the other Jamie, or a dark part of your soul which is already there and this world draws it out.'

'Yes, that worries me, but I don't know what the answer is,' he admitted.

'I don't know either. You see a lot of the same people in each world, but some you will never see again.' She paused. 'Your children,' she continued, 'your two children, you will never see again. But there will be other worlds where you will have different children.'

What she was telling him made her seem crazier than he was.

'You think I'm crazier than you are.'

'Shit!' he said in surprise. 'How can you read my mind? How do you know so much about me?'

'Oh, my darling, you told me.'

'I'm struggling to understand. I've not met you yet, but I've told you about all this.'

'More than told me.' She laughed. 'I'm sorry, you told me how surprised you would be, and I love seeing it.' She ran her hand over his face. 'I'm teasing you a little.'

'What about the crimson dream I have? I see you in them, between each jump. Are you there as well?'

'Yes. It's indeterminate time. We both go there between each world we jump to. Gabriel doesn't talk to me, only you. It's difficult to remember what happens; it's like a dream. But I see you and feel you while I wait.'

'Gabriel told me about indeterminate time. A waiting

room between worlds, but with no time.'

'Yes, we wait between worlds.'

'We are both anomalies. Something caused us both to become a time anomaly, Gabriel told me.'

'I know how I became an anomaly. I've come to rescue you from this world, so you can rescue me in mine.'

'How?' Jamie said, still struggling to understand.

'When you jump from this world, you will be in my first timeline. I won't know you, and it will surprise me what you must tell me. In fact, more so, because it will sound absurd. What I tell you now is what you will tell me. It's been such a long time since I've seen you, my darling.'

'How many years?'

'It's been over fifty years,' she said, tears filling her eyes. 'Oh Jamie, it's been so long. This isn't long enough.' Her voice was only a whisper.

'What do you mean, it isn't long enough?'

'Never mind, my darling. What else do you want to know?'

'Everything.'

Amelia poured them both a refill and clinked her glass on his.

'Cheers. A toast to you and me, to our ephemeral meetings and the eternal lives we lead.' She lifted the glass and drank nearly half the tumbler before putting it down.

'Now, you made me promise when I met you in this world, we wouldn't become intimate. You haven't met me yet and I should wait until we both know each other. I'm desperate for you to make love to me; I can't tell you how much. But you're right, you need to know me first. I would like a hug; it's been fifty years.' Her voice sounded so sincere, so passionate.

She sat back on the settee and pulled him towards her. The warmth of her body felt comforting, especially as she knew what had happened to him. A fellow traveller in these strange worlds. He drifted away.

A soft hand on his shoulder gently roused him. 'Jamie, I need to tell you more. You can't go to sleep yet. I had planned exactly what I needed to tell you, but now it seems most of it has evaporated. Strange, so many years to be prepared and now, as I sit next to you, it's all jumbled up.' She smiled and stroked his arm.

'I know it must feel strange for a woman you hardly know to be so intimate with you. I know you so well and though it may not be fair to you, I don't care. It's been fifty years since I saw you last in the flesh. I loved you then, and I have loved you ever since. You will understand what I mean in time. And now, though you are bewildered, it's you. I can feel it's you. I wish I could transfer my feelings to you, but you will find out in your next jump.'

'When do I jump?'

'Soon, my darling, soon.'

He looked at her and saw a tear trickle down her cheek.

'What is it?'

She shook her head and smiled, a mixture of sadness and happiness.

'You told me a lot of things when you met me for the first time – sorry, I mean my first time. I'm thinking about the first time now. It's such a long time ago. Strange how after so many years and so many memories, some remain with you like they happened yesterday. When you told me we would meet again in the future, I didn't think I would have to wait quite so long. And now I don't know how long it will be before we meet again, if we ever do...' Her voice trailed off.

They sat silently for a while as Jamie churned over what she had said.

'There's a lot I don't understand, but how can I meet you before your first jump?' Jamie asked eventually. 'It's not logical.'

'It's not logical because it's outside what we can understand. It's real because it happens to us. The world outside, the universe, is so vast we can't even begin to understand it.'

'I'm still struggling with this simultaneous time shift. If I meet you in my next jump, is it you?'

'Yes, in my past,' she paused and added, 'my simultaneous past.'

'What about all the other Amelias in all the other timelines? And all the other Jamies?'

'I've only met you, my darling. All the other Jamies die a day earlier than me, so in all the timelines I've been in, they are never there. This is the second time I've met you. The first time is in your next jump.'

'So when does it end?'

She smiled wearily. 'I don't know. I haven't worked it out yet.'

'We jump forever?' The horrific reality dawned on him.

She shrugged her shoulders. 'I've no idea.'

He reached for his whisky as Amelia did the same.

'How do we meet? When?' he asked.

'Well, you jump into your Jamie the night before I'm due to go on holiday. Two weeks in Spain, meeting up with my Spanish friend. The Jamie from your next timeline is a little different, but you have such talents. I won't tell you anymore; you'll find out for yourself. You asked me not to tell you. You must get to Charlwood Airport by eleven o'clock the next morning after you jump. It is important you get there by eleven o'clock. I was ready to check in at eleven thirty when it opened, but you stopped me.'

'Why–' but before he could complete his question, she placed her finger on his lips.

'The plane I was about to board crashes on take-off.'

She continued, 'I remember it clearly, even after all these years. I was so excited. It was to be my first time on a plane. I hadn't slept much the night before, but I wasn't tired. I arrived hours before I needed to, had breakfast, and wandered about the shops waiting for the check-in to open. I wore a yellow and white striped summer dress, even though it was October and quite cold, and on my trolley I had a big straw sun hat with a yellow ribbon. It's important, remember it.

'I remember as I walked towards the check-in desk, a man approached me and before I could react, he had slipped a handcuff on my left wrist. A gentle act, natural. As I looked down, I saw the other end of the handcuff attached to his wrist. At first, I didn't know what to think, it was so unexpected. I looked up and saw a handsome man. You spoke calmly, your voice steady and clear. “Amelia,” you said, “you need to stop thinking about the lecture you’re giving when you get back. Enjoy your holiday with Maria in Spain and don’t worry about the mug you broke this morning.” The overriding shock was that you knew what I had been thinking. You said, before I had chance to think anything more, “My name is Jamie, I have come to save you. I mean no harm to you.” I believed you, deep down. I didn't scream or do anything. I just asked who sent you?

‘“You sent me.” Your answer was simple, but made no sense. “You sent me from your future. Please don’t be frightened. Will you listen to what I have to say?” Your eyes never left mine. I must have nodded. “Good. I will explain all once we’ve sat down over there.”

‘You turned and pointed to the rows of seats which looked out over the planes and runway. “I know you are shocked and don't know what to think or do. Whether to shout and try to break away from me or whether you should stay and listen. I will not harm you and just ask that you let me explain before you do anything. Come, let’s sit down.” Your voice was so steady and calm that although shocked, I didn't feel frightened.

‘I parked my trolley at the end of an aisle and we sat down on the seats. You were close to me, our cuffed hands touching. You settled back in the chair and I followed. “Are you comfortable? As comfortable as can be expected, obviously?” you asked. I felt a little reassured by your consideration. “You will not believe any of what I tell you now, but in time you will believe all of it.” I remember you paused for what seemed like forever. I was completely lost for words, thinking it must be some terrible joke.

'You carried on in your steady voice. "The plane you are about to board crashes on take-off. If you get on it, you will not survive." All sorts of wild thoughts went through my mind. Was this man responsible for the plane crashing? Why was he saving me and letting the other passengers board?

'You responded a few moments later with, "I'm not going to blow the plane up, it crashes because a huge flock of birds takes out the engines. And I can't save the people on the plane because firstly they wouldn't believe me and secondly, as you will see later, the impact of what I am doing comes with huge consequences."

'You kept reading my mind, which I found a little unsettling. "Look, I'll make a deal with you. You will have to miss your flight, because I can't let you get on the plane. But if the plane takes off and it doesn't crash, then I am in the wrong timeline and I will let you go. You can go to the police and get me arrested; I will pay for another flight. I want you to sit with me and wait for your plane to take-off."

'I spoke for the first time saying I thought you were crazy asking me to believe you, but some of what you said made me a little wary. I remember I wanted to scream. I wanted to get on my plane, but at the same time I was intrigued. You're a handsome man and I felt no malice in your voice or intentions. I agreed to sit with you until my plane had taken off. Our hands touched the whole time.'

Amelia sat up, drank more of her whisky and handed

Jamie his glass. She leant back into the sofa and continued, 'We sat there for the next two hours. You told me about the timelines, how we jump between different worlds, all the stuff I've told you.

'Strange, when you jump next you will see me in the airport. I'm holding your hand now. You're the most important man in the world to me. But when I sat in the airport, I thought you were completely crazy. You told me so much while we waited for the plane to take off, most of which I didn't take in. As a scientist, everything you told me went against everything I had ever studied. You needed help.'

She stroked his face. 'There isn't enough time, my darling, there isn't enough time.' He looked at her, tears in her eyes, and as he went to sit up, she firmly put her hand on his shoulder. 'No, lie next to me. Don't do anything, just listen.'

He relaxed back beside her, felt the warmth of her body, and let the calmness take him.

'The last call for my flight came. I felt a little angry, but you calmly said I wasn't to be angry. I suppose I felt unnerved by all of it, but you soothed me and I resigned myself to the fact I had missed my flight. You didn't say anymore, just watched the planes take off. I felt a sort of tension, an unsettled nervousness.

'About twenty to two, you pointed to a plane which pulled onto the runway. "Your plane. It crashes at quarter to." We watched the plane come down the runway and lift off. Nothing appeared wrong.

'We watched as it climbed away from the ground and I glimpsed tiny flecks. I immediately knew it was the birds. I don't think the plane shuddered, rather it seemed to slow, even from where we sat. At that moment, I knew you weren't crazy. The plane hung for a moment in the air, suspended, but then the nose dipped down and it started to fall.

'We rushed over to the windows as the plane, in slow motion, fell to the ground. I should have been on the plane. You took hold of my hand as we watched. The plane hit the ground and a few moments later a huge fireball engulfed it. I remember the brightness of the fire mixed with fear and relief. It frightened me, but I also realised something much bigger existed out there. Before I noticed, you had released me. "You're safe now," you said.

'That's when I fell in love with you. I put my hand on your arm. "You're safe now," you whispered again, and I felt something I had never felt before. Just like I feel now.' She touched his face again.

They both sat up and she poured another whisky. She touched his glass with hers. She smiled and drank the whole glass down in one. He drank most of it, but she nodded for him to drink all of it, which he did. They leant back into the sofa. He felt drowsy as he leant against her.

'What happened next?'

'We went for a drink, whisky, and sat in the lounge for a long time. You told me more about how we travel between timelines, and I struggled to understand what you were saying. I held your hand and stayed close to you. I needed to feel safe after what happened, and you seemed to know everything.'

She paused for a while before continuing. 'I felt more in those few hours than I had my whole life. It's still powerful.

'We made love later in the evening. You have burned inside me ever since then. We made love many, many times, but never enough.' She smiled wistfully.

'So we were together as a couple?'

'Oh yes, we were, my darling. You moved in with me and we both worked at the university. You were so talented. We lived comfortably, and we had each other. We both lived for each other. You were my life and little did I realise it, but you would become my life throughout time.'

'How long were we together for?'

'Not long enough. I won't tell you how long, you expressly asked me not to, but enough for me to search for you throughout time. '

'I've got so many questions to ask about our relationship and what happens. How much time do we have together in this timeline?' He felt her stiffen.

'Have some more whisky, please,' she said, her voice emotional. He leant forward, poured out half a glass and drank it down. As he turned to ask her if she wanted another glass, the alcohol drained away and his mind sharpened as he saw Amelia standing with a gun in her hand.

'That was the question, my cue,' she told him.

'I don't understand.' His mind tried to catch up with the unfolding events. 'Are you alright?' The whisky was mixing with his confusion.

'No. The question, the one you asked now, it was the signal.'

'What signal?'

'You are about to jump into my first timeline and save me,' she spoke fast, her voice nervous. 'I don't want you to go. I want to stay with you, but it must be this way. You told me I had to shoot you now, otherwise you won't jump into my timeline.' Tears ran down her cheeks.

'You also said I had a choice, now at this point. But I love you, my darling.' She moved away from him and lowered the gun. 'I love you,' she said, barely a whisper.

'Are you going to shoot me?' he said without moving.

'I love you too much. I'm so sorry,' she said. 'I'm so sorry.'

They looked at each other. Then he felt the tingle in his arms and a violence roared through his body. He reached for his gun, but Amelia had it.

He leapt off the sofa, the violence on the other side of the door. Billy burst in, a gun in each hand. Jamie paused for a moment, a disconnect between the sudden violence and Billy. Billy fired and a searing pain ripped through his chest as he reeled back onto the floor and knocked the coffee table over, scattering the whisky bottle and glasses.

'Jamie!' Amelia screamed. Billy fired again and as Jamie looked round, he saw Amelia collapse on the sofa.

'Billy?' Jamie's voice was weak, the pain intense.

Billy walked over to Jamie and looked down.

'Billy?'

'Sorry mate. Your price went up to a mill. Too much. If I don't take it, some other bastard will. Joe and Paul whispered about you. I popped them and decided it might as well be me.'

'Julia?'

Billy shrugged his shoulders and put the gun against Jamie's forehead. 'I'm afraid it's a mill. Dead.' He pulled the trigger.

The thick green liquid held him and washed away all his thoughts. The coldness of the glass touched him every now and again, and he reeled away from it. Time didn't exist for him, just the endless struggle against the thick liquid. Indeterminate time. Then the liquid swirled away and left him on the precipice again. The crimson castle stood in front of him, clearer this time. He looked for Gabriel and Amelia.

'James.' Gabriel said, his voice faint.

'Gabriel?' Jamie looked round but couldn't see him. 'Gabriel, where are you?'

'James. I'm right next to you,' Gabriel appeared.

'What's going on? I had such violence in me.'

'Your soul comprises an infinite number of combinations. You are who you are, but other parts of you may have developed different tendencies. You feel them inside you now. Fighting you.'

'Yes, I do. How do I make it stop?'

'Undo the anomaly. You must close the loop.' Gabriel faded into the crimson landscape as quickly as he had appeared.

As Jamie looked over to the castle and moved towards the precipice, his calmness vanished. He searched for Amelia, scanning the castle and beyond into the misty red fields. He saw a flicker of a shadow and Amelia appeared.

Her face wasn't clear, but he felt her agitation.

'I'm so sorry, my darling,' she said, her voice shaking. 'I want to hold you forever, but I can't. It can't be. Jamie, save me, please save me!'

An unease developed, 'Amelia, I'm here.' As he moved out over the void, he shouted louder, 'Amelia!'

'I don't know if you are still there, my darling. I'm so sorry I've left you alone.'

'Amelia! I'm here,' but he felt the ground disappear from underneath him.

The crimson world slipped away from him, the thick liquid waiting as the bottle wrapped around him. His instinctive struggle resumed, and restlessness flooded his being.

Chapter 9

25th October 1985

Jamie rushed towards consciousness and snapped awake. He was in a room; the curtains drawn. The room was dimly lit and covered in stuff – on the floor, on the desk and on the bookshelves. Several large batteries sat on the floor with a mass of coloured wires which ran into many other boxes. A burnt odour hung in the air, his aching hands covered in black streaks. Thick smoke rose from one box, and he instinctively reached across to the batteries on his left and pulled the wires off the terminals. A sharp pull released the stiff wires. A burst of pain rushed across his head from the sudden exertion, so he sat back, breathed deeply, and waited for it to recede.

The room was littered with books – open books and

books stacked in piles – with most of the titles either comprising mathematics or physics. Formulas covered the wall and a part of him seemed to understand what they meant. The numbers and strange formulas played before his eyes, and he could smell the numbers as he breathed in. It was a sensation he had never experienced before. Despite everything, there was a strange comfort in the numbers. His headache faded, and he pulled himself off the floor, leant against the door to the room and flicked on the main light. All the colours of the room rushed at him. The formulas around the room seemed to come alive. He watched them and time seemed irrelevant. He needed to find Julia; she was close, and this latest Jamie knew her.

Stepping into the hallway, he heard voices further down the corridor and walked towards the noise. It was a communal kitchen. A few people sat at the table whilst others leant against the counters. As he entered, the talking stopped and all eyes turned towards him. Sensations hit him: coffee, alcohol, perfume, body odour, mouldy wood. He struggled to stay in control, filtering the different smells as he stood by the door. A tall lad stepped towards him and spoke, but his voice was muffled. Jamie stood there frozen to the spot before snapping back to reality as the sensations filtered away and the person who spoke became clear.

'... you staring at you half-wit? Crawl back to your room...' His words were a little slurred, but his vicious intent was not.

'Dave, leave him alone,' a woman said.

Jamie stepped to one side to see who had spoken. The

lad stepped in front of him, closer. The violent Jamie slipped out from inside his mind, changing his emotional state. His breath shortened, and he felt a sudden surge of violence throughout his body.

'Don't get any closer,' Jamie said, his voice a low growl with his heart beating faster.

The lad backed away immediately. The woman at the table got up and approached him.

'Did you speak?' she said, her voice gentle, and he recognised it from somewhere.

'He got too close,' Jamie said as the violence abated. He continued, his voice gentler, 'I'm looking for Julia Parker. Does anyone know where she is?'

'You are speaking, such a nice voice,' she said. 'Julia might be in the Union bar. I saw her there a while ago, when we left.'

Jamie felt a sudden relief. 'Thanks,' he said to the woman, turned and left the room. The new Jamie took him down a flight of stairs and out into the cool night air, leading him towards the Union. Again, he experienced a surge in sensations as the fresh aroma of the grass and soil next to the path mingled with the many unfamiliar smells swirling around him. Julia was his focus, but it was a struggle to block out all these extra sensations.

He walked across the campus, and there were some similarities with his earlier lives, but this was a different world. He entered the Union and small crowds of people were scattered around the room. As he circled round, looking for Julia, a group of lads approached. They stopped in front of him and his breath shortened again.

'What's the weirdo doing in here? You don't belong here.'

Jamie struggled with the violence, but he spoke first to see their reaction. 'I'm looking for Julia Parker,' he said, his voice steady and sharp. The man closest to him stopped mid-sentence, his mouth hanging open.

Jamie spoke louder and asked for Julia. Everyone stopped and looked.

A woman approached him. Again, he recognised her from somewhere, from another timeline. 'I think she's gone to the coffee bar,' she suggested, giving him a sympathetic look.

'Thank you. I'll try there.'

He stepped back into the night air and followed the flow of people to the coffee bar. Many people milled around outside and others packed the inside. As he approached, he stopped as if something was holding him back. Despite wanting to go in, he couldn't. He experienced a myriad of aromas: coffee, alcohol, cigarette smoke, the smell of so many people. He didn't know how long he stood there, but he couldn't move. His senses were overloaded and he couldn't function.

'Jamie!' Julia's voice drew his attention as she stood in front of him. 'What are you doing here so late?' She smiled, but didn't come any closer. 'I'm on my way home. I'll walk back with you to your room.' She didn't wait for an answer, but turned to walk away.

'Julia. Don't go.'

She spun round. 'What did you say?'

'I said don't go. Why is everyone so shocked when I

speak?'

'Oh my God! You are talking, you are bloody talking!'

'Yes, I am talking, but why is everyone so shocked?'

'I've never heard you speak. You don't speak – never have. Oh my God, you have a beautiful voice. You are talking. This is the best!'

'What do you mean, I don't speak?'

'This is amazing. How? Why? When did this happen?' She walked around him, laughing.

Jamie stepped forward and caught hold of her arm, and she stopped with a look of shock again.

'What is it?'

'You're touching me!'

Jamie let go of her arm. 'I'm sorry.'

'No, don't be sorry. You don't like touching people or them touching you. I'm so shocked by you speaking and then taking hold of my arm.'

'Julia, I need to speak with you.'

'Oh, don't stop speaking, it's wonderful.'

'No, Julia, I need to talk to you alone. It's important and I have little time. Please.'

'Sure, why don't we go back to my room? I've got the green tea you like.'

'Yes, let's go! I really need to talk to you.'

'It's unbelievable, you speak so beautifully. Come on, my talking genius.'

The delicate aroma of the tea entered the room before Julia. The room mesmerised him – books with different smells, the colours around the room too bright. The strong aroma of tea as Julia came back into the room pulled him out of his locked-in sensation.

She smiled and placed his cup on the desk, then sat down on her bed. 'So, I'm shocked. What happened? Tell me, you said you wanted to speak to me.'

There were too many inputs, too many sights and smells for him to focus. For a while, he sat on the chair by the desk. Again, time seemed irrelevant, as if stuck.

She reached over and touched him on the knee and he came back. His mind cleared.

'Are you OK?'

'Yes, I'm fine. I need to tell you everything.' He paused a moment, relaxed, and continued. 'The Jamie you've known is gone. He died earlier when his experiment, or whatever, went wrong.'

'Your quark diffusion?'

'It must have gone badly wrong. I'm another Jamie, from another timeline, another world.' Senses continued to impinge on the fringes of his mind, but he told her everything while she sat still and stared at him.

He paused and drank some of his tea, giving her time for his crazy talk to sink in. 'From what you say, I've not had much in the way of speech, and from what I know, I have sensory issues. I see the world differently. I still have those, so many sensations I've never experienced before.'

'I can't believe what you're telling me, but also the fact that you are telling me. I've never heard you talk. You have such a lovely voice. I don't know what to believe.'

'Julia, I'm not the Jamie you know. I'm the same in a way, but not in the way you think of Jamie. He's gone.

The difference in my speech and what I talk about must make you question if what I'm telling you could actually be true. There is so much we don't know. The timeline we live in is narrow and there is so much more beyond it.'

'I don't know what to say.' Her voice was quieter than before. 'None of what you say makes any sense.'

'I meet the same people in different timelines. I've been married to you twice. In the first timeline we had two beautiful children.' He paused. 'I miss them terribly, and I miss my Julia from my first timeline. I'm sorry, it sounds weird.'

He could sense her disbelief.

'We are linked. I don't know how, but we are.' He carried on. 'Before I jumped into this timeline, I was with another anomaly. She told me about this timeline. Her name is Amelia and I have to save her life tomorrow. I have to stop her boarding a plane which will crash on take-off. I have to save her.'

'You sound even weirder now. Are you sure your experiment didn't go wrong, confused you and somehow kick-started your voice?'

'I'm a different Jamie to the one you know. I know it all sounds crazy, but I need to be at Charlwood Airport tomorrow morning to save Amelia. Her plane will crash on take-off. I need to get there early tomorrow. Can you help me?'

'Of course, but you don't need to go to Charlwood.' The tone of her voice was placating.

'I have to get to Charlwood to save Amelia. Please, I'm not making this up.'

A sudden surge of stress produced a level of discomfort he had never felt before, all calmness gone. 'I have to get to Charlwood. I need you to help me get there early tomorrow morning,' he repeated.

She reached forward and placed her hand on his arm. It felt heavy and uncomfortable.

'Don't get stressed,' she said. 'Take deep breaths and we'll work it out together. It's not a problem.'

'But I have to get to Charlwood.'

'OK, Jamie, we'll sort it out.' He felt a weight lift as she took her hand off him. 'Don't get stressed about it. We'll sort it out.'

'No, you don't understand what I'm telling you. Amelia will die tomorrow morning if I don't get to the airport and stop her from boarding her plane. I know you think I'm crazy, and in a way I don't blame you, but I need you to listen to what I tell you.'

'OK, Jamie. I'm listening, but I struggle to believe what you say.'

'I know what I told you is unbelievable, but I need your help to get to Charlwood tomorrow. I don't know how to get there. I don't know why, but I need your help.'

'OK Jamie, it's not a problem. I'll see if Steven can take us. We'll sort something out.'

'Who's Steven?' But as he asked, he knew it was her boyfriend. He liked Steven, or at least the other Jamie did. 'I know Steven,' he said.

'Yes, you know Steven. I'm sure he'll take us. He'll be here later on. We've always been there for you, you know we have.'

'You have, but not as you think.' He paused and then continued. 'I'm an anomaly and Amelia will be one soon.'

'What do you mean – Amelia will be one soon?'

'Well, normally when a person dies, they will do so across all timelines, all at the same time. Amelia's time is tomorrow and when I save her, she becomes an anomaly.'

'Why do you save her?'

A simple question, but it made Jamie stop. He hadn't considered the why. Gabriel brushed against the turmoil in his mind, and the crimson dream tugged at him. He hadn't saved Amelia yet, but his instincts told him he had to. Yesterday she didn't shoot him.

'I don't know why I save her,' he admitted after a pause.

'But you haven't saved her yet.'

'No, you're right, I haven't.' He hadn't saved Amelia yet. He had jumped into a different situation and the past and future were not fixed. He assumed he had to save Amelia, but it hadn't happened yet. 'When I save her, she becomes an anomaly, like me.'

'How did you become an anomaly?'

'I don't know, to be honest. I have a dream between each world; I call it the crimson dream. I wait there between jumps. It's clear and calm, but when I jump into the next world, it's like a dream you think you should remember but it eludes you. There's Gabriel, he explains it to me. I think he says I'm the cause of the anomaly, but I don't know what I did in my original world to cause it.'

She smiled. 'I'm amazed.'

'Why are you amazed?'

'You! You can talk, you can communicate. After all these years I've known you, you can talk. It's crazy talk, but you're talking.'

They both sat silently for a few minutes. Jamie reached for his tea and drank it.

'Can I ask you a question?' he said, eventually. She nodded, finished her tea, and placed her empty cup on the floor.

'Put yourself in my position, a person who jumps between different worlds. I know it's hard, but try to imagine. Imagine I made you an anomaly which caused you to jump into different worlds. You could relive your life, but it would always be different. There would be no end to the number of times you jump. It would be eternal, to jump forever. In effect, you would never die.' He paused. 'Would you want me to save you?'

She looked at him, a little perplexed. A look he recognised.

'Think about it, don't answer straight away.'

'I don't know. I suppose your initial reaction is to live forever, but I don't know.'

'Are you happy with your life, here in his world? Answer truthfully.'

'Well, yes, but I've only lived for twenty years.'

'It's twenty years or eternity. I suppose it's the question I face with Amelia, to save her or not.'

'I don't know.'

'I'm not asking you to believe what I tell you, just think about the question hypothetically. Please, for me, it's important.'

'OK, OK. Let me think. I think we should have a drink, a proper drink.' She got off the bed and pulled a bottle from a cupboard above her desk. 'You'll have to use your teacup.'

Jamie lifted his cup, and she poured a good measure. She reached over and filled her cup before sitting back on her bed. 'Cheers to my silent and strange friend. To your beautiful voice,' she said, raising her cup.

Jamie returned the toast. 'To you in all the timelines.' The harshness of the drink made him a little dizzy.

'I don't know what to say. Your question about immortality, and the unbelievable things you've told me, all seems so far-fetched.'

There was a knock on her door.

'Steven, it's open,' Julia called.

Steven stepped into the room. Jamie smiled. Steven had a good colour, a good glow. The instinctive reaction was a strange sensation for Jamie.

'Jamie! You're out late.'

'Hello, Steven.'

Steven stopped closing the door and turned wide eyed toward Jamie. 'You spoke!' he said, surprised. 'Julia, he just spoke.'

'I know. He's been speaking a lot.'

Steven sat down on the bed next to Julia.

Jamie told Steven the same as he had Julia. They both listened carefully, but disbelievingly.

Jamie saw a packet of sweets on Julia's desk, the different colours on the wrappers drawing his attention. The packet said "Heaven's Pebbles" and as he picked them up, he shook a few onto the desk. The different colours slowed him a bit as they spun on the desk, but he managed to pick out four sweets.

'Can I have your hands?' They pushed their hands towards him. 'This is from a film I saw in a different dimension. I'll put a red sweet in your right hand and a blue one in your left hand.' He placed one colour in each hand. 'If you choose the red sweet, you want immortality. The blue sweet is the real world, your world. One which starts and ends. A world which makes sense. Think about it and decide which you would choose.'

He sat back on the chair as they looked at each other with a sweet in each hand.

'You both think I'm totally insane,' Jamie said, 'but just go with it.' They both nodded, Jamie not sure which part of what he had said they were nodding to.

Jamie drank some more from his mug. A few minutes later, Steven opened his left hand and showed the blue sweet.

'For me, it's easy. I want my world, not some strange immortality.' He popped the blue sweet into his mouth.

Julia opened her left hand as well. 'I'm with Steven. I want my real world, as it should be. The world you describe sounds like an eternal hell.'

'It is,' Jamie replied as she popped the blue sweet into her mouth.

He woke easily from his fitful sleep when he heard the gentle knock on his door. 'Jamie, you awake?' Julia called softly.

'It's open.' He sat up as Julia came in.

'We need to get going if we want to get to Charlwood Airport by eleven. Steven is getting ready. Have you slept in your clothes again?'

Jamie nodded, a wave of apprehension swimming inside his head. He needed to clear his thoughts. 'I'm ready, just need my coat.' As he went to pick up his coat, he saw a pair of handcuffs on his desk. Amelia told him yesterday about handcuffing her. He picked them up and put them in his coat pocket.

Jamie watched the countryside slide past as he stared out the car window. Confusion and doubts swamped his mind. Steven was driving with Julia in the passenger seat and they were chatting, but Jamie ignored them, consumed by doubts about the upcoming decision. Amelia had told him what to do later this morning, but his doubts grew. The prospect of no end to his eternal jumps between timelines filled him with a deep dread. But if he let her board the plane, she would have only lived a short, and maybe unfulfilled, life.

'What are you thinking?' Julia turned and looked over her shoulder. 'You've been quiet all morning.'

'I'm thinking about Amelia. She is alive in this world at the moment. What I will tell her later today will sound unbelievable, but she has asked me to save her even though she doesn't know it at the moment.' What he said sounded absurd. 'In the Crimson dream, she asked me to save her. Maybe she meant let her board the plane.' The thought became clear suddenly.

'From the dream you told me about last night?'

'Yes, it's come back to me a little clearer. When I left the dream she shouted for me to save her, but I'm not sure if she meant eternal life or let her board the plane and she will only have one short life. I don't know. How much longer to the airport? Will we be there by eleven?'

'It's not far. We'll arrive well before eleven,' Steven said.

'How exactly do you intend to stop her?' Julia asked. 'You can't go up to a perfect stranger and tell them you're from the future, or the past, whatever it is, and ask them not to board their plane.'

'Well, Amelia told me how I do it. I handcuff her wrist to mine, then we sit down and I tell her everything. She misses her flight, and she stays alive.'

'Handcuffs?!' She looked directly at him.

'She told me.' He realised why she was worried. 'I'm not going to harm her. She told me it prevented her from running away, and all we do is talk. You want to know if I will be inappropriate?'

'Well, yes, along those lines. I'm worried.'

Amelia had told him about the handcuffs but had made no mention of Julia. How had he got to Charlwood last time? Stop, stop, he thought. The future hasn't happened yet. 'Don't worry, I won't do anything wrong.'

Julia laughed out loud.

'Don't say anything, just go with it,' he said. 'Enjoy the wild ride.'

'It's definitely wild.'

'Stay with it. If nothing happens and it's all in my

head, I'll let you officially classify me as crazy.'

'Alright, as long as you do nothing silly, you know, I mean anything illegal.'

'I won't.'

'Promise?'

'Yes, I promise. You don't think Amelia exists, do you?'

'I'll be honest with you as always, no.'

'OK, I'll tell you what she looks like, so when we see her, you know I'm not making any of this up. She's about five foot eight, with brown eyes and dark shoulder length hair. A slim build, elegant I would say, in her late twenties. She'll be wearing a yellow and white striped dress, and on her trolley she has a large straw sun hat with a yellow ribbon.'

'How do you know so much detail? From the dream?'

'No, I was with her yesterday when she told me.'

She shook her head a little. He smiled to himself. A sliver of doubt floated around his mind. He had to save her, but how? When he saves her, she becomes immortal, to live for all eternity. Did Amelia want to live forever? Why not ask her? It came to him – obvious.

'Julia, I've got an idea. I'm just going to ask her.'

'I don't know what you're talking about.'

'I want to know if Amelia wants to live forever, and I thought why not ask her?'

She paused for a moment. 'OK, let's assume Amelia is at the airport. You can't go up to her and ask if she would like to be immortal.'

'Well, not that bluntly. I'll speak to her, and well, I'll just wing it. Something will come to me.'

'No, you can't. You can't ask a stranger if they want to live forever.'

'You don't think Amelia exists, so what does it matter?'

She paused for a moment longer and nodded. 'Well, that's true. Let's get to the airport first.'

The intense assault on his senses continued as he looked out the window. A fog of visual images clouded his mind as he tried to think clearly about Amelia and about immortality, and it frightened him. His world had died, but he hadn't. All the worlds he jumped into, real but not his world.

Yesterday Amelia had asked him to save her, but he didn't know what she meant. She told him how he saved her, but in the last few moments with her yesterday, something was wrong. He hadn't saved her yet, it hadn't happened. What he did now was real. But none of this was real to him. His soul belonged to the world he was born into, not drifting, lost through different time dimensions, having no anchor and no ending. Having no ending was the real nightmare. What if it went on forever? How would he feel after five hundred years or even a thousand years? What about ten thousand years, or a hundred thousand years or a million years? It was a nightmare of a proportion he could not even begin to comprehend.

As they strolled into the airport, Julia suggested getting something to eat. There was still plenty of time. Steven paid for their breakfast, and as Jamie sat down, he felt ravenous. The food smelt different, more intense. No one spoke as they ate.

Half an hour later, they sat by the huge windows in the departures terminal. This must be where he sat with Amelia the first time, Jamie thought, as he looked out across the airport with the runway in the distance. The sky was clear, the autumn sun reflecting off the parked aircraft.

'What time is it now?' Jamie asked.

'It's just gone eleven,' Julia said with a quick look at her wrist.

He drew his focus back. A plane rolled down the runway, gradually gathering speed, and as it went past him, the nose lifted off the ground. It climbed into the vast blueness of the sky until it was only a tiny speck.

'I need to walk around by the shops. She'll be along soon.' Jamie stood.

Julia and Steven walked with Jamie towards the shops.

They strolled down the main thoroughfare. Jamie felt agitated, scanning the crowds, wanting to find Amelia. He wanted to shout her name and call for her. Then, in the newsagent, he saw her.

Jamie stopped, Julia nearly crashing into him. Amelia stood and flicked through the pages of a magazine. The strangest sensation ripped through his body, an intimacy he was quite unprepared for. Yesterday, in another world, she had been in love with him although he had not met her. Now she had not met him yet, and he had an inkling of what she must have gone through.

'What's happening?' Julia asked.

'It's her, in the newsagent, over there.'

Julia looked over. 'Where?' then, 'Oh my God! It's her,

exactly as you described. Oh my God, how did you know? Steven, it's her. Jamie, what are you going to do?'

'Don't know yet.' Jamie stared at Amelia.

They all watched her as she continued to browse. Amelia returned the magazine back to the rack and looked as if she was about to pick up another, but changed her mind and pushed the trolley out of the shop.

'I've got to talk to her,' Jamie said and walked towards her, leaving Julia and Steven behind. Jamie didn't know what he would say, but knew he had to go over to her.

As he approached, he said in a gentle voice, 'Amelia.'

She stopped. 'Do I know you?'

'No and yes, I'm Jamie.' With an easy smile, he stepped a little closer.

'Hello,' she said, and a moment later, 'maybe we have met before?'

He didn't answer, he couldn't.

'I'm sure we have.'

'No, we've not really met, not yet at least. It's complicated.' Jamie paused. 'You need to stop thinking about the lecture you're giving when you get back. Enjoy your holiday with Maria in Spain.'

'How did you know that?'

'As I said, it's complicated, but you told me – in the future. This isn't coming out right. Can we sit down for a few minutes? I need to talk to you, tell you something.'

She stared at him. 'I don't know what you're saying...'

'When you made your tea this morning, your mug split in two when you poured in the hot water.'

'How...?' Her eyes opened a little wider.

‘Please, don’t be alarmed, I’m not some psychic or anything, or some weirdo. It’s complicated, that’s all. Please let me explain.’

She nodded.

‘Let’s go over there by the window.’

For a moment she paused, then followed Jamie and sat down in front of the large glass walls which looked out over the runway.

‘How do you know me?’ she asked.

‘We were together yesterday, in a different time and place. You told me those things to help me get your attention, so I could ask you a question. You asked me to come here to save you.’

She said nothing.

‘It’s complicated, but I need to ask you one question and then you can get your flight to Spain.’

Again, she remained silent.

‘Immortality,’ Jamie paused. ‘If you had the chance, would you want it? Simple question but difficult to answer.’

She continued to stare at him.

Jamie felt a flutter on his shoulder, a breath against his ear. Gabriel, but as he looked to his right, there was no one there. Then again, he felt it. Gabriel. A part of his mind recalled the red dream, Amelia shouting, ‘Save me.’ Then it was gone.

‘I don’t know what to say. Is this really happening?’

‘Please, it’s important. This question is key to everything. Give it a few minutes’ thought.’

As she shifted in her seat, Jamie could see a certain

confusion in the way she looked at him. A minute passed before she replied.

'I suppose everyone would want to be immortal, to live forever.'

'Yes, but what about the downside?'

She shook her head.

'The downside.' Jamie repeated. 'Everything has a downside. When your friends die, when the people that mean the most to you go away, you are left alone, alone forever, then there is no peace.' Jamie stopped and again he felt Gabriel on his shoulder.

'No, I think everyone would still want to be immortal. There are downsides, but think about what you could achieve in your life, how much you would learn. I would want that. I think there would only be upsides. I'm a scientist and what a wonderful way to explore the whole world. You would have time to understand the universe. Who wouldn't want that?'

Again a flutter on his shoulder. Gabriel. 'You have to stop it.' Another thought, but not enough to help. How was he supposed to save Amelia?

The Amelia in front of him wanted to live forever, the scientist in her was too strong. 'Save her, close the loop,' Gabriel whispered in Jamie's ear.

The more he looked at her, he realised how different she was from the woman he met yesterday. The Amelia in front of him had a fresh innocence, a desire for knowledge whatever the cost. Amelia, the anomaly, was desperate, lonely.

Yesterday, in the last few moments, she said she loved

him too much, but it was the last thing she said. 'I'm so sorry.' He hadn't understood, but now he did. She was sorry because she didn't shoot him. Sorry she left him alone in time. She didn't want to be an anomaly.

'Thank you, that is the question I had to ask, and you've answered it.'

'Is that it?' Amelia said.

'It will seem strange to you, but in time you will come to understand this conversation. Put it out of your mind and enjoy your holiday.'

She looked even more bewildered.

'Go, enjoy your holiday.'

She returned his smile, a little wary. 'You are a strange man, not sure if you're just chatting me up, or something else.'

'I could just be chatting you up.'

Amelia stood up and took hold of her trolley, gave Jamie one last look, and then walked back to the main aisle.

He watched her walk across the concourse, blend into the crowds, and disappear altogether. Julia and Steven came over and sat down next to him.

'What happened, are you alright?' Julia said.

'No.'

'I don't understand. Were you not supposed to stop her, to save her?'

'I am saving her. As she spoke, the last time I saw her became clear. I had told her she had to shoot me when I gave the signal. I would then jump to her first timeline and save her. She wanted to, but couldn't. She kept saying she was so sorry. She was sorry for leaving me an anomaly; she didn't want to be one. I think she decided then. I feel terrible; she will be dead in a few hours. Far from immortality, she will not live one full life.'

'I don't know what to say. We're having a surreal—no—insane conversation. That we're even having a conversation is extraordinary. You met a woman you described to me yesterday, exactly, talked to her, and now she's boarding a plane which you say is going to crash. That's so bizarre.'

Another flutter on his shoulder made him shiver.

'Are you alright?' Julia asked.

'Yes. It's Gabriel, like a red breeze blew across my shoulder. It's the only way I can describe it.' He shivered again. 'Will you sit with me until her plane takes off?'

'Of course,' she said.

They sat there in silence, watching the planes take off in front of them. Jamie felt an intense moment of anxiety and guilt as each plane rushed down the runway and into the sky.

'It's her,' he said as another plane rolled down the runway.

'Are you sure? How do you know?'

'I know, I can feel her, the last moments of her life.' He breathed in deeply. 'What have I done?'

The weight of what he had done crashed down on him. She asked him to save her and he had let her down. He had taken her future away. A sense of fear blew through him, a dark fear, a cold fear. 'What have I done?' he said as he stood up.

'Jamie, calm down. It's alright.'

He took another deep breath. His body needed more air than he had ever known. The plane was gaining speed down the runway. 'Oh my God, Amelia, I'm sorry, so sorry.' He ran to the window, Julia following as he pressed his face against the glass, his breathing deep and sharp. Julia had her arm around him.

'Oh no, I'm so sorry,' he repeated. A constant rush of fear swam around his body as he saw the plane leave the tarmac. It lifted higher into the air, then the flecks of movement in front of the plane. The birds. The plane seemed to slow a little. Amelia was no longer an anomaly. She would not jump into another timeline.

'Oh my God!' Julia exclaimed. The plane had slowed enough for her to notice. It juddered. At first, hardly a perceptible movement, but it quickly became more obvious. As if in slow motion, the great bulk of metal fell from the sky.

'Oh God! How did you know?' Julia said.

The plane hit the ground. It didn't bounce, but a cloud of debris shot up into the air. A flame on the wing and a moment later the whole plane burst into flames. In those few moments, he felt horrific anguish and wanted to go back an hour.

The redness of the flames filled his vision. His legs gave way, and he fell. The redness became crimson, a swirling vortex surrounding him. His crimson world developed as he slowed, stopping in front of the crimson castle. This was different though, clearer, a sharpness he had not experienced here before.

The crimson fields and castle were empty as he looked for Amelia.

'James.'

'Gabriel, what have I done?' Jamie turned to him, desperate for an answer.

'You have closed the loop and resolved the time anomaly. You made the right decision.'

'Why does it feel so wrong?'

'It always does when someone closes the loop. Despite the catastrophic consequences of an infinite time loop, the conscious act of ending it for someone is difficult.'

'But Amelia hadn't even had a full life.'

'It's not for us to decide.'

'What happened to Amelia, the Amelia I knew?'

'She doesn't exist anymore. In all future timelines, she will never live beyond this point of time.'

'What about all the future lives she lived?'

'Those futures haven't happened yet and never will.' Gabriel's voice was clear and gentle.

'I don't understand.' Jamie felt drained. The crimson world seemed real, far too real. He tried to find logic in what Gabriel told him. A thought hit him.

'What happens to me?'

Gabriel looked at him for a few moments before he spoke. 'You closed the loop. You were the cause of it and now you have closed it. The anomaly doesn't exist anymore.'

'I don't exist anymore.' The realisation dawned on Jamie.

'No, James, you don't.'

'My lives I have lived, the many lives.'

'They haven't happened. They will never happen.'

'What now?' Jamie felt his shock disturb the crimson countryside.

'The time loop has to close completely. You will go back to where you belong. Maybe a few hours before the end, maybe a few days, maybe more.'

'How much more? I need to know.'

'We have no control. Probably no more than a week. If too long, you could cause another anomaly.' Gabriel paused again. Jamie understood, but he told himself this was a dream, a nightmare.

'You have done well. It is always difficult to close a loop, but you have. It's done now and the time continuum will return to balance. As it should be.' He smiled. A radiating smile which filled Jamie with calmness and a deep warmth. 'We won't meet again. Goodbye, James.'

Gabriel faded into the crimson fabric. Jamie looked over to the castle and he thought he could see Amelia, a faint outline, no expression on her face.

'I'm so sorry, Amelia. I had to let you board the flight. When I saw you after fifty years, you were so unhappy compared to this morning. I had to close the loop, I had to.'

The crimson world closed in on itself, and the black chasm wrapped itself around Jamie.

Chapter 10

Jamie rushed through the darkness with all his thoughts squeezed and, unlike the green bottle, a constricted tightness surrounded him. Gradually the rushing slowed until it came to a near stop, then the constriction loosened and he accelerated away. A sense of colour developed – a familiar crimson. His thoughts were in freefall, released from his nightmare. His soul unloading into a waterfall of emotions. No particular thought held his attention, just a certain calm. Whether lasting an instant or an eternity, he had no idea.

Then he opened his eyes. Dark, quiet and calm. The emotional race from the crimson castle was only a dream. The darkness surrounded him, but slowly he saw outlines of shapes. As he inhaled, the smell hit him. It comforted him, a familiar smell. Again, he inhaled deeper. After the plane crash, the jump took him straight to the crimson castle, no green bottle. Gabriel was clear, the crimson dream real. Gabriel said he had closed the loop, and he had to go back. For a third time, he inhaled, and he knew his timeline. He was home. After all the emotions of the last jump, he was content to stay still and slowly drift off to sleep.

But a thought at the back of his mind started to niggle. The calm so pleasant he didn't want to disturb it. But a progressive thought gained speed and pushed all the comfortable, pleasant emotions away from his mind. The date? In all the other jumps, the date was always the same. But this jump was different.

With one sweeping motion, he rolled his legs off to his left and sat up. The shapes became clearer and, as he sat on the edge of the bed, he recognised his final year room at university. To his left, the outline of his desk by the curtains, a small bookcase to its right, a big plastic chair next to it, and the mirror opposite him. The familiar air filled his lungs again.

The date? He needed to find out. He stood up and expected to be disorientated, a little weak, but felt clear-headed, his legs strong, and he instinctively reached over to the light switch by the door. A weak light filled the room. He stepped up to the mirror. Young, as always, but his reflection seemed more familiar. For a long time, he stared into the mirror. Back in his own world. But had it all been a nightmare? The mirror offered no further clues.

'Need the date,' he said to himself, running his fingers through his hair, thick and too long. 'Need to find Billy.'

The night air was fresh, not quite cold, but it

heightened his senses as he ran over to Billy's block, taking the stairs two at a time to the third floor. He knocked quietly at first but had to bang on the door to get any response.

'Shit, it's the middle of the night!' he heard Billy mumble. The door opened and a tired and rough looking Billy stared back at him. It was his Billy, the real Billy. He stared for a moment.

'What do you want?' Billy asked. 'I thought you had passed out earlier.'

'I need to know the date?'

'What?!' Billy's voice sounded a little louder.

'I need to know the date. It's important.'

'What?! You wake the whole floor up to ask for the date. Have you gone nuts!'

'I'll explain tomorrow, if it's not too late, but tell me the date. It's not a trick question.'

Billy didn't reply.

'The date, Billy, nothing else.'

Billy stared at him for a moment longer. 'It's Wednesday, I think.'

'Not the day of the week,' Jamie's impatience crept in, 'the number of the month and year.'

'Shit, I don't know. It's the middle of the night. It's October, middle of October.'

'I need to know the exact date: day, month and year.'

'OK, let me think. Monday was the 14th, today was Wednesday, no wait, Wednesday was yesterday. Today was Thursday, so tomorrow is Friday...'

'So this morning will be Friday the 18th?' Jamie said.

'Yeah, the 18th.'

'OK, and it's October?'

'Yeah.'

'Sure?'

'Yes, yes, I'm positive.'

'And the year?'

'Oh, come on...'

'No, the year?'

'1985.' Billy gazed at Jamie. 'Are you on something?'

'No, I'll explain later. It's important, life and death stuff.'

'Are you serious?'

'I'm serious, Billy. I'll see you later.'

'Yeah, OK.'

'Thanks, mate.' Jamie left and sprinted along the corridor, down the steps two at a time, and felt the fresh air fill his lungs as he left Billy's block.

His thoughts ran wild with his legs already taking him towards the top of the campus, a desperate energy as he sprinted up the hill. Only a week before he died. It made little sense, but he knew the conclusion.

A row of benches waited at the top of the path. The one on the left was their bench, which he sat on and looked out over the town. The yellow glow of the streetlights spread out in front of him, the night quiet.

Amelia was no longer an anomaly and in letting her board the plane, he had himself ceased being an anomaly. Only a week – only a week before his time. He didn't know what he could do in a week, but he had a clear awareness he needed to find meaning. A resolution.

The need to walk overwhelmed him, and he started back through the campus and then on into the town. As he strode through the empty streets, a sense of purpose grew as his thoughts dragged along behind him.

Then he saw it as he stopped outside the bookies. Of course, he knew the future, in this timeline at least. The results of every major event in the next twenty years – in the financial markets, politics and sports. At that instant, he knew what he had to give Julia, something he didn't in their first life together. He could make her rich.

An urgency crept through him, and he had to get back to campus to talk to Billy. He broke into a run.

It was nearly dawn when he reached Billy's block. He sprinted up to Billy's room and banged on the door, but had to bang a second time before he heard any movement.

'What do you want now?' Billy said, opening the door, his voice hoarse with sleep.

'I need to talk to you. Now!'

'What! It's still the middle of the night. Can't it wait until later, like when everyone's awake?'

'No, mate, it can't. Time is short and I need you right now. This is life and death.'

Billy stepped back a little. Jamie saw he wanted to go back to bed.

'I need to talk, but there's so little time. It's important.'

'OK, mate. You make some coffee. I'll get dressed and see you in the kitchen.'

Jamie nodded and headed to the kitchen, further down the corridor. He poured out the water as Billy came into the kitchen and they sat down opposite each other, steaming coffee between them.

'Right, you have my attention now. This better be good!'

'OK, what I'm about to tell you will seem crazy weird. But I haven't got time to skirt around what's happened to me.'

Jamie noticed Billy show a little more interest. His body leant forward.

'Don't quite know where to start.' Jamie paused. 'I jump between different time dimensions.'

Billy's eyes widened a little. 'What are you on, mate? You turn up in the middle of the night and ask for the date. Now you drag me out of bed to tell me some shit about you time travelling!'

'I said it would seem weird to you. There are thousands, hundreds of thousands of timelines, which all run parallel to each other. For some reason, I became an anomaly and I jump between different timelines. However, we cease to exist at exactly the same time through all timelines. I met another jumper, and I closed the loop. I'll tell you later, and I think I've ceased being an anomaly. I jumped back to my original timeline earlier this morning, but unfortunately I die in a week's time.'

Billy stared at him, picked up his coffee, and took a loud sip.

'I don't know what to say. You're clearly high on something, which is fine. In fact, I wouldn't mind some. But you're clearly off your head.'

'No, no! I said it was a little weird. OK, maybe

completely off the wall. But you have to hear me out. Every timeline has a different history, a different world. And we're connected. I meet you in these different timelines. We're all a little different. The worlds are different, some a little and some a lot. But what's different now is I've come back to the world where I know the future for the next twenty years.'

Billy stared and drank his coffee.

'OK, let's think about this as a concept,' Jamie said. 'Say, a person, let's call him Jamie, lives until he's forty and, for all intents and purposes, jumps back twenty years. This Jamie knows the future for the next twenty years. Say he was interested in sports and worked in the financial markets for those twenty years. What would the possibilities be?' Jamie picked up his coffee.

'So, as a concept, I can see a great deal of possibilities. You're clearly nuts, but to know the future would be kind of handy.'

'Well, I know the future.'

'You're not serious? You sound serious. You drag me out of bed in the middle of the night to have a weird conversation, but what you've said is complete shit.'

'Maybe, but I need to ask you a few questions to make sure I'm in the timeline I think I'm in.'

'What!' Billy's eyes opened wider. 'You need a doctor at a secure hospital. I don't believe I'm sitting here listening to this.'

Jamie ignored his remarks. 'Who won the FA Cup this year?'

'What?!'

‘Was it Man U one nil against Everton?’

‘Yeah, of course it was.’ Billy finished his coffee and went to make another. ‘You want another one?’

‘No, I'm fine. Who's the Prime Minister?’

‘Maggie Thatcher.’

Jamie continued the questions and Billy answered mechanically. They all made sense for his timeline. But he already knew. This was his best friend. The other Billys had been similar, but not quite the same.

‘You think all I’ve told you is crap, but you have to believe me.’

‘Well, you say you know the future. Who wins the Man U game this weekend?’

‘It's twenty years ago. I can't remember that sort of detail. I can remember most of the key events in sports and finance, but I can't prove it in the next week. For the moment, you need to trust what I’ve told you.’

‘I'm struggling, mate. I'm worried you've flipped out. You need help.’

‘I need you to listen carefully. I've dealt with this weird shit for years and it still seems crazy, but it's not. There's stuff out there you would not believe. I don't believe it and I don't understand it. Gabriel explained most of the stuff to me.’

‘Whoa, who's Gabriel?’

‘It’s a long story, maybe for another time, but he gave me enough detail to work out my time is next week.’

‘Your time?’

‘When we die, when our soul dies through all timelines. Next week is my time, I cease to be. The first time I was an anomaly, and I lived another twenty years before I jumped out of this timeline into a different one. Exactly at the same instant I jumped to, the other Jamie had died and I sort of took over. This is the first time I have jumped back to before my time.'

'Shit, mate. You're clearly completely out of your mind!'

Billy didn't believe him, but he easily understood why.

'OK, what if I tell you something that you tell me in the future? You've not told anybody, but in the future you tell me.'

Billy looked at him quizzically. 'OK, but I don't know what you're on about.'

'Your mate, Dave, from school. His mum Alison, you knew her really well, didn't you?' Jamie smiled and raised his eyebrows. Billy stared at him with eyes wide open.

'Shit! How do you know?'

'I'm trying to tell you I've already lived this life once. You don't tell me for many years.'

Billy shook his head.

'Look, Billy, I need you to go with me on this one. In time you will believe, but for the moment I need you to trust me.'

Jamie stopped and looked over at Billy.

'I think you're completely off your head, but we're mates and if you need me to roll with you, despite how absolutely insane you sound, I'll be there for you.' Billy nodded as if to confirm the agreement.

'Good. Let's have another coffee.'

* * *

Jamie sat in the Union at lunchtime and waited for Billy. A long shower and a shave had refreshed him, made him feel a little stronger, but still terrified. As he waited, his hunger grew. Julia was at the forefront of his thoughts, with only a week to get to know her. Torn between his desperate need to see her again or, if less selfish, he would have no contact with her and she wouldn't be involved in the last week of his life. There was no rational way to think about it, but he had an unstoppable urge to talk to his Julia. Billy's reaction earlier made him wary of saying anything to her. She would run a mile and rightly so.

The only option was to stay away from her, he told himself. But he knew he needed to get to know her a little, at least. No plan came to him which would let him get close to her, but he never had clear plans, as was evident when he stopped her marrying John. The smell of fried food disturbed his concentration. The resolution he needed to find with Julia was clear, but he had no idea how to achieve it. Eventually, the smell of the food got the better of him – he needed to eat.

He picked up a tray and ordered a burger, large chips, and a large cola. The girl in front of him counted out her pennies, literally. His hunger made him impatient – he wanted her to hurry up, get out of the way, his time limited. Instead, he took a deep breath; she was scraping out a meagre budget. A young girl. It made him think of Holly; she could be at university, like the girl in front of him. Suddenly he felt sad. There would never be a Holly. The girl finished, so he stepped up to the till and paid. As he picked up his tray and turned to walk back to the tables, Julia stood right behind him. She looked so young, but it was definitely his Julia.

There was a crash at his feet and, as he looked down, he realised he no longer held his tray. The burger and chips were scattered across the floor, the cola splashing onto Julia's shoes and jeans. He stared at the mess on the floor.

'Are you alright?' he heard her say. She touched his arm. 'Are you alright?' She sounded concerned.

Jamie snapped out of it. 'Shit, I'm so sorry. I don't know what happened, it just fell.' He felt terrible. This was a disastrous way to meet Julia.

'It's alright, just an accident,' she smiled.

'I don't know what happened. I'm sorry, what an idiot!'

Julia walked over and spoke to the cashier, who returned a moment later wheeling a bucket and mop.

Jamie bent down and began clearing up the spilled food.

'I'm so sorry, I feel terrible.'

'It's alright, don't keep apologising. I'll help clear it up and it'll be OK.'

'I spilled cola all over your jeans and shoes.'

'They'll wash.' She scooped up the top half of the burger.

'Let me pay for your lunch. It's the least I can do.'

'You don't have to.'

'Please, let me.'

'OK, let's get this cleared up first,' she said.

Jamie scooped the last of the food off the floor and onto the tray, and handed it to the girl who stood by the end of the counter. Julia had the mop and wiped the spilled cola off the floor.

'Go and get your lunch and I'll wait for you.' She smiled again.

His heart raced as he walked back down the counter and ordered the same again. Julia waited by the cashier.

'I'm sorry, your food must be cold now.'

'Stop saying sorry, it'll be fine.'

Jamie paid again, and he followed her to a table by the window. The autumn sun shone through the window and reflected off the tables.

'Hi, I'm Julia,' she said as they both sat down.

'I'm Jamie. I don't know what happened there. I saw you and next thing the tray, the floor...'

'It doesn't matter. I've been treated to lunch with some company.'

Jamie smiled at his Julia.

They sat at the table for over an hour and talked. The conversation flowed easily. The only thing he had to remember was she had just met him. He couldn't get too intimate or mention things he couldn't possibly know.

The uneaten food had long gone cold when Julia said she had to get off to a lecture. They walked out of the Union into the cool sunshine.

'Julia, I know it's a little hasty, but do you fancy going for a drink tonight? I know I threw my lunch all over you, which isn't the best introduction, but please say you'll come for a drink.'

'I can't tonight,' she said and smiled. 'Maybe another night. I'll see you around.'

She walked away from him. 'Julia, I'm a time traveller.

I've only got a week before I go. You have to come out with me!' She had stopped and turned to face him. 'I've travelled a long way to meet you. There's no time for another evening. Life is too short; every moment counts.'

'You're crazy!'

'Yes, absolutely. Once I started travelling in time, I realised I was. But don't hold it against me.'

'No, I can't, even for a time traveller.'

'Look, I'll be at the King's Head at seven o'clock tonight.'

'Oh, I don't know.'

'Well, I'll be there tonight. The invitation is open and I'll leave it there.'

'OK, Mr Time Traveller Man, I probably won't be there, but thanks for the invitation.'

He spent the entire afternoon in the library, which was quiet this early in the academic year. With several new pads of paper in front of him and lots of pens scattered on the desk, he wrote furiously, so much to get down on paper. Far from having eternity, he now didn't have enough time.

At six o'clock he left the library, stopped briefly in his room to leave his papers, and hurried down to the King's Head. He sat at a table close to the door, sipped his pint, and hoped Julia would come. But he felt pessimistic. The spilt food and how he had pleaded with her were probably all a little too much in one meeting. Every time the door opened, he expected it to be her, becoming more unsettled and anxious as the minutes ticked by. By nine o'clock, he realised she wasn't coming. The cool night air felt good as he made his way back to the campus, but there was a panic in the hours he had sat in the pub, wasted hours.

He settled down in front of his desk and sorted through what he had produced earlier. As he continued to write, he found some relief and when he put his pen down, it was half-past eleven. More time had gone and his room became too small. He needed to get out.

Once out in the cooler air, he headed back to the top of the campus. He paced back and forth, a brewing restlessness. When he looked at his watch, another hour had passed. Time slipped away too quickly. He headed back down into campus, his legs taking him to Julia's block. With rational thought receding, he sprinted up the stairs to Julia's room.

He didn't hesitate to knock when he reached her door. A few moments later, the door opened. Julia peered out, her face a little puzzled.

'I'm sorry, but I needed to see you.'

'It's late,' she said.

'Look, I'm not weird, don't be alarmed. I'm possibly a little crazy, but I have a real reason why I need to see you urgently.'

The door remained open. 'Go on, I'm listening.'

'When I told you I was a time traveller earlier, well, I am a time traveller. Don't shut the door, please hear me out.'

'You are a little crazy, aren't you?'

'Well, I did say I was.'

'Look, it's late and I've got a busy day tomorrow.' She pulled away from the door and began to close it.

'Look, don't go! Wait! Your middle name is Louise and you hate it. Your favourite number is nine, you like the colour blue but you love purple.' The closing door stopped. 'Your favourite author is F. Scott Fitzgerald, and your favourite poem of all time is The Ecstasy by John Donne.' She came closer to him.

'How do you know all this?'

'I know it's difficult to believe, but I know you, Julia, I know you.'

'How can you?'

'You tell me in the future.'

'What?! That's ridiculous!'

'When you were eleven, you went skiing in Austria and your dad broke his leg. When you were fourteen, you spent Christmas in Sydney. Your dad's best friend lives there, and you went to visit. You had your first real crush on Brad, the surfer from Manly beach.' Her eyes widened.

'How the hell do you know that? I haven't told anyone, and I mean anyone.'

'You tell me in the future.'

'This is way too weird.'

'Can we take it I know you better than someone you just met earlier today? One possibility is I am from the future and you have already told me. I have a lot more I could tell you.'

'I'm confused. I haven't told anyone – but I tell you in the future? That's not possible.'

'Well, it's actually far more complicated than simple

time travel.'

'Are you making fun of me?'

'No, no. Can we get a coffee and maybe sit down and I'll explain? The kitchen's empty.'

She considered him for a moment. 'OK, you put the kettle on and I'll be out in a minute.'

Jamie went to the kitchen and put the kettle on. A few minutes later, she walked in wearing her big purple jumper, a jumper he had forgotten how much she lived in.

'You sit down, I'll make these,' he said.

'I suppose you know how I have my coffee.'

'I do. In fact, you come to think I make the best coffee.'

Jamie told her everything. About each timeline, about each jump, the crimson dream, about Gabriel, about Amelia, and his irrevocable act in the last timeline to bring him back home. Time ran away and finally, when he finished his second cup of coffee, he paused. Julia had only listened, always such a good listener.

'What do you think?' he said.

'You're completely mad,' she said and laughed. 'But how you know me, I don't understand. There's something about you. I know you, or maybe you know me. It's strange.'

'So much we don't know or understand.'

'I just don't know what to believe.'

'Do you want another coffee?'

'No, I've had too much caffeine. Wait, go on, I'll have another. You do make an excellent coffee.'

As he made the coffee, he looked over at Julia. It was

his Julia. Home to his time, but so little time.

'I need you to understand why I have to see you,' he said as he sat down with the coffees. 'I've only got a week and I have so much I want to talk to you about. I haven't got time to go through all the touchy feely process of courting you slowly.'

'You're fairly crazy,' she said, her hands cupping her mug. 'Not totally bad crazy, I think. A little intense, maybe.'

'Hang out with me for a week. Only one week and then I'll leave you alone. It'll be fun, I promise.'

'I don't know.'

'Come on, one week. You'll live long, you can afford a week.'

'It's just a week,' he insisted, when she didn't answer.

'OK, Mr Time Traveller Man. One week.'

'Thank you.'

'So what's the agenda, then?'

'How about I surprise you? We start tomorrow afternoon. I'll meet you in the Union at two o'clock. In the main bar. Dress smart.'

'I'll be there.'

'Right, I'm off. Much to do.'

'What have you got to do?'

'In time, you will see.' He downed his coffee. 'See you tomorrow at two.'

He rushed back to his room, to his desk, and wrote through to dawn.

One thirty on Saturday afternoon and Jamie stood in the

Union bar. A constant pressure pushed on his senses as his minutes ticked by; a second chance to find redemption in his life – in this life.

People came and went. Old faces he remembered, and it felt strange he knew some of their futures. A little before two o'clock, he saw Julia walk in. She looked stunning, smartly dressed, so young. As she walked further into the room, he stepped forward and, as he did, she caught sight of him. She smiled and walked over to him.

'I'm glad you came,' he said.

'I promised, one week.'

'Do you want a quick drink before we head off?'

'Yes, why not? I'll have half a lager. I'm quite thirsty.'

'You go and sit down and I'll get them.' He headed over to the bar.

'So where are we going?' she asked as he sat down opposite her with the drinks.

'Well, it's a surprise. We'll finish these drinks, then we're off to the station.'

As he picked up his drink, he looked at his wife, who didn't know him yet. Amelia flashed through his mind. When he met her for the first time, she was in love with him. They had spent a life together. She had missed him and knew all about him. But he didn't know her. He felt for Amelia, as a person who suffered in the same way as he did.

The table moved and Julia's drink spilled over the top of her glass. A person stood next to him. Pete, big Pete. Jamie turned round to see more clearly and noticed his boys behind him.

'I see you're all dressed up. Didn't know we had a date today,' Pete said to Julia with loud slurred words.

Jamie instinctively got up and moved around towards Julia.

'Oh, is this your lover boy now?'

'Pete, we never went out. You bought me a drink in the Union – once!'

'Shut up,' he told her and turned his attention to Jamie.

'So you think you can muscle in on my woman?'

'You're drunk, Pete, and you never went out with Julia. She's not your woman.'

Pete moved surprisingly quickly towards him. Julia stood up from her seat and intervened between them.

'Pete, stop! Who I see is none of your business.'

'I thought I told you to shut up. This is between me and lover boy.'

Jamie heard a ruckus behind Pete. It was his friends, egging their leader on. Jamie noticed how frightened Julia looked.

Jamie felt the rush, and the violent Jamie surged to the fore.

'Please, Pete, leave it. Julia's not your girl.' Jamie spoke slowly, part of him wanting to stop the violence, but he knew that wouldn't happen.

Recalling Pete's knee injury, Jamie stepped forward with agility, darting his foot forward and digging his heel sharply into the side of Pete's right knee. A moment of disbelief crossed Pete's face, but as Jamie pulled his foot back, his fist arced round towards Pete's head. The impact jolted through his arm, and he watched as Pete's disbelief turned to a grimace of pain. Jamie took a step back, prepared to strike again. But Pete's eyes rolled and, slowly at first, his great bulk fell backwards, scattering tables and chairs as he crashed onto the floor.

A complete silence fell over the Union. Jamie looked at Julia, her eyes wide open in disbelief. The boys' expressions were shocked.

'You boys want some?' The other Jamie's deep violence cut through his voice and they all took a step back. 'If not, sort this piece of shit out.' He pointed to Pete, who lay still on the floor. 'When he comes to, tell him to stay away from Julia, but me, he can come and talk to anytime.' His voice had an edge to it and he couldn't help but smile. The boys looked terrified. 'Are you boys listening?'

They all nodded in unison and edged towards Pete, but all eyes remained on Jamie, who stepped over to Julia. 'Sorry,' his voice was quiet and calm, 'bullies piss me off.'

Every eye in the Union was on him. 'Shall we go? I think it would be best. Come on.' He took her hand and led her out of the Union. The cooler air felt good as they stepped outside. After a few paces, he stopped and let go of her hand.

'Sorry, this was my week, and I didn't need Pete's interference.'

'No, it's alright. I'm a little shocked you dropped Pete.'

'Are you angry with me?'

'No, just a little shocked.'

'Not quite the start I imagined, but shall we try to

leave it behind?'

'Yes! He was a bully, and I was always a little afraid of him. You're different. You're crazy enough to stand up to Pete, but I feel safe with you. Doesn't make much sense, does it?'

'No, life generally doesn't make sense. Especially mine. Let's not dwell on it. We've got places to go.'

'Sounds good to me. Where are we going?'

'Let's get a train.'

Jamie kissed her gently on her lips. Her eyes were closed. He rolled over to lie next to her, and she moved her arm as he settled in beside her.

'What a day!' she said after a few minutes.

'Good day, I hope.'

'Oh, yes, very good! Brilliant!'

Jamie breathed in and felt a sense of calm he had not felt for a long time. Not since he was in this timeline all those years ago. The warmth of her thigh, her skin under his fingertips. They had checked into The Savoy Hotel on the Strand. It was past midnight now.

'What are you thinking?' he asked.

'I'm thinking good thoughts,' she said, her voice low.

She smiled, and he felt her radiance. Right at this moment, he knew he had to capture the feeling, as it would soon be gone. He stroked her cheek, and she took hold of his hand and kissed it.

'I don't know what you have done to me. You, well, it seems weird, but you know my body better than I do. I've never felt anything like it. I don't know who you are, a stranger who has swept me off my feet. It'll probably all be over tomorrow, but I don't care. Once is wonderful.'

'You have me for a week.'

'What exactly do you mean? Yesterday I wasn't sure what to make of you, but now, you don't seem such a stranger. It's not the sex, there's something else. And the one week business. What happens at the end of the week?'

'We'll deal with it when we get there. Let's enjoy the moment. You can't imagine how much this means to me, such pleasure.'

'Same here.' She smiled a lazy smile. He moved closer to her, their bodies touched. Even though he still had much to do, a drowsiness took hold of him. Julia breathed quietly and regularly, asleep.

Sleep took Jamie just as quickly.

The room was bright when he opened his eyes. Julia sat next to him on the bed in a white dressing gown.

'Julia.'

'Ah, you're awake.'

'Yeah, what time is it?'

'About ten.'

Jamie sat up. 'Shit, how long have you been awake?' A hand gently pushed him back onto the bed.

'Relax. It's Sunday morning. I ordered room service earlier as I was hungry when I woke up. I hope you don't mind.'

'No, of course not. I can't remember the last time I

slept so well.'

'Same here, but I was tired.' She smiled. 'Why don't I get room service for you too?'

'That would be great; I'm starving.'

'Full English?'

Jamie nodded as she picked up the phone. This had been the best night's sleep in a long while: no dreams, no nightmares.

'How are you feeling this morning?' he said as she put the phone down.

'I'm great. I'm the best I've ever felt.'

'How long have you been awake?'

'A few hours, I think.'

She lay down quietly next to him while they waited for the knock from room service.

When it arrived, Jamie ate quickly. 'I can't believe how hungry I am.'

'I wonder why,' she said with a smile.

'What a day yesterday,' she said as they settled down with a cup of tea. 'It's strange how your life can change so quickly. Two days ago I hadn't talked to you, then Friday lunchtime you spilled your lunch all over me – never in a million years would I have imagined waking up with you in The Savoy on Sunday morning. Maybe your craziness is wearing off on me.' She laughed. 'How did you know I wanted to see Evita? It was great. And the meal last night. Are you rich? You look like a poor student, like the rest of us.'

'I'm not rich, but I will be. Or at least you will be.'

'There you go again, cryptic words.'

'In time, all will be revealed. Let's enjoy the week.'

'Our room must cost a small fortune.'

'Yes, but it doesn't matter. You will see.' He took her hand. 'I don't want to go back to Uni yet. Shall we get another train once we're up and ready?'

'Where to?'

'Do you want to know?'

'Yes, I want to know.'

'South, out of London. I won't tell you anymore.'

She rolled on top of him and pushed his arms over his head. 'You are going to tell me,' she said close to his ear.

A few hours later, they stood at the end of the Palace Pier in Brighton. The breeze was cool and heavy with salt. They leant against the railing, standing close.

'I've never been to Brighton, but I like it.' Julia smiled at him.

'Thought you might.'

'This is such a mad weekend. I never believed you could go from feeling so little to feeling so much.' She squeezed closer. 'Are we going back tonight?'

'No, we'll stay here tonight. Tomorrow I need to go to Littlehampton, and I need you there with me. Then we'll go back. OK?'

'Absolutely. If you make me feel like last night, I'm yours completely.'

'Well, I will certainly do my best. And speaking of last night, I think we should go and find a hotel to book into.'

'Sounds like a smart idea.' She leant over and kissed him.

'I'd like to stay here a little longer. I want to feel the sea air fill my soul and clear my mind.'

She nodded and leant into him. The closeness of her body made his desire for her rise again. He wanted it to last forever.

They stepped off the train at Littlehampton, lunchtime on Monday. The sun shone, but the cold bite of autumn cut through his jacket. He held Julia's hand as they walked from the train station towards the harbour. It all looked similar, maybe a little newer than he remembered. The wind strengthened as they walked out towards the sea. They sat on a bench close to where he left twenty years in the future.

'Are you alright?' Julia asked after a few minutes.

'Yeah. A lot of emotions at the moment. A lot.'

'I don't want to ask, but I don't understand why we're here.'

'Yeah, I'm sorry. In time, it will all make sense.'

'I'm more confused than ever now.' She squeezed his hand harder.

'This place is deeply emotional. This is where I left this time dimension,' he paused, 'in twenty years' time.'

Julia made no response.

'All the stuff I told you a few days ago is true. I know you think it's not, but on the 20 August 2005, I went fishing with my family here. You, my wife, and our two children, Holly and William. Many years ago, many years in the future, which will never be. I'm sad, as I realise my children will never be born now. My future has not happened yet and never will. I've already lived a life with you – a wonderful life. I never told you enough, always too worried about the little things in life.'

He stopped. Julia sat close to him, her face quizzical.

'Look, don't try to make any sense of this. In time, you will see I am not crazy. Well, maybe not how you think now. I needed to come here. I don't expect you to understand, but I needed to sit here for a while to find closure.'

'I should be worried about what you're telling me, but I think about how you make me feel. I trust my feelings and they say you're different from anybody I have ever met. It's like I've known you forever.'

'Don't try to rationalise it. Trust your feelings.'

'I'm a little sad sitting here.'

'Come on, I don't want you to be sad. Let's get lunch. Let's see if the fish and chip place is already here.'

Jamie looked at the small alarm clock on the desk, holding it close to see the faded luminous dots. Four o'clock in the morning. He placed the clock back on the desk, quietly pulled the chair out, and sat down. Julia lay behind him, fast asleep.

They came back to her room on their return from Littlehampton yesterday. He had picked up his letters on the way back and they lay in front of him on the desk. The desk light was on, pointed away from Julia but with enough light to write. About half the letters had been written now, but he needed to write the first letter to Julia. With a clean sheet of paper in front of him, he picked up his pen and wrote the date carefully at the top. For a while, he sat there and pulled his thoughts together. The first letter to Julia, for her to read after Friday. Don't think, he told himself, just write.

My dearest Julia,

When you read this, you will know I am Mr Time Traveller. I am sorry for leaving you like I did. I don't know how it will happen, all I know is when. I feel bad for bringing you into my life for only a week, but it couldn't happen any other way. Please don't hold it against me. Time will heal all. There are twenty-one letters attached to this letter. One for each year. It will tell you what will happen in the financial markets and what you need to do to profit from it. I want you to be comfortable. I want you to have choices and use this money for those choices. We always struggled with money and I don't want you to. Give some to charity if you have too much. I leave it up to you to do with this information as you see fit.

Of course, you may think I'm completely crazy, but start slowly with the information I give you. I hope you find someone who will make you happy. You don't know how hard it is to write, but please keep a little part of me somewhere tucked away inside you.

We had a wonderful life, but you will never experience it. The future, my future, will never happen, so you will never know. I hope your future life is as beautiful as the one we had together. Use the money to ease the burden. This is the reason I am doing this. I felt I never told you properly how wonderful you were, in all those years we were together. I suppose it was unsaid. But when

I left you on the pier in Littlehampton, part of my life was unfulfilled. I needed to say things to you which I never got chance to.

However screwed up you think I am, you're the one I love completely. Just so you know.

And don't be sad, I've lived a life longer than intended. And to finish with such pleasure, it couldn't be better. The alternative for me was to live forever, constantly jumping into strange timelines. Never finding any resolution. Life is short, it's the natural way. My life has been a little different, but my goal is the same, and though I desperately don't want to leave you now, the course I set in motion a time dimension ago is unalterable.

So read each letter at the start of the year and do as I say in them. You will become a rich woman. And when you read this letter, think of the resolution I have found.

I have some letters to finish. It's Tuesday morning, about four thirty, and you are sleeping gently behind me. A truly beautiful moment.

I love you. Through all time.

Jamie.

He folded up the letter and placed it into an envelope without reading it. From the heart, no editing. On the envelope he wrote: 'Julia – to be opened after 25 Oct 1985... when you're ready.'

He placed the envelope into a green folder and put it aside. He had many letters to write, as he had only reached halfway through 1997. A few moments of thought took him back to what seemed like a long time ago and, though a little hazy, it soon came back to him as he wrote.

* * *

'Where have you been?' Billy asked, slapping Jamie on the shoulder. Jamie sat in the Union nursing a pint. Billy sat down opposite him.

'I've been around.'

'You certainly have. I couldn't believe it when I heard you'd dropped Pete. I saw him on Sunday, and you did some damage. He must have really pissed you off.'

'He messed with Julia and I didn't have time for his shit.'

'Where did you learn to punch? I never knew you had the killer instinct. I mean Pete, he's huge.'

'I suppose I snapped.'

'So where have you been?'

'Went to London with Julia, ended up staying there for the night.'

Billy grinned and nodded. 'Alright, was it?' He raised his eyebrows.

'Yes, if you must know, fantastic. We went down to Brighton on Sunday and came back last night.'

'You certainly didn't hang around.'

'As I said, I haven't got much time left.'

'You still on about dying? How much time do you have left?'

'Friday night.'

'Bit precise.'

'Look mate, no point me explaining because you won't believe a word. But after Friday, maybe you will have fewer doubts. I've written several letters for you to open next year. Read them with an open mind, and the information I give you about sports events will be enough to make you comfortable. Bet wisely, maybe small to start with, to see for yourself if the information is correct.'

'What are you on about?'

'Billy, you might think I'm crazy, but let's assume I'm not. Assume I am a time traveller. I'm giving you the future. You don't believe me, but as you have the result before it happens, it should be fairly easy to see if the results are correct.'

'Yeah, I suppose.'

'OK, I need you to do something for me.' Billy nodded. 'I want you to promise to look out for Julia.'

'You seriously think you will die on Friday?'

'Well, if I don't, it'll be a bonus. But if it's as I think, I will. I need to sort out a few loose ends – last time I didn't. I need to find resolution with Julia and, well, our place in the universe.'

'If you're a time traveller, why don't you jump out now into another time?'

'It's not how it works. I have no control over it. Only at one point did I have control, but the decision I made meant I am now here and there's nothing I can do to change it.'

'This is heavy shit, mate.'

'Remember, look out for Julia and place some bets.'

'OK. I need to get a drink, though. Do you want one?' Billy said as he stood up.

'No, I'm good, mate.' Billy walked off to the bar.

Jamie finished his drink. He felt a hand on his shoulder, a gentle touch.

'Julia!' he said as she sat down next to him.

'What do you want to do right now?' she said close to his ear.

Jamie stood up and took her hand. 'Let's go.' He waved to Billy as they quickly left the Union.

Jamie sat at Julia's desk once again in the early hours of Wednesday morning. He finished the last of the letters, labelled them, and made sure they were all in order. He had one last letter to write, the last one. For the pier at Littlehampton in 2005. It would be the last contact he would have with her and the most important one. She would understand then. He wrote slowly, his emotions flowing freely onto the paper.

The light started to filter through the curtains when Julia stirred. Jamie had finished his letter a little while ago. He sat quietly and thought through all his madness.

'What you doing, love?' she asked, her voice sleepy.

'The last few jobs. I'm finished now.'

He quickly stripped off and slipped into bed with her. Her body was warm and welcoming.

'I've got a lecture this morning, so I'll see you about one. We can grab lunch in the Union; I'm always hungry at the moment!' Julia laughed. 'Then, if we're bored in the afternoon, we can think of something to do!' She smiled and winked.

'I'll look forward to the afternoon then,' Jamie laughed. 'Are you sure you have to go to your lecture?'

'Yes, I am. I've already missed some, thanks to you

leading me astray. I need to go. I'm all yours for the rest of the day.'

'Fair enough. I will miss you.'

'Don't be so soppy. I'll see you at lunch.' She kissed him on the mouth, her lips hot against his. She pulled away, about to leave, when he grabbed her hand.

'One last kiss before you go,' he leant forward and gently kissed her again.

'Are you OK?' she asked as he pulled away.

'Yeah, yeah, I'm fine,' Jamie felt his eyes well up. 'I'll see you at lunch.'

'OK, see you at lunch, in the Union.' She smiled and left for her lecture.

Jamie knew he needed to find a quiet place and instinctively headed up to the benches at the top of the campus. Fortunately, they were empty, with no one around. As if a floodgate had opened, he sat down and cried. Too much pent-up emotion, too many lifetimes, too many timelines, too many worlds. He didn't understand any of it. Julia, the only real person and emotional force in his life. And somehow he seemed to have said goodbye. It was the last time, and it frightened him. He had to let it all out.

He breathed deeply and took control. He felt worn out, drained. The tears dried on his face. Eventually, he stood up and looked out over the town, wiped his face as best he could, breathed in deeply and walked back down into the campus. Ordinary life around him helped give him some perspective again.

As he passed the bookshop, something caught his eye.

He stepped up to the noticeboard by the door. It gave a list of all guest lectures. In amongst all the names, one stood out. A lecture by Amelia Shaw from Oxford, called 'The Physics of Time Dimensions'. Jamie stared at the board, trying to find some rationale why he had stopped by that notice. Someone came up right next to him. It was Amelia – he knew before he turned to face her.

'Amelia,' he said, almost as if he was expecting her.

'Jamie.'

'How?'

'You told me in my dream last night. You were sorry, you said over and over again. I saw your face so clear, just like now. I knew I would see you today. It was the strangest dream, so clear and some of it just out of reach.'

'I know you, but not in this life. This is wrong.'

'I need you to show me the way,' she hesitated, 'the way into town.'

Jamie thought for a moment, the request so strange but at the same time almost natural. 'Sure,' he replied.

She turned and walked down through the campus towards the car park. He followed. Part of him wanted to stop and understand why this was weird, but there was a magnetic draw to her request.

As he waited by the passenger door of her small red car, he felt an unsettled shift in his emotional state. A foreboding slid round the outskirts of his mind. He wasn't sure why he was going with Amelia; it felt surreal, almost a dream. She leant across the seat and popped the lock and, before he had time to ponder his darkening thoughts, he slipped into the seat beside her.

She drove gingerly out of the car park, and onto the slip road which took them out to the dual carriageway.

'We need to go into town. Is it this way?' she asked.

'No, take the next exit. It's only a few hundred yards. You can see it over there. We can go round and come back on the other carriageway.'

She nodded. 'I saw you in my dream last night,' she turned to look at Jamie, 'just like you look now.'

Jamie didn't know what to say. Even after his long journey, things still surprised him.

'What dream?' he said.

'It was like a red dream. You were there, talking to me.'

'Do you remember what I said?'

'Very clearly. "I'm so sorry, Amelia. I had to let you board the flight. When I saw you after fifty years, you were so unhappy compared to this morning. I had to close the loop, I had to." I don't understand any of it. Do you know what it means?'

Jamie felt Gabriel's breath again on his shoulder. Tiny electric currents brushed up his body, heightening his awareness.

They pulled off the carriageway and drove down to the roundabout, taking them under the main road and back onto the carriageway in the other direction.

'Gabriel was there as well,' she said as she accelerated up the slip road.

He looked at her and wondered if she was Amelia, the Amelia he knew. It didn't make any sense. 'What did he say?' he asked.

'He said I had to close the loop. I had to meet you

today and take you into town. That's all. I don't understand the first bit. Do you?' She accelerated onto the carriageway.

'Yes,' Jamie said, as he turned to look over his shoulder. Everything became clear the instant he saw the lorry bear down on them.

He looked back at Amelia, and she was transfixed on him. A part of her was the Amelia he knew from the previous time dimensions. She was his link, why he was no longer an anomaly. She had come for him and now they were in her car, driving directly out in front of a lorry. She was his reason for leaving, and he was her reason for leaving. All the Crimson Castles converged, everything became instantaneous, everything Gabriel knew came into his mind. In the next moment, before the impact of the lorry, the whole universe made sense. A billion pieces of information all lined up. It was beautiful.

'It's beautiful, isn't it?' Amelia said, taking hold of his arm.

'Yes.'

'Thank you.'

Time, for a moment, seemed to slow. Everything happened in a moment, but somehow it seemed to take more time than it should. As the lorry hit, his whole physical world started accelerating. The car spun as it hit the barrier at the side of the road and it continued to spin, up and over with glass flying and uncontrollable chaos spreading in his tiny world. But in all the developing mayhem, he saw a calm Amelia, her eyes fixed on him. Then it all went blank.

Chapter 11

Littlehampton 20 August 2005

Julia sat in the sunshine, letting it warm her face. She looked out over the harbour at Littlehampton, looked out over the difficult day ahead. But she felt close to him. Many years had passed, but it didn't feel such a distance since she sat here with him. Time would heal, he had said, and he was right. But not in the way he had thought. Her grief had tempered, but her love for him remained as strong now as then.

'Are you alright, Mum?'

Julia felt a hand on her shoulder.

'I'm fine, Holly.'

'I've never understood, with Dad and you.'

'We're here, so I can try to explain. You probably won't

believe it, I still don't in a way, but there can be no other explanation.'

She looked at her daughter, nineteen years old and beautiful. They sat close to each other.

'Right, I might as well.' Julia reached into her handbag and pulled out a yellowed envelope.

'What's that?'

'This is the last letter your Dad wrote to me, and as always they were marked when they should be opened.'

'He wrote more?'

'Oh yes, one for every year, but I'll come back to them. I need to read this first and then I'll explain.'

Holly nodded, and Julia reached down for a letter opener and carefully opened the letter. Her hands shook a little as she unfolded the letter and read it quietly to herself.

My dearest Julia,

I hope you read this on the harbour at Littlehampton, for no other reason than it ties up all the loose ends. This is where I leave you in the life I lived, so I suppose it's the final goodbye, in a sense. I hope by now you have heeded my advice through the years (and the advice I gave you was actually correct) and you are wealthy, with choices. I hope you are married, and I mean happily, even though it does tug at me a little. I hope you have children, as you always were a great mother. And I hope you have good thoughts of me.

I'm sitting at your desk. It must be about four in the morning and you are asleep behind me. A part of me feels guilty about bringing you briefly into my life, but I hope you have forgiven me and you have enjoyed life as much as I did with you.

When I left in 2005, I always searched for some resolution and never knew what it was. When I was taken away from you and the kids, I felt complete emptiness, not to mention all the confusion of waking up in hospital in 1985. It took me a while to work out the whole time-dimension craziness. But through all the jumps I made, I still looked for resolution. I didn't know what resolution, but I knew it existed. When I jumped into Amelia's original time line to stop her boarding her plane, I saw life and death clearly.

If I didn't stop Amelia becoming an anomaly, she would live forever. She would never find any resolution. Resolution is with the people you are close to. In my case, a resolution with you in this life. When I came back and met you, my Julia, I saw the resolution I needed. We always struggled with money, but despite everything, we had each other. You never wavered, and I felt desperately guilty when I left you. Now, as you will hopefully have seen, I have given you some financial help, options to enjoy life so much more. This is my gift for the life I lived with you, but unfortunately, you will not have lived with me.

I suppose this is the resolution I need to find and if you are sitting on a bench at Littlehampton, in the early morning sun (there's a thunderstorm coming), with a reasonable bit of wealth, I can rest easy in these last few days.

You are stirring behind me. I have found my peace, so I'm going to finish and slip in beside you and wrap you in my arms.

Take care now and in the future, I have no more letters to write. You were always in my soul and I hope somewhere in your heart I will have a small place, obviously tucked out of the way.

I will be with you through all time, for I am a time traveller.

Jamie

She remembered Jamie slide into bed with her after he had signed his name and an utter moment of pleasure, comfort and contentment which she thought then would last forever. All her senses stirred as those emotions swam around her thoughts.

'Are you alright, Mum? You're crying.'

Julia looked up at Holly and realised her shoulders shook slightly, and she felt the tears roll freely down her cheeks. 'I'm fine. It's his final letter. It's brought back a wonderful memory. I'm not sad, just thoughts of your father in the last days he was with me.' She closed the letter carefully and placed it slowly back in the envelope.

'You've never said much about my father, even when I asked you about him. Only that you knew him briefly and he passed away before I was born.'

'I had my reasons. But I think it's time now to tell you about him.

'Where to start? Your father was a time traveller.' Holly's eyes widened. 'I knew him for a week before he died. I loved him in a way I have never loved anybody else, and still to this day I love him no less. I could never marry; I didn't love the other men in my life the same way.

Don't think of it as sad. Although only a week, the way he captivated me, loved me intensely, I'm glad I had the opportunity to feel it once in my life. Even if only for the briefest time. And he left me you.' She smiled, and Holly leant in and hugged her gently.

'I don't know what to say.'

'Don't say anything. You will struggle to believe what I tell you. But over the twenty years since he died, he has given us all our wealth.'

'What do you mean?'

'As I said, he was a time traveller. He had already lived his life here, and he wrote me a letter for each year, which I opened on the first of January. They told me what to do and how to become rich. He already knew the future. I did as he told me and we became rich. I don't think Jamie could ever have imagined how rich we would become, and he never knew about you. He would have loved you so much.'

'I can't take it in. I thought it was a short affair; you never talked about him.'

'That couldn't be further from the truth. I couldn't tell you when you were younger. I waited until you were old enough to understand, or at least try to understand. I should have told you earlier, but I felt today was the right day. When you're ready, I will let you read the letters, then you can see for yourself and maybe get to know your father a little.'

'I don't understand; it sounds unbelievable.' She shook her head and looked at her mother. 'Why are we here?'

'In his future he died today, if that makes any sense,'

'It makes no sense, Mother, no sense at all.'

'I met your father on a Friday, in the canteen at university. He dropped his tray when he saw me.' Julia turned and smiled to Holly at the thought of a distant memory, still clear in her mind.

'He told me he was a time traveller, and he only had a week, during which he wanted to go out with me. I thought he was crazy, but he had something about him I couldn't quite put my finger on. He came to see me late on the Friday evening and told me things about myself nobody else could have possibly known. A little disturbing, a little strange, but his charm worked, and I agreed to one week with him. Give me one week, he begged. Little did I know one week was all I was entitled to.' Julia paused for a moment as she looked out over the harbour and out to the shining sea.

'He took me to London to see a musical, and we stayed in The Savoy, then he took me to Brighton and we stayed in The Grand, and on the Monday we came here. He told me about this Saturday and how he died. We sat here a long time, but by then I had fallen hopelessly in love with him. As much as I am still today. It's a feeling I never tire of; it fuels me every moment of every day.'

Julia felt emotion build up inside her. 'And by the next Friday, our week was up. In that week, I reached both extremes of emotions and nothing has ever been the same since. I will tell you more later. It's getting too much.' She stopped and felt a constriction in her chest, her breath heavy. The pain, and the love, all within her.

Holly placed her arms tightly around her mother, feeling her pain and tears as she held her. They sat there in silence. The warmth of the sun grew as the morning wore on.

After a while, Julia straightened herself and smoothed out her dress.

'I don't quite know what to say.' Holly broke the silence.

'I know it's a lot to take in, but I couldn't tell you until you were older. I suppose now is a good time. I have much to tell you and I will in due course.'

'So what was he like?'

'He was, well, my Jamie. I can't do him justice by describing him. I hope you one day feel as much happiness as I did knowing him. Today I say goodbye to him, where he died in his life. It sounds weird, but I have always had him next to me. His letters every year have guided me all the time. The boyfriends and partners over the years never worked. Always Jamie, there in my presence, even more powerful than if he were alive. He was always there, in my mind. It would never have been fair to marry.'

'It sounds awful, Mother.'

'Far from it. He gave me purpose, firstly through you and then through the wealth he gave me. I have never regretted anything in my life. Those first few years were hard: grief stricken, pregnant and trying to get my degree. I managed it all. Billy, your father's best friend, helped me those first few years. But as I made money and found my feet, he drifted off into his own life. He became wealthy but unfortunately he died in 1996. You were probably too young to remember.

'I remember the letter in 1997. Jamie knew Billy had died the previous year. It was weird, but I suppose reinforced what your father knew. He said in the letter there would come a point at which I would either have to settle down to a quiet life or, if I carried on, become more public as my wealth increased. I would lose some of my freedom. I chose to carry on and with all the charitable trusts we now have, I feel good about the decisions I made.' She gave a little laugh.

'What?'

'It's just a thought. In his life, he strived to find a resolution, as he called it, with me. We were happy, but we struggled to make ends meet and he wanted to put it right. His resolution, to give me wealth, so I could make decisions free from the worry of money. But with all the wealth we now have, we're effectively trapped. I can imagine Jamie and me down here today, fishing, with kids. Eating a picnic, being a family. Trapped but free. And we're free but trapped.'

Holly looked at her.

Julia reached into her handbag and pulled out a worn wallet. She opened it and pulled out several items. 'This was your father,' she said and handed Holly the items.

Holly looked through them one at a time. Jamie's Student Union card, then his library card, and finally a strip of four passport pictures with Jamie and Julia. 'Oh my God! This is my father!' Holly stared at the pictures. 'He was handsome – and you looked so happy. I can see it in your eyes. Where was this taken?'

'In Brighton, I had already fallen hopelessly in love with him.' She smiled at the thought. 'These are the only pictures I have of your father. When he died, his parents didn't know about me. I tried to talk to them but, in our grief, it never worked out. They never listened and never wanted to know me.

'I found out I was pregnant and I carried you and my grief with purpose. I didn't need anyone else. It wasn't until ten years later his letter told of his parents dying in a car accident in the previous year. I felt guilty for not getting in touch with them, but I don't think they would ever have believed me.'

Holly stared at the pictures. 'This is too much to take in.'

Julia took the pictures back and placed them carefully back into the wallet. 'Don't try to take it all in. We will have time together to talk about it and once you have read his letters, you will know him better.'

'It sounds desperately sad. But in the picture of you and my father, you looked so happy and free.'

'I am happy. You are everything to me, you embody what my life with Jamie has been all about. It's not conventional, but what life is? I have you and we do make a difference.'

She paused, stood up, and walked over to the harbour railings. She wanted to get closer to the water and the sun. A beautiful day, too beautiful to die. Tears rose as she grieved again, those faded memories from the unimaginable grief she felt twenty years ago surfacing again. This was goodbye. Holly came over next to her.

'Are you OK?'

'I'm OK, I'm saying goodbye.'

Holly pushed her arm through her mother's. They leant against the railing and watched the sea ebb and flow.

Julia noticed Liam, her bodyguard, in the corner of her eye. Always just in the corner of her eye. He was nervous about this trip. It was too exposed, he had said. She noticed the growing crowd, with Liam and his team closing in around her. She turned and nodded and instantly he was next to her.

'Your Grace?' His voice was low and gentle.

'I think I'm done here. I've said my final farewell.'

'We can stay as long as you need, Your Grace. I have contacted the local police and they will pull the crowds back. You need to say goodbye. If the situation needs, I will signal an evacuation.'

'Maybe a few minutes more.' She looked round and saw the crowds. 'Why don't you get the cars ready and I'll have another five minutes?'

'Understood, Your Grace.' He hurried away from her, his gruff voice issuing orders into his mic.

'Just you and me from now on,' Julia said as she turned back to Holly.

'No, he'll always be with us,' Holly said quietly. They stood there for the next few minutes and felt the heat of the sun grow. 'Come on, Mum, we need to move on.'

Holly gently pulled Julia away from the railings. The gathered crowd shouted warm greetings, police officers standing between them and her entourage. Liam walked next to Julia with the rest of his team around them. The array of cars waited, doors open, and Julia and Holly headed for the silver Mercedes. As Julia settled herself into the back seat, the door closed.

Her PA sat in the front. 'Your Grace, the PM called and would appreciate your attendance at Chequers tonight.'

'Not tonight, Jane. You will have to reschedule.'

'Yes, Your Grace.'

Julia turned and smiled at her daughter, hers and Jamie's. No, he would always be there. It lifted her heart. He would always be there, through all time. He was, after all, a time traveller.

Printed in Great Britain
by Amazon

61635466R00180

VIVAVOCE

FEDEZ

L'ACQUA È PIÙ PROFONDA DI COME SEMBRA DA SOPRA

MONDADORI

mondadori.it

L'acqua è più profonda di come sembra da sopra
di Fedez
Collezione Vivavoce

ISBN 978-88-04-79830-9

I edizione ottobre 2025

Indice

L'acqua è più profonda di come sembra da sopra

Prologo

ROTTURA

Sanremo, 2023

Quello è il momento in cui tutto crolla. Volevo quel palco.

Lo volevo da morire.

Era diventato un'ossessione, una febbre.

Ci pensavo la notte, ci pensavo mentre bevevo il caffè al mattino. Ma non avrei mai immaginato di arrivarci così, in quella situazione del cazzo. La peggiore che potevo immaginare.

E invece era proprio quella.

Lì, sotto i riflettori, a sanguinare senza farlo vedere. E non invidiavo Chiara. Non la invidiavo, no.

Noi abbiamo sempre fatto due mestieri diversi.

Due pianeti che si sfioravano ma non si toccavano mai davvero.

Era lei, semmai, che diceva di invidiarmi.

«Tu sei un artista» diceva, «tu puoi parlare col sangue, puoi trasformare la merda in musica.»

E aveva ragione. Ma io intanto stavo lì, a mangiarmi le mani perché non ero su quel cazzo di palco.

A guardare i riflettori da lontano, mentre sentivo le vene tirare dalla voglia di essere lì sotto.

Il pubblico, il sudore, il microfono che pesa come un'arma.

Io avevo bisogno di quello.

Mi faceva male non averlo. Non provavo rancore.

Solo un'inquietudine sottile, come febbre bassa.

Il palco era tutto quello che avevo desiderato, e lei era lì.

Ma non c'era veleno.

Non c'era gara.

Solo la coscienza precisa, scientifica, di essere fuori.

Fuori dal tempo, fuori dal gioco, fuori dal mondo. Avrei voluto parlare, ma non ne ero più capace.

La voce mi si era consumata dentro, insieme a tutto il resto. Oggi non ricordo più nemmeno cosa accadde dopo. Sarà colpa della depressione, dei farmaci, che ne so.

So solo che da quel momento in poi le cose iniziarono a disfarsi. Il panico era lì, come un animale accovacciato sotto lo sterno.

Sapevo riconoscerlo.

Era antico, mio.

E sapevo anche che non se ne sarebbe andato. Il caos non lo puoi gestire, se sei lucido al massimo lo puoi accettare, altrimenti lo subisci e basta. E qui i fatti si confondono con le leggende. Ci sono più fili nascosti che verità condivise. Nel frullatore dei media e dei social chiunque è un'invenzione di qualcun altro. Difficile distinguere la verità quando tutto crolla. Con il panico appiccicato al cuore. E il panico è paura incontrollabile, anche quando se ne è consapevoli. Noi restiamo lì, a guardare il caos con il cuore contratto. Perché di certi demoni ci si libera soltanto raccontandoli. Vomito inchiostro. Penso al tuo volto e non ti riconosco. Valori e ideali, perle ai maiali. I nostri cazzi messi in Piazza Affari. La nostra è una gara a chi corre ai ripari. Finché magistrato non ci separi. Ricordi Sanremo? Si è tinta di nero per una vicenda di cronaca rosa. Tu che mi butti fuori di casa e io che butto il blister del Prozac. Fine corsa. La giostra si ferma, il buio comincia.

Il panico – quello vero – è freddo.

Razionale.

Come un algoritmo impazzito.

E non se ne va mai del tutto.

Bisogna raccontarlo.

Dargli un nome, anche se mentendo.

Perché mentire, a volte, è l'unico modo per sopravvivere. Dall'inizio della mia vita, si è sempre trattato di non essere più solo davanti alle cose che fanno paura. Cercare armi, corazze, cercarle negli uomini più grossi, più fighi, nelle donne più abbaglianti. Confondere protezione e amicizia, amore e autostima. Cercare rimedi per la sensazione di essere solo davanti a cose più grandi e più forti di me. Da solo di fronte al fondo nero che mi sono messo negli occhi, simbolicamente, sul palco. Lo stesso che, in questi anni, ho frequentato davvero. Perché spesso la soluzione che troviamo è questa: quel baratro lo assorbiamo, ce lo portiamo dentro.

Non credo nella distinzione vittima-carnefice: se mi si chiedesse di posizionarmi, definire chi sono, non saprei cosa rispondere. La soluzione che continuo a trovare è quella di arrivare così in basso da dimostrarmi che, almeno, posso rinascere. Una volta una persona mi ha detto che il mio talento più grande – il solo che ho – è quello di dare esattamente ciò che le persone vogliono. Se presa alla lettera credo sia la cosa più vera che mi sia mai stata detta. Sin da bambino la mia solitudine non era né malinconica né tragica, era autosufficiente. Sono cresciuto a dispetto di tutto, di me stesso, contro me stesso, creandomi un po' un doppio che ha bisogno di sfidare il mondo. Sempre. E quasi sempre viene sconfitto. Prende botte. Dal mondo. Danziamo con i nostri demoni, abbracciamo le nostre debolezze, mentre fingiamo di non vederli, di non sentirli, ma eccoli lì. I demoni. Io demone. Il respiro affannoso della lotta più temuta, quella contro noi stessi, in cui viviamo accompagnati dai nostri fantasmi, danziamo con le nostre debolezze. Nel silenzio. Nel vuoto che rimbomba più forte di qualsiasi applauso o fischio.

Ma perché lo sto raccontando in un libro? C'è chi sosterrà che è per i soldi, forse è vero, non m'importa, ma ha senso se anche solo una persona dopo averlo letto si sentirà meno sbagliata, imperfetta, fallita soltanto perché il mondo intorno urla che lo è: un fallito, un coglione, un nulla. Io non sono un buon esempio, forse sono il peggiore che esista, ma forse proprio per questo posso diventare il migliore degli esempi possibili. Esiste un momento in cui comprendiamo che il coraggio più grande non è la fuga, ma il guardarsi negli occhi. Smettere di ignorare quel vuoto assordante che smania per essere ascoltato perché è l'unico modo di esistere davvero. Non possiamo controllare ciò che accade intorno a noi, ma possiamo decidere come reagire a tutto questo. È la caduta, è il crollo, a costringerci a cercare un senso. Non ci domandiamo mai perché abbiamo vinto, ma il fallimento ci obbliga a interrogarci, a cercare risposte, a ricostruire. Cadiamo per imparare a rialzarci. Cadiamo perché la vita non smetterà di riproporci la stessa lezione, finché non la faremo nostra. Una spirale ciclica che vuole solo essere ascoltata. Una storia, quando ci sei in mezzo, non è una storia, è solo caos, confusione. È soltanto dopo che diventa una storia, che prende una forma. È quando la racconti a te stesso o a qualcun altro. Non è più tempo di scappare, è tempo di cadere.

Atto I

NON ESISTE UN CAZZO DURO COME LA VITA

Non mi va di parlare della mia infanzia

Non mi va di parlare della mia infanzia; lo trovo un tema noiosissimo, ma il mio editor insiste. Quindi, parlerò di me come se non fossi io. In terza persona, per avere il distacco che sento verso quegli anni.

Federico Lucia nasce nella periferia milanese, precisamente in un anonimo condominio al confine tra Buccinasco e Corsico. Zone non esattamente paradisiache. Buccinasco era un avamposto della 'ndrangheta nel Nord. Corsico, un posto di periferia, con tutti i disagi che si porta dietro la periferia, anche a Milano. In particolare c'era una strada, a Corsico, via Cavour: senza amici potenti, eri un bersaglio ambulante. Ti scippavano, assicurato. Federico detiene un record: sette bici rubate nello stesso mese, tre mentre era ancora in sella. «La Graziella è di mio cugino» dicevano, e ti ritrovavi circondato da dieci di loro. Prova a rispondere che non era del cugino. Dovevi dargliela per forza. Va be', ora basta con la terza persona ché sembro un megalomane.

A scuola, i compagni erano figli dei capi della 'ndrangheta. Una realtà che ho scoperto leggendo un libro di Renato Vallanzasca, qualche tempo fa, in cui elenca i nomi della malavita milanese. Sembrava l'appello della mia classe. Non ho ricordi vividi, ma avevo attorno strani suicidi, morti sospette.

Ho avuto un'infanzia okay, tutto sommato. Mio padre lavorava come orafo, mia madre era impiegata: poi è arrivato un momento di difficoltà, nel 2001, e mio padre ha perso il lavoro, finendo a fare il magazziniere. Mio padre è arrivato dalla Basilicata senza sapere una parola di italiano. E mia madre è cresciuta nelle case popolari del Giambellino. Si sono incontrati in una discoteca quando avevano tredici anni. Mi disgusta solo il pensiero di immaginarli, i miei che limonano.

Stanno insieme da allora e non riescono a parlare senza urlare uno addosso all'altra. Una vita intera a gridarsi contro, e io lì in mezzo sono cresciuto così, con questi che urlano e si insultano ogni cinque minuti. La mia assistente dice che io ora sto facendo lo stesso, con tutti quelli che mi stanno attorno.

Mio padre, lavorando molto, era sempre in trincea. Mia madre si è messa a fare la mia manager perché, in questo mondo, volevo qualcuno che non mi pugnalasse alle spalle. A volte succede che ti inculano anche i genitori, però hai meno rischi che possano farlo.

I miei sono stati dei buoni genitori ma, come tutti, hanno lasciato qualche cicatrice, pure senza volerlo. Una volta ho fatto un test della personalità, ed è saltato fuori che ero un figlio senza radici solide. Mio padre ha trovato per caso i risultati e, tutto preoccupato, mi ha chiamato dicendo: «Ho letto questa roba, da chi diavolo stai andando?». Pensava che mi stessero facendo il lavaggio del cervello, plagiandomi. Gli ho risposto: «Se vuoi, posso farti un elenco di cose che sono state difficili, cose di cui non vi siete accorti».

Non hanno percepito un sacco di cose. Erano attentissimi su certi fronti, meno su altri. Poi va detto che la mia adolescenza è stata terribile. Ho frequentato le peggiori compagnie di Milano. Che erano anche le più belle, per altri versi. Ho collezionato esperienze, ho fatto conoscenze che mi hanno portato dove sono ora. Ma erano ambienti pericolosi. Se oggi sapessi che mio figlio esce e va a fare quello che facevo io, sarei molto preoccupato per la sua incolumità. I miei mi lasciavano libero e non si rendevano effettivamente conto di cosa facessi: avevano una visione parziale, non sapevano che frequentavo dei giri importanti, un ambiente non molto sano. Microcriminalità, spaccio, e non solo. Anche se poi è vero che, se nasci in un contesto di quel tipo, devi farci i conti. Credo sia inevitabile.

Ero un caso a parte a Buccinasco: la periferia ti cuce addosso un'immagine, che a pensarci bene non è cambiata molto nei decenni. Già allora aveva la sua divisa: tute da ginnastica e motorini truccati. L'immaginario collettivo tra i ragazzi era netto, preciso, tutti più o meno ci adeguavamo. All'epoca si vestivano tutti quanti Lonsdale London. Io ero l'eccezione, il robboso, il punkabbestia del posto. Non ero ben visto. Sono cresciuto in un ambiente in cui il menu era sempre lo stesso, e il piatto del giorno era il bullismo, la prevaricazione, la legge del più forte che campa sottomettendo il più debole. Se eri diverso, non solo esteticamente, ma anche giusto un po' introverso, avevi già perso in partenza. Io frequentavo i tipi più problematici, uscivo con quelli famosi per le risse. Non ero ben accetto, nemmeno da loro, ma continuavo a girarci lo stesso.

Le giornate si assomigliavano tutte: giri in paese, giostre, risse. Sempre risse.

Coi miei ci siamo spostati tanto.

Quando ho finito le medie ci siamo trasferiti a Binasco: un piccolo paese in mezzo ai campi, tra Pavia e Milano. Non è stata la scelta più brillante che si potesse fare: siamo andati a stare in una casa più grande ma completamente isolata. Di fronte avevamo una cartiera: tutt'intorno c'erano solo pantegane e prostitute col bidone del fuoco. Che io frequentavo. Non ricordo la mia prima volta e credo sia perché ho perso la verginità con una prostituta di Binasco. Quindici euro per il primo rapporto orale, trenta per il resto.

Per andare a scuola, da Binasco, dovevo svegliarmi alle cinque di mattina e prendere una serie infinita di autobus. Oppure farmi un'ora abbondante di motorino: lo stesso tempo che ci vuole per fare Milano-Torino. Non ho mai capito perché, ma era freddo anche ad agosto. La periferia è così, a volte senti un freddo esistenziale che ti si infila dentro e non te lo togli più, neanche ad agosto. Neanche quando cresci e arrivi a vivere in un attico in centro a Milano. Quel freddo lì te lo porti dentro e basta.

Dopo qualche anno, per via anche di una serie di problemi famigliari, a un certo punto i miei genitori si sono resi conto che non potevamo continuare a stare lì, e alla fine ci siamo trasferiti. La terza superiore l'ho fatta a Rozzano, dove loro vivono ancora adesso. Un paese piccolo, ma non troppo, all'estrema periferia sud di Milano, costruito in mezzo ai campi e alle risaie. Qualcuno lo chiama il Bronx del Nord, ma ci vive anche tanta gente perbene, a cui nella vita è andata com'è andata. Nel 1990 ci costruiscono la gigantesca torre della Telecom, un po' il simbolo di quel posto. Centottantasette metri: più alta di tutto il resto. Di notte sparisce: rimangono soltanto le luci, che si vedono anche a decine di chilometri di distanza. Quante sere, rincasando, è stata una specie di stella polare, l'indicatore che, da qualunque parte stessi arrivando, ti ricordava dov'era la base. La torre di Rozzano, il posto da cui vengo io, quello da cui me ne sono andato, per combinare qualcosa, per prendermi le cose che desideravo. Per fare di più, fare meglio di ciò che la vita aveva messo in conto per me, per noi.

Quando con Chiara abbiamo comprato l'attico a CityLife, dal terrazzo, la prima notte, ho visto quella torre in lontananza: mi sono emozionato, mi sono commosso. Corriamo all'impazzata, senza renderci conto di niente: poi ci sono delle scene, delle prospettive, che in un secondo ti restituiscono il senso di anni e anni di guerra e di caos. Per me è quella torre di centottantasette metri che scompare nella notte ma che mi ricorda la sua presenza con delle luci intermittenti un po' tristi.

La prima rissa

Non ho molti altri ricordi della mia infanzia. Anzi, un ricordo ce l'ho. Non so bene perché mi è rimasto sempre in testa, o forse sì, in realtà. Perché in fondo secondo me rimaniamo quelli che siamo stati da bambini. Io, per dire, lì nella periferia mi sono sempre sentito diverso. Ma diverso non vuol dire migliore, vuol dire solo diverso. E pure lì, non ho mai avuto l'istinto all'attacco, ma quello della difesa, della sopravvivenza che può diventare anche violenza. È una cosa che poi mi sono portato dietro tutta la vita, difficilmente sono il primo a istigare uno scontro, a cercare di scoprire le vulnerabilità di chi mi sta di fronte, ma se mi sento attaccato, invece, reagisco e, a volte, esagero.

Insomma, c'era questo bambino, all'asilo, che mi faceva di continuo un gesto strano. Sembra una specie di trailer della mia vita. L'asilo in cui andavo era in Barona, zona sempre un po' gangsta. Non so se in tutti gli asili facevano 'sta roba, ma mi ricordo che c'erano dei lego giganti e ognuno si faceva un cubo. Passavi l'intervallo a correre in cerchio per la scuola, spingendo questo cubo. Forse questa attività pedagogica si faceva solo in Barona, non escludo fosse propedeutica per lavorare come corrieri della droga e scappare dalla polizia.

A ogni modo, mentre costruivo il mio cubo e correvo in cerchio, c'era questo bambino che ogni volta si fermava davanti a me, immobile, e mi faceva il gesto col dito medio alzato. Correva, correva, mi vedeva, si fermava e mi faceva quel gesto. In silenzio. Io non capivo. Gli chiedevo: «Vuol dire uno? Cosa mi vuoi dire?». Andavo a casa e lo raccontavo a mia madre. «Mamma, questo bambino mi ha fatto così col dito.» Lei: «No, ma non ti preoccupare». Non voleva spiegarmi il significato di quel gesto. È andato avanti settimane a farmelo, fino a che un mio vicino di casa mi ha spiegato il significato. In Barona i bambini si allenano per trasportare la droga e mandare affanculo la gente. Tornato a scuola, gli ho lanciato in faccia il cubo e l'ho menato. La mia prima rissa.

Come ho smesso di andare a scuola

Io non sono il tipo a cui è facile insegnare qualcosa, lo riconosco. Ho la testa dura, penso spesso di aver ragione, sono diffidente e per ogni mio professore deve essere stato un incubo avermi come studente, lo ammetto. Però anche io vivevo la scuola come una gabbia in cui non solo ero imprigionato. In ogni scuola in cui sono stato ero sempre il più odiato, ed è un ritornello che riempie da sempre la mia vita, sarà lo stesso quando divento un cantante e inizio a frequentare l'ambiente musicale o dopo con Chiara per giornali e media.

Direte: se sei sempre il più odiato fatti qualche domanda. Magari è vero, in qualche modo può essere colpa mia, ma le cose guardate con i miei occhi, dal mio punto di vista, con la mia vita addosso sono diverse. Io non sono un bullo, ma è capitato che lo diventassi, come a scuola. La catena è sempre quella: ti senti diverso, gli altri ti vedono come un corpo estraneo da attaccare, lo fanno e, solo a quel punto, tu reagisci, ti lecchi le ferite e ti riprometti che non lascerai più che ti ricapiti una cosa del genere ed è lì, in quel preciso momento, che a tua volta rischi di diventare tu il bullo. Il bullismo alla fine è un cerchio, una catena di cui si è, allo stesso tempo, anello forte e debole. Era tutto un ciclo di prevaricazioni: io a scuola subivo da alcune persone e mi sfogavo su delle altre.

Il mio rapporto con la scuola, comunque, viene marchiato a partire dal momento, alle medie, in cui i professori ti fanno fare i corsi di orientamento per scegliere le superiori. È quando i prof ti danno il loro consiglio. Quei corsi di orientamento erano labirinti di scelte per il futuro: ti sedevi, ascoltavi, e poi, come degli oracoli, i professori ti svelavano il percorso: il liceo ti elevava, il tecnico ti relegava a una sfiga amara, il professionale ti cancellava del tutto. La gerarchia è: se ti dicono liceo sei un figo, se ti dicono tecnico sei Fantozzi, se ti dicono professionale sei una merda totale. Alle medie non brillavo sui libri, ma nel disegno, sì. Ero tra quelli che disegnavano meglio di tutta la scuola, e questo mi aveva fatto ottenere il compito di decorare e adornare gli spazi comuni. Così mi orientano verso l'artistico. Mi iscrivo – convinto delle mie capacità di disegnare bene – al Boccioni di piazzale Arduino, vicino a quella che oggi è CityLife. Poi però arrivano i test: copiare un manichino. Lo faccio ma, buttando un occhio al lavoro degli altri, mi rendo conto che il mio talento è rilevante giusto a Buccinasco. A Milano, tra gli aspiranti artisti della città, sono scarsissimo. La professoressa di Discipline pittoriche, in particolare, non ci gira attorno: «Non sei tagliato per questa scuola».

Sono andato comunque a un liceo artistico, ma sperimentale, al terzo anno si prendeva un indirizzo: grafico pubblicitario, arti figurative, architettura o beni culturali/restauro. Chi non sapeva disegnare optava per beni culturali, l'indirizzo più teorico. Scelgo quello ed è lì che partecipo a un concorso della Fondazione Pomodoro (ora sede di Fendi). C'è una specie di test, di prova, come guida museale: la vinco, e divento guida alla mostra di Kounellis e addetto della catalogazione delle opere di Pomodoro. Quest'esperienza mi ha insegnato tantissimo: innanzitutto, che se sei molto ricco la gente ti deve chiamare "maestro" (quando arrivava il signor Pomodoro tutti lo dovevano chiamare così, ma io ovviamente mi rifiutavo); e poi di non parcheggiare mai l'SR di Spiderman senza mettere la catena, dato che l'ho fatto e non l'ho più ritrovato. Lo stage era non retribuito: non ho guadagnato nulla, né in termini di arricchimento personale né in termini di patrimonio. Giusto quello che ho detto, oltre ad avere imparato a mettere la catena al motorino.

Però per un paio di cose devo dire grazie alla scuola: la politica e la musica. Il mio interesse per la politica, infatti, nasce alle superiori. Era abbastanza frequente, all'epoca, tra i banchi delle scuole pubbliche. È da lì che viene il primo contatto con le realtà politiche: è in quella fase che in me si sono sedimentati slancio e passione per il dibattito pubblico e le dinamiche del potere. La mia scuola, il Boccioni, era di fianco a un centro sociale chiamato Cantiere. Ne respiravo l'energia, il fermento, la rabbia. Ricordo le volte che quelli del Cantiere venivano a fare casino fuori dall'istituto, picchiando ragazzi per ragioni che in realtà non sempre perfino i malcapitati capivano. Una volta hanno preso a botte un mio compagno di classe, dicendogli: «Ti vesti da fascista». Ma il tipo stava lì, spaesato, non sapeva nemmeno cosa volesse dire "fascismo". Io devo dire che rimasi affascinato da quel brivido di squadrismo di sinistra, mi gasava, cominciai a frequentarli, a immergermi nella loro realtà fatta di contestazione e serate di rap improvvisato. Inizio a fare rap all'interno di quella che poi era una casa occupata.

La politica entrò prepotente nella mia vita, tra workshop e le prime manifestazioni, dove le bombe carta volavano come coriandoli di un carnevale rovesciato. Mi ricordo di quel periodo con un misto di orgoglio e rimorso: non fu diretta opera mia, ma poco dopo che avevo iniziato a frequentare il Cantiere, spuntò il Cuore Nero, un centro sociale di stampo fascista. I giornalisti che si accalcavano all'entrata, e quei tipi, con le loro bretelle e i basettoni, pronti a sfoderare mazze al posto degli argomenti. Non durò molto, il Cuore Nero. Pochi giorni dopo l'inaugurazione, fu ridotto in cenere. Non posso dire di esser stato parte dell'operazione, ma quel fuoco, in quel momento, aveva un che di liberatorio. Quell'epoca mi ha formato, per certi versi nasce lì la persona che sono oggi, consapevole delle complessità della lotta politica, delle contraddizioni. Ma, riflettendoci a posteriori, non posso negare che sia stato anche un luogo molto violento. Forse è per questo che poi negli anni ho continuato ad avere questo atteggiamento nei confronti di ciò che per me è politica, perché è nato in un luogo di dibattiti accesi e di passione reale.

Per me la politica è ancora quella che vidi fare tanti anni fa al Cantiere, una politica talmente concreta che la potevi quasi toccare come la musica, lì era una cosa vera, che grattava l'anima più cruda del quartiere.

Al Cantiere, comunque, si facevano anche delle gare di freestyle, dove tu entravi, pagavi un ingresso a offerta libera o comunque molto basso. Le birre costavano due, tre euro. Era molto frequentato, anche perché era l'unico posto in cui potevi cantare su un palco di fronte a centinaia di persone. Le gare di freestyle erano come tornei: ti iscrivevi e ti esibivi in una specie di sfida contro un altro rapper. Saliva l'adrenalina: un minuto a testa, a suon di insulti in rima. Alla fine il pubblico decretava il vincitore. Ho vinto parecchie gare: nessuno sa perché, su internet non ci sono i miei video, tranne forse uno. E quando mi rivedo non riconosco la mia voce: avevo ancora le tonsille. C'erano anche dei tornei nazionali in quel periodo: al "Tecniche Perfette", che era il più complesso, con selezione regionale fino alla sfida finale, tipo "Mortal Kombat". Io vinsi in Piemonte, Emis Killa spadroneggiava in Lombardia. Siamo arrivati entrambi alla semifinale nazionale, dove poi vinse Emis. Era estenuante, un martello nella testa: vivevamo in funzione di quello. Ti svegliavi al mattino e pensavi tutto il tempo alle rime da trovare. È un'ossessione: quando fai freestyle devi tenere sempre la mente allenata, ogni cosa che vedi diventa un verso, pensi a un'ipotetica rima che ci puoi fare. Emis Killa era un dio nell'improvvisazione. Io me le preparavo, ma ero bravo a spararle come se mi venissero lì per lì. Denny l'ho incontrato al Cantiere. Organizzava una serata di freestyle, ma a un certo punto i ragazzi del centro sociale hanno deciso che era troppo per loro. Gli rubano la serata, lo fanno fuori semplice e diretto. Una sera c'ero anch'io a esibirmi: Denny si presenta ubriaco fradicio. Sale sul palco e inizia a vomitare parole contro il centro sociale e il capo, un tizio detto Mangiapanini. Denny ha tirato fuori tutto, senza freni. La situazione è andata a puttane: era il loro territorio, era casa loro. Io mi trovavo lì, davanti al palco, e ho visto questi tipi avvicinarsi. Denny viene preso e riempito di botte. Iniziano ad arrivare calci anche a me, allora salgo sul palco e vedo Denny circondato da duecento persone che lo sommergono da ogni lato, letteralmente. Si sono trasformati in una squadra di calcio, pronta a fare un fallo dietro l'altro, Denny era la palla. Gli hanno spaccato lo zigomo e il naso. Io e lui abbiamo iniziato a legare quella sera, mentre aspettavamo l'ambulanza fuori dal centro sociale. Da lì, siamo diventati amici. Lui era di Baggio, quartiere Olmi, sempre posti pittoreschi. Anche Denny era un musicista; insieme avremmo fatto, tempo dopo, il mio primo tour, il "Sig. Brainwash".

Al liceo, comunque, mi hanno bocciato due volte. Il primo anno perché avevo in classe una ragazza che secondo me fingeva di avere problemi. Sua madre chiedeva l'insegnante di sostegno per la figlia, quando lei era assolutamente in grado di seguire le lezioni. A un certo punto per un mese non è venuta a scuola: si è inventata che ero io la causa per cui non veniva più. Diceva che la bullizzavo. Il che era vero, ma non più degli altri. Poi ho dato una spinta a una prof, perché mi aveva dato uno schiaffo. L'ho spinta giù dalle scale. Ma erano pochi gradini, tipo quattro. Quindi bocciature sempre per la condotta, non per i cattivi voti nelle materie. Avendo compromesso il rapporto coi professori, cambio indirizzo e vado a fare architettura. Ma io ho le mani che mi sudano, col Tratto Pen è un casino. Faccio delle cose ignobili, impresentabili. All'artistico funziona che, nel corso delle settimane, porti avanti sempre lo stesso lavoro, per cui hai una data di consegna fissata a lungo termine. Quindi, nel work in progress, prendi i fogli e li metti in un armadio. Armadio dove c'erano anche le tavole di tutti i miei compagni di classe. Io le rubavo, scegliendo quelle dei più bravi, prendevo la lametta da barba, grattavo via il nome, mettevo il mio e peggioravo un po' la tavola, per renderla credibile. Sono andato avanti così fino a che una tipa non ha riconosciuto il suo lavoro in una delle mie tavole. Lì il gioco è finito. Comunque a un certo punto ho smesso di andare a scuola ed è forse l'idea migliore che abbia mai avuto perché è lì, in quel preciso momento, che ho cominciato davvero a fare musica.

Frequentavo – per la seconda volta – la quarta superiore. Quell'anno il liceo viene diviso in due. Scoprono, dopo tanti anni, che in quella scuola c'è l'amianto. Metà alunni rimangono nella sede principale e metà vanno in una specie di scuola di riserva, che è a Bonola, ancora più lontano. Io – nota a margine –, nonostante poi mi sia venuto lo stesso il cancro, rientro tra i fortunati a cui è stato concesso di non respirare più l'amianto.

Ma non è stato per l'amianto che ho abbandonato la scuola, lo ammetto. C'entra la voglia di evadere, di provare a capire di che pasta ero davvero fatto, di trovare il mio posto nel mondo. E non è un caso, secondo me, se è proprio in quel periodo che ho cominciato a sperimentare con le sostanze. Non capivo bene quello che facevo, ma erano uno strumento facile, veloce, spesso idiota, per spalancare una finestra sul mondo che non fosse quello grigio in cui vivevo, quella scuola di periferia, quei professori, quei compagni. Poi, ovvio, essendo non sempre propriamente lucido mi venivano anche idee del cazzo, una delle quali è stata la pietra tombale del mio rapporto con la scuola. In poche parole, avendo scopato con l'ex fidanzata del mio migliore amico Niccolò, ho pensato bene che per evitare le sue mazzate l'idea migliore fosse farmi pestare prima dal mio amico Dose. Ovvio, no? Una mattina, parlando con Dose, gli dico: «Ho avuto un'idea per evitare le mazzate di Niccolò». Io lo portavo a scuola in motorino, in quel periodo un vecchio rottame con un enorme adesivo di Gesù Cristo sul retro. Lo lasciavo giù al suo istituto e poi andavo al mio. Gli ho detto: «Se mi presento già pestato, Niccolò smette di menarmi». (Spero che Dose legga questo racconto, perché so che suona folle, ma vi giuro che è andata così.) Quindi espongo il mio piano e chiedo a Dose di darmi dei pugni in faccia, abbastanza forti da lasciare dei segni evidenti. A quel tempo avevo un sacco di piercing, me li levo tutti e dico a Dose: «Fallo». Non so se avete mai chiesto a qualcuno di picchiarvi di proposito, ma non è semplicissimo. Stavo lì in cucina, fisso in piedi, a ripetere: «Vai», «No, no, aspetta». Dopo un'ora di tentennamenti lui mi colpisce in faccia, un dolore bestiale, ma mi guardo allo specchio e non vedo niente. Nessuna traccia, nessun segno. Mi son dovuto far dare tre, quattro pugni. A un certo punto, devo dire, prendi il ritmo. Prova dopo prova riesco a ottenere un occhio nero e il naso sanguinante, sangue che non mi pulisco, così da essere più drammatico. Arrivo a scuola, Niccolò vede che sono messo male ma mi mena lo stesso. A quel punto dico basta. Torno da mia madre e le racconto tutto: «Niccolò mi picchia ogni giorno, posso smettere di andare a scuola?». Lei mi risponde: «Va bene, ma trovati un lavoro».

Mi hanno picchiato in modo gentile

In realtà la lezione non l'ho imparata subito come sperava mia mamma e, infatti, un lavoro non era proprio nelle mie priorità. Dovevo sentirmi vivo, dovevo sentirmi libero e, per questo, nella prima vacanza della mia vita, a Tarifa, mi sono fatto picchiare da un paese intero. Dev'essere quella mia componente masochistica, quella per cui per imparare davvero una cosa devo sbatterci la testa una volta e poi un'altra a costo di farmi male, di mettermi in pericolo. Però, evidentemente, è un mio modo per funzionare, per tirare fuori da me tutto ciò che posso, per "sentire" davvero qualcosa.

Tarifa è nella punta più a sud della Spagna, da dove si vede il Marocco. Ci vai per due motivi: fumare gli ovuli o fare kitesurf. E io non so fare kitesurf. Avevo diciassette anni, i miei genitori vanno in vacanza e io rimango tutta l'estate a Milano da solo. Non sapendo cosa fare, ma non avendo neanche soldi, decido di partire con un volo da venti euro per andare a Tarifa con un amico, un writer di Milano, ai tempi molto conosciuto nell'ambiente, uno un po' matto. Se c'era da fare qualcosa di sbagliato, lui riusciva sempre a fare precisamente quella cosa. L'itinerario va tenuto presente perché è importante sul finale della storia: non esiste il volo Milano-Tarifa. Bisogna fare Milano-Malaga, e da Malaga prendere un pullman, e poi il taxi. A Tarifa c'erano dei nostri amici, leggermente meno poveri di noi – cioè, almeno mangiavano –, che avevano affittato un appartamento in sei. Noi non avevamo i soldi neanche per quello.

Arrivati a Tarifa, non avendo prenotato niente, non troviamo posto da nessuna parte. E così scopro cos'è l'ostello della gioventù: non viaggiando non ne avevo mai visto uno. Entro in questo posto convinto di entrare in un brutto hotel. Ci accompagnano in camera ma non ci danno le chiavi: non capivo perché. Entro nella stanza e mi ritrovo in mezzo a un sacco di gente. Chiedo: «Scusate, ma la camera?». In tutto ciò mi si rompe la valigia. O meglio: non mi ricordavo il codice del lucchetto, così ho chiesto un martello all'ostello e ho iniziato a prenderla a martellate, passando poi tutta la vacanza a trascinarmi dietro la valigia aperta. In più i nostri compagni di stanza puzzavano come fogne. La situazione era davvero da film horror: raggiungiamo i nostri amici nella casa che avevano preso in affitto, e li imploriamo di ospitarci. Loro accettano ma comunque si tratterà purtroppo di una vacanza molto breve. Non so ora, ma ai tempi a Tarifa la popolazione era, in gran parte, stile sinti e giostrai. Questi uomini dal codino, alla Roberto Baggio, un po' gipsy, per intenderci. La seconda sera, per fare qualcosa, decidiamo di andare in uno dei mercatini locali: ci sediamo su una panchina e davanti a noi compaiono due ragazzini della nostra età, un po' più giovani di noi forse, dal mood giostrai, appunto. Iniziano a fissarci. Noi eravamo in sei o sette: loro ci fissano, noi facciamo altrettanto. Eravamo di più, avevamo il vantaggio del gruppo. Andiamo a comprare le caramelle, ci risediamo sulla panchina e i due riprendono a guardarci e ridere. Non capiamo perché. A questo punto il mio amico writer riesce a dire la cosa più sbagliata: «Io lo so perché stanno ridendo ma non vi dico perché». A posteriori so che era completamente falso, lo diceva solo per mettere zizzania. Ma in quel momento la sua mossa attecchisce. Ci dice: «Ci hanno sputato sulla panchina, siamo seduti sullo sputo». Al che uno dei nostri amici piglia, si alza e va a prenderli a schiaffi. I due ragazzini a quel punto ci guardano e ci dicono: «Aspettateci qua». E noi decidiamo di fare la cosa più saggia di tutte se sei in villeggiatura in un Paese straniero e dei locali poco raccomandabili ti dicono di aspettare là: decidiamo di aspettarli davvero. Passano alcuni minuti e arrivano una decina di ragazzini, sempre sui quattordici anni. Erano piccoli: noi tutti a ridere, a dire «che cazzo volete». Solo che poi, subito a seguire, arrivano anche una ventina di tipi della nostra età, e già iniziamo a preoccuparci. Poi arrivano due trentenni, uno, ricordo, col dente d'oro.

Qui va chiarito il mio ruolo in questa vicenda: totalmente passivo. Non volevo trovarmi in quella situazione, non avevo fatto nulla di male, tanto che, mentre tutti discutevano sotto un porticato, e le cose si mettevano sempre peggio, io ero in un angolo in disparte a farmi i fatti miei, perché proprio non ero parte della faccenda. A un certo punto i due trentenni, da dietro, iniziano a prendere a pugni il mio amico. Al che cominciamo a scappare, ma la domanda che io mi facevo, mentre correvo, era: "Scappare dove, che sono qua da un giorno e non so niente di questo posto e di che strada fare per tornare a casa?". In più, dato che io stavo in disparte, ho iniziato a correre più tardi rispetto agli altri. Tanto che, mentre scappo, mi rendo conto che sto correndo di fianco agli aggressori dei miei amici. Per rimediare prendo e mi butto di lato, verso il molo. Era tutto scuro, il mare nero. E io avevo delle scarpe giallo evidenziatore, una giacca con delle stelline arancio fluo e il cappellino verde. In pratica illuminavo tutt'attorno a me. Nel panico mi nascondo dietro un muretto, e mi dico: "Che culo, me la sono sfangata. Vuoi vedere che sono il più intelligente della compagnia?". Faccio capolino da dietro il muro per vedere se qualcuno mi stia seguendo e ai miei occhi si presenta questa scena: un tizio che cammina con un ombrellone in mano e un'andatura da zombie, vagamente zoppo, e altri tipi con dei bastoni. Il problema era che, dopo il muretto, c'erano un tratto di mare e poi un altro muretto. Mi rendo conto che dovrei fare un salto troppo rischioso. Ma la paura, si sa, risveglia l'istinto animale: mi lancio e riesco, fracassandomi un ginocchio, ad approdare sull'altro muretto. Mi dico: "Sono salvo". Con grande fatica e il ginocchio sanguinante, giro l'angolo e lì trovo una recinzione con dietro tutto il paese che mi aspetta. Una marea di gente. La roba estenuante è stata dover aspettare che, uno per uno, tutti scavalcassero la recinzione per venire da me. Ci tengo a fare un plauso alla popolazione di Tarifa, comunque, perché sono stato picchiato in modo gentile: non hanno optato per l'approccio cavolfiore o petalo di rosa, quando ti inglobano e te le danno tutti insieme: hanno preferito la tecnica del "mi metto in fila, ti dico una frase in spagnolo e ti do un pugno". Avevo il sangue che mi colava ma non sentivo dolore, avevo l'adrenalina a mille: la fila era lunga, erano davvero in tanti, così a un certo punto, per cercare di interrompere la cosa, fingo di avere le convulsioni. All'ennesimo pugno mi butto a terra e inizio a tremare: non so se ci hanno creduto o gli ho solo fatto pena, in ogni caso ha funzionato. Mi rubano le scarpe e vanno via. Io mi ritrovo scalzo, sporco di sangue e senza sapere la strada per tornare a casa. In lontananza vedo una volante della polizia: trascinandomi mi avvicino, la fermo e chiedo di essere portato a casa. Solo che poi, durante il viaggio, mi rendo conto del passo falso: i miei amici erano pieni di fumo nell'appartamento. Quindi li chiamo, e senza far capire niente agli agenti cerco di avvisarli, in modo che nascondano il tutto. I poliziotti intanto decidono di fare una piccola pausa in un bar. Io rimango in macchina, coi finestrini aperti. Aspetto, aspetto, finché non mi ritrovo davanti alcuni di quelli che mi avevano picchiato. Stavano andando in giro in branco in cerca dei miei amici. Circondano la macchina e iniziano a deridermi. Uno di loro, prima di andarsene, mi allunga un oggetto: era la scarpa di un mio amico. Alla fine, a ogni modo, riesco a tornare a casa: i miei amici si incazzano perché gli ho portato gli sbirri. Ma ce la caviamo senza conseguenze e ci riprendiamo dal delirio. Però il problema, a quel punto, è: cosa fare nei successivi sette giorni di vacanza, dato che c'è un paese intero che ci vuole ammazzare di botte?

La risposta che ci siamo dati è stata: rimanere in casa a giocare ai videogiochi e fumare gli ovuli. Ovuli che ci portavano due gemelli del tutto rispettosi della tradizione di Tarifa, e cioè andare in Marocco a recuperare gli ovuli, ingoiarli per poi tornare indietro ed espellerli lì, in Spagna. Solo che in quei giorni qualcosa era andato storto: uno dei gemelli era riuscito a farli uscire, l'altro no. E infatti aveva un colorito decisamente verdastro. Non so se si è più ripreso. Siamo rimasti rintanati tutto il tempo, ma ogni tanto in qualche modo bisognava mangiare. Io e il mio amico writer avevamo finito i soldi, quindi mi sono dovuto ingegnare. Pantaloni ascellari, cappellino in testa e fingendo di essere claudicante, andavo a fare la spesa, ovvero andavo a rubare. Non sono mai stato un bravo ladro, quindi puntavo a saccheggiare l'angolo più nascosto del supermarket: quello di budini e crème caramel. Per sette giorni ho mangiato solo quello. E qui torna significativa la questione dell'itinerario per andare e tornare da Tarifa: taxi, pullman, aeroporto. Un viaggio lungo, a tappe. E se mangi per una settimana crème caramel le conseguenze sull'apparato digestivo sono quelle che tutti potete immaginare. La provvidenza però si è ricordata di me: sul pullman, tipo oasi nel deserto, perché non avevo ancora mai visto un pullman che ce lo avesse, c'era anche il bagno. Credo che a Tarifa la vita mi abbia voluto dare una lezione, che non so quale sia, e comunque temo di non averla imparata.

I più disagiati di Milano

La vita in sé non ha senso, solo guardandola dalla fine, da un punto di vista privilegiato possiamo creare una narrazione, mettere al loro posto degli episodi e tracciare un arco del personaggio. Ci permette di dire: ah ecco perché ha fatto questa cosa, a posteriori. Mi sento un po' così ripercorrendo quella fase della mia vita adesso. Quand'ero lì nel mezzo non aveva senso, non aveva senso Niccolò, la scuola, la vacanza a Tarifa né l'invito a cercare un lavoro da parte di mia mamma, ma oggi quella vita alla Charles Bukowski, quelle avventure di paura e delirio sono il terreno in cui mi sono davvero formato come artista. Infatti, in quel periodo più che un lavoro io cercavo la musica. Le droghe, le risse o l'abbandono della scuola potevano essere un sintomo di quell'esigenza di evasione, quel desiderio di trovare un senso, ma la musica no, la musica era invece la causa, era la propulsione a fare qualcosa di diverso, a non omologarmi, a elaborare in qualcosa di concreto quella profonda necessità di emancipazione che provavo.

A Milano c'era un luogo dove le persone più disagiate si incontravano, ma non pensate alla solita periferia. È il

Muretto, in pieno centro, accanto a corso Vittorio Emanuele, dove una scala ti portava dritto al McDonald's. Un po' un luogo storico, quasi simbolico, per il rap di varie generazioni.

Per diverso tempo c'erano stati solo rapper e breaker. E per fermare i breaker, ricordo, il Comune aveva piazzato sul pavimento una serie di lastre metalliche dorate, così che si facessero male ai gomiti quando ballavano. Ma noi eravamo già la generazione di quelli a cui non fregava molto della cultura hip hop classica: quindi c'erano rapper, ma anche magrebini (che stavano molto coi rapper), rumeni e albanesi insieme, i neri, e poi, più verso il Duomo, c'erano i pigoldini, quelli che andavano al P:Gold, a una serata che si chiamava "Pervert", caratterizzata da ragazzini piastrati con felpe piene di stelline fluo che si sfondavano di pastiglie e dicevano tutti di essere bisex, perché andava di moda dirlo. Erano gli emo che si facevano di MDMA e ballavano la tech-house di Obi Baby.

Al Muretto c'erano tanti ragazzi delle comunità, o che comunque vivevano un po' ai margini. I vari sottogruppi mal coesistevano in quel corridoio umano molto stretto, ma noi, i rapper, eravamo un po' la Svizzera: parlavamo con chiunque. Tra tutti, ricordo che c'era Cosmin, il rumeno con l'istinto da ladro, che se ti chiedeva in prestito il cellulare finivi sempre per dovergli ricordare: «Cosmin, dove hai messo il mio telefono?». «Ah scusa, deformazione professionale» rispondeva, mentre cercava di fregare anche noi, i suoi amici. Con gli estranei, invece, di gentilezza ne aveva poca.

Questo ecosistema vedeva noi, disagiati, incrociare la Milano bene che faceva shopping proprio lì dietro. Il centro della città, le élite, toccavano con mano le periferie, quelli che cercavano quotidianamente in tutti i modi di non vedere, di marginalizzare. Gli servivamo per alimentare il loro benessere finché facevamo lavori sottopagati, ma quando ci vedevano lì, a casa loro, non erano più così contenti. C'erano le Messaggerie Musicali, i negozi fighi di abbigliamento. I ben vestiti incontravano i mal vestiti, e talvolta i ben vestiti diventavano mal vestiti. Non che io volessi fare il moralista, il puro, ma spesso stavo fuori dalle dinamiche più a rischio. Al massimo, mentre facevo freestyle, Cosmin arrivava con la refurtiva e io nascondevo il bottino. Puntualmente spuntava un ragazzo in lacrime, senza giacca, che chiedeva se avessimo visto qualcosa. «Non ho visto niente, mi dispiace» era la risposta unanime. La polizia ci faceva spesso visita, il questore ci conosceva tutti.

La scena rap underground di quegli anni era lì, i più forti del freestyle erano al Muretto: Piuma, Cianuro, in quel periodo i numeri uno. Anche se poi non sono riusciti ad avere successo. Da lì siamo usciti solo io ed Emis Killa. Ci sono passati anche i Club Dogo, Vacca, Kaos One, ma era la generazione prima della nostra. Quel posto è un pezzo di storia: se eri un rapper emergente, finivi lì per forza, anche se eri del Sud. Ragazzi di tutta Italia venivano a sfidarsi a freestyle, in cerchio, insultandosi le madri.

Non si andava a scuola e si andava invece al Muretto. Ci si piantava lì fino alle sei o sette di sera. Non oltre: dopo, il posto diventava una tana di scarafaggi.

Così, a una certa ora, migravamo verso la "vietta", altro punto di ritrovo, vicino alle Colonne di San Lorenzo. Una via lunga e stretta che porta al parco Vetra. Lì si mescolavano tutti: noi del Muretto e quelli che venivano dai quartieri di Giambologna, da via Antonini, Corvetto, Prealpi. Una fauna varia. Una sera ero lì con tre amici, di fronte al parcheggio dei motorini, mentre il resto della banda era nascosto dietro un muro. Arrivano questi sei-sette tipi su scooter Scarabeo con le ragazze. Si fermano, ci guardano storto e dicono: «Che cazzo guardate?». Non sapevano che dietro il muro c'erano i nostri. Tre, due, uno, e gli rubiamo tutto: motorini, giacche, tutto quanto. Il giorno dopo sui giornali: "La gang delle Colonne di San Lorenzo".

È al Muretto che ho iniziato a fare davvero musica: provando, fallendo, scrivendo cose buone o cose di merda.

Non giocare mai in tre a "Final Fantasy"

Avevo diciassette anni: un mio amico, writer e skater, si ritrova senza casa. Aveva la mamma malata di tumore al cervello, a cui avevano assegnato una casa dell'Aler a Crescenzago, non lontano da Loreto. Casa sfitta da anni, di cui però non si decidevano a darci le chiavi. Così decidiamo di sfondare la porta e occuparla. Non so se fosse proprio legale. Ci ritroviamo una casa in condizioni pietose: topi, scarafaggi, polvere, materassi luridi di tutti i colori. Il mio amico decide di entrare in questa casa così com'è. Ho dormito più volte in mezzo a quello schifo. Una volta abbiamo pranzato e ricordo il portaposate: pensavo fosse stato pulito, guardo e dentro c'erano i vermi. In quel periodo non ero schizzinoso. Comunque, piano piano la situazione si inizia a sistemare, cominciamo a buttare un po' di roba, i mobili messi peggio. Non è che ci vivessi proprio: dormivo dai miei, ma passavo le giornate lì.

A un certo punto lui trova un coinquilino, che era un mio amico, Fadamat, altro rapper. Famoso perché aveva fatto un album che si chiamava *Mister Nice* e diceva in giro che Fabri Fibra gli aveva copiato il personaggio di Mister Simpatia. Dinamica a cui io non credo: semplicemente Fibra era più bravo di lui. Era un ragazzo più grande di noi: io ed Emis Killa gli facevamo le doppie, era uno un po' intrallazzato nella scena rap. Più famoso di me, in quel momento. Quando lui e il mio amico iniziano a convivere, io porto una Playstation 1, o forse 2, e loro di fatto passano le giornate a fumare e giocare ai videogiochi. Qui si aggiunge la figura di G.: non ricordo bene da dove fosse saltato fuori, frequentava la nostra compagnia del Muretto, lo conoscevo solo di vista. Era un tizio molto alto, magrissimo, la faccia da Frankenstein, gli occhiali, veramente brutto. Credo non abbia, a oggi, ancora scopato. G. era facilmente soggiogabile, diciamo, tanto che viene convinto ad andare a vivere a casa di questi due ragazzi e a pagare un affitto per dormire in una casa che era una casa occupata. E nemmeno in una camera: gli hanno messo una brandina di fianco alla cucina. Quello tra i due e G. era, in sostanza, un rapporto di dominanza. Veniva bullizzato, picchiato per nulla, costretto a fare cose terribili.

Un giorno succede questo: loro giocavano continuamente a "Final Fantasy", avevano una memory card in comune e ognuno si salvava la sua partita. G. è alla Playstation, arriva Fadamat e gli dice: «Togliti che adesso gioco io. Muoviti sennò ti meno». G. gli risponde: «Salvo e te lo do». Ricordo che Fadamat si siede, si fa una canna e dice: «Dov'è finito il mio salvataggio vecchio?». Sulla card c'erano solo i salvataggi di G. Fadamat inizia a dare i numeri: «Io passo la mia vita a giocare a "Final Fantasy", ho perso un mese di vita». Quindi inizia a menarlo, e gli dice: «Adesso mi ripaghi il danno». Quel minutaggio giocato e perduto si converte allora in soldi, in un debito monetario che a quel punto G. ha nei confronti di Fadamat. Non avendo una lira, G. decide di barattare il debito con ore lavorative: gli lavava la biancheria, gli stirava la roba, gli puliva la camera.

Poi però è arrivato il jolly, ovvero: G. aveva l'opportunità di scalare un maggior numero di ore facendo delle cose particolari decise da Fadamat. Fu una delle cose più umilianti viste in vita mia: eravamo in camera di Fadamat, con un altro amico, Enzi, che ai tempi era famosissimo, a fargli sentire un po' di pezzi nostri. Per intrattenere Enzi, Fadamat chiama G. e gli dice: «Fai degli orgasmi». Lui ha ubbidito. Per farsi scalare, non so, cento euro, G. era in mezzo alla stanza, con delle persone che non aveva mai visto, a fingere degli orgasmi. Lo racconto perché oggi vorrei sapere che fine ha fatto G., mi piacerebbe sapere la sua storia e se è riuscito a non uccidere nessuno dopo aver subito tutto questo: credo, e spero, sia diventato un serial killer di successo.

Sputavo nel caffè

Sono stati anni strani quelli, anni a volte di noia, a volte di euforia, di creazione e di ozio, gli anni che per tutti, anche per chi fa l'ingegnere o l'idraulico, sono gli anni di formazione. Le cose le impari a vent'anni o non le impari mai più. Fatto sta che io ero senza un soldo e con i miei genitori a un passo dal perdere la casa perché le rate del mutuo li stavano schiacciando.

Una sera mi chiamano, sento quella voce che già sai che qualcosa non va, mi dicono: «Federico, svegliati, datti una mossa o la musica te la scordi». Ero iscritto a una di quelle scuole di recupero per chi si è giocato gli anni scolastici. Ma era la versione povera. La versione premium, quella per i ricchi, funzionava che tu ti andavi a iscrivere a una scuola tipo a Napoli, facevi finta di studiare durante l'anno qui, poi tornavi a Napoli, loro ti davano le risposte e tu passavi l'esame. Però costava, troppo. Invece io andavo alla versione povera: corsi a caso, in un indirizzo che non c'entrava una mazza con l'arte che avevo studiato prima. Come il cinema, io non sapevo niente di cinema. Alla fine dovevi fare l'esame come privatista: pensate andare a fare la maturità in una scuola pubblica, dove non ti conosce nessuno, avendo studiato poco e le cose sbagliate. Era la scuola dei disadattati, raccoglieva gli scarti e i casi problematici di tutta Milano. Il ricordo più bello che ho di quei giorni è di quando ho visto un compagno di classe, completamente fatto per le canne che fumavamo, alle otto del mattino sul balcone dell'istituto, che dava sull'Arco della Pace, lanciare una lattina piena di Coca-Cola contro un'auto degli sbirri. I poliziotti si fermano, salgono e iniziano a fare un interrogatorio e tutta una predica sull'omertà, avvertendoci che il silenzio ci avrebbe resi complici di attività mafiose (spoiler: nessuno ha parlato).

Ogni giorno, dopo la "scuola", lavoravo al bar che i miei genitori avevano incautamente comprato, facendo ciò che detestavo di più: interagire con gli esseri umani. E il bar ne attraeva di tutti i tipi: i gentili e i maleducati. Ce n'era uno in particolare, un operaio di Copenaghen, che lavorava in zona. Me lo ricordo ancora, ogni volta arrivava al bancone e, per chiamarmi, schioccava le dita. Chiedeva sempre un caffè macchiato. Servire le persone per me era un inferno, non è proprio la mia cosa, come è facile capire a chiunque mi conosca da più di cinque minuti. Per vendicarmi sputavo nei caffè. Per non farti beccare, piccolo tutorial, non puoi semplicemente sputarci dentro direttamente: se sputi al momento, la saliva galleggia. Ti beccano al cento per cento. Quindi io preparavo una tazzina personalizzata per questo tizio, solo per lui, già sputata. Dopo un po' di tempo, siccome veniva tutti i giorni, ormai sapevo a che ora sarebbe arrivato. La mettevo nel banco frigo dove tenevo il latte (appunto perché lui, il caffè, lo chiedeva sempre macchiato).

Quando prendevo il latte prendevo anche la sua tazzina speciale e, come se niente fosse, con grande nonchalance gli facevo il caffè.

In quel periodo, a un certo punto, decido di tentare il tutto per tutto. Dovevo produrre il mio primo disco. Lascio la "scuola", che ormai era diventata un luogo senza senso, e insieme a Silvia, la mia ragazza di allora – con cui, per inciso, siamo in ottimi rapporti –, troviamo un piccolo locale in comodato d'uso. Era un'offerta da parte di un'amica ebrea di sua madre, situato in un angolo non proprio stupendo di Milano, piazzale Selinunte. Decidiamo di lanciarci: un negozio di tatuaggi. Io facevo lo store manager, cioè prendevo gli appuntamenti, mentre Silvia tatuava. Con i primi soldi guadagnati mi sono comprato una videocamera, una Canon da ottocento euro. Ho imparato da solo a girare e montarmi i video. Ed è stato allora che, con altri mille euro che avevo tirato su, ho registrato *Penisola che non c'è*, in cui parlavo quasi solo di politica, tutto riflessioni sociali. Un territorio pressoché inesplorato dai rapper della mia generazione, in Italia, tutti fissati con denaro e virilità. In quel periodo andavano molto Marracash, i Club Dogo: ho il cazzo grosso, ho i soldi, un po' quello che va adesso. La trap alla fine non è che sia così diversa da quello che c'era all'epoca. Io scelsi una strada solo mia, concentrandomi su ciò che realmente mi interessava. Contro ogni previsione, nonostante quelle tematiche, il successo è straordinario. Sono riuscito a emergere.

Penisola che non c'è uscì lo stesso anno dell'esplosione del mixtape, negli Usa, di Wiz Khalifa, quello di *Black and Yellow*. Khalifa pubblicò i dati dei download, in America, e io facevo più o meno i suoi stessi numeri, ma in Italia. Era folle.

Dopo *Penisola che non c'è*, intanto, pubblicai *Jet set*, un video che fece crollare i server di YouTube Italia a causa del traffico senza precedenti. Diventai la parola più cercata su Google a livello nazionale. Quando lo racconto oggi i miei amici mi prendono per il culo, ma è vero. Il video fece il record di visualizzazioni nelle ventiquattro ore. I server di YouTube in Italia non reggevano quel quantitativo: spalmarono le visualizzazioni su vari Paesi e, quando cliccavi, e si illuminavano le mappe delle nazioni, figurava che c'era gente che guardava i miei video, non so, in Kazakistan. Oggettivamente non aveva senso. Infatti circolarono accuse di statistiche manipolate, numeri truccati, che spinsero YouTube a confermare ufficialmente l'autenticità delle visualizzazioni. Ci fu uno, ricordo, che aveva un canale anonimo, con la voce camuffata, tutto contro di me. E diventò supervirale, questa cosa. Era tutto vero, però. *Jet Set* fu il video più visto dell'anno. E tutto questo da indipendente. Ho ottenuto un successo mainstream senza firmare con un'etichetta: mi montavo uno dopo l'altro i video a casa e facevo numeri da major.

Il mio primo concerto al Leoncavallo, quattordici anni fa, è stato uno spettacolo; mi hanno salutato come un rivoluzionario, un Che Guevara dell'era digitale. Gli instore erano affollatissimi, con la fila chilometrica che prendeva intere vie, e tutto semplicemente annunciando l'evento su internet. Non andavo in televisione, non avevo un ufficio stampa. Non c'era ancora neanche Instagram, in rete avevo detto alla gente: "Ci vediamo oggi e firmo le copie del mio disco in free download".

In rete il video dell'instore milanese c'è: una marea di gente, tutti urlano e mi salutano, nessuno ha il telefono in mano.

Iniziare da indipendente mi ha fatto fare più soldi: sono arrivato in major che valevo dieci volte di più.

L'inizio della fine

È strano a dirsi, da fuori non si direbbe probabilmente, ma io non ho mai cercato l'ebbrezza della celebrità, del successo. Quei numeri che crescevano, quelle persone che cantavano le mie canzoni, i soldi che entravano non mi hanno mai dato una sensazione di onnipotenza. E, forse, è una delle poche cose per cui devo dire grazie al mio temperamento infelice, al mio pessimismo innato, che per molte questioni è controproducente ma per la gestione di quella botta di adrenalina che ti dà il successo secondo me è indispensabile, altrimenti perdere la rotta è questione di un secondo. Ti credi 'sto cazzo e il gioco si rompe.

Io, invece, ho sempre vissuto le fasi più alte della mia carriera come l'inizio della fine. Io convivo quotidianamente con la fobia del fallimento e non importano i dischi di platino, gli stadi, Sanremo o i soldi, ogni volta riparto da zero, ogni disco, ogni canzone, ogni singolo verso che scrivo è come se lo scrivesse sempre il me di vent'anni fa, quello che nessuno ascoltava, quello odiato, quello a cui tutti dicevano che non ce l'avrebbe mai fatta. Eppure questa perenne sensazione di precarietà è il fuoco che alimenta la mia creatività, mi spinge a cercare di fare sempre qualcosa di diverso, a prevedere cosa potrà succedere nella musica, a capire quali tendenze si imporranno per non diventare vecchio, logoro, inutile. Ho sempre vissuto tutto cercando di prevenire quello che arriva dopo, e le mie previsioni non sono mai positive, quindi anche quei primi anni di successo, come poi tutti i momenti più alti, li ho sempre vissuti come l'inizio della fine, cioè come l'orlo del baratro, e non la conquista di una vetta.

Avevo poco più di vent'anni, ed ero già famoso, un astro nascente del rap, e tutti i rapper mi amavano (è durata poco, una fase, breve ma intensa, di cui ho nostalgia). Ero sotto l'etichetta di Guè e DJ Harsh, Ghali mi faceva le doppie ed era uno dei miei migliori amici. In quel periodo, parentesi, Ghali era il rapper più odiato della scena, perché aveva fatto uscire un video col suo gruppo, i Troupe d'Elite, di cui faceva parte anche Ernia. Erano odiati senza apparente motivo, il pezzo non era grandissimo ma nemmeno una merda. Erano stati insultati da tutti, l'unico a difenderli pubblicamente ero stato io. Guè se ne sbatteva. Spero che Ghali abbia ricordi di quel periodo come li ho io.

In quei giorni, dicevo, avevo ricevuto la mia prima mazzetta di soldi veri, guadagnati con date e dj set. Ho dato quasi tutto ai miei genitori perché saldassero i loro debiti. Con quelli avanzati mi sono ritrovato i miei primi diecimila euro in tasca: mi sentivo ricchissimo. Così sono andato a Forte dei Marmi, con i soldi, Ghali, Ernia e qualche altro amico al seguito. Ricordo il problema di quella vacanza: ero già molto famoso tra i giovanissimi, ma non abbastanza da potermi permettere una guardia del corpo. Quando andavamo in giro beccavamo o gente che mi diceva "grande" o gente che mi diceva "sei un coglione". Pollice in su o dito medio. Ghali, devo dire grande amico, non si risparmiava mai se qualcuno mi insultava. Alla prima parola storta si lanciava e si andava a picchiare. E aveva questo strano superpotere: sanguinare dal naso anche al tocco più leggero. Bastava guardarlo per farlo sanguinare. Una spinta? Sangue. Nuotare? Sangue. Qualunque cosa facessimo, sanguinava a secchiate.

La vacanza, insomma, fu vivace: passai il Ferragosto nel recinto del kids club di uno stabilimento, circondato da gente. Era impossibile vivere. È stato in mezzo a quel caos che ho scritto il testo di *Pensavo fosse amore e invece...* Conobbi questa ragazza molto carina, che aveva un tenore di vita stranamente alto. Faceva sesso con me gratuitamente ma con gli altri, ho scoperto, no. Una sera ci fu proprio l'apice: credo che ancora alla Capannina si ricordino di questa rissa, perché fu bellissima. Ero con Ghali e gli altri. E in discoteca c'era questo tizio, a torso nudo, che mi chiedeva di firmargli i capezzoli. A palese presa per il culo. Io sorrido e me ne vado. Parte una discussione col gruppo di questo ragazzo. Ghali spinge uno contro un tavolino di vetro, che va in frantumi. Ma i proprietari, non si capisce perché, cacciano fuori gli altri ragazzi, non noi. Poi però sono arrivati i poliziotti per portare via Ghali: io, totalmente ubriaco, riesco a fare una requisitoria e a convincerli a non portarselo via. Siamo rimasti lì fino a tardi. Solo che a quel punto all'esterno c'era una folla che ci stava aspettando. Un buttafuori ci ha avvisato: «Le sentite tutte queste persone qua fuori? Sono qui per pestare voi». Come a Tarifa, ma al posto dei giostrai c'era la gente dei locali di Forte dei Marmi, con la camicia bianca e i mocassini. La sicurezza ci ha suggerito di sgattaiolare via dalla spiaggia, passando per le cucine. Così, ho lanciato le chiavi della Peugeot 207 di mia madre, che avevo sfondato contro un guardrail nel viaggio per arrivare fin lì, alla ragazza probabile sex worker, chiedendole di andare a recuperare l'auto e dandole appuntamento due bagni più avanti. Pensavo che i buttafuori, dicendoci "vi accompagniamo", ci scortassero fino alla macchina. Invece aprono il cancelletto e ci chiudono fuori: noi eravamo in quattro o cinque, tra cui Ghali, completamente al buio, in mezzo agli ombrelloni. A dividerci dalle persone che volevano aggredirci c'era solo un lembo di spiaggia. Non sapevamo come uscirne. Nessuno fiatava perché altrimenti ci avrebbero sentiti immediatamente. Ma di colpo Ghali, preso dalla paranoia, inizia a dire a raffica: «Sono qui, sono qui, sono qui». Al che ci nascondiamo tutti sotto i lettini del bagno, per renderci poi conto che in realtà Ghali non aveva visto nessuno.

Ne siamo usciti incolumi, ma l'estate ha continuato a essere movimentata: DJ Harsh a un certo punto viene a Forte dei Marmi perché era previsto un dj set di Salmo, Gemitaiz, MadMan ed Ensi. In quel periodo, come ho detto, molti avevano insultato il gruppo di Ghali ed Ernia, tra questi anche il tour manager di Salmo, Stevie Lametti, che lavorava per l'etichetta mia e dei Troupe d'Elite stessi. Li aveva insultati su Facebook e noi eravamo incazzati neri e non vedevamo l'ora di incontrarlo per sistemare le cose. La scena fu questa: lui seduto su un muretto, con Ghali che lo affronta. «Dài, cos'è che dovevi dirmi?», e fa la mossa alzando il braccio, come per dargli un pugno. Il tizio, spaventato, si ribalta, cade all'indietro al di là del muretto. Scoppia un casino, si mettono in mezzo altre persone. Ensi voleva prendermi a schiaffi, ed era il doppio di me: poteva benissimo farlo, ma non l'ha fatto, quindi colgo l'occasione per ringraziarlo. A un certo punto ci diamo appuntamento davanti a un hotel per la resa dei conti, l'atto finale, davvero con le peggiori intenzioni. Se non che Salmo mi chiama per dirmi che ha sonno: «Andiamo a letto, non litighiamo». Morale della storia: se Salmo è il più saggio, figurati gli altri.

"X Factor" in MD

Insomma, sì, sono anni movimentati, divertenti, euforici, ma come dicevo con la perenne sensazione che dovessero finire da un momento all'altro, quindi da una parte li vivevo con la fame insaziabile di chi non vuole perdersi nulla e dall'altra con la leggerezza incosciente di chi dice chissenefrega, tanto l'apocalisse è dietro l'angolo. Avevo ventiquattro anni, era appena uscito *Sig. Brainwash*, il mio primo disco sotto major. Ero ancora apprezzato dagli altri rapper. Di quel periodo ricordo i dischi d'oro per terra, nella casa che condividevo con uno dei pochi ancora oggi miei amici, Denny LaHome (quello che ho conosciuto al Cantiere), che veniva anche in tour con me. Abitavamo insieme a casa della nonna di Charlie Charles, in via Savona. Casa arredata anni Sessanta, molto bella (spaccava, sembrava un club d'epoca per scambisti), ma con la moquette tutta zozza.

Comunque, era quel periodo quando una volta, al The Club, un mio amico mi fa bere da una bottiglietta e poi mi dice: «Dentro c'era l'MD!». Io mi prendo male: era già tardi. Penso: "Se mi sale a quest'ora, non dormo più". Nel mentre finiamo pure a casa con delle tipe. Premessa: quando prendo l'MD io regredisco a bambino di sei anni. E infatti ho passato la serata a fissare ipnotizzato degli adesivi dei Pokémon che brillavano sul muro.

A un certo punto provo ad andare in camera mia, ma trovo un mio amico che sta scopando. Mi dice: «Partecipa anche tu». Ma io sono regredito a un'età presessuale. Quindi prendo e torno ai miei adesivi sul muro. Poi ci ripenso: rivado in camera e trovo lei sdraiata, lui in piedi, nudi. Mi avvicino a lei, le do una pacchetta sulla pancia, tipo: "Uè, come va?". Ma mi rendo conto che la sua pancia è ricoperta dei loro fluidi corporei, soprattutto di quello del mio amico. Disgustato, vado in bagno a lavarmi con tutto quello che trovo: alcol, detersivi, candeggina, qualsiasi cosa, e mi ricordo che dallo schifo mi metto un guanto da forno sulla mano, e dormo così tutta la notte.

Alle dieci avevo appuntamento in Sony per parlare con la curatrice di "X Factor", Eliana Guerra. Il problema è che mi sveglio ed ero ancora fatto, con le iridi completamente nere (come a Sanremo, ma non per via delle lenti a contatto), alteratissimo. In quel periodo la sede della Sony Music era in via Larga. Gli ascensori erano veramente piccoli e stretti, mentre saliamo per andare all'appuntamento il mio manager di allora, Franco Godi, mi guarda in faccia e mi dice: «Federico, ma che occhi neri che hai». Era il provino per fare il quinto giudice in una puntata speciale, solo l'anno dopo sarei entrato nel cast fisso del programma.

Arrivo, mi siedo, vedo Eliana Guerra, ed ero veramente teso: non volevo sembrare fatto. Per avere l'aria di un ragazzo intelligente, sagace, adatto al ruolo, la prima cosa che mi viene da fare è gridare: «Comunque "Amici di Maria" fa cagare». Poteva finire tutto lì, invece quelli del programma accolgono con grande entusiasmo questa mia uscita. La situazione prende una piega positiva, solo che io non riesco a stare fermo. Avevo le mani esagitate, continuavo a far roteare il telefonino con un dito. L'ho fatto girare così velocemente che a un certo punto mi è volato via. È andato a sbattere contro il muro e si è sfasciato. Comunque, gli sono piaciuto.

Se ti chiedono una foto spera che non ci siano bottiglie nei paraggi

Avevo da poco partecipato per la prima volta come giudice a "X Factor", e avevo dato la stura alla mia vena politica: erano iniziati gli scontri diretti con gli esponenti dei partiti. Qualche mese prima Gasparri mi aveva dato del tossicodipendente, del "coso dipinto", e aveva insultato una mia fan. Non mi ero ancora reso conto di cosa fosse il Movimento 5 Stelle: avevo pensato e sperato che potesse salvare questo Paese dalla rovina, invece ha contribuito solo a rovinarlo ancora di più.

Il mio primo disco, *Penisola che non c'è*, è totalmente incentrato sulla politica: ovviamente è un'analisi fatta da un cantante di vent'anni, non il saggio di un politologo, ma il tema era quello. Era un grido di denuncia, la prospettiva personale di un ragazzo che viveva gli anni del berlusconismo e l'ascesa dei 5 Stelle, il movimento di Grillo e Casaleggio che prometteva di incanalare la rabbia popolare in forme democratiche. Inizialmente vedevo in loro una speranza, una possibilità di cambiamento autentico. Col passare del tempo, la mia visione è mutata. Oggi credo che la presenza dei 5 Stelle abbia contribuito a sopire quella rabbia, anziché renderla il presupposto per una reale trasformazione. Il mio primo contatto diretto con il Movimento, da personaggio pubblico, avviene subito con Gianroberto Casaleggio. È lui ad avvicinarmi, vuole conoscermi, così vado alla sede del Movimento, che è nel cuore pulsante del lusso milanese di via Montenapoleone, lontano anni luce dall'immaginario di chi veniva dalla periferia e dai centri sociali. Casaleggio mi aveva colpito per le sue teorie: era un complottista bello estremo, ma con delle intuizioni geniali. Un po' il nostro Elon Musk, ma senza quella capacità imprenditoriale. Mi ricordo che la prima cosa che mi ha detto è stata: «Federico, devi stare attento alla stricnina». E io: «In che senso?». «È un veleno inodore, non te lo trovano nel sangue.» E ha aggiunto che Chávez era stato ucciso proprio con la stricnina. Di lì a poco ho scritto la prefazione del suo libro, un gesto che ha consolidato la nostra connessione intellettuale. Poi ovviamente ho conosciuto anche Beppe Grillo.

Va detto che fin da subito ho avuto contrasti anche con loro, nonostante per me fossero l'unica possibilità di voto, ma andavo per esclusione. Tutti pensano che io abbia scritto l'inno dei 5 Stelle: in realtà la mia collaborazione con il Movimento si tradusse in una canzone per un evento chiamato "Notte dell'onestà", un nome che evocava trasparenza e rinnovamento. Il tema era quello dei pregiudicati in parlamento: l'idea della manifestazione era bella, rispetto a valori e idee, ma dissi loro che mi sembrava un po' meno intelligente associarla ai simboli del partito. L'uso di quei simboli creava una divisione innaturale, una barriera tra "noi" e "loro" che andava contro lo spirito dell'iniziativa. Secondo me sarebbe stato meglio dare la possibilità anche a chi apparteneva ad altri partiti di partecipare a una protesta che era ipercondivisibile, trasversale. Il mio discorso in piazza del Popolo, davanti a centomila persone, fu così un tentativo di ricordare l'importanza di un'azione condivisa, libera dai simboli di partito, dalle tifoserie. Grillo si incazzò. Quella sera capii che il Movimento era già troppo immerso nelle dinamiche del potere per poter rappresentare un reale cambiamento: non era più un "portiamo le idee in piazza", promuovendo così una democrazia partecipativa e attiva, era questione di portarsi voti a casa. Erano già stati totalmente risucchiati dal palazzo. Da quel momento, pur mantenendo rapporti formali, ho iniziato a prenderne le distanze.

E anche a sinistra non ho certo avuto un'impressione tanto migliore. Con Matteo Renzi ho un rapporto molto travagliato. Quando lui era presidente del Consiglio, io avevo appena iniziato a frequentare Chiara, e insieme andammo alla prima di *Inferno*, tratto dal libro di Dan Brown, quello del *Codice da Vinci*. In quell'occasione Renzi fece un discorso inutile (e non si capisce perché il premier debba andare a parlare di politica prima della proiezione di un film che non c'entra niente), e io andai a pisciare: mentre pisciavo, dissi alla mia guardia del corpo una cosa del tipo: «Renzi ha fatto davvero un discorso stupido». Esco e chi mi trovo davanti? Renzi che si lava le mani. Non siamo mai stati amici. Lui è uno che non sa proprio gestire la permalosità, secondo me dovrebbe ritirarsi dalla politica e fare quello che sembra stia facendo ora: il consulente in Arabia Saudita.

E anche con Zan il discorso è complesso: tutti mi hanno descritto come "paladino arcobaleno", perché purtroppo, in questo Paese, ormai ogni cosa viene ridotta a un'etichetta. Ma se si va a riprendere il motivo per cui ho difeso la legge Zan, si scoprirà che non mi riferivo ai contenuti del disegno di legge: la mia critica era più verso il fatto che un singolo – il leghista Andrea Ostellari – stesse ostruendo il processo democratico. Forse è vero che tanti politici lo fanno, ma io credo sia sbagliato che un singolo abbia la facoltà di bloccare la macchina democratica. Non sono mai entrato nel merito dei contenuti del disegno di legge: tanto che, quando feci la diretta con Alessandro Zan, il passaggio in cui dichiarava di voler dare gli ormoni ai bambini me lo sono perso, non l'ho sentito. L'ho recuperato a posteriori. E su questo, per esempio, io sono totalmente in disaccordo. Il mio discorso sulla legge Zan, appunto, era a monte: prima ancora di discutere la legge, facciamo sì che l'iter democratico abbia il suo sviluppo normale e non venga ostacolato. Poi non si può negare che, prima che iniziassimo a parlarne io e Chiara, non ne parlava quasi nessuno.

Il tema della sinistra è che ti usa: chiaro, tutti in politica ti usano, ma quantomeno la destra, umanamente parlando, sa relazionarsi con le persone. Molti politici di destra sanno parlarti da persona a persona, mentre gli uomini di sinistra ti spolpano e dopo ti voltano le spalle. Sempre. Voltare le spalle non significa che io avrei voluto favori che poi non ho ricevuto: non li ho mai cercati. Ma quando sei in una situazione di difficoltà – vedi il caso Balocco – con quelli di destra puoi confrontarti, ci puoi parlare. Quelli di sinistra, se li chiami, non ti rispondono più. Sono meno affidabili, sempre umanamente parlando.

Poi, intendiamoci, fanno schifo tutti, la politica è quello che è, e la destra forse ha fatto più danni della sinistra (o se la pareggiano). Ma quando puzzi di merda quelli di sinistra si allontanano da te, invece quelli di destra, dato che alla puzza di merda ci sono abituati, riescono a continuare a rivolgerti la parola, non spariscono. E poi si sanno divertire molto di più degli altri. Sono oggettivamente più simpatici. E, per quanto siano delle merde, sono più pane al pane e vino al vino, se ti devono dire una cosa te la dicono, sono meno melliflui.

Ho sempre avuto più rapporti umani con persone che, nei fatti, hanno idee diverse dalle mie. Quando mi sono ammalato di cancro, per esempio, Salvini è stato quello da cui sentivo, quando mi scriveva, della vera empatia. E questo nonostante avessimo idee diverse e ce ne fossimo dette di tutti i colori. Per un mese, ogni settimana mi ha scritto per sapere come stavo. L'ho apprezzato. Il che non cambia la mia valutazione rispetto al Salvini politico, ma cambia la mia valutazione rispetto al Salvini uomo. Persone con cui avevo rapporti migliori invece non ci sono state: Di Maio, Conte, non pervenuti. Ti scrivono solo quando hanno bisogno di te, quando gli serve usarti.

Tornando alla lotta per la legge Zan, è sempre stata attribuita a me come se io fossi "Federico Arcobaleno", ma la verità è che non ho mai detto: "La legge Zan è una bomba". Per me era un provvedimento scritto male. Non ho grande stima di Alessandro Zan, credo che reciti una parte e, quando gli chiedi di partecipare a un confronto con Adinolfi, lui non lo fa: «Non devo avvicinarmi a questa gente sennò gli do popolarità». Invece è perché lo teme. Dialetticamente, Adinolfi lo uccide. E quindi apprezzo più Adinolfi, che nonostante abbia idee totalmente diverse dalle mie non si tira mai indietro di fronte a un confronto.

Non che a destra siano messi tanto meglio. L'unico mio rammarico è non aver conosciuto bene Berlusconi. A un certo punto fummo davvero a un passo dal portarlo a "Muschio selvaggio". Mi chiamò durante la pandemia per fare i complimenti, a me e Chiara, per quello che stavamo facendo. Per organizzare l'ospitata parlavo con Licia Ronzulli, ma ogni volta che stavamo per accordarci Berlusconi stava male e quindi non se n'è fatto niente. L'ho incontrato una volta, per caso, nel ristorante del papà di un compagno di classe di Leone. Ero con Chiara e ci disse, a me e a mia moglie: «C'è solo una persona più famosa di voi in Italia: io».

Morale: se ho mai pensato di impegnarmi attivamente in politica? No, al massimo, per me, qualche lavoro dietro le quinte. Più che dai politici, sono affascinato da figure che agiscono sotto, nell'ombra. Se rappo voglio stare sul palcoscenico, se agisco politicamente preferisco il dietro le quinte. Nei corridoi labirintici del potere italiano, i veri architetti del potere preferiscono gli angoli silenziosi delle retrovie ai riflettori. Personaggi come Gianni Letta e Luigi Bisignani incombono come i moderni Richelieu, orchestrando più di quanto appaia a livello superficiale. È un luogo comune che la politica sia l'apice del potere: sotto questa facciata si nasconde una forza più incisiva, un teatro nascosto di operazioni in cui le fila del controllo sono tirate da lontano. Il vero potere, ho capito, non risiede tra i palazzi della politica o nelle dichiarazioni pubbliche dei funzionari eletti. Prospera nell'ombra, in un regno in cui le decisioni vengono prese e i destini sono determinati non dai voti, ma dal silenzio.

Questo potere nascosto gioca un gioco molto simile a sasso-carta-forbici, e trionfa invariabilmente sulle istituzioni visibili della politica. È palpabile, tangibile, innegabilmente reale. Non posso divulgare dettagli specifici, entrare nel merito più di così: sono racconti che si avvicinano troppo all'intrigo nazionale. Ma ho assistito in prima persona al manifestarsi di questo potere nascosto. Non è roba da teorie del complotto: questi poteri occulti hanno volti, sono persone concrete, con due braccia e due gambe, non qualcosa di astratto.

Fatto sta che nel 2015, in quel periodo delle manifestazioni No Expo, ero un piccolo Che Guevara mentalmente instabile. Nel contesto delle proteste erano scaturite anche delle indagini legate a collaboratori di Beppe Sala. Manifestazioni normali, ma la stampa iniziò a dipingere Milano come se fosse diventata di colpo Beirut, quando in realtà succedevano le classiche cose che succedono in manifestazione: qualche scritta sul muro, qualche coro, nessuno scontro reale con la polizia. Mi sembrava tutto esagerato, pompato apposta. A un certo punto sento un mio amico di un centro sociale e gli chiedo di mandarmi, nello specifico, i temi per i quali protestavano. Tutti parlavano di una Milano messa a ferro e fuoco, quando non era neanche vero, ma nessuno parlava delle ragioni della protesta. Pubblico su Twitter questa sorta di manifesto, evidenziando che si trattava di una protesta legittima, basata su questioni concrete.

Il giorno dopo arrivano i black bloc a Milano e iniziano a vandalizzare macchine e vetrine in corso Magenta: secondo me i poliziotti decidono di stare a guardare, in segno di protesta contro la votazione sul reato di tortura, avvenuta qualche settimana prima. I giornali di destra prendono le mie dichiarazioni di Twitter sulla protesta confondendo le date, facendo sì che sembrasse che le avessi scritte *dopo* i fatti dei black bloc. Il sindaco Pisapia mi tira merda addosso, invitandomi ad andare a ripulire la città dai disastri. Io faccio un video e sputtano tutti. In quel periodo se facevi un video per spiegare qualcosa la gente più o meno ti ascoltava, c'era ancora un minimo di razionalità nel dibattito. Quindi sembrava che la cosa fosse risolta. Ma il giorno dopo è successo che delle lavoratrici precarie hanno lanciato un uovo al presidente del consiglio Matteo Renzi e sono state manganellate. Io ho pubblicato una foto di una di queste donne, col volto insanguinato, scrivendo: "A Milano black bloc lasciati liberi di agire, a Bologna donne precarie manganellate a sangue. Avete invertito gli ordini?". Mi risponde a questo tweet il profilo ufficiale del COISP – il sindacato di polizia che ha avuto l'ardire di offendere più volte la madre di Federico Aldrovandi, difendendo invece i suoi assassini –, scrivendomi: "Invertito ci sarai tu".

Cambio di scena: qualche giorno dopo, compleanno del mio amico Luca, andiamo a festeggiare al Just Cavalli, locale in cui avevo messo piede tre volte in vita mia. Non ero certo un habitué. Prendiamo un tavolo e di fianco a noi c'è un gruppo di ragazzi della Milano bene, tutti parecchio molesti. Uno viene a chiedermi una foto mentre sputazza, lo fa in modo palesemente provocatorio, per infastidirmi. Ci arriva anche addosso del ghiaccio. A un certo punto uno di questi, che stava spiaggiato su un divanetto, mezzo morto, tipo *Pulp Fiction*, di botto si rianima e corre verso di me gridando. Talmente eravamo dalla parte della ragione che anche i buttafuori del locale arrivano a malmenare questi tizi. Nel trambusto poi cadono delle bottiglie per terra, viene un ragazzo da me e mi dice: «Guarda che una ragazza del tavolo di fianco si è fatta male alla testa, perché è scivolata». Mi preoccupo, vado a vedere. Un taglio piccolo, ma necessitava di punti.

Era circondata di gente. Chiedo che sia portata in ospedale, e alla fine sono io a chiamare l'ambulanza, non rendendomi conto che i gestori del locale sono parecchio indispettiti, evidentemente non vogliono grane. Sono lì che cerco di telefonare ma mi strappano il cellulare dalle mani e un buttafuori mi molla un pugno in faccia, aggiungendo: «Tu da qua non esci vivo». Allora chiamo la polizia: mossa geniale. Arrivano sette volanti, e proprio del sindacato con cui avevo avuto problemi.

Mi portano in caserma e, una volta fuori, la notizia che esce è: "Fedez: una fan gli chiede una foto, lui si rifiuta, le spacca una bottiglia in testa. Poi chiede alla polizia di difenderlo in quanto vip".

Tutte le accuse a mio carico sono cadute, c'erano i video del locale. Ma per una settimana buona sono stato quello che, se gli chiedi una foto, ti spacca una bottiglia in testa.

Non sono mai stato avido

I soldi mi piacciono ma non devono farti vendere l'anima. I soldi sono un obiettivo ma non possono diventare mai un fine, altrimenti crolla tutto e in pochi anni ti bruci. I soldi sono lo specchietto che i discografici ti sventolano davanti per prenderti, sfruttarti, masticarti e sputarti via, tanto dopo arriva il prossimo. E per questo forse non sono mai piaciuto troppo al mondo musicale. Per questo fin da subito ho sentito che quelle dinamiche di controllo mi stavano strette.

Quando ho iniziato a fare i primi dj set, venivo pagato bene e con quel denaro, nel giro di un anno, come dicevo ho estinto i mutui e i debiti di famiglia. Poi, con i primi diecimila euro tutti per me, ho organizzato quella vacanza a Forte dei Marmi, con Ghali e amici al seguito. Poi c'è stato *Sig. Brainwash*, disco che è diventato il più venduto dell'anno, scalzando i Modà e Fabri Fibra dalla vetta. Coi miei primi grossi guadagni ovviamente ho festeggiato: la mia prima Porsche, una Boxster, spettacolare, ma credo di averci fatto giusto dieci chilometri. E la Lamborghini, comprata un po' più tardi, con cui penso di averne fatti altri dieci. Le macchine, a dire il vero, non è che mi siano mai interessate molto. Poi, ai tempi di Chiara, mi sarei preso qualche orologio vistoso, con diamanti, ma non ho mai avuto un vero interesse per il lusso ostentato. Anche perché non si usava all'epoca: è con Sfera Ebbasta che in Italia è arrivato il connubio trap e diamanti. Prima si parlava di soldi, sì, ma non di lusso ostentato.

La prima vera spesa? Lo stesso anno in cui ho incontrato Chiara, l'attico a CityLife. A cui sono approdato dopo aver dovuto lasciare la mia vecchia casa.

Fatto sta che, nonostante il successo del disco, in quel periodo gli occhi della Sony, mia etichetta, erano puntati altrove. In particolare, su Baby K, e infatti hanno fatto uscire prima il suo disco, spostando il mio. Peccato che in una settimana io ho venduto quello che Baby K ha totalizzato in tre mesi.

Ero a un bivio, dovevo scegliere dove andare adesso, e le proposte non mancavano, proprio come due anni prima. Nel 2011 Fibra aveva appena lanciato la sua etichetta, Tempi Duri, e per me lui era come un dio. Ma dall'altra parte c'era l'offerta di Guè, che aveva deciso di fondare una nuova etichetta proprio a partire dal mio contratto, se avessi deciso di firmare con lui. Tanta Roba, così si chiamava, avrebbe raccolto sotto la sua ala i nomi più promettenti dell'hip hop italiano: Gemitaiz, MadMan, Salmo, i Troupe d'Elite, e quindi Ghali ed Ernia. L'annuncio di nascita dell'etichetta, ancora visibile su YouTube, ci ritrae, io, Guè e DJ Harsh, nell'atto di fondazione. Il primo album pubblicato dall'etichetta, nel 2011, è stato appunto il mio, *Il mio primo disco da venduto*, seguito da un mixtape di Guè e da *Death USB* di Salmo. La scelta è caduta su di loro, devo ammettere, anche per una certa antipatia verso Paola Zukar, la manager di Fibra.

Comunque sia, Fibra mi aveva promesso di portarmi in tour con lui, ma le promesse, si sa, lasciano il tempo che trovano. Quando esce il mio disco, è a RTL, lo stanno intervistando. Commentano la classifica di iTunes, dove io ero primo. Gli chiedono: «Conosci Fedez?». E lui dice di no. Faceva finta di non conoscermi perché non avevo firmato con lui. Quando il mio successo è diventato innegabile ha tentato di recuperare, lodandomi su Twitter. Ma non ho risposto. Anzi, ho iniziato a dissarlo apertamente. Durante i miei concerti, prima di cantare *Alfonso Signorini (eroe nazionale)*, mandavo in onda un'intro di Signorini stesso che annunciava: «E adesso abbiamo un fantastico artista, il numero uno in Italia: Fabri Fibra!», e poi salivo io sul palco. Sfottevo l'immagine del Fibra che insultava tutto e tutti nello star system ma che poi aveva fatto il jingle per un suo programma. Da lì i rapporti non si sono più risanati.

Nel 2014 è uscito il mio disco successivo, registrato interamente a Los Angeles, *Pop-Hoolista*. Un concept album che ha come tema principale il sistema politico italiano. È composto da venti brani, con la partecipazione, tra gli altri, di Elisa, Malika Ayane, Noemi e Francesca Michielin. Fu una trattativa magnifica: andavo in giro a prendere offerte da tutti. Lì c'è stata la firma del mio primo contratto da un milione di euro. Tutto questo grazie a un'idea: *Kill the middlemen*.

Quando ho iniziato, il mio manager era Franco Godi, quello degli Articolo 31, l'uomo dei jingle di "Carosello". Un gigante, ma io volevo fare a modo mio, e mi rendevo conto troppo bene dell'opportunismo dell'ambiente.

Godi, per dire, per un anno, un intero anno dall'uscita del disco, non s'è fatto vivo. Poi mi scrive: «Ho ascoltato il tuo album: molto bello». Gli ero caduto dal cielo. Godi era un uomo del Novecento, con le maniere da discografico degli anni Novanta.

Capisco subito che c'è spazio per ottimizzare i costi, spendere di meno, dividere meno la torta. Io non vengo da una famiglia che ha sempre avuto tutto, cioè non mi è mai mancato nulla, ma abbiamo sempre dovuto sudare per fare una vita normale. Però mio padre da giovane era un intrallazzone, era un ottimo venditore: orologi, cachemire. Devo aver appreso da lui un certo intuito negli affari, e poi il fatto di essere nato povero mi rende insopportabile l'idea che qualcuno me li stia "rubando". Quindi ho preso Ax e gli ho detto: «Senti, perché non facciamo una società insieme, io e te?». La mia idea? *Kill the middleman,* appunto. Stipendiare i manager anziché lasciar loro una percentuale sui contratti, come si è sempre fatto. Più soldi per noi, ma soprattutto una vera azienda, diventare imprenditori. E avevo solo ventiquattro anni. Così sia io che J-Ax ci stacchiamo da Godi e nasce Newtopia – ora Doom –, con me e lui soci al cinquanta per cento. (Dopo ho rilevato le sue quote per centomila euro: oggi la società vale milioni.) Siamo nati come società di management discografico, quindi abbiamo iniziato a lavorare anche con i brand, quando ci siamo accorti che tutte le campagne di marketing migliori le partorivamo noi. E poi, diciamocelo, gli artisti musicali sono un palo nel culo ed è molto di più il sangue che ti fanno buttare che i soldi che ti fanno guadagnare, per questo con la Doom gestiamo i content creator: danno molti meno problemi degli artisti e ti fanno fare più soldi.

Ma, a parte tutto, la Newtopia e Doom per me valgono perché mi permettono di avere il controllo creativo totale in quello che faccio, non ho intermediari che possono cambiare le carte in tavola, che possono inquinare una visione artistica, che possono rubarmi i soldi per limitare la mia libertà. Che, se ci pensate, è un paradosso.

Il mondo della musica è fantastico

Al mondo discografico questa voglia di libertà, questa dichiarazione di emancipazione che è la Newtopia, e poi Doom, non sono mai andate giù davvero. Chiariamoci, non sono Robespierre, non sono un rivoluzionario, ho solo fatto i miei interessi, quello che reputavo meglio per me, però anche un atto di insubordinazione individuale a un sistema lobbistico come quello delle major non piace per niente. Perché crei un precedente, crei un modello vincente a cui altri potrebbero ispirarsi. Poi ammetto che anche io non sono una persona simpatica, o meglio sono selettivamente simpatico. Se mi stai sul cazzo si vede e non faccio niente per non fartelo capire, e invece l'ambiente musicale si fonda sull'amichettismo, sul sorridersi anche quando ci si sta sul cazzo, sul collaborare anche quando disprezzi qualcuno, sul far finta di essere grandi amici quando non ci si può vedere a vicenda. E se non stai al gioco il mondo discografico te la fa pagare.

Per esempio, mi ricordo quando uscì il mio disco *Paranoia Airlines*, nel 2019. Sotto Sanremo successe un casino perché era stato deciso che dovesse essere il punto più basso della mia carriera, il mio disco meno venduto. E per assurdo è stato invece il disco con il sell out più alto della mia carriera, perché ho molti difetti, ma sono molto bravo a stare a galla. Ho usato una mossa di marketing che aveva fatto Travis Scott in America, ma che nessuno aveva mai sperimentato in Italia, ovvero: se compri il disco ricevi in regalo un prodotto del merchandising. Sembra un'idea del cazzo, ma in realtà è parecchio complicato metterla in atto, perché bisogna avere un rivenditore certificato da rilevazione GFK che poi vada in classifica. Fatto sta che la persona che mi ha aiutato a mettere in atto la mia idea aveva questa certificazione, ma le due major competitor hanno spinto affinché venisse revocata e a me hanno fatto un esposto per privarmi del primato del disco di platino ottenuto in una settimana. Ricordo che in quei giorni mi chiamò Pico Cibelli della Sony, che mi disse: «Io non ho mai visto una persona tanto odiata nel settore discografico come te».

In un modo o nell'altro io ne sono sempre uscito più o meno in piedi, ma alla lunga tutti questi colpi bassi mi hanno reso sempre più diffidente. Per questo mi piace lavorare da solo. Ci sono carriere che stanno in piedi grazie alle relazioni. Non faccio nomi ma ci sono artisti che vivono grazie al fatto che con le collaborazioni riescono a ottenere certi numeri, cosa che spero prima o poi finisca perché questa dinamica crea un circolino per cui, se io, etichetta o management, ho gli artisti che ti fanno il featuring e che ti possono svoltare una carriera, allora posso chiedere favori a destra e a manca. Io sono sempre rimasto abbastanza fuori da tutto questo, un po' perché per natura sono un solitario che non si fida mai del prossimo, un po' per le delusioni che ho ricevuto. Posso dire di avere dei rapporti veri, nel bene e nel male, con le persone con cui collaboro. Anche quando tutto finisce di merda.

Per esempio, nessuno sa che io non parlo più con Tananai proprio per quella natura fantastica del mondo della musica per cui c'è chi riesce a infamarsi, insultarsi di brutto e cinque minuti dopo a mostrarsi in amoreggiamenti artistici. Lui ha iniziato a lavorare con una persona con cui avevo collaborato io, e che è diventata il suo manager, Stefano Clessi. Ogni volta che ci vedevamo, Clessi mi implorava di fare un pezzo con questo giovane emergente, per dargli una mano. A un certo punto Tananai si presenta a Sanremo Giovani e per fare un favore al suo manager, che era appunto un mio caro amico, inizio a supportarlo nonostante non sapessi chi fosse. Accetto di fare delle storie Instagram e una serie di altre cose, perché a quel punto era, diciamo, nella mia squadra. Dopo Sanremo Giovani decido anche di offrirgli un feat nel mio disco *Disumano*.

Nel 2022 Tananai va Sanremo: arriva ultimo ma devo dire che affronta la cosa in modo esemplare. Alberto è una persona molto positiva, un preso bene. A volte anche troppo per i miei gusti. Ha un po' questa gioia ingiustificata verso la vita. Ha quella che io chiamo "la sindrome di Jovanotti".

Dopo Sanremo, per l'estate gli propongo *La dolce vita*. Superiamo una serie di peripezie e registriamo il brano, che va molto bene. È sulla scia di quel successo che Tananai, con *Tango*, viene preso nuovamente a Sanremo, il Sanremo in cui io ero imbottito di psicofarmaci e stavo malissimo. Lui e il manager continuavano a chiedermi di sostenerlo al televoto. Ricordo ancora questo mantra "codice 6, codice 6", me lo scrivevano a martello, "mi raccomando, siamo una squadra fortissima". Mi dicevano proprio così, che eravamo una squadra, che avremmo fatto grandi cose, che eravamo uniti. Ora, vorrei dire: per me "squadra" significa indossare la maglietta di quell'appartenenza e accollarsi oneri e onori di esserlo, una squadra. Uno che indossa la maglietta di una squadra indosserebbe allo stesso tempo quella della squadra rivale? Secondo me no. E soprattutto, in ogni caso, te lo direbbe.

Succede invece che, a un certo punto, e senza che nessuno me lo dica direttamente – ed è questa la cosa che mi fa girare di più il cazzo, perché se me lo dici mi dà fastidio, ma un po' meno... –, scopro che Tananai sta lavorando a un brano sul campionamento di un pezzo di *Born Slippy .NUXX* degli Underworld, dalla colonna sonora di *Trainspotting*. Era tipo da due anni che chiedevo al mio amico, il manager di Tananai, insomma, di fare un pezzo su questo campionamento, e lui ogni volta mi rispondeva: «No, no, perché su questo pezzo abbiamo scritto *Notti in bianco* di Blanco». E io gli dicevo: «Ok, ma siete solo partiti da lì, poi è ne uscito un altro brano». Insomma, io lo volevo proprio usare, quel campionamento. E alla fine scopro che lo stanno facendo con Tananai. Nessuno mi coinvolge e, ciliegina sulla torta, fanno il featuring con Marracash, che è uno che da *Status* in poi mi insulta in ogni cazzo di album e intervista che fa.

All'inizio non sapevo come prenderla, mi dicevo che in fin dei conti ognuno collabora con chi vuole. Ma non è stato un bel comportamento, il loro.

Fatto sta che quello che io chiamo "karma Federico", una forza sottile e scientificamente verificabile per cui quando mi fai del male è quasi certo che un destino avverso arriverà a punirti (ma mai proporzionale al male che mi hai fatto), colpisce anche stavolta. Non gli viene dato il campionamento, e nello stesso anno in cui esce anche il mio *Disco Paradise* fanno uscire il brano monco, senza metà dell'architrave. Risultato: non è certo stato uno dei più grandi successi sia di Tananai che di Marracash.

Anche con Blanco la dinamica è stata simile.

Nessuno sa che faceva reggaeton, prima che Clessi decidesse di lanciarlo in un altro genere. È lui che ne ha plasmato il suono, insieme al produttore Davide Simonetta, influenzando profondamente quello che poi Blanco è diventato. Il talento c'è, la sua voce è incredibile, ma il suono è in buona parte un'invenzione di Simonetta. Per convincerlo, hanno usato il mio nome. Al padre di Blanco – che era minorenne –, per convincerlo a firmare il contratto di management, hanno sottolineato che lavoravano con me. E io ero d'accordo: «Usate il mio nome, non voglio niente, vi aiuto a spingerlo». La cosa va in porto, Blanco firma. Sono stato io il primo a promuovere *Notti in bianco*, un anno prima che esplodesse. Era parte del mio team: lo considero ancora oggi un artista davvero valido. Tutti mi ringraziavano, mi piaceva sul serio come artista, continuavo a dire: «Vorrei andare in studio con lui». Mi rispondevano: «Vediamo, vediamo». Poi arriva il pezzo con Salmo, *La canzone nostra*, che esce senza che nessuno mi dica niente. Sono rimasto di merda: perché nascondermelo? Quando servivo andavo bene, poi sono diventato un reietto.

Karma Federico: Blanco lascia Clessi. Quando va a girare *Mi fai impazzire* con Sfera Ebbasta, passa al manager di Sfera. Poi il disastro delle rose a Sanremo. Dove, sia chiaro, Blanco non ha fatto niente di così grave, ma è stato ingenuo. Se vuoi fare la rockstar, devi essere come i Placebo: prendi i fischi, ma è parte del gioco. Se fai la rockstar, devi fregartene e andar via senza dire nulla. Non puoi distruggere la roba e poi scusarti. Perdi di credibilità. Spero non demorda, perché la sua musica è bella, ha una carriera davanti, e gli auguro davvero tutto il bene possibile.

Molti dicono che mi avvicino a chi brilla per rubare loro la luce e poi scartarli, abbandonarli. Modalità vampiro. Ma Drake, tanto per dirne uno, fa esattamente la stessa cosa con gli emergenti. Per me, è semplicemente un *do ut des*. È ridicolo che si pensi che io cannibalizzi altri artisti, come se fossero lì ad aspettare di essere sfruttati da me. È sempre uno scambio: io prendo da loro e loro da me. Annalisa o Tananai non collaborano con me perché sono figo come Beyoncé – cosa che purtroppo non è –, ma perché valutano e decidono se gli interessa o gli risulta strategico farlo.

Io non attacco mai per primo. Mai. Non è il mio stile. Se guardate tutti gli scazzi, tutti i casini in cui sono finito, non sono mai stato io a iniziare. Mai il primo colpo. Se però mi spari, io rispondo. E non con un colpo. Con cinque. Sempre. Sparo a chi mi spara. Senza pietà. Ma mai alle spalle. Mai. Col tempo ho capito che certe volte è meglio tacere. Invece quando ero giovane, reagivo subito. D'istinto. Uno mi dava uno, io davo cinque. Non c'era proporzione. Ma mai codardo, mai infame. Mai alle spalle. Faccio tanto casino, ma poi non affondo la lama a uno che è per terra. Non l'ho mai fatto, non l'ho fatto con Rovazzi, non l'ho fatto con J-Ax. Anzi, Ax a un certo punto, dopo aver fatto insieme *Disco Paradise*, mi dice: «Ti devo dire grazie», perché lui veniva da un crollo, una carriera in difficoltà. Io invece stavo in alto, potevo anche mandarlo affanculo e farlo da solo. Ma no. Lui mi era stato vicino quando non serviva fingere. E quel momento, quella tregua, io me la sentivo vera. La separazione mi aveva fatto male, sì, perché pensavo fosse un amico. Uno vero. E quando perdi un amico vero, non è scena, è carne che si strappa. Poi lui mi manda un messaggio e mi dice quel "grazie", perché sapeva che potevo mollarlo, che lì potevo finirlo. Sarebbe bastato un colpo, una frase, un post.

La gente ama vedere cadere gli altri. Ma io non lo do mai, il colpo di grazia. Non è nel mio sangue. Anche se di colpi ne ho presi, Cristo se ne ho presi. Da ogni parte. Gente che aspettava solo un mio passo falso per colpire. Ma io ho un istinto. Non è cervello, è fegato. È sopravvivenza. È come l'Immortale in *Gomorra*. Ti sparano, ti pugnalano, ti seppelliscono, e tu riemergi sempre. Mezzo morto, ma ancora con gli occhi aperti. Più che un bullo mi sento spesso bullizzato e reagisco, al bullismo degli altri, con altrettanto bullismo. Però è vero, sono vendicativo. O meglio: progetto molte vendette solo che, alla fine, davanti all'opportunità di colpire veramente, di affondare la lama, mi fermo quasi sempre. Questa è la realtà. Vivo nella progettualità di una vendetta che raramente porto a termine. Ma che mi cova dentro, e soprattutto mi logora. Sono in piedi, sono ancora vivo, ma ne porto le cicatrici addosso.

Chiara

Sarà un caso, ma io al caso ci credo poco, credo di più al karma, piuttosto. Fatto sta che, in quel periodo di cambiamento totale nella mia carriera artistica e imprenditoriale, dopo *Pop-Hoolista* incontro Chiara. La prima volta che l'ho vista ho notato che aveva la faccia lucida. All'epoca ero fidanzato. E lei lì, lucida come la vita che scivola via o ti fa specchio. Non so bene cosa ho pensato. Forse niente.

Lei è entrata nella stanza e non c'è stato nessun colpo di fulmine, nessuna musica in sottofondo, nessun ralenti da film romantico. Solo un dettaglio così apparentemente superficiale come la lucentezza della pelle. Ed è questo che, secondo me, l'ha resa così vera per me fin dal primo momento. Non so, magari mi nascondo dietro quest'immagine della pelle, forse è una sorta di meccanismo di difesa per inibire qualsiasi forma di romanticismo, e che mi porto dietro da un botto di tempo. Dai diciassette anni, per la precisione, dalla mia prima fidanzata. Lì qualcosa si è rotto dentro e nessuno l'ha più aggiustato. Io ero pazzo di lei, e lei nel frattempo si stava scopando mezza Milano. Lo scoprivo un pezzo alla volta. Un amico, un conoscente, uno che passava per caso. E io lì, con in mano questa idea infantile dell'amore, che si scioglieva come ghiaccio nel piscio.

Qualcosa in quel momento si è incrinato. Lo sguardo. Il modo in cui guardavo le donne. Non era rabbia, era sfiducia. Era delusione. Non è giusto. Lo so. Non è la realtà. Ma cazzo, quando ti prendono a pugni nel cuore a quell'età, cominci a camminare storto e a dire a te stesso che tanto sono tutte così. Non mi fidavo più. Più di nessuna. Non perché volessi vendetta, ma perché la testa aveva messo un cartello con su scritto: "Attento Federico. Zona minata". Un mio amico diceva: «Le donne non sono tutte troie. Sono una più troia dell'altra». E lo diceva ridendo, con una birra in mano e il cuore in pezzi. Io ridevo, anche. Ma non ci credevo. Non davvero. Solo che non avevo più voglia di credere in altro. Ecco, non era odio. Era stanchezza. Era paura. Era quel senso di essere fregato per sempre. Una volta ti basta, sai? Una sola. E ti porti la scheggia nel petto per sempre.

Per questo forse io, di quel momento, di Chiara mi ricordo la pelle lucida. Ma il corpo sa quello che la testa non vuole dire. Il corpo si emoziona. Non ci sono ragionamenti e pensieri profondissimi. Non con le trombe del destino, ma con la voglia di toccarsi, di stare bene, di scomparire un po' nella pelle dell'altro. E allora si scopa. Questa cosa che bisogna sempre avere una frase epica per quando vedi la persona che diventerà importante... Stronzate. Nei libri ti diranno "folgorazione", ti venderanno il colpo di fulmine, le parole giuste, i segnali, il destino.

Io ho pensato: "Stiamo bene".

E allora avanti così. Che c'è di male? La verità è che

a volte non succede niente di speciale. Solo che ci si comincia a stare addosso e ci si trova comodi. E poi magari ci si affeziona. O ci si fa del male. O tutte e due le cose. Io ho una testa semplice, va bene? Non ho bisogno di leggende. Mi bastano i fatti: lei era lì, viva, con il suo mondo abbagliante, e per qualche motivo io ci sono entrato. Succede così, a chi ha fame. Sono una mente semplice. Trovo più interessante la descrizione della realtà così com'è che il voler truccare la realtà a proprio piacimento per dare un racconto più disincantato. L'idea del "non c'è niente di particolare, alle volte le cose succedono": è la testa di Federico. E alle volte succede che per caso trovi una complicità che non avevo mai avuto con nessun'altra.

Nessuna. Con lei ho parlato delle mie paure più grandi, quelle che non confessi nemmeno allo specchio quando sei strafatto. Con lei mi sono spogliato davvero. Non il corpo. La testa. Il cuore. Le schifezze dentro. È stata la mia confidente. La mia spalla. Quella che non ti fa sentire solo quando tutto fa schifo e non sai più dove sbattere la testa. Non rinnego niente della vita fatta insieme. Tra tutte le donne che ho avuto tra le mani e nella mente, nessuna mi ha mai fatto pensare: "Forse con questa ci posso costruire qualcosa che dura." Eravamo diversi, sì. Mondi lontani.

Ma ci incastravamo. Come due pezzi storti di un puzzle difficile. Storti, ma funzionava. Il problema è che anche le cose che funzionano a volte fanno male. I conflitti c'erano. Certo che c'erano. Ma servivano, cazzo. Credo che in una relazione gli elementi di conflitto siano fondamentali per non spaccarsi i coglioni. Servono per non diventare dei vegetali che guardano la tv a cena senza parlarsi. Il punto è quando quei conflitti cominciano a pesare più del resto. Più delle risate, più del sesso, più di quel modo strano che hai di toccarti la fronte quando pensi. C'è stato un momento felice in cui il peso specifico degli elementi di conflitto non sovrastava la complementarietà sinergica che avevamo tra noi. Quando quei cazzo di conflitti ti soffocano, allora lì si rompe qualcosa.

E quando si rompe, non suona nemmeno. Fa solo silenzio.

Ma, finché abbiamo funzionato, la nostra diversità – lei centro, io provincia, lei candida, io tatuato, lei bionda, io moro – è stata la nostra forza sia come coppia sia come "immagine pubblica". È strano quando il tuo nome si trasforma in un marchio, magari Chiara che viene dalla moda era più abituata a immaginarselo, ma per me è stato strano diventare "i Ferragnez", anche perché nel mondo dell'intrattenimento, dell'esposizione mediatica, puoi programmare, prevedere determinate cose, però quello che in realtà devi fare è semplicemente essere pronto quando l'onda arriva, riuscire a cavalcarla e non esserne travolto.

Si tratta di essere nel posto giusto al momento giusto. E noi siamo stati evidentemente ciò che il pubblico voleva nel momento in cui lo voleva. È come un allineamento di pianeti, e noi ci siamo fatti trovare pronti.

Atto II

QUANDO L'ANIMA VUOLE SMETTERE

Il giorno più importante della fine

L'ho detto, ho sempre vissuto i picchi come se fossero il ciglio di un burrone. Anche quando ho fatto il concerto a San Siro. Tutti urlavano, tutti postavano: "Questo è il tuo giorno". E io invece lo sentivo già finito. Già andato. Già vecchio. Perché il successo, per me, è sempre stato una trappola con la carta dorata. Appena ci arrivi ti rendi conto che non hai vinto niente, hai solo alzato la posta in gioco.

Avevo la fobia del fallimento piantata nel petto come una scheggia. Ogni volta che le cose andavano bene io sentivo l'odore della merda che arrivava. Ogni applauso mi sembrava un addio in anticipo. Ogni traguardo la curva prima della discesa. Ho sempre vissuto tutto con la testa rivolta al dopo. Mai un brindisi, mai una risata vera. Solo previsioni. E mai buone.

Avevo percepito un'inversione di tendenza verso la musica trap, poi c'erano i nuovi, artisti più giovani, c'era la sensazione che i tempi stavano cambiando e che io ero ancora lì, con la mia faccia di ieri.

Quel giorno a San Siro non l'ho vissuto come il giorno più importante della mia carriera. Ma come l'inizio della discesa della fase ascendente della mia carriera. Ero il passato che fingeva di essere ancora presente. Ma, paradossalmente, è questa maledetta angoscia a tenermi in piedi. A farmi resistere.

Non ho mai creduto nel mio stesso mito.

E questo mi ha tenuto vivo. Longevo, dicono. O forse solo troppo paranoico per fermarmi.

Non sono cambiato in meglio

Tumore. Tre sillabe del cazzo. Vengono pronunciate in un secondo, ma è un secondo che rischia di cambiare totalmente il tuo mondo. Perché proprio a me? È tutto ovattato, è tutto lentissimo, ma è anche velocissimo. Sei al tempo stesso scosso dall'adrenalina, ma anche anestetizzato.

Tumore neuroendocrino del pancreas, per la precisione. È una forma molto rara, la stessa di Steve Jobs, notizia non molto rassicurante quando anche uno degli uomini più ricchi del pianeta, che aveva accesso alle migliori cure del mondo, non è sopravvissuto. Però essere riuscito a parlare subito con Gianluca Vialli mi ha aiutato. La sua serenità, la sua pacatezza, il suo essere sincero senza retorica mi hanno dato sollievo dopo quella notizia devastante.

L'ho scoperto per caso tramite un esame di controllo, sono ipocondriaco e faccio continuamente dei check-up, tra i quali una TAC ai polmoni per un pregresso problema respiratorio, che aveva evidenziato qualcosa che non andava. Da lì era partito l'iter di analisi e questo è stato il mio vero grande privilegio. Non c'erano metastasi e l'esame istologico ha poi evidenziato che la neoplasia non aveva intaccato i linfonodi. Quindi non ho dovuto fare chemioterapia, è bastato l'intervento chirurgico. Bastato si fa per dire, perché mi hanno asportato cistifellea, testa del pancreas, duodeno e un altro pezzo di intestino. Il mio corpo, insomma, è diverso, è cambiato, è monco di alcune sue parti, eppure io non mi sono sentito cambiato in meglio. Quella cosa che la malattia ti rende una persona migliore con me non ha funzionato, e credo che alla fine sia tutta retorica fatta dai sani che, impauriti che un tumore possa capitare anche a loro, sperano almeno che li cambi in meglio. Poi, ovvio, ci sono persone illuminate come Gianluca Vialli, che affrontando la malattia raggiungono un grado di consapevolezza profondo, però credo sia raro, che ci sia bisogno di una sensibilità particolare, che per la maggior parte della gente non funzioni così. O, quantomeno, per me non ha funzionato così.

Forse anche per il fatto che la mia esperienza con il tumore è stata intensissima ma anche rapidissima, è stata una malattia al passo coi tempi, tutto estremamente veloce, in cui un giorno stavo morendo e dieci giorni dopo, in seguito all'operazione, mi hanno detto che praticamente ero guarito. È come se non avessi avuto il tempo di metabolizzare. Ho dovuto affrontare tutti gli step che si affrontano per una malattia, ma in modalità iperaccelerata. Da sano mi sono ritrovato come uno con una spada di Damocle che oscilla sopra la sua testa, ogni secondo più vicina a decapitarlo. E anche se è andata bene, e il tumore era incapsulato, non c'erano metastasi, e sono stato fortunato e tutto quello che volete, pensare che forse stai morendo, anzi, pensare che stai davvero per morire per me è stato uno shock.

Provate a concentrarvi e a riflettere sul serio, a sentire sulla pelle la sensazione che si può provare avendo la consapevolezza di essere una persona con pochi giorni di vita davanti a sé. Non è bello, no? È per questo che essere un condannato a morte, anche se risparmiato dagli eventi, non mi ha reso una persona migliore, anzi, forse ne sono uscito più incazzato con la vita, più paranoico, più chiuso in me stesso di quanto lo fossi mai stato prima. Forse, a pensarci bene, qualcosa di positivo però me l'ha lasciato. Da quei giorni di primavera del 2022 ho imparato ad abbracciare le cose per come arrivano. E di merda da abbracciare n'è arrivata tanta, da lì in poi.

La sindrome di Jovanotti

Il 2023: è il momento in cui siamo tutti all'apice della popolarità. Chiara è invitata a Sanremo. Qualche mese prima avevo iniziato la terapia di psicofarmaci come si comincia una relazione che sai già che finirà male. Con entusiasmo. Con speranza.

Con la testa piena di merda e il cuore vuoto. Quindici giorni dopo camminavo per New York e mi sembrava di vedere tutto per la prima volta. I colori, i rumori, i volti. Come se avessero acceso il mondo e io ero l'unico a saperlo. Ridevo per niente. Amavo tutti. Ero felice di essere felice, anche se non c'era un cazzo da essere felici. "Ipomania", la chiamano. Io la chiamavo "ubriacatura farmacologica". Un'esaltazione da cocktail chimico, la felicità che ti viene somministrata come una dose. Poi arriva il tracollo. E quello non lo vedi mai arrivare. Per me, per noi, è stato quel Sanremo.

Quando mi è venuta l'idea di portare "Muschio selvaggio" al Festival credevo fosse una buona mossa per il podcast. Ma, sono sincero, soffrivo anche il fatto di non esserci come cantante. Il Festival mi fa sempre stare di merda ma, allo stesso tempo, è come una sirena che mi chiama e a cui non riesco a dire no. Portare il nostro podcast lì era un modo per esserci, senza partecipare davvero. Anche perché, piccolo particolare, in realtà era nei piani che io, a quel Sanremo, partecipassi come cantante: poi non è più stato possibile perché Chiara aveva accettato la proposta di Amadeus. Mi ero sentito con lui: «Ma è un problema se io partecipo e c'è Chiara che presenta?». Lui mi ha rassicurato: «No, tranquillo, anche l'anno di Ambra Angiolini e Renga si era già creata la stessa situazione».

Alla fine, abbiamo deciso che era meglio evitare: già nell'edizione in cui ero stato in gara con Francesca Michielin, e Chiara aveva fatto delle storie su Instagram per spingere a votarmi – cosa normalissima –, era scoppiata la polemica. Se avessi partecipato con lei lì a condurre, addio, apriti cielo.

Però, e magari sbaglio, per me quel palco è sinonimo di musica: pensavo che la priorità, nella nostra coppia, avrebbe dovuto essere mia, in quanto cantante. È il mio lavoro, il mio ambito, il lavoro di Chiara non è presentare. Insomma, più o meno consciamente, me la vivevo male.

Non ero lucido, evidentemente, e infatti in quel Sanremo è successo di tutto, un vero casino: sveglia alle sei, colazione con Beppe Vessicchio – che, a proposito, ha poteri paranormali, ma questo non lo sa nessuno –, giravamo le puntate del "Muschio" all'alba, per poi montarle nel pomeriggio in vista della messa in onda serale. Un delirio. Io non sentivo la stanchezza: ero come un mix fra Johnny Depp in *Paura e delirio a Las Vegas* e Usain Bolt. Non dormivo mai. Bevevo, fumavo, prendevo tutti quegli psicofarmaci, facevo dirette senza senso, organizzavo festini in casa.

Faccio anche il freestyle in cui attacco tutti. Polemico e accusatorio, come sempre. Attiro molta attenzione. Durante il collegamento dalla nave della Costa Crociere, ormeggiata al largo di Sanremo, sputo rime nel freestyle inedito prodotto da Salmo. Tra noi, negli anni, c'era stata una lunga faida a colpi di barre e frecciatine: si era conclusa nell'estate del 2022 con la riconciliazione pubblica sul palco del megaconcerto di Salmo a San Siro. Nel collegamento sanremese dalla Costa mi concentro sui temi di attualità e sparo a zero su ministri e politici. La prima stoccata è per la deputata Maddalena Morgante di Fratelli d'Italia, che ha accusato Rosa Chemical di portare all'Ariston la rivoluzione gender fluid: «Se va a Sanremo Rosa Chemical scoppia la lite, forse è meglio il viceministro vestito da Hitler». Il riferimento è al viceministro delle Infrastrutture Galeazzo Bignami, fotografato a una festa in divisa da nazista, fotografia che io strappo in diretta. Ce n'è poi pure per il Codacons: «Guarda Codacons come mi diverto». Riprendo anche le dichiarazioni del ministro per la Famiglia, la natalità e le pari opportunità, Eugenia Roccella, sull'interruzione di gravidanza: «Purtroppo l'aborto è un diritto, sì, ma non l'ho detto io, l'ha detto un ministro. A volte anch'io sparo cazzate ai quattro venti ma non lo faccio a spese dei contribuenti». Poi faccio riferimento alla mia malattia, e alla morte di Gianluca Vialli: «Ho avuto il cancro e come un vero duro sono andato in tele e ho pianto, se penso a chi mi ha dato la forza guardo in alto il ricordo di Gianluca che porto su questo palco». Le conseguenze, è ovvio, sono state toste: ho litigato pesantemente col direttore dell'intrattenimento del prime time Rai, Stefano Coletta, che ha preso le distanze dal mio freestyle e dagli attacchi politici contenuti nel testo della canzone. La posizione della Rai è stata netta: «Mi dissocio, inammissibile attacco personale» ha detto Coletta.

Ovviamente Chiara non era contenta, ma il colpo di grazia è stato il bacio con Rosa Chemical. Ora lo posso dire: ci eravamo messi d'accordo. Gli avevo proprio mandato la foto del mio posto in platea. Lui era in gara con il brano *Made in Italy*, durante l'esibizione mi ha raggiunto, abbiamo mimato un rapporto sessuale e poi, dopo avermi portato sul palco, mi ha baciato sulle labbra. Com'è noto, si è scatenato il finimondo. Onestamente, non avevo pensato che la cosa potesse turbare Chiara. Ero lì, tra l'altro in mezzo a tutti i parenti di mia moglie, e nessuno sembrava essersi fatto troppe paranoie, in quel momento. A parte Charles Leclerc, seduto lì dietro, che è rimasto scioccato. Poi, durante la pubblicità, sono andato dietro le quinte e ho capito che lei era a pezzi. Per me era una cazzata divertente, lei l'ha vissuta come se fosse la fine del mondo. È scoppiato un dramma. Siamo finiti nei camerini e io, sentendomi trattato come un lebbroso da lei e dal suo team, me ne sono andato. Mi sono sentito nella fossa dei leoni. Ero circondato da gente che mi guardava come se fossi un mostro. Luis Sal era dietro di me, e ha subito anche lui quel momento.

Io alla fine sono scappato e quella notte sono rimasto in giro. Eleonora, la mia assistente, ha dovuto dormire con tutti i coltelli perché dicevo che volevo tagliarmi le vene. Ero uscito di testa. Lì è arrivato il burnout totale. Giusto mentre Selvaggia Lucarelli iniziava a sparare merda sulle mie uova di Pasqua e io dovevo fare quel video dove non riuscivo nemmeno a pronunciare per intero le parole. Sempre in quei giorni dovevo girare uno spot per McDonald's, dire "Crispy McBacon" è stato un inferno: quattro ore di tentativi. Mi sono sentito un caso umano, vedevo la pietà negli occhi della gente sul set. Una vera umiliazione.

Chiamo il mio psichiatra, e lui decide di farmi smettere con tutti i farmaci. Solo che, per un equivoco, credeva io prendessi una dose molto più leggera: invece ero a triplo regime. Quindi, stop ai farmaci e buongiorno crisi di astinenza da film horror (infatti poco dopo avrei dovuto ricominciare). Due settimane a letto senza riuscire a muovermi, crampi alle gambe da urlare, non distinguevo più realtà e allucinazione. Sognavo di essere fidanzato con Gigi Hadid e ho finito per credere che fosse vero, tanto da prenotare un volo per Los Angeles per raggiungerla. E in tutto ciò, mentre sono lì a letto, completamente perso, Luis mi chiama per dirmi che vuole mollare il podcast. Anzi, che vuole chiuderlo.

Dillo alla mamma, dillo all'avvocato

Luis l'ho conosciuto nel periodo in cui ero stato "tradito" da J-Ax e Rovazzi, e quindi mi ero attaccato moltissimo a lui. Lo trovavo una persona davvero matura, sotto certi punti di vista era più risolto di me. Mi ha dato una grossa mano, a livello psicologico, e tanta forza. Da lì è nata un'amicizia importante.

Come nella musica, io se collaboro con qualcuno è perché lo sento davvero vicino, lo sento quasi parte della mia famiglia. Sarò ingenuo, sarò un coglione, ma mi affido totalmente, in particolare quando si tratta di avere rapporti d'amicizia. Probabilmente è sempre per via di quel senso di fragilità, del bullo che è stato bullizzato che mi porto dietro da quando sono bambino. Fatto sta che con Luis, a un certo punto, ci viene l'idea di fondare "Muschio selvaggio", che diventa poi il podcast più forte in Italia, a testimonianza anche della nostra sinergia: insieme funzionavamo. Ma il rapporto, poi, si incrina. Lui inizia a soffrirmi, e secondo la mia assistente è per la mia tendenza a vantarmi molto, anche davanti a lui, dei miei successi. Io invece non l'ho mai vista come una competizione, quella fra noi: Luis ha fatto fortuna ed ero sinceramente felice per lui. Se ho detto cose che gli hanno dato fastidio, le ho dette scherzando: lo chiamavo "il prossimo Rovazzi" o lo prendevo in giro sugli steroidi (senza mai davvero pensare che li prendesse). Ma evidentemente lui ha cominciato a nutrire un risentimento crescente, convinto forse che le mie battute fossero delle reali cattiverie. Non lo so.

In ogni caso Luis, dopo mesi di silenzi, alla fine mi vomita tutto addosso. Mi dice cose forti, molto cattive, in maniera violenta. Sosteneva che io lo volessi sminuire, quando, giuro, non era mia intenzione farlo. Non ne avrei avuto motivo. Quando ha fatto "Celebrity Hunted" con me, non è che l'ha chiamato Prime: ho imposto io a Prime di prenderlo. Quando Luis ha fatto un botto di soldi tramite la partnership con una banca, il contatto gliel'avevo girato io. E non ho mai preteso niente. Era mio amico. Ci sono rimasto male per questa rottura, ho pianto tantissimo, per una settimana dallo psicologo ho parlato solo di questo. È stato un lutto. Alla fine, comunque, sembrava che avessimo sistemato le cose. Io ho sottolineato quanto lui fosse importante per me, ho insistito sul fatto che avremmo dovuto sempre parlare dei problemi, evitando di trascinare malumori e tensioni. Solo che poi la nostra amicizia ha subito un'altra fase di tensione nel mio periodo più pesante con gli psicofarmaci. Il tutto aggravato dai miei problemi a casa: quando io e Chiara litigavamo, infatti, lei aveva la cattiva abitudine di cercare supporto in qualcuno vicino a me. E così scriveva a lui, buttandogli addosso tutta una serie di cose nostre. Dinamica che lo fagocitava e, comprensibilmente, lo logorava.

Facciamo questa telefonata, in cui ci mandiamo affanculo. Lui ha intenzione di chiudere il podcast, io sono incazzato perché sono assolutamente contrario. Avevo trovato degli investitori che valutavano "Muschio selvaggio" alcuni milioni di euro, era previsto che cedessimo delle quote. Ma il podcast aveva quel valore anche sulla base della sua presenza. Di conseguenza ha perso valore, Luis, mediaticamente, pure. Però io ci sono rimasto malissimo, l'ho vissuto come un lutto enorme: era una persona a cui ero veramente tanto affezionato. La cosa che più mi dispiace è che il male che io posso avergli fatto non è stato fatto in cattiva fede, invece lui ha progettato ogni cosa a freddo, proprio per farmi del male.

E, comunque, quelli di Bologna sono dei taccagni.

Mondi lontani

C'era stato il tumore, c'erano gli psicofarmaci, c'era stato Sanremo e c'era stata la rottura con Luis. Un anno di merda di cui però avevo assaggiato solo l'antipasto di quello che sarebbe davvero arrivato.

In quei mesi sentivo di non avere il controllo, e non era solo una questione di paranoie indotte dai farmaci. Quell'onda mediatica, che per più di dieci anni ero riuscito a controllare, piano piano mi stava invece sommergendo, travolgendo, lasciandomi sconvolto e alla deriva, in cerca di un appiglio in qualsiasi cosa sembrava potesse darmi sostegno, senza pensare se fosse buona o cattiva. Era una sensazione quasi fisica, una sensazione di abbandono, di profonda solitudine, nonostante in teoria avessi una moglie a cui poter chiedere aiuto.

Solo pochi anni prima mi sarei aperto, ci saremmo trovati vicini per superarla insieme, e invece adesso eravamo due isole che si stavano allontanando irreversibilmente l'una dall'altra. Cose, persone, eventi che avevo sempre sopportato per Chiara ora mi diventavano insostenibili. Le nostre differenze emergevano come iceberg pronte a far affondare la nave. Faccio un esempio: durante il matrimonio ho subito, per osmosi, le frequentazioni di mia moglie. Avevo accettato passivamente di stare a quel tipo di pensiero lì, di accettare l'architetto superfancy di Milano, quello della moda iperinserito e un'altra serie di figure insopportabili. Una confezione bellissima. Ma dentro, per me, puzzavano tutti. Preferisco frequentare uno che vedi subito quanto fa schifo, piuttosto che un pacchetto stupendo di cui però a poco a poco ti accorgi che puzza di marcio. Meglio chi si presenta per quello che è, piuttosto che per quello che dovrebbe essere. L'azienda di mia moglie io la vedevo come il Rotary Club, e di conseguenza trattavo tutti come tratto gli snob. Ovvero peggio di come loro trattano gli altri.

In particolare, i rapporti con Fabio Maria Damato sono sempre stati difficili. Damato e Chiara erano amici, lui era proprio nel club degli amicissimi. Potrei fare una lista delle volte in cui negli anni l'ho insultato, e ci siamo presi a parole. Sembrava più un ballerino di flamenco che il CEO di un'azienda. Viveva della luce riflessa di mia moglie: si sentiva onnipotente, esercitava il suo ruolo facendosi figo in giro, e spesso trattava le persone come pezze da piedi. Con lui ho sempre avuto forti scontri, specie sulla gestione della serie tv. Io ero per tenere tutto. Sono un pornografo: se devi raccontare la tua vita non puoi farti sconti. Bisogna andare fino in fondo. Avrei tenuto un sacco di merda in più, invece dall'altra parte c'era un po' la voglia di pilotare la narrazione, senza comprendere – perché loro non avevano mai fatto televisione – che se vuoi fare una docuserie devi far vedere le luci e le ombre, sennò non funziona quella roba lì. Se vuoi far vedere che sei solo bello e figo allora diventa un documentario governativo del Partito comunista cinese. Erano più per l'artificio, insomma, il controllo rigido dell'immagine. Non è questione di virtù o di sincerità: noi la televisione la sappiamo fare. È da quando ho ventitré anni che lavoro con la televisione: so come far uscire un prodotto fatto bene, che appassioni il pubblico. Loro il mezzo non lo conoscevano: il loro unico obiettivo era far vedere la donna forte, emancipata, leader, realizzata. Il modello aspirazionale. Che ha senso, ma a forzarla così tanto poi ottieni il risultato opposto, ovvero il rigetto da parte delle persone. Io sono sempre stato il matto della famiglia: nonostante avessi un'azienda che fatturava come la sua, nonostante abbia dimostrato più volte di avere capacità imprenditoriali vere, solide, venivo trattato come il saltimbanco. Quello che, sì, va bene, è divertente, fa lo show, ma le cose serie sono altre. Va anche detto che dovevano sopportare che li insultassi tutto il tempo: classificarmi come matto era anche un modo per tollerarmi. Il sottotesto era: lasciamolo fare, tanto è così. Non ho mai nascosto il mio rigetto nei loro confronti: accettavo di essere attorniato da questo circo di fighetti vanitosi e più o meno parassiti, ma lasciavo chiaramente intendere di non digerirli. Li pigliavo per il culo alla grande. Alle feste, poi, arrivava inevitabilmente il momento "foto in posa": tutto un po' eccessivo e affettato. Certo, ero parte del teatrino, ma ci credevo molto meno. Trovavo tante cose patetiche. Oggi, se mi invitano a una cena parlo con la gente: sono una persona più o meno normale. All'epoca stavo tutto il tempo a fissare il cellulare. Non li guardavo nemmeno in faccia. Li trovavo insopportabilmente noiosi. Convintissimi in modo immotivato. Dopo sette anni di pettegolezzi del mondo della moda – chi va a letto con chi, il designer che viene licenziato... – alla fine davvero non ne potevo più.

Anche i rapporti tra le nostre famiglie sono sempre stati pessimi. Veniamo da estrazioni sociali diverse. La mia è una famiglia della periferia milanese: ci diciamo "ti voglio bene" mandandoci affanculo. Però i miei genitori sono persone presenti: stanno sempre coi bambini, non hanno ambizioni mediatiche, né velleità social. I social li usano, sì, ma sembrano degli ottantenni. Mia madre ha come immagine del profilo l'avatar di WhatsApp da superboomer, mio padre posta, ma a caso: si gode la pensione, fa le cose solo per divertirsi. Dall'altra parte, invece, erano tutti degli aspiranti influencer. Ho assistito a liti in cui la mia ex suocera chiedeva alla figlia quanti post avrebbe fatto per il suo nuovo libro. Insomma, era chiaro: eravamo mondi diversi destinati a tornare lontani.

Uno tsunami di merda

Quando arriva uno tsunami di merda e ti ci trovi sotto e non sai più dove stava la superficie, come si va avanti? Non lo sai. Vai avanti per inerzia. Io di tutta la storia del pandoro non sapevo niente fino a quando a Chiara non hanno rifilato quella multa da un milione. L'Antitrust aveva i suoi bei fascicoli spalancati, ma a guardare mia moglie tranquilla, fredda come il ghiaccio, non mi immaginavo ci fosse un casino di quelle proporzioni. Una volta sola mi aveva parlato di soldi, ma le cifre che aveva citato erano molto diverse rispetto a quanto aveva incassato.

Era stata un'estate di merda, ero impantanato fino al collo. Sette psicofarmaci mi avevano prescritto, tutti insieme, una ricetta per il disastro. Ho dovuto tagliare con tutto quanto perché la bocca mi si era bloccata, ve l'ho detto, non riuscivo neanche più a parlare. Gli approcci medici a volte funzionano, altre volte incasinano ancora di più. Ogni malattia è un mondo a sé, un buco nero che risucchia al suo interno il tempo, e la vita di chi sta intorno. Perché i problemi mentali sono difficili anche per chi ti vive accanto. Ti isolano in un egoismo cieco, ti ributtano indietro all'essere primordiale che vede solo il suo dolore. E io, come sempre, sono stato il mio peggior nemico.

Depressione, pensieri di farla finita: ho provato di tutto, terapie di elettrostimolazione al cervello comprese. Dopo l'estate, il colpo di grazia: il fuoco di Sant'Antonio e le emorragie interne. Avevo la testa da un'altra parte, e non certo pronta a immaginare che la faccenda di Chiara si trasformasse in un casino nazionale. La sera prima che scoppiasse il caso, alla cena aziendale, ero lì, microfono in mano, a fare il gradasso, esaltatissimo: «Quest'anno spacchiamo tutto, ragazzi». Brindisi, risate. Poi, a letto e buonanotte. La mattina dopo, sveglia con Chiara in lacrime accanto a me. «Un milione di multa» dice. «Ma che cazzo stai dicendo? Avevi incassato solo trecentomila.» «No, era un milione.» «Porca troia, Chiara, ti rendi conto… tu mi parlavi di tre, quattrocento…» «E gli altri con un'altra società…» «Ho capito, ma quella società sei sempre tu, è la tua, non è esattamente un dettaglio.»

Mi sono messo a leggere le carte, ho scoperto insieme al mondo esterno quello che è successo veramente. E mi sono incazzato: indipendentemente dai cavilli legali, se avessi saputo dei milioni e dell'entità delle donazioni, le avrei detto chiaro e tondo: «Hai fatto una stronzata pazzesca». Quello che nessuno sa è che a non volere quel milione di euro in casa, quindi a dirle di donarlo, sono stato io. «Trova il modo, ma questi soldi qui non li voglio» le ho detto. E lei li ha donati, ma la decisione era stata mia, non della squadra di comunicazione che aveva tirato fuori quella buffonata di messaggio video che aveva solo peggiorato le cose.

Aveva deciso di appoggiarsi allo studio di Auro Palomba, quello che aveva fatto fare il discorso di scuse di

Maurizio Costanzo quando gli avevano trovato la tessera della P2. Bravissimo, fortissimo, ma il mondo della comunicazione è un po' cambiato rispetto ad allora. Questi superesperti hanno dimostrato di non sapersi muovere nella contemporaneità, nel digitale. Io continuavo a dirle: «Guarda che secondo me ti stanno consigliando male, difenditi». Solo che lei non aveva e non ha tuttora compreso che non era tanto importante il parere del tribunale: per la gente lei era già colpevole. E lei aveva tutti gli elementi per potersi difendere, ma non ha voluto farlo.

Dalla sua bocca non è mai uscito: "Abbiamo sbagliato, restituiamo tutto".

Il senso del messaggio video per me avrebbe invece dovuto essere: è stato detto che la condotta con cui ho guadagnato questi soldi è ingannevole, i processi faranno il loro corso, nel mentre io, siccome voglio avere la coscienza pulita, questi soldi li dono tutti, poi mi difenderò nelle sedi opportune. Forse in quel momento un'affermazione del genere non era funzionale alla strategia di difesa a livello giuridico. Si è scelto invece di parlare del famoso "errore di comunicazione". Ma è stato dire quelle cose il vero errore di comunicazione.

Io, in ogni caso, non avevo voce in capitolo. Ero fuori dal gioco, e tanto meglio, perché, se avessi aperto bocca, lei avrebbe fatto tutto il contrario.

Il caso Balocco, insieme ad altre vicissitudini personali e professionali, ha messo a dura prova il nostro rapporto, portando alla luce profonde divergenze di valori e visioni. Queste tensioni hanno influenzato non solo la nostra relazione, ma anche le nostre carriere e le interazioni pubbliche.

A partire dal caso dei pandori, hanno iniziato a fare

le pulci anche a me, in fatto di beneficenza. È iniziata la caccia alle streghe. Ancora oggi evito di parlarne perché mi rendo conto che, se lo facessi, non riuscirei a controllare la narrazione. L'unica maniera che ho è querelare le persone che fanno illazioni sui miei progetti e sul mio modo di far beneficenza, e aspettare che ci sia una sentenza che dica che mi sono sempre mosso in maniera supertrasparente. I giornalisti ci hanno provato ancora, sono andati ovunque: non c'è nessun ente, nessuna associazione che dirà di non avermi visto, di non aver avuto i soldi, a partire da TOG. E questo indipendentemente dalle cifre raccolte, che variano a seconda del tipo di progetto.

Mia moglie e io abbiamo sempre avuto aziende e interessi separati, nonostante venissimo percepiti come un unico brand, i Ferragnez. I nostri team non si stimavano reciprocamente, e questo generava una frizione costante. Mia madre e il mio team lavoravano controvoglia con quello di Chiara, e soprattutto con Fabio Maria Damato, e viceversa. Insomma, per noi loro erano degli snob che se la tiravano e pensavano solo alle stronzate, e per loro noi eravamo dei poveri arricchiti che venivano da Rozzano.

Nella nostra cooperazione professionale, come la serie Amazon, abbiamo gestito insieme i contratti, ma le differenze nella scelta dei contenuti, l'ho raccontato, hanno accentuato i nostri dissensi. Non c'è mai stata armonia tra i due gruppi, meno che meno in un momento di crisi come quello del caso Balocco.

Io avevo limonato Rosa Chemical a Sanremo, quindi come ho già detto ero il pazzo della famiglia, non avevo voce in capitolo. Venivo da stati depressivi, problemi con gli psicofarmaci: non mi avrebbero mai permesso di coordinare le comunicazioni. A posteriori, ripeto che sarebbe stato comunque meglio se me ne fossi occupato io. Anche perché di peggio non si poteva fare.

Forse era la prima volta che Chiara mi mentiva, o forse no. Non so nemmeno se voleva davvero tenermelo nascosto o se credeva alle sue stesse stronzate: distrazione o confusione, chi se ne frega? Mi fa incazzare solo a pensarci. Non voglio nemmeno saperlo.

Non sono qui per essere un modello o esempio, per nessuno. Non credo di essere una brava persona. Non voglio che gli altri mi vedano come un santo: non mi sono mai sentito, né mi sento, moralmente superiore a Chiara. Non sono uno che giudica le persone in base alla loro morale. Ma ho i miei principi. Pochi, ma ci sono. Non negoziabili. Su alcune questioni, non ho problemi a dire che Chiara e io eravamo agli antipodi. Abbiamo avuto molti scontri: un sacco di attriti tra noi, anche prima che esplodesse tutto il casino di Balocco.

È iniziato quando ho scoperto che era coinvolta in qualcosa chiamato il *fashion trust* della moda, in cui c'è Umberta Gnutti Beretta, parte di una famiglia che produce armi e che guadagna montagne di soldi grazie alla guerra, compresa quella in Palestina. Potrebbero facilmente fabbricare solo armi da caccia, e invece scelgono di andare avanti a produrre e vendere armi da guerra. E, ancora peggio, fornirle in contesti con cui non voglio avere niente a che fare. Non capisco ancora bene cosa facciano in questo *fashion trust*: credo diano soldi ai giovani stilisti, non proprio una priorità in questo Paese. Quando ho scoperto il coinvolgimento di Chiara in quel giro le ho detto che non ero d'accordo e che era mio dovere prendere pubblicamente le distanze: «Se fai così, devo dissociarmi».

La situazione famigliare, insomma, era tesa anche prima di Balocco. In quell'anno abbiamo affrontato tre gironi infernali, tutti insieme. La prima grande scossa c'era stata poco prima del mio tumore. Poi la malattia, con tutto lo shock che ha comportato, per un po' ha cancellato i dissidi, riunendoci. Tutti i problemi che avevamo in qualche modo sono momentaneamente spariti. Ma, dopo la malattia, un turbine di squilibri ha preso il sopravvento, e io ero agitato per via delle prescrizioni sbagliate di psicofarmaci. È stato un periodo tosto: riconosco tutta la mia pesantezza, ero difficile da gestire. Lei, d'altro canto, sembrava non cogliere la profondità del mio malessere, credo molti segni le sfuggissero.

Del suicidio

Non è il salto.

Non è il colpo.

Non è l'atto in sé.

È tutto quello che succede prima.

È la gestazione. Figlia di un lungo periodo di progettazione di tale atto. Un feto che cresce nel buio del cranio, che ti sussurra piano, ogni giorno, "basta". Io ci sono arrivato dopo aver mollato gli psicofarmaci di botto come si butta via un pacchetto di sigarette vuoto.

Uno dice: "Sono solo pillole." Ma quelle bastarde erano diventate la mia pelle, la mia lingua, il mio pensiero. E appena le ho interrotte il cervello ha cominciato a urlare. Come quando ti disintossichi dall'eroina. Dieci giorni. Crampi. Le gambe come blocchi di carne molle. I sogni si mangiavano la realtà, mi svegliavo e non capivo se ero sveglio o solo in un altro livello di inferno. Un tunnel. Ma mica con la luce in fondo. Solo cemento e buio e i miei occhi. Il dopo è stato peggio. Perché il corpo ha smesso di tremare, ma la testa era una stanza chiusa a chiave. Il mio cervello gridava per avere la sua dose e non c'era nessuno a rispondere. Passavo le giornate sul divano.

Sdraiato. A dormire o a cercare di farlo, per non sentire il peso di stare sveglio. Per non dover pensare, guardare, respirare. Dormire diventava una specie di suicidio parziale. Una morte a tempo. Dormire, tentare di dormire il più possibile per non vivere e, quando vivevo, percepire il peso di vivere. Pensare che svegliarti per vivere un'altra giornata è più pesante che non risvegliarsi più. E a un certo punto ti dici proprio: "Ma sai che forse sarebbe meno faticoso non svegliarsi più?". Ecco, è lì che si piazza il pensiero. Calmo, freddo, lucido. Non tragico. Solo stanco. Quella roba, quella cosa che ti fa dire: "Oggi no. E forse neanche domani. Forse mai più".

Scrivo ai bambini da dentro una cabina armadio, circondato da bottiglie vuote e da un mucchio di psicofarmaci. Mi lascio collassare là dentro. Mi ha trovato Chiara. Lei era esasperata da quella storia di Balocco, e io continuavo a giocare con l'idea di farmi fuori, finché non ci ho provato sul serio. Mi sono ritrovato in ospedale: sai, quando tenti di suicidarti scattano tutti quei protocolli. I carabinieri ti piombano in casa. Grazie a un dottore amico, ho evitato che venisse fuori il vero motivo del mio ricovero.

Tra parentesi, ne scrivo in *Allucinazione collettiva*.

Giornalismo che uccide

In quei giorni, con la mia solita sconsiderata impulsività, avevo scritto una lettera a una giornalista invece che a Chiara, causandole un evidente disappunto. Le ha dato fastidio che, in un momento del genere, non avessi pensato a lei.

Non aveva colto il mio intento, però. Temo che non lo abbia ancora capito. Nella mia lettera, tentavo di spiegare come un certo giornalismo non si limiti a narrare fatti o a fare inchieste, ma si cimenti nella demolizione sfrenata morale delle persone, fino al punto di spingerle verso il baratro della disperazione. Un simile giornalismo può annichilire fino al desiderio di morte.

E, a proposito di giornalismo che può annichilire così, se sono diventato nemico di Selvaggia Lucarelli è anche perché osavo risponderle.

Perché nessuno risponde mai a Selvaggia Lucarelli, non l'avete notato? Lei ama instaurare questo regime del terrore. La visione che ha di se stessa è quella di una monarca.

E, da una che è diventata una ghostbuster delle truffe, una *truffbuster*, un baluardo del giornalismo d'inchiesta, insomma, io un modo di fare del genere non me lo aspetto. Mi aspetto tutto un altro atteggiamento. Integerrimo. Lei, invece, ha un modus operandi che ho imparato a conoscere nel tempo: Selvaggia Lucarelli non attacca e non fa scoop perché trova la notizia. Selvaggia Lucarelli cerca cose contro di te, e le utilizza per farti del male, perché sei il suo nemico. E ce l'ha quasi fatta anche con me.

Non lo fa con tutti, però.

Per esempio, dagli attacchi di Hamas del 7 ottobre 2023, e dalla brutale reazione di Israele, la Lucarelli è una grande indignata per il genocidio di Gaza (giustamente, ci mancherebbe). Quindi mi verrebbe da pensare che anche prima del 7 ottobre fosse vicina alle sofferenze del popolo palestinese.

E quando, nel luglio 2023, Giulia De Lellis va con il suo fidanzato dell'epoca (erede della famiglia Beretta, di nuovo loro, tra le cui armi ci sono anche quelle che vengono usate quotidianamente da Israele contro la popolazione palestinese) a fare feste insieme alle milizie israeliane, che solo quell'anno avevano ucciso più di centocinquanta bambini, sarebbe lecito aspettarsi che Selvaggia Lucarelli, la giornalista che non si lascia scappare nessuna occasione di segnalare le storture del mondo, dica qualcosa, castighi il comportamento della De Lellis e di Beretta.

Invece cosa fa Selvaggia? Non lancia una delle sue solite battaglie contro la De Lellis, ma si limita a commentare la poca sensibilità dovuta all'ignoranza delle condizioni del popolo palestinese da parte sua. Tutto questo quando invece a Chiara è stata messa una lente di ingrandimento sotto il culo, e da ben prima del caso Balocco.

Sapete perché? Perché la Lucarelli – anche se in teoria è una giornalista – ha un management come se fosse una influencer, la Newco Management, la stessa agenzia di Giulia De Lellis, di cui uno dei fondatori è Francesco Facchinetti. Uno che, tra le sue case history da imprenditore, annovera svariate attività dalla dubbia moralità: Stonex One, oppure la promozione di Catge, una criptovaluta molto ambigua e discussa, oltre alla rivendita di materiale sanitario durante il Covid.

E Selvaggia Lucarelli i suoi amici li tutela sempre. Per questo, secondo me, il suo metodo non nasce da una vera esigenza giornalistica di ricerca della verità, ma dalla voglia di avere seguito e consenso, una dinamica da social in cui i suoi articoli diventano un'arma, un mezzo, con cui accumulare follower e potere.

Ma il moto che guida un giornalista non dovrebbe essere la ricerca della verità? (Chissà che ne pensano i colleghi del "Fatto Quotidiano"... io qualche cosa la so, ma tanto lo potete immaginare anche da soli.) Selvaggia Lucarelli non cerca la verità, Selvaggia Lucarelli incute paura. Per questo io contesto il metodo Lucarelli, perché l'ho vissuto sulla mia pelle, perché ho rischiato di esserne vittima fino in fondo. Se le stai sul cazzo, se ti vuole abbattere, farà tutto ciò che è in suo potere per riuscirci.

Solo che non tutti poi, com'è già successo nel recente passato, hanno le spalle larghe, l'esperienza e la scorza che posso avere io nel gestire l'onda mediatica, il maremoto d'odio che ti sommerge e che finisce per non lasciarti scampo.

Una questione di tradimenti

La vera rottura con Chiara arriva per una questione di tradimenti. Lei pensa che la tradisco e io non mi metto nemmeno a discuterne, sapevo che aveva ragione ma non ritenevo fosse il momento giusto per parlarne. Le dico: «Abbiamo già un problema gigantesco, vuoi davvero aggiungerne un altro ora? Affrontiamoli uno alla volta, non tutta la merda insieme». Non c'è stato verso. Al che vado a Miami per lavoro. Ma lì iniziano le scene di gelosia, grosse, che tirano dentro anche Eleonora, la mia assistente. Chiara pensa che io abbia una storia con lei, ma Eleonora per me è come una sorella. Poi, anche quando ha capito che era una stronzata, e che quello che diceva non aveva senso, ha continuato comunque a essere gelosa del rapporto che avevo con lei.

Ma è vero, avevo la testa altrove. Da una parte c'era la vita come la casa del Mulino Bianco. La perfezione impacchettata. C'era Chiara. Io ci vivevo dentro, ci stavo dentro fino al collo. Era tutto giusto, tutto esposto. Tutto da vetrina. Ma dall'altra parte c'era un'altra storia. C'era Angelica. Una storia senza luci puntate, senza palchi, senza il circo intorno. Una storia che sembrava vera proprio perché stava nascosta. Lei non voleva apparire. Non cercava di venire allo scoperto. A me bastava questo per crederci.

Mi sembrava che lì dentro, in quell'ombra, ci fosse più verità che nella casa coi biscotti e le pubblicità. Poi ti svegli. Poi lo capisci. Lo capisci che l'avevi idealizzata.

Che tutti e due l'avevamo gonfiata come un pallone con l'elio. Perché l'impossibilità di viverla davvero la rendeva più intensa, più viva, più drogata. Era amore sotto steroidi. E gli steroidi, lo sai, ti fanno volare un po', ma poi ti inchiodano il cuore. Non me la sono mai vissuta bene, quella cosa. Era tossica, era dolorosa, faceva male a entrambi. Stavo male. Stavamo male. Non è che mi mettevo a ridere, dicendo: "C'ho l'amante", tipo il cattivo del film che accarezza il gatto sulla poltrona. Io non ridevo mai. Io annegavo a giorni alterni.

Io e mia moglie eravamo diventati nel frattempo una specie di famiglia icona pop, un fenomeno di costume, la più ingombrante favola mediatica della nostra epoca. "Il grande amore." "L'unione perfetta." Uno di quei trucchi di prestigio che, se li guardi bene, ti accorgi che non c'è niente di magico, solo tanta fatica, e colla, e molte mani dietro al sipario. E allora sì, a un certo punto ho voluto mostrare i fili. I meccanismi. Le crepe. Non per distruggere tutto. Ma perché c'è qualcosa di liberatorio nel dire: guardate che non è tutto vero. Guardate che anche le favole sanno di merda quando apri le finestre. Come si fa a distinguere la verità dalla finzione in chi ha ammesso di aver recitato per anni la parte del marito ideale? La verità è brutta. È scomoda. Anche ora non è facile capire se vi stia raccontando i miei segreti più intimi o se reciti per voi una parte scritta a tavolino. Una cosa, che agli occhi di tutti era talmente perfetta da sembrare finta, anche se non si è svelata del tutto, ha comunque finalmente mostrato un po' di verità. E la verità, come la vita, è una merda.

Ho incontrato Angelica poco prima di sposarmi con Chiara. Era un sentimento forte, sì, qualcosa che ti prende il petto e ti fa sanguinare. Ma non è vero che l'ho chiamata cinque minuti prima di mettere l'anello, dicendole: "Se tu non vuoi, io non mi sposo". Con tutti i parenti, a Noto, in Sicilia, che aspettavano il mio arrivo all'altare e io che, se lei mi avesse detto "non sposarti", avrei preso un pony alato e sarei tornato a Milano, come un pazzo che scappa dalla realtà. È una scena che non sta in piedi, non è reale. È una scena da film di seconda mano, surreale come un sogno ubriaco. Quello che non si dice è che non è stata una relazione di anni, non è stata un'amante con cui ti vedi ogni giorno, ogni notte, sei mesi, un anno, due. Era un legame forte, sì, che sopravviveva anche senza che ci vedessimo, come un fuoco che brucia sottoterra, invisibile. E forse era anche peggio, perché se ti vedi è facile mantenere la brace calda. Se non ti vedi, diventa qualcosa di più profondo, o forse solo più triste.

Uno non può scegliere cosa provare e cosa no per qualcuno, siamo solo carne e ossa, e le emozioni sono un casino che ti prende senza chiedere permesso. D'altra parte, puoi mandare all'aria il matrimonio? No. Perché no? C'hai dei figli. E allora tenti di sistemare le cose e cerchi di farle funzionare. Il sentimento per Chiara era reale. Quello per Angelica era diverso. Si possono tenere vivi due sentimenti contemporaneamente? Non mi sono mai chiesto se si possono amare due persone nello stesso momento. Non avevo tempo per domande del genere. Ci sono finito dentro, tutto qui. È come la guerra: nessuno è pronto, nessuno la vuole davvero. Ma poi ti ci trovi dentro, con la divisa sporca e il cuore che pesa. È come chiedere a un soldato: sei pronto per la guerra? Ti dirà di no, poi però sputa per terra e ci va comunque. Così è successo anche a me. Mi ci sono trovato. Punto.

Una cosa era la vita che doveva essere con Chiara: casa, progetti, cani, la lista della spesa e finestre da aprire alla mattina. L'altra era un miraggio, ma aveva tutto quello che mancava alla prima. Una roba silenziosa, senza trucco né filtri. Lei ti guardava e non voleva niente. E cazzo, quanto vale una cosa che non vuole niente da te? Con Chiara volevo costruire qualcosa. Davvero. Ma lei – l'altra – aveva il profumo delle cose che non si ottengono. C'era qualcosa che non avevo mai avuto. Un silenzio buono, una carezza che non chiedeva nulla. Era un'illusione, forse, ma cazzo se sembrava vera. Non ho mai pensato che la mia storia con mia moglie fosse interessata. Né io né lei siamo fatti così.

Ma è il mondo a essere fatto così: ti infili in una situazione, pensi che stai camminando dritto, e invece stai già sbandando da un pezzo.

Con Chiara volevo costruire. Con lei volevo sognare. Ma l'altra aveva quello che Chiara non aveva, e non era colpa di nessuno. Succede.

Era lontana dal rumore, lontana da tutto quello che brilla solo in apparenza. L'ho detto, non voleva niente. E io lì, stanco, affamato proprio di niente.

Ma c'era una cosa, una di quelle cose che non puoi dire a voce alta. Una specie di ombra che ti cammina accanto quando spegni la luce.

E allora resti lì, con due storie in mano e nessuna che riesci a tenere davvero.

Questo crea confusione, ma scoprirsi crea sempre confusione. Però le emozioni svelano una prospettiva doppia. Passioni e immagini che grazie alla stereoscopia acquistano tridimensionalità.

Ho scritto di entrambe in tutte le canzoni.

Perché solo nelle canzoni non riesco a mentire.

È stato tutto sbagliato. Alla fine, c'è stata una grossa lite, e Chiara mi ha sbattuto fuori di casa. A marzo 2024 c'è stata la rottura definitiva. Una sera le dico: «I bambini sono grandi, ormai capiscono. Non facciamo uscire niente prima di parlargli. Non voglio che lo sappiano dai compagni di scuola». E il giorno dopo, manco a farlo apposta, esce tutto. Qualcuno dei suoi aveva deciso di diffondere la notizia. Da quel momento le ho vietato di pubblicare foto dei bambini: perché quello che è successo dimostrava che c'è qualcuno che lavora per lei disposto a sacrificare il bene dei nostri figli. Pur di trovare una exit strategy. Per questo qualcuno spingere a livello mediatico l'idea che Federico fosse un cattivo marito era la scusa perfetta per oscurare il danno di immagine derivato dal caso Balocco. Vuoi giocare così, alla guerra di comunicazione? Va bene, ma non giochiamo con la salute mentale dei nostri figli. Ora non vivo più con i bambini. Quando un matrimonio arriva al capolinea, pensi a loro, certo, ma rimanere insieme solo per i figli non ha senso. Specie nella situazione in cui siamo finiti io e Chiara. Lei era diventata ossessiva nel controllo, non potevo fare nulla in casa senza essere spiato, seguito, monitorato. Venivo controllato quando parlavo con il mio medico, era una situazione insopportabile. Da un certo punto in poi si è trattato solo di sopravvivenza.

Io sono uscito di casa dopo aver tentato il suicidio, dopo un'emorragia, dopo aver perso la sensibilità nella schiena a causa del fuoco di Sant'Antonio, incapace di piegarmi anche solo per allacciarmi le scarpe, dovevo fare riabilitazione tutte le settimane con gli ottantenni. Cagavo sangue, mi avevano mandato una lettera di estorsione. Una lettera pesante: minacciavano i miei figli, mi chiedevano dei soldi. Una lettera strana: mi si accusava di cose folli, come "Noi sappiamo che il tuo tumore è finto". Ma facendo anche riferimento a fatti molto privati miei, avvenimenti molto specifici che riguardavano me e Chiara, delle crisi di cui però nessuno, al di fuori del nostro cerchio ristretto, sapeva. Nella lettera mi invitavano a pubblicare una storia su Instagram con il solo fondale nero se volevo ricevere ulteriori istruzioni. Si comprendeva che era una persona molto vicina a noi: impossibile non essere preoccupati. Ho denunciato, c'è stata un'indagine, ma non è emerso nulla.

In tutto ciò stavo morendo. Se le cose fossero andate avanti così sarei morto. Dovevo rimanere in quella situazione solo per i miei figli? Ho scelto di causargli un dispiacere, ma di continuare a vivere. E l'ho fatto per loro, per i bambini, perché per me sarebbe stato più semplice lasciarmi andare, farla finita.

Allucinazione collettiva

Chiara per me è stata un po' un'allucinazione collettiva, e probabilmente io lo sono stato per lei.

Ovviamente parlo dal mio punto di vista, non posso conoscere il suo, ma credo sia così. Ribadisco che, nella nostra storia, santi non ce ne sono. L'ho sempre stimata sul lavoro per tutto quello che ha saputo fare. E mi prendono in giro quando io dico che avevamo un'intesa sessuale forte, ma quella è una componente fondamentale per me, non so per gli altri. Siamo due estremi che per un certo momento si sono integrati perfettamente, ma rimaniamo due estremi opposti che prima o poi dovevano necessariamente tornare a scontrarsi come Montecchi e Capuleti, élite e periferie, la Bella e la Bestia che, finché l'incantesimo dura, possono resistere ma una volta che svanisce c'è poco da fare, una rimane la Bella e l'altro la Bestia.

Io e lei veniamo da posti troppo diversi, l'ho detto: estrazioni sociali diverse, famiglie completamente diverse. Io e i miei genitori ci diciamo "ti voglio bene", boh, una volta ogni tre anni. Dimostrazioni affettuose non ne vedi mai, tra me e mia madre. Sono più le volte che ci insultiamo. Ma con i miei figli è proprio la nonna classica. Non che l'altra non sia una nonna, semplicemente i miei sono quelli che, nella vita quotidiana, ci hanno dato una mano consistente. Sono persone più pratiche: dimostrano l'affetto coi fatti. Mentre la sua famiglia è tutto un mondo di cuoricini rosa, nomignoli, carezze. Col tempo ho messo a fuoco che apparteniamo quasi a specie diverse: quello che è importante per lei non lo è per me, e viceversa. Oggi ho raggiunto una consapevolezza tale da comprendere che ciò che facevamo è stato completamente sbagliato, e ha creato un proselitismo tossico, con migliaia e migliaia di replicanti che cercavano di imitare quello che facevamo noi.

Nella serie lo si vedeva: tanti hanno pensato fosse pilotata, finta, invece era esattamente così. Ci sono stati momenti in cui la differenza tra di noi diventava un valore aggiunto, fasi in cui stavamo bene ed eravamo belli nell'essere diversi. Questo fino a quando le difficoltà esterne hanno trasformato queste stesse differenze interne in scogli insormontabili.

Io, per esempio, da Sanremo in poi, da un punto di vista ideologico, ho iniziato a rigettare un po' la retorica progressista portata all'estremo, la retorica femminista e LGBTQIA+ infilata ovunque. Avevamo delle discussioni forti anche su questo: io ascoltavo "La Zanzara" di Cruciani, a lei faceva schifo. Per me quindi era impossibile anche solo pensare di invitare a casa Cruciani. Oggi lo sento e lo vedo. Prima invece non potevo avere rapporti umani con persone che per lei erano infrequentabili.

Mi hanno attribuito il ruolo di paladino woke, ma io non sono mai stato quella roba. Non che non sia a favore dei diritti, ma ci sono eccessi che non mi appartengono. Invece Chiara era più per seguire quasi in automatico tutte le battaglie progressiste veicolate dai social. Perché ci credesse o per posizionamento, non so dirlo. A un certo punto volevo sentirmi libero di avere rapporti umani senza sentirmi giudicato o in colpa perché frequentavo persone che dicevano cose diverse dalla retorica imposta dai social.

Io, tanto per dirne una, non sono per darsi delle regole in termini di linguaggio: lo trovo stupido e preferisco un linguaggio crudo e diretto. Quello che sto cercando di usare senza finzione e retorica nella stesura di questo libro. Cruciani, per esempio, a me fa ridere, lo trovo anche una persona intelligente, con un modo di esprimersi di rottura, per certi versi.

Forse, dopo una fase di attivismo performativo, che io stesso a tratti ho praticato, ho visto i limiti di quell'approccio così polarizzato e unilaterale. Mi sono reso conto che non ha senso rinchiudersi in uno schema morale rigido: a volte ci sono cose che ci incuriosiscono o che ci fanno ridere, anche se non sono proprio quelle giuste. Insomma: tutto va sempre contestualizzato. Mentre adesso mi sembra che il contesto sia morto.

Non ho mai veramente discusso con Chiara del perché è finita. Dal suo punto di vista, sono io il cattivo e, per un verso, non posso non essere d'accordo. Credo che lei fosse molto sicura di sé. Io periodicamente uscivo di testa perché nascevano polemiche inutili su di noi. Chiara riusciva a sbattersene. Io no. Come lo scandalo ridicolo sull'acqua in bottiglia Evian. C'è anche l'acqua di Armani che costa tanto, ma nessuno si scandalizza. Erano tutti pretesti per sminuire la sua figura e i suoi risultati. Su molte questioni io la difendevo, ma lei non ha mai visto, in questa cosa, un atto d'amore. Per lei non contava: esigeva in altri modi. Dimostrazioni d'affetto esplicite, dire "ti amo" ogni cinque minuti. Una visione del rapporto molto dimostrativa. Cose che io magari non riuscivo a darle. Ed è per questo che lei non riesce a capire che l'intera debacle di Balocco, pur non essendo – secondo me – penalmente perseguibile, è moralmente e politicamente grave. Se anche Chiara non traeva beneficio dal vendere più pandori c'è, infatti, una questione di valori. E questo non significa che io abbia valori migliori dei suoi. Ammetto che su tante cose io non ho una morale. Su altre (poche) ce l'ho. E, per esempio, la faccenda della beneficenza è un valore non negoziabile.

Lei non capisce che quella roba, per me, era grave tanto quanto un tradimento. Così come altre cose che faceva e andavano contro le mie idee. Sulla beneficenza ci siamo scontrati molte volte, perché secondo me delegava troppo, era poco coinvolta. E attenzione: se lei si fosse lasciata coinvolgere di più – e io so che è una persona anche emotiva, sensibile, quanto e più di me –, probabilmente avrebbe donato di più, avrebbe fatto scelte diverse. Il problema è che non si interessava quanto doveva. Poi su altre cose è più empatica, più sensibile. Ma in quel frangente forse aveva altre priorità, e sicuramente è stata anche mal consigliata.

Il problema è che questo atteggiamento ha generato tutto quello che sappiamo. Se io ne fossi stato al corrente sarebbe stato un conto, tuttora non so perché mi abbia detto delle cifre diverse. Sarei stato il primo a dirle: "Che cazzo stai facendo?".

In più, io non le ho detto: "Ti lascio per questa cosa", nonostante mi avesse dato molto da pensare. E ho dovuto subire la gestione di un problema che era anche mio. Perché, così come quando io facevo le figure di merda, gli schizzi arrivavano anche a lei, lo stesso valeva per me. Qui, però, altro che schizzi di merda.

Per il carattere che ho io, se mi vogliono giustiziare sulla pubblica piazza, non sto con le mani dietro la schiena. Faccio un bordello prima che mi sparino. Oppure, se tu mi vuoi sparare io sono quello che ti abbraccia e si lancia dal balcone insieme a te. Così moriamo entrambi.

Tra l'altro, di cose da dire ne avevamo: il disegno attorno a ciò che è successo a Chiara è lampante.

Sono certo che quello che faceva lei lo facevano anche altre mille aziende, da sempre. Questo non dico che annulli il problema, ma la questione era più grande.

Quando Chiara Ferragni viene coinvolta nello scandalo, chi c'è tra le prime persone che rilasciano dichiarazioni pubbliche? Giorgia Meloni. Chiara ha prestato il fianco: non ha compreso che era un confronto tra fazioni politiche, a tutti gli effetti. Quando ho fatto le mie dichiarazioni di carattere politico le ho fatte con la consapevolezza delle mie azioni, lei come ho già detto non ha una consapevolezza politica. Mi seguiva, dicendo cose che, certo, pensava, ma poi non era in grado di sostenere le tesi che portava avanti. Per questo si esponeva meno di me. E lo faceva solo quando era semplice esporsi. La politica non è il suo territorio. Ma non si è resa conto che, a un certo punto, noi eravamo a tutti gli effetti delle figure politiche. Quando ti esponi così, devi essere più immacolato degli altri. Noi siamo stati un simbolo, rappresentavamo delle cose. Che sono di colpo crollate. L'errore c'è stato, e non solo di comunicazione: il suo continuare a non volerlo dire, più il tempo passava, più diventava ridicolo. Lei parla del 2024 come l'anno più brutto della sua vita, ma dev'essere onesta intellettualmente e riconoscere che è stata lei stessa a contribuire a renderlo tale.

Auguro a Chiara un futuro luminoso e felice, soprattutto per i miei figli, perché meritano di crescere in un ambiente sano. Ho dubbi sul suo lavoro, perché lei di business, in realtà, non capisce un granché. Ha sempre delegato. Io sono nato con il pallino dell'impresa, sono un accentratore, non mi fido di nessuno. Lei si è sempre fidata molto, e spesso ho reputato una virtù il suo delegare, visto che io su molte cose non ci riesco. E soprattutto resto dell'idea che non puoi lasciare che l'identità della tua azienda sia la proiezione del tuo CEO: mia madre è il mio CEO, ma è la proiezione delle *mie* idee, del *mio* concetto di fare azienda. Poi, un sacco di cose pratiche le delego, ma ho una visione molto specifica di dove andare. Lei si faceva dare dagli altri anche la visione: quindi, a quel punto, l'azienda è tua o della gente da cui ti fai suggerire la direzione da percorrere? Alla fine, chi è che comanda? Quando lei ha conosciuto Pozzoli, le redini dell'azienda, di fatto, le teneva lui. Quando io e Chiara ci siamo incontrati, lei aveva quaranta dipendenti e guadagnava meno di me. «Come è possibile» le dicevo «che tu sia conosciuta in tutto il mondo e io incassi il doppio di te?» Ci è voluto un po' per farle vedere che il problema era il suo ex. Certo, sembrava una questione di gelosia o di antipatia da parte mia, ma era pura analisi oggettiva. Le ho fatto capire che non erano i suoi soci a essere i cattivi, come pensava lei (e infatti non erano loro i cattivi): il problema stava tra quelli che lei riteneva fossero dalla sua parte.

Nel mondo degli affari digitali, le apparenze contano

più della realtà. Questa è stata una lezione che Chiara, credo, ha imparato a caro prezzo. Io ho seguito da vicino la sua ascesa, inizialmente sono stato abbagliato dalla facciata glamour delle operazioni, da tutti quei dipendenti e dai case studies a Harvard. Ma la verità, dietro le quinte, era tutt'altro che dorata.

A conti fatti, per me, quello che conta è il fatturato. Noi, come azienda, non abbiamo mai ostentato i nostri risultati, se lo avessimo fatto avremmo potuto rivelare guadagni doppi rispetto a quelli di Chiara, all'epoca. E nonostante avessimo solo dieci dipendenti (ora ne abbiamo una trentina). Il punto di svolta per Chiara è stato l'arrivo di Fabio Maria Damato, una figura chiave per ridefinire la traiettoria dell'azienda. Che inizialmente è fiorita sotto la sua guida, va riconosciuto: è Damato che, in buona parte, ha portato Chiara a essere quello che è diventata, coi suoi pregi e i suoi difetti. Solo che Damato è diventato troppo influente, lei gli dava troppo retta. Accorgendosene troppo tardi. Poi Chiara si è scusata con me, mi ha detto di essere stata manipolata. Ma quelle scuse, arrivando così in ritardo, mi hanno fatto uscire di testa. A quel punto la faccenda ce l'eravamo lasciata alle spalle (con pianti, terapia e sensi di colpa a manetta). La verità è che, su molte cose, avevo un'idea sbagliata, e ho capito che mia moglie era davvero ingenua.

Inoltre quella positività irrefrenabile verso la vita non è fatta per me. Lei è davvero come si vede: molto gioiosa, molto sbrilluccicosa, molto *shiny*. Io invece sono molto cupo. Ho tentato di assimilarla, quella sua gioia sfrenata, quella lucentezza che sembrava emanasse in modo quasi involontario. Ma io non sono così. Quell'entusiasmo non mi appartiene. E penso che la filosofia di vita di

Chiara sia davvero migliore della mia: se dovessi consigliare a qualcuno, tra la mia e la sua, scelgo la sua, senza esitazioni. Ma presto o tardi uno deve accettare la propria natura: si può provare a cambiare per l'altro, sì, ma fino a un certo punto. Sennò tanto vale cercare un'altra persona. Le persone vanno accettate per come sono. Se ti accorgi che vuoi continuamente cambiare il modo in cui è fatto l'altro, è meglio trovare una persona diversa. Io ho cercato di diventare altro, ma non ci sono riuscito.

Ci siamo fatti molto male durante il matrimonio. Ci siamo danneggiati a vicenda con questo rapporto. Sempre su lunghezze d'onda troppo diverse, con temperamenti e culture che non potevano essere più distanti. Per un po' ci siamo bilanciati: a tratti sembrava che avessimo trovato un equilibrio. Precario, come diceva anche il nostro terapeuta, quello che compare nella serie: lei una portaerei che va dritta, io una mina vagante che non riesce a non raccogliere le provocazioni e si butta nella mischia. L'incastro disfunzionale era ovvio a tutti, tranne che a noi stessi.

Il divario si è allargato quando ho ripreso a frequentare certe compagnie. Una reazione a quel mondo patinato che ho respirato negli anni di matrimonio. Preferisco la compagnia di chi è storto, sbagliato, perché lo trovo più autentico rispetto a quelli che sembrano perfetti ma in realtà sono vuoti dentro, come brioche. Le brioche vuote non mi interessano. Voglio stare con gente che ritengo interessante, e me ne frego delle aspettative altrui. Non ho bisogno di mantenere una facciata. Mi circondo di chi mi piace, punto. Non esiste un crimine in questo senso, mi pare, non esiste il reato di cattiva frequentazione. E io non ho incarichi pubblici: non vedo perché debba rendere conto a qualcuno delle persone che frequento. Perché dovrei giustificarmi? Non ha questa premura chi ricopre ruoli pubblici, non vedo perché dovrei avercela io. Voglio frequentare dei criminali? Dei miliardari? Io ho sempre avuto amicizie che vanno dalla punta della piramide sociale, le persone più ricche e potenti di questo Paese, fin giù agli ultimi livelli. La vita, per me, è interessante solo se vissuta costantemente ai suoi margini più estremi, che sia nord o sud, povertà o ricchezza, destra o sinistra, santi o delinquenti. Non è che queste cose io le studio, no. Le faccio, senza pensarci troppo. Non sono molto bravo a capire cosa voglio, cosa decido. Sono andato dall'altro lato, alle radici, alle cose semplici: dall'estrema e paranoica cura dell'immagine a sbattermene, cercare di provocare, di stuzzicare.

La delusione Marco Travaglio

E, a proposito di provocazione, mentre ero nel mezzo della separazione con Chiara ho sentito la necessità di difenderla, di difenderci. Non accettavo la posizione remissiva, a capo chino, che lei aveva assunto. Sicuramente avevamo sbagliato, ma non c'era ragione di lasciarsi fustigare così. In particolare non sentivo fosse giusto essere umiliati dai giornalisti che per anni avevano banchettato sulla nostra vita.

Tra le tante discussioni, quella che mi ha più deluso è stata quella con Marco Travaglio che io, specialmente da ragazzo, ho stimato molto. Col "Fatto Quotidiano", fino a un certo punto, avevo avuto un ottimo rapporto. Il giornale mi voleva pure come editorialista: scrissi un articolo, dopo la strage alla redazione di "Charlie Hebdo", che fu messo in prima pagina. Mi sono accorto però che Travaglio ha un problema: non puoi contraddirlo, ha bisogno di essere incensato, e non puoi non pensarla come lui.

L'ultimo incontro tra di noi si è rivelato spiacevole e a suo modo memorabile. È venuto ospite a "Muschio selvaggio", insieme con Daniele Capezzone. Per anni l'avevo considerato un punto di riferimento. Avevo sempre visto in lui un baluardo dell'informazione italiana, un uomo che aveva fatto della ricerca della verità la sua arma primaria. Leggendolo e ascoltandolo per anni, io mi ero formato, ero cresciuto politicamente e intellettualmente. Sono anche stato ad "Annozero", dove Travaglio era ospite fisso, per un dibattito con Giovanardi quando avevo ventidue anni. Era una figura che rispettavo. Ho persino scritto canzoni in cui elogiavo il suo lavoro. Ma alla fine si è rivelato esattamente come gli altri, uno che adatta i suoi principi a proprio vantaggio. E mi sono reso conto che i fascisti sono più sinceri: ti dicono subito che non valgono nulla, non fingono di essere i nuovi Indro Montanelli. C'è più coerenza, perlomeno.

Quando Travaglio è venuto a "Muschio" io arrivavo dall'intervista a Matteo Mariotti, il ragazzo attaccato da uno squalo, in cui lui aveva detto di aver pensato al suicidio per colpa della shitstorm scatenata da Selvaggia Lucarelli. Quindi mi sembrava doveroso chiedere al direttore di Selvaggia Lucarelli cosa ne pensasse del suo metodo. Sentirsi rispondere: «Non mi piace fare i processi agli assenti», da uno che ha scritto, tanto per dirne una, un libro su Berlusconi dopo la sua morte, e ha basato tutta una carriera sui processi agli assenti, mi ha fatto capire la totale disonestà intellettuale del personaggio. Non c'era niente di così anomalo nella mia domanda. Se fosse stato Travaglio a intervistare me, mi avrebbe di sicuro interrogato sul caso Balocco. Era altrettanto inevitabile che io interrogassi l'editore di Selvaggia Lucarelli sul suo modus operandi. La reazione di Travaglio è stata di un'irritazione puerile. Poi quando, con semplicità, gli ho chiesto: «È veramente necessario, in un articolo su una raccolta fondi, menzionare che il ragazzo non è simpatico?», lui si è alterato: «Ma tua moglie è Wanna Marchi». Travaglio ha avuto la libertà di criticarci, insomma, ma si è offeso per le critiche rivolte a lui. Sosteneva anche che gli avessi teso un'imboscata solo perché a "Muschio selvaggio" facevamo commentare tutte le puntate a qualcuno. Nella puntata di Travaglio c'era David Parenzo, che ha criticato Travaglio per le sue parole. Noi permettevamo a tutti di esprimersi liberamente, anche a costo di essere attaccati a nostra volta, senza censurare niente: erano liberi anche di prendersela con me. A volte qualcuno ha detto che come intervistatore faccio cagare, che parlo sopra gli altri, eccetera eccetera. Travaglio pensava invece che io avessi orchestrato l'attacco di Parenzo, che fossero critiche su commissione, ma è completamente falso. È talmente megalomane e narcisista che, in un'intervista tv, è arrivato a dire: «Spero che Fedez non abbia lasciato Chiara Ferragni per colpa mia». Come se io potessi chiudere un matrimonio di sette anni a causa sua. Gli mando un messaggio dicendogli, in sostanza, che è un mitomane. Da lì tutta una serie di messaggi folli in cui parliamo di Chiara, Selvaggia Lucarelli, Wanna Marchi e del fatto che non ho finito gli studi per colpa di una dislessia molto complessa. Gliene mando uno anche molto lungo, in cui cerco di spiegargli con calma e per bene il mio punto di vista. Lui mi risponde senza la minima empatia. E io, in quel momento, mi sono chiesto: "Ma io, finora, in cosa ho creduto?". Da lì non abbiamo più avuto rapporti.

Nemmeno mia madre può rompermi le palle su chi frequento

A completare un anno di merda, nella primavera del 2024 è scoppiato il caso Iovino. È dall'adolescenza che frequento cattive compagnie: se mi beccano a delinquere con loro, pagherò il prezzo e risponderò dei reati. Ma ricordo che si può delinquere anche con le buone compagnie. Bisognerebbe giudicare le azioni, non se le facce con cui mi accompagno sono quelle giuste o quelle sbagliate.

Ho trentacinque anni: nemmeno mia madre può rompermi le palle su chi frequento. Sono libero di uscire con chi voglio. Non mi sono mai macchiato di crimini, ma mi capita di frequentare persone che ne hanno commessi: dunque? E poi, lo Stato predica che il carcere dovrebbe rieducare, no? Passo il tempo con uno che è stato dentro per narcotraffico: ok. Però un magistrato di sorveglianza lo ha ritenuto anche un detenuto modello, gli sono stati concessi i domiciliari, è libero di andare dove vuole in Lombardia dalla mattina alle otto fino alla sera alle undici, pure allo stadio. Se il magistrato lo ha visto così, che dovevo vedere di diverso, io? Io realmente quello vedevo. Poi lui e gli altri erano persone violente? Sì, e allora? Io non ho mai compiuto atti violenti con loro.

Quello che mi scandalizza è che stanno contestando alla curva del Milan reati di cinque anni fa, reati che nulla hanno a che vedere con la curva. I reati della curva non si capisce quali siano, se non quattro birre e quattro parcheggi, di cui sia la Digos che il sindaco di Milano erano a conoscenza.

Dei reati della curva dell'Inter, però, se n'è parlato molto meno. Sebbene ci siano stati tre morti in quattro anni, infiltrazioni della 'ndrangheta, omicidi, tentati omicidi. Alcuni miei amici sono in carcere ingiustamente: sono dentro per un'associazione a delinquere che non esiste, lo dico serenamente. Da amico ho sempre avuto l'impressione che è come se prendessero tanti piccoli reati e li mettessero insieme per riuscire a dare il reato di associazione a delinquere. Ma sono reati singoli commessi da singoli individui, non c'è l'associazione. Se, per ipotesi, dei tizi della curva vanno a picchiare della gente, e Luca Lucci è ai domiciliari, cosa ne sa lui di cosa combinano queste persone? Luca Lucci non sapeva nulla di cosa facevano queste persone. Ci sono intercettazioni in cui Luca Lucci cazzia alcuni della curva quando scopre che facevano risse e cose del genere, perché si stavano ripulendo. E comunque non erano solo miei amici: erano amici di tutti.

Oggi non prendo più psicofarmaci. Mi davano un sacco di effetti collaterali. Era una depressione farmacoresistente a generarmi quegli istinti suicidari così importanti. Invece ora non sono più depresso. Fumo le canne, mi diverto, esco con della gente orribile, ma almeno non sto più male come alla fine del matrimonio. Non faccio neanche più psicoterapia: semplicemente per una questione di tempo. Dovrei tornarci, o forse no. Quello che Freud doveva darmi, credo me l'abbia dato. Per ora mi sono avvicinato a metodi diversi, tipo il mental coaching. A volte giusti, altre meno. È un terreno insidioso, perché puoi beccare quello bravissimo così come il truffatore.

Adesso sono migliorato: alle provocazioni rispondo con la musica. Almeno per ora, non so quanto durerà. Sotto la luce al neon dell'esame dei media, dove ogni post viene sezionato e ogni passo falso ingigantito, ho imparato la lezione: basta con la risposta perpetua. Ora, ciò che devo dire lo dico con i pezzi. Ho capito che il dibattito online è una terra desolata, non ha senso: le persone ascoltano i primi tre secondi del tuo argomento. E fine. Le parole sono ridotte a rumore incoerente, è come vomitare suoni nel vuoto. A un certo punto, neanche io so perché, quello che facevo con la scrittura dei pezzi avevo iniziato a farlo nelle storie di Instagram. Non ha senso portare avanti una conversazione sui social. Meglio le canzoni: è una cosa che avevo dimenticato.

Atto III

UNA BELLA CANZONE

Le foglie del destino

Circa un anno fa ho scoperto che in India ci sono queste biblioteche secolari, dove si custodiscono rotoli di foglie di palma incisi in sanscrito. E, secondo la tradizione, su ogni foglia c'è scritto il destino di una persona, il destino di un'anima. Questi antichi archivi spirituali ospitano milioni di scritti: per accedere alla propria vita passata, è necessario innanzitutto lasciare un'impronta digitale. I veggenti, tramite quest'impronta, scovano il fascio di foglie che potrebbe contenere quella col percorso della tua vita. Anche se in realtà queste foglie non narrano le sorti di ogni essere umano, ma esclusivamente di coloro che, in qualche modo, sono destinati a incrociare l'India nel corso della loro vita.

In effetti io, a diciotto anni, mi sono tatuato sulla pelle il simbolo di Ganesha, uno degli dèi indiani. E senza sapere il perché. Modificandone anche l'iconografia: al posto di una mano, un uncino. Quando, anni dopo, un amico affascinato da teorie alternative e complottismi vari ha cominciato a parlarmi dell'esistenza di queste foglie del destino, questa circostanza mi è sembrata una specie di segno premonitore. Il mio amico mi racconta che in queste foglie ci sono scritte le tue vite passate, ma anche gli eventi attuali e futuri, fino alla morte. E non in modo vago. C'è proprio scritto come muori, con una precisione disarmante.

La vita, effettivamente, aveva iniziato a giocare con me: nel periodo in cui Chiara mi ha sbattuto fuori di casa, seguivo una life coach. Una poco spirituale, più sull'improve yourself, sul miglioramento di se stessi, sul raggiungimento dei propri obiettivi. Cose piuttosto concrete. Avevo iniziato a vederla da poco, non eravamo in confidenza. Durante gli incontri con lei succede una cosa strana: contro ogni aspettativa, mi propone di esplorare proprio le foglie del destino. «Pensa che me ne hanno parlato giusto qualche settimana fa» le dico. E lei: «E tu invece pensa che ero titubante nel dirtelo, perché so che non sei una persona interessata a questo genere di cose, magari mi prendevi per pazza». La coincidenza mi colpisce, così decido di accettare. Durante il periodo in cui mi preparo alla lettura delle foglie (non vado in India, ma faccio la versione luxury, zero-sbatti, quindi da casa), la vita sembra avvolgermi in una serie di eventi inspiegabili e coincidenze pazzesche. In quel momento nessuno sapeva che io ero stato sbattuto fuori di casa, e io vivevo da nomade in vari Airbnb di Milano, mi ero ribattezzato "gipsy dell'area C". Un giorno, in pieno centro, mi si avvicina un Hare Krishna per offrirmi libri sul karma e sulla reincarnazione. Diverse persone, non collegate tra di loro, mi suggeriscono di guardare *Kung Fu Panda*, per motivi che mi sfuggono: «Guardalo perché ti potrebbe essere utile». Un mese dopo, una specie di guida spirituale, un po' sui generis: «Tu l'hai mai visto *Kung Fu Panda*? Dovresti guardarlo». Sì, anche lui.

Ma arriviamo al momento in cui devo effettivamente fare la lettura. È importante contestualizzare il luogo. Un referente italiano mi mette in contatto con un lettore di queste foglie, il mio si chiama Vinod. Il referente italiano arriva nell'Airbnb, e non è consapevole di dove siamo: avrebbe potuto essere uno studio, un ufficio, una casa d'appoggio, qualsiasi cosa. Entrando chiede se ho visto *Kung Fu Panda,* io e la mia assistente non ci possiamo credere. Poi inizia a farmi una serie di domande, perché prima di leggere la foglia deve appuntarsi la mia data di nascita e altre informazioni, in modo da poter dare conferma al lettore, dato che questo parla un inglese a dir poco zoppicante. Secondo la tradizione, chi ti legge la foglia interferisce col tuo karma: spesso i lettori muoiono molto giovani, perché si fanno carico del karma di molte persone. Però progrediscono anche, dal punto di vista karmico, quindi l'idea è che rinasceranno in una condizione migliore. L'obiettivo delle letture è che loro ti diano dei rimedi. Cioè, per come l'ho capita io, magari sbaglio: se devi morire in un incidente d'auto, loro ti forniscono dei rimedi – che non so quali siano perché la mia lettura è in corso da più di un anno – per far sì che in quell'incidente tu non muoia, ma magari, non so, ti ferisca gravemente. Con le foglie funziona che il lettore inizia a esaminare il bandolo rintracciato a partire dall'impronta digitale e ti fa delle domande. Ti dice, che so: «Tua madre si chiama...». Oppure: «Hai un fratello che lavora...», «Tuo padre ha problemi di cuore...». Se le informazioni non coincidono con la foglia che ha in mano, la scarta e passa alla successiva.

Prima di iniziare la ricerca della mia foglia, Vinod mi fa però presente le difficoltà: il karma, attivandosi, potrebbe frapporre degli ostacoli. E non era un presagio vuoto:

eventi inquietanti hanno iniziato davvero a disturbare la lettura. La corrente è mancata improvvisamente nel tempio in India. Telefonate incessanti hanno squassato il silenzio qui in Italia e, dopo un periodo in cui non ci eravamo sentiti per niente, Chiara ha cominciato a inondare il mio telefono di messaggi in cui mi insultava. Anche mia madre di colpo ha iniziato a chiamarmi per segnalarmi tutta una serie di problemi sul fronte lavorativo. Qualcuno si è messo a trapanare nella casa di fianco. La percezione di una resistenza è diventata intensa, era come se delle forze si fossero coalizzate contro quel contatto. Mi hanno detto che evidentemente il mio karma era molto forte, e stava cercando di ostacolare la seduta. Intanto il mio lettore procedeva con le domande, confrontandosi con informazioni che non appartenevano alla sua comprensione linguistica e ripetendo fonemi alieni alla sua lingua madre.

Poi, all'improvviso, ecco una foglia che sembra proprio la mia: il nome, la situazione famigliare, tutto corrisponde. Vinod, a un certo punto, mi dice proprio: «Tu sei stato appena mandato via da casa». E non lo sapeva nessuno. Dev'essere proprio la mia, mi dico. Solo che quando gli dico che sono nato nel 1989 lui scarta la foglia: la data di nascita non corrisponde, è il 15 ottobre 1988. Cerco di impedirglielo, mi sembra un errore trascurabile, gli dico: «Ma sono io, solo la data è sbagliata». Ma lui risponde dicendo che l'universo in cui viviamo non è l'unico, per cui può esistere benissimo, in un altro universo, un Federico Lucia nato il 15 ottobre 1988. Insomma, un altro io in una dimensione diversa dalla nostra. La tensione è palpabile: la sincerità, mi è stato detto, è fondamentale, poiché ogni menzogna può avere conseguenze drammatiche. L'italiano che fa da interprete ci ha raccontato che una volta avevano letto la foglia a una signora che aveva dei problemi con un mafioso. A loro aveva detto che lui era uno stalker, che lei l'aveva mollato e lui, ossessionato, la perseguitava da tempo e voleva ucciderla. In realtà, si è poi scoperto che la donna gli aveva rubato dei soldi. E infatti Vinod, che lavorava sulla base di una convinzione sbagliata, il giorno dopo si è rotto tutt'e due le gambe, ed è rimasto in ospedale per mesi.

Alla fine, la mia foglia viene trovata. Ma quando la comincia a leggere, Vinod di colpo sbianca, e visibilmente turbato mi dice che secondo le profezie avrei dovuto essere già morto, di cancro. Poi in tutta fretta dice: «Io devo andare», e chiude, si disconnette. L'interprete italiano mi offre due spiegazioni: o io, in questa vita, ho smaltito tanto karma, perché ho fatto tanto bene, e quindi sono in una specie di vita bonus. Oppure sono un'anomalia del sistema, un errore nella matrice cosmica. Sono confuso, molto confuso. La mia lettura, comunque, continuerà, e sta continuando. Resta il fatto che questa rivelazione, in un periodo già di per sé gravoso, ha aggravato il mio stato depressivo.

C'è poi l'episodio di Iovino, qualche giorno dopo io faccio la lettura e Vinod mi dice: «Questa cosa non va bene». Tra l'altro lui mi aveva messo in guardia: durante il periodo della lettura della foglia sarebbero potuti accadere eventi particolari, che avrebbero stimolato la mia reattività. Oltre alla questione con Iovino, effettivamente, si erano materializzate altre provocazioni. Così per diversi mesi ha dovuto commissionare a dei bramini delle preghiere, per me, nel tentativo di sciogliere il mio karma. Però talmente avevo sbagliato, e talmente il mio karma era potente, che per sei mesi lui non mi ha più voluto sentire. Abbiamo anche dovuto far nascere dei vitelli, ho fatto delle donazioni di cibo a un villaggio indiano (parliamo di pochi euro, ci tengo a precisarlo, cifre irrisorie, sennò potrebbe sembrare che mi stessero estorcendo dei soldi).

Solo da poco abbiamo iniziato la lettura vera e propria: il lettore parte leggendoti dei racconti allegorici che si trovano scritti nella foglia, cose che dovrebbero parlarti della tua vita. Ma io a quel punto non avevo più voglia di continuare, era andata troppo per le lunghe, mi ero stufato. Sono partito controvoglia, con lui che parlava in indiano, non capivo niente, e mi veniva da ridere. Poi però a un certo punto ha detto delle cose che mi hanno fatto piangere: c'è una ciclicità nella mia vita, una ciclicità numerica, basata sul nove. A nove anni mi è successa una cosa traumatica, a diciotto pure, a ventisette ho conosciuto Chiara, e ora sono entrato nell'anno dei trentasei. «Adesso capisco perché abbiamo dovuto aspettare che tu entrassi nel trentaseiesimo anno, perché hai questa ciclicità» ha detto Vinod. «Adesso hai Naandi dalla tua.» Naandi è il braccio destro di Shiva, il toro sacro che lui cavalca. Questi, mi ha spiegato, sono gli anni in cui posso diventare illuminato o essere definitivamente risucchiato dall'oscurità. In teoria, dovrei aver smaltito molto karma con tutte le cose che mi sono successe, e questo è l'anno in cui Nandi è mio alleato per combattere e sconfiggere un certo demone, salendo di livello. O muoio, dice Vinod, o divento spirituale.

E così è arrivato Sanremo.

Quel palco

Avevo una bella canzone. Avevo voglia di risalire sul palco. *Battito*. Segna un grande cambiamento nella mia vita. Prima di separarmi da mia moglie lavoravo con un team musicale creativo. Cambio totalmente perché succedono delle cose non sempre belle. Quindi *Battito* è l'inizio di un nuovo percorso con delle nuove persone, che sono Federica Abbate, Cripo e Alessandro La Cava. E durante la mia vacanza in Sardegna costruisco questo piccolo studio per un nuovo inizio di gestazione creativa. Scriviamo, scriviamo insieme. A un certo punto sono dovuto entrare dentro il brano e capire che quella cosa che avevo scritto racconta tantissimo di me, ma per una volta racconta tantissimo pure per tante altre persone. Anche perché ormai i trapper, quando ottengono il successo, poi ti parlano solo di come sono diventati ricchi. Perché? Perché ora non sono più poveri, non vivono più quella roba lì e quindi ripetono costantemente come hanno fatto i soldi, le macchine, le donne e alla lunga non parlano più a nessuno. Non frega più niente a nessuno. Io invece mi sono guardato davvero dentro e mi sono reso conto che dalla merda nascono i fiori. Che essere artista, quando vivi la merda, ha un lato positivo, ti crea veramente una nuova linfa vitale per la scrittura. Ringrazio di soffrire ancora d'amore perché mi fa scrivere delle cose molto belle.

Ci sono brani che quando li scrivi sono liberatori e ci sono brani che quando li esegui sono liberatori. *Allucinazione collettiva* è un brano che ho scritto piangendo. *Battito* non è un brano che ho scritto piangendo, ma l'ho cantato piangendo internamente. E ho pensato seriamente di non riuscire a cantarlo su quel palco. I mesi, le settimane precedenti sono state un vero inferno. Io venivo da un Natale marcio, emotivamente ero un rottame, ma stavo ricominciando a respirare. Pensavo di essermela buttata alle spalle, Chiara, Iovino, la depressione, Angelica, quella roba lì. Poi esce quel maledetto video di Corona e boom: tutto riemerge. Il lutto che pensavi sepolto ti salta addosso di nuovo come un cane rabbioso. E fidati, sfido chiunque. Quando pensi di averla superata, e poi la vedi ovunque. Su TikTok, in tv, per strada. La faccia di Angelica che ti sorride dai muri, come una pubblicità del dolore. E il peggio? Che lei credeva fossi d'accordo con lui. Ma, dentro di me, speravo che lei stesse vivendo lo stesso casino. Che magari, magari, la fine non era fine davvero.

Corona sapeva che non ero d'accordo, mi aveva avvisato, quello sì, ma se n'è sbattuto. Sapevo benissimo che non potevo fermarlo anche se sapevo che quei video avrebbero fatto male a tantissime persone, oltre che a me. È come vedere da un elicottero un'onda anomala che si abbatte su una città, tu vorresti urlare, fare qualcosa per avvertire gli abitanti, ma qualsiasi cosa tu faccia non potrai mai fermare l'onda. Ed è stato proprio all'uscita di questi video che mi sono davvero reso conto di che cosa voglia dire essere così popolari da averne paura. C'era stato il pandoro, Sanremo, la musica, i concerti, i Ferragnez, ok, ma in quei giorni lì ho capito davvero quanto fosse morboso tutto ciò che gravitava intorno a me e, paradossalmente, proprio quando mi sono reso conto di quanto fosse enorme e incontrollabile il fenomeno, è lì che sono riuscito a ridimensionare ciò che mi arrivava addosso. La faccenda era diventata talmente mastodontica da risultare quasi ridicola, grottesca. Vedere come le persone si interessassero alla mia vita privata più di quanto me ne stessi interessando io mi rendeva tutto assurdo, così come l'indignazione finto moralista che si era generata.

Poi ovviamente, per quanto ridicolo, fu bruttissimo, ma la preoccupazione nasceva anche dal fatto che di lì a poco mi sarei dovuto buttare su un palco come quello di Sanremo con una canzone inedita, un salto nel buio dove i giudizi delle persone sarebbero contati davvero, perché non sarebbero stati giudizi su di me, ma sulla mia musica. E l'aspetto più frustrante per me non era ammettere di aver sbagliato a fare determinate cose, ma pagare le conseguenze di una ricostruzione fantasiosa, di azioni che altri avevano ricostruito per me. E che queste ricostruzioni avessero un impatto pure sui miei figli. Anche se, a mente fredda, credo che tutto questo casino non possa aver davvero fatto male ai miei figli, perché viviamo in una società talmente veloce che, quando Vittoria e Leone saranno abbastanza grandi per capire ciò che è avvenuto intorno ai loro genitori, alla loro cerchia famigliare, tutto sarà quasi dimenticato. I social sono così, hanno bisogno di content, di content, di content, ogni giorno, ingurgitano persone, storie, vite, le cacano e poi se ne dimenticano.

Perciò sono arrivato a Sanremo a pezzi. Rotto. Pronto a ricadere nel buio, ma ci sono andato. Non per lo spettacolo. Non per il pubblico. Ma per me. Per lei. Per cercare di riconquistarmi con *Battito,* di riconquistarla con *Bella stronza,* anche se sapevo che era tossico. Tossico come una sigaretta bagnata fumata per dispetto. Ma c'era un'altra parte di me, più viva, più lucida, che diceva: vai lì e spogliati. Mostrati per quel relitto che sei. Senza filtro. Senza trucco.

I buchi allo stomaco che mi sono fatto / per tutto lo schifo che ho accumulato.

Perché alla fine gli esempi positivi sono belli, certo. Ma i negativi… i negativi ti insegnano di più. E io, lì, ero il negativo perfetto. Il fallimento ambulante. La rovina romantica. Ed è stato bello, cazzo. Bello esserlo fino in fondo sopra quel palco.

Battito

Buio. Sipario. Scale. Base. Cicatrici.

Le luci rosse tutte intorno, i miei occhi chiusi.

La voce che temevo non uscisse.

Le mani tremanti, la bocca arida come quella di un cadavere.

Il fuoco e lo zero assoluto, portarsi dentro questa contraddizione.

Uno scontro tra due parti di se stessi, che non prevede che entrambe sopravvivano.

Il corpo resterà in vita dopo l'amputazione?

Ero su quel palco, incapace di gestire il caos, ma anche in mille altri posti.

In tutte le case dell'ultimo anno, su tutti i letti d'ospedale, sui divani dei litigi, nei locali dove mi sono rifugiato e ho fatto casini. Davanti alle facce che ho lasciato si coprissero di lacrime, le facce di chi, sfinito, sfinita, mi ha detto basta. Ho tenuto gli occhi chiusi per non essere travolto, per arrivare alla fine della sola canzone che avrei potuto cantare in questo momento: tornare su quel palco, lì dove è iniziata la fine di tutto. Dove ho esagerato, mi è stato detto, urlato. Dove non ho avuto rispetto.

Tornarci con un pezzo che è stato il mio modo di vedere davvero quello che ci è successo, quello che ho fatto. Poi ho aperto gli occhi, le pupille nere, ultradilatate. Petrolio, buco nero, "il paziente non è cosciente". Come con le sostanze, come coi farmaci che avrebbero dovuto salvarmi e non l'hanno fatto. Questa che leggerete è la storia di uno che non ce l'ha fatta.

Le persone credono che io decida, pianifichi, organizzi: io sono il manipolatore, lo stratega, io sono la falena. Ma la verità è che, dall'inizio, c'è una parte di me che non ha deciso quasi niente. Sin dal principio è stata una corsa, una fuga. Assecondare tutti gli impulsi, specie quelli sbagliati. Come l'attacco della base di *Battito*. Avevo vent'anni: era esattamente già così. Non voler più prenderle, non voler accontentarsi solo della seconda scelta, umanità di serie C. Dai margini al centro. Così, inizi a correre: arraffi, agguanti, fai male agli altri, ti fai molto male. Dai margini al centro, per poi tornare indietro, e ricominciare. La fama è simile a un girone infernale: c'è tanta luce ed è un massacro che tutti amano spiare.

Ambizione? Narcisismo? Io so solo che ho quasi smesso di vivere: io non so quanto mi resta da vivere. Quando sto da solo, i demoni arrivano. Proprio i demoni, senza volto o con il mio: con gli occhi neri, come i miei a Sanremo. Dita lunghe e sguardi vuoti. E quindi esco. Parlo con gente. Gente che conosco da sempre o che ho appena conosciuto, non importa. Tutti loro hanno lo stesso problema. Le persone che frequento soffrono della stessa patologia. L'incapacità di essere soli non è più un tratto patologico, è diventata una condizione antropologica. Una forma di panico diluito nella normalità. Non riusciamo a stare soli. Neanche per un'ora. Ci troviamo nei soli-ti posti. Siamo tutti là fuori a evitare qualcosa. A fingere di divertirci, a prenderci in giro, a raccontare storie che non finiscono mai. Usiamo nomi veri per cose false. Siamo un branco di ragazzi spaventati, addestrati a sorridere e a consumare. Nessuno dice che stare soli fa paura. Così una notte ho spento tutto. Nessuna uscita. Nessun contatto. Nessun rumore. Mi sono seduto nel buio e li ho aspettati. Per vedere se i demoni mi vogliono davvero. Non so se sono venuti o se erano già dentro. Non è successo nulla. Nessun cambiamento interiore, nessuna epifania. Solo il lento scivolare verso un'assenza. Un'assenza precisa, senza redenzione. Ma anche senza dolore. Applausi.

Un nuovo inizio

Quando ho riaperto gli occhi dopo la prima esibizione di *Battito* è stato come se mi fossi scrollato di dosso gli ultimi due anni, il tumore, il divorzio, il pandoro, Iovino, la depressione, vaffanculo. In quell'esatto momento al di là del consenso, degli applausi, dei complimenti ho percepito profondamente come la musica abbia un potere davvero magico, taumaturgico. La musica può coprire ogni cazzo di rumore di fondo, il chiacchiericcio di chi vuole distruggerci, sfruttare le nostre vulnerabilità, deridere le nostre fragilità. La musica ha il potere di farci sentire ascoltati, per una volta. Di poter dire una cazzo di cosa, e gli altri in silenzio la ascoltano e può darsi che la capiscano, che ti capiscano, che mi capiscano. Non hai bisogno di urlare, di sbracciare, di dire: "Ehi, guardate, sono qua". Sul palco, come in un rito religioso, cala il silenzio e puoi finalmente parlare davvero davanti a persone che per quei tre minuti ti sentono e capiscono che sei ancora lì, magari ferito, dolorante, ammaccato dalla vita, barcollante, ma ancora in piedi. Se canti una bella canzone è una bella canzone, punto. E puoi essere veramente la persona più dimenticata del mondo, quella che nessuno in questo pianeta del cazzo si fila, ma se canti una bella canzone qualcuno che ti ascolta lo troverai. Per questo credo che io a Sanremo ho vinto. Mi sarebbe piaciuto vincere davvero, ovvio. Mi sarebbe piaciuto essere nei primi tre, anche solo per fare la copertina di "Tv Sorrisi e Canzoni", perché mi gasa quella roba lì. Ma ho vinto perché le aspettative verso me stesso erano talmente basse che mai avrei pensato di raggiungere quel senso profondo di redenzione al di là della vittoria effettiva o meno. Ah, e comunque Angelica con *Bella stronza* non l'ho riconquistata.

Epilogo

NON SONO UN ESEMPIO

Credo di aver imparato alcune cose

Sanremo è andato bene, insomma. Ma è un frullatore emotivo molto intenso. Sei come uno sportivo, in quella settimana. Uno sportivo che corre a cento all'ora per sei giorni. Giorno, notte. Giorno, notte. Giorno, notte. Quando arrivi in fondo vuoi solo che finisca, ma quando finisce poi rimani lì da solo. E ora? Che ci faccio qui da solo? Dove sono tutti? È una scarica di adrenalina grossissima, come in *Pulp Fiction*, può resuscitare i morti, ma poi quando l'effetto finisce rischi di riaffacciarti al baratro. E infatti anche io non sono stato bene nelle settimane successive. Alle luci, al casino, alla gente che ti applaude, anche ai giornalisti ti abitui, ma quando quel rumore non c'è più che si fa? Come si riempiono le giornate? Un tempo l'avrei vissuta malissimo, quel vuoto mi avrebbe inghiottito perché avrei provato a colmarlo con altro rumore, altro casino, altra gente, altre luci. Ma sarebbe stato solo un palliativo, una triste replica, una ripetizione annacquata delle emozioni di quella settimana pazza. Ho capito invece di essere una persona diversa, non necessariamente migliore, ma più consapevole, perché a questo giro ho saputo gestire quel vuoto. Una persona in cambiamento, in evoluzione, che è riuscita a non sbandare quando ha dovuto affrontare un grande problema: imparare a stare da sola. Io se sto a casa da solo vengo risucchiato dai demoni, motivo per il quale frequento continuamente altra gente. E invece stare da solo ti può arricchire, per questo mi sono imposto, dopo Sanremo, di non uscire forzatamente, di darmi tempo, di lasciar sedimentare tutto il buono che avevo sentito su quel palco.

Per la promozione di *Battito* volevo solo luoghi che mi permettessero di cantare e basta senza fare interviste e l'unico luogo era "Amici" di Maria De Filippi. Volevo mantenere sana l'esperienza e non tramutarla in una cosa tossica per me. Credo di aver imparato alcune cose. Non tante. Abbastanza però da farmi rendere conto che la vera difficoltà non è imparare, ma trattenere. Trattenere ciò che si è appreso, impedire che svanisca, che venga sostituito da quei meccanismi automatici, deprimenti, che regolano il pensiero da sempre. Per farlo, bisogna continuamente riattivare quella conoscenza nuova, tenerla in vita come un malato cronico attaccato a una macchina.

Credo di aver imparato il valore della solitudine. È una conquista. Non perché sia piacevole, ma perché almeno è reale. E poi c'è l'altra cosa, quella più fastidiosa: la mente crea scenari di catastrofe. Sempre. Non perché siano realistici, ma perché è il suo modo di giustificare l'inerzia. E così non fai nulla, non agisci. Ti paralizzi davanti a un'ipotesi che, il più delle volte, non si realizzerà mai. E quando finalmente affronti il problema, ti accorgi che non era niente. Che il disastro era nella tua testa. Ma intanto te lo sei già vissuto, il disastro. L'hai sofferto per intero, senza che accadesse. Una sofferenza gratuita, priva di oggetto. Una sofferenza teorica. Ed è forse la peggiore. Ho imparato anche a non voler controllare tutto come avrei fatto un tempo, a fare meno strategie, a tornare a fidarmi, a lasciare libero sfogo alla mia autenticità cercando però di non ripetere gli stessi errori di un tempo. Ho imparato, come dice il mio amico delle foglie del destino, che bisogna accettare l'amaro per riconoscere il dolce. Il gusto non esiste in sé. Il bene e il male non esistono. Esistono solo contrasti, differenze di temperatura. Il dolore può salvarti, il piacere può rovinarti. È tutto così instabile, così profondamente ambiguo, che a volte vivere sembra solo un esperimento mal riuscito di resistenza mentale. Succederà quello che deve succedere.

Non è mai troppo tardi per vivere un passato migliore

Se incontrassi il Fedez di quattro o cinque anni fa gli direi: "Enjoy your depression". Goditi la tua depressione. Cioè, se stai dentro alle cose, che siano belle, brutte, dolorose, meravigliose, non rifiutarle. Perché se le rifiuti non è che magicamente spariscono, stanno là a covare, a distruggerti nell'ombra e tu non stai facendo altro che allungare il brodo, perdere tempo. Se devi ingoiare una pastiglia di cianuro, tanto vale prenderla tutta insieme piuttosto che spezzettarla e diluire la pena un pezzettino alla volta. Accetta quel momento, arriva quasi a goderne, cerca di avere una visione positiva, che senso ha vivere nell'apprensione che un giorno, prima o poi, sarai costretto a vivere male, a soffrire, a sparire?

Vorrei fra trent'anni guardarmi indietro e poter dire di essere effettivamente diventato quella persona. Sempre che sia ancora vivo, lo spero. Un po' più diplomatico, più ragionevole e magari anche un po' più ricco di tutto, pure di soldi. Ma vivo. Anche se non so nello specifico cosa esattamente cambierei ora di me stesso affinché questo avvenga. Secondo me non ha senso fare questo tipo di strategie perché poi alla fine la vita ti spiazza, ti butta giù o ti tira su e se tu sei stato lì a farti i tuoi castelli, lei arriva e quei castelli te li spazza via con un solo colpo di mano. E tu rimani lì senza avere risposte, come un coglione che non sa più articolare una reazione. Per questo non voglio pensare alle prossime cose da cambiare, perché si cambiano quando è il momento di cambiarle. Si calibra la risposta a ciò che la vita ci mette davanti, non preventivamente. In questo momento c'è questo, bene, quello che verrà verrà. Sapete cosa succederà? Quello che deve succedere. E lo so perché il mio corpo ha imparato a respirare anche quando l'anima vuole smettere. E allora dici basta. E lo dici sul serio. Per la seconda volta nella vita ci pensi. Solo che non è soltanto un pensiero: è un buco dove ti ci sdrai dentro. A me è andata di culo perché sono riuscito a reagire in maniera positiva. Poi, o lo fai, o non lo fai. E se non lo fai, ti ritrovi lì, che provi a ripartire da zero. Ma zero non esiste. Zero è una bugia. Tu riparti con tutti i cocci nel carrello. Con tutta la merda che ti sei portato dietro. Solo che ti dici che sei cambiato. Io lo dicevo. Dicevo: sono cambiato. Lo urlavo anche. Ma lo facevo per convincere me stesso. Era una bugia necessaria. Ora non lo dico più. Non ne ho bisogno. Lo so. E questo basta.

Perché questo libro non è un atto di vanità, non è difesa, non è strategia. È solo una cazzo di radiografia dell'anima. E fa male. Non sono un esempio. Non sono un eroe. Non sono neanche un uomo buono. Sono uno che ha perso il controllo e che ha dovuto imparare a camminare sulle macerie. E prima di ricostruire ha dovuto distruggere tutto. Radere al suolo. Mettere le mani nella merda e dire: ok, vediamo se c'è ancora qualcosa di vivo qui sotto. E poi c'è quella parte che nessuno ti racconta:

quando cambi tu, deve cambiare tutto. Anche il contesto. Anche le persone. E allora lo capisci che cambiare fa più male che restare fermi. E a volte ci resti, fermo, proprio per quello. Perché cambiare è uno sforzo da bestia. È scavarsi via le unghie, è spaccarsi in due, è dire addio a un pezzo di vita solo perché non ti salva più. E quando finalmente lo fai non è mai per un grande gesto eroico. Lo fai perché non ti resta nient'altro.